Praise
Brian Moreland's Books

"Brian Moreland's *Shadows in the Mist* is a smashing debut of a major new talent...equal parts horror story and spine-jangling thriller."
—**James Rollins**, *New York Times* best-selling author of *Map of Bones* and *Black Order*

"Brian Moreland's fiction is taut and spellbinding, often blending varied themes to form a dark genre very much his own. From his WWII occult thriller *Shadows in the Mist*, to the haunting chiller *The Devil's Woods*, Brian's work is at once versatile, original, and deeply engaging."
—**Greg F. Gifune,** author of *The Bleeding Season*

"*The Devil's Woods* is a force of nature. A complex, chilling foray into the darkness of a forbidden land, and man's tortured soul."
—**Hunter Shea**, author of *The Jersey Devil*

"*Dead of Winter* is a thrilling, wholly-engrossing read that masterfully crosses multiple genres and leaves the reader breathless. Highly recommended!"
—**Brian Keene**, best-selling author of *The Rising*

"Sharply written and scary as hell, this one is a must-read for all horror fans."
—**Ronald Malfi,** author of *Snow* and *Night Parade* on reviewing *Dead of Winter*

"Witchcraft, sacrifices, an abandoned house and a thing that has hungered for decades set the stage for this must-read expedition to *The Witching House.*"
—**John Everson,** author of *NightWhere* and *Violet Eyes*

"For horror fans wanting a healthy dose of the small-town stuff a la Stephen King."
—**Hellnotes**

Books by Brian Moreland:

Shadows in the Mist
Dead of Winter
The Witching House
The Devil's Woods
The Seekers
Darkness Rising
Tomb of Gods

THE
DEVIL'S
WOODS

The Devil's Woods

RISING
HORSE
BOOKS

Published June 2017 by Rising Horse Books
Dallas, Texas

2nd Edition, Printed in the U.S.A.

The Devil's Woods was originally published by Samhain Publishing December 2013.
Republished by Rising Horse Books June 2017.

Cover design: Brian Moreland
Images licensed through Fotolia.com
Foggy Forest - Nebel im Dachauer Moor © Second2None
Elk skull © baphomets
Bull skull© smokedsalmon
Coyote skull © emu

ISBN: 978-0-9986846-9-7

THE
DEVIL'S
WOODS

Brian Moreland

RISING
HORSE
BOOKS

Prologue

British Columbia, Canada
Lake Akwâkopiy Cree Indian Reserve

Five days after the tragedy, Jon Elkheart returned to the forbidden forest. With a vengeful glare, he challenged the looming wall of aspen, spruce and vine-choked pines that guarded this unsacred land. The only entrance was a trail that disappeared into a black hole inside the jungle-thick brush. The darkness within Macâya Forest was an impenetrable void, a shadow world of shape-shifters, and yet its mysteries beckoned him.

There are places in the world where lost spirits never rest, Elkheart thought with a coppery taste in his mouth. *And man is considered prey.* Standing by a swamp at the edge of the rainforest, he peered through the scope of his assault rifle, searching the woods for sudden movement. He listened for the slightest snap of a twig or brush of a leaf. The June morning was still and windless, as if all of nature sensed what he was about to do.

You should turn back. You can't do this on your own. The scholarly part of Elkheart understood this logic. As an archaeologist, he had always put his research first, above all else. Until this last mission went haywire. Now the guilt and anger pumping through his veins would not let him rest. *You have to go back in there,* spoke a voice that was not ruled by logic. *You have to find Amy.*

Elkheart looked up at the sun creeping over the mountains. Clouds drifted across the valley, as if shielding the forest from the approaching light. Soon only the tips of the branches pierced the white smoke. Stretching out his arm, he turned a small video camera toward his face. "June 10th, 7:00 a.m. My name is Jon Elkheart. I am a professor from the University of British Columbia. I am also one of the last surviving members of the Lake Akwâkopiy Cree band. Most of my people abandoned this reservation years ago. Those who stayed behind have suffered nightmarish visions from a forest that has haunted our

7

reservation for more than a century. A week ago I led a documentary film crew and four mercenaries into Macâya Forest, an uncharted patch of rainforest located at the northeastern tip of the reservation." A heaviness burdened Elkheart's chest as he remembered that tragic night. The screams and gunshots echoed in his mind and guilt twisted his guts. "Most of my crew was slaughtered by something that attacked us from the woods. My assistant, Amy Hanson, was taken alive. I'm going back into Macâya Forest to search for her. I pray the spirits of my ancestors will guide me."

Never enter Macâya Forest with impure thoughts, Grandfather Two Hawks had warned. *You must call in your animal spirit guide and enter with the heart of a warrior.*

Elkheart blessed a large knife with an elk-horn handle. Grandfather had given him the hunter's blade on his thirteenth birthday after killing his first elk. He had eaten the slain animal's heart and earned his name. Now, Jon Elkheart dipped two fingers into a coffee can of elk's blood and wiped red streaks across his cheeks, as if a mask of war paint could channel the ancient warriors of his tribe. The ceremony did nothing to settle his nerves. He faced the mouth of the forest where few men had survived before him. "This time I will not run."

Nervous whimpers broke the silence. Elkheart's German shepherd pressed against his leg. He stroked his dog's bristled neck. *Should have left him back at the cabin.* "Scout, run on home." He shooed the dog. "Go on." But Scout refused to leave his master's side. Elkheart sighed. "You're just as foolish as I am."

Taking a deep breath, Elkheart sheathed his knife. He gripped his M4 Carbine. The semi-automatic assault rifle had belonged to one of the mercenaries who had died for this mission. Trying not to think of the soldier who had been decapitated, Elkheart turned on a flashlight that was attached to the barrel. A long beam pierced the dripping green-gray gloom that shrouded the rainforest. Wary of every sound, he passed through the threshold. His dog followed.

As Elkheart crept down the narrow path between spiky pines, firs, and cedars tangled spruce, ghostly voices filled his head, pulling his thoughts in every direction. His Cree ancestors would not give him peace until he returned to these unsacred woods and exposed its secrets.

A blanket of dew covered the bracken and surrounding leaves. Only splinters of sunlight lanced the dense canopy. The morning fog drifted between the trees, making visibility even more difficult. Elkheart could only see a few feet around him.

Scout sniffed along the ground a few feet ahead, a silhouette in the haze. They weaved between trees, crossing cold-water creeks and climbing up fern-covered hills. The darkness faded into a gray gloom, as the morning sun finally filtered through the tops of the trees.

Untying his green parka, Elkheart loosened the hood to cool off. Sweat soaked his black-and-silver hair. Slightly winded, he inhaled the pine-scented air. A branch shook above him, dropping pinecones onto his shoulders. He jerked the rifle upward. An owl swooped from its perch and disappeared into the mist.

Elkheart released his breath. *Okay, stay alert. Be ready for anything.*

Steadying his rifle, he stepped through a thicket. Large fern leafs and dangling vines made his efforts difficult. Only the twisting path separated the trees and underbrush enough to travel through the woods. To venture from the trail would be like wandering into an uncharted jungle.

The fog thickened. Smokey plumes circled his feet, covering his boots and the moss-covered trail. Scout began to fade in the mist. Elkheart bird-whistled the German shepherd to come back. Elkheart's heavy backpack burdened his spine. Easing the pack off, he leaned against a tree. Scout sat on his haunches, watching the forest.

Fishing into his backpack, Elkheart retrieved his video recorder and a bottle of Stoli. The vodka had been a birthday gift from Wynona, his…what? Ex-girlfriend? No, their relationship had never been that formal. Ex-drinking partner was more fitting. "Friends with benefits," his students would say.

Studying the clear liquor, Elkheart felt a brief tightness to his chest, remembering the drunken, lust-filled nights he and Wynona had shared before the whole mess started. He still loved her, still caressed the empty spot in his bed where she once slept. But some pasts just couldn't be healed. And Wynona's wounds ran deep as canyons. Letting her image fade, Elkheart swallowed a gulp of vodka. He glanced around warily, thumbed the camera's record button.

"So far, so good. I'm about a half mile deep and all's quiet." Elkheart paused to listen to the forest a moment, turning his camera toward the surrounding trees. "For over a century, my people have feared Macâya Forest. The landscape here is different from the woods that surround the reservation's compound. Here, the trees tower to enormous heights and intertwine with one another as if trying to conceal something the land never wanted man to discover." He gazed up at the giant trees, the sacred elders, wondering if they were listening. He felt as if eyes were watching him. "I'm about a quarter mile from the strange ruins my team and I discovered before their deaths. I only got a glimpse, but what I saw was beyond belief. I should be there shortly, where I hope to find Amy. If I come across what killed my crew, this time I'm prepared."

Elkheart hit the stop button. A strong wind blew along the trail, and the fog began to swirl. He half expected an ancient trickster to emerge from it. Or a threat much more real.

Elkheart rubbed the antler handle of his knife, drawing courage from his spirit animal. When that didn't work, he drank another fiery gulp of vodka. He then slipped his backpack over his shoulders, grabbed his rifle and stepped toward the swirling fog. Scout sniffed the trail a few feet ahead.

As Elkheart grew closer to the ruins, his asthma kicked in. The fifty-year-old professor started wheezing. Fear paralyzed him as questions rolled through his mind.

What the hell are you doing here? Why is revealing the secrets of this forest worth more than your life?

Part of him wanted to return to Vancouver with the evidence they had found. He had plenty of artifacts and footage to open up an investigation. He would be on CNN and every major talk show around the world. *Time* and *National Geographic* would cover his story. He would finally be respected in his field, and more importantly, earn the respect of his three grown children. But Elkheart couldn't leave Amy behind. He took another step, a warrior's vengeance surging through him. He jerked his rifle at a sudden sound. Low, huffing grunts.

Scout growled.

Elkheart tensed, raising the rifle. "Shh, boy."

The shepherd silenced, but remained poised to attack.

Ahead, something lumbered through the pines with heavy footfalls that sounded like a grizzly. But this predator had run off all the bears from these woods.

Remain still. Wait it out. It's only passing.

The heavy footsteps tramping over damp earth echoed off the pines.

Scout watched the path, waiting for his master's command to attack.

Elkheart remained still, holding his breath. Out here, the slightest gasp could be heard a great distance. The asthma tickled his lungs like centipede legs.

The unseen animal lumbered away, its thundering footfalls and cracking branches growing softer.

The wind carried the beast's familiar stench, stinging Elkheart's nose, and memories filled his mind: images of a moonlit night, gunshots firing, his crew wailing as their shredded bodies flew through the air. Amy screaming as the thing dragged her off.

Now, Elkheart's lungs clenched up. He groped for his inhaler, sucked in.

Somewhere beyond the trees, the beast stopped walking.

Elkheart fought to control his wheezing, pumping several gasps of asthma medicine into his lungs. The centipede legs abated and he finally silenced his panicked breathing.

Too late.

The snapping of branches rushed toward him.

Scout turned and barked.

The predator circled them, staying hidden within the fog.

Elkheart hugged his rifle with shaking arms. Staring through spiky branches, he aimed at the forest. *God, the beast's right here! Behind the fog!* His heartbeat quickened as he realized he was about to see the thing in the light.

"Come on! Show yourself!"

A cacophonous roar erupted from within the forest.

Barking, the German shepherd dashed into the mist.

"Scout! No!"

The dog's growling soon blended in with the roar of the unseen beast. Branches cracked, or were those bones? A fatal ripping followed by a canine yelp.

"Scout!"

A long, drawn-out shriek echoed across the valley. Branches snapped. Snarls filled Elkheart's ears. He raised the rifle and fired a three-round burst into the fog. The shots whizzed between the trees, their final reports echoing across the valley. At least one bullet hit something solid.

The forest grew silent again.

Was it dead?

Elkheart flattened against a tree, watching the mist swirling with the wind. He dug through his backpack. Pulled out the vodka bottle and a jar that contained a rag soaked in kerosene. He stuffed the rag into the bottle, allowing a long strip to hang out. *I will not back down.* Holding the flame of his lighter beneath the wick of the Molotov cocktail, Elkheart advanced along the path. The forest remained so dead calm he could hear his own heart hammering his chest.

From somewhere in the infinity of trees a twig snapped.

Elkheart stiffened. He listened for the faintest sound. The surrounding pines, like silent observers to this game of cat and mouse, offered nothing.

Another twig cracked, this time sharper.

Closer.

He lit the wick of the Stoli bottle and threw it toward the sound. The makeshift bomb exploded against the trees, torching two of them. A tall shadow beyond the flames roared and lumbered back into the fog.

Elkheart gripped his gun, backing away. The research couldn't end like this. Not after all his work. Twenty years of expeditions. Who would be left to warn the ignorant world? He had to escape. He was the last Cree descendent who knew enough to expose the secrets of Macâya Forest.

A woman screamed.

"Amy!" Elkheart left the trail, running between the evergreens toward her crying voice. Branches clawed at his clothes with wooden talons. The girl's moans echoed off to his left, then shifted to his right, and then strangely, back behind him.

He stopped, confused. "Amy, where are you?"

Her crying changed to mocking laughter, and then Elkheart's heart seized as he realized he had been tricked. He tried to fire his rifle, but it jammed. He tossed the gun and pulled out his knife. He challenged the fog, "Show yourself!"

From above, hot, blistering air heated Elkheart's scalp. Something wet and sticky hit the nape of his neck, oozing down his back. He tilted his head up toward the trees and saw a large mouth with a rack of fangs. A shadowy thing was hanging upside down from the branches. Its hands gripped Elkheart by the throat, lifting him high into the air. He released a warrior's howl and stabbed at the beast with his knife. Elongated fingers noosed around his throat, choking off his air. His dangling legs kicked the tree. His beloved knife fell from his limp hand. As the forest went black, Jon Elkheart heard the lost spirits of his ancestors calling him deeper into the cold and visceral darkness of Macâya Forest.

Part One

The Journey

My shrink says the best way to face your fears is to go back to your roots. To return to the time before innocence was lost. Before a child's mind witnessed something so horrific that it was forever scarred. The moment of trauma is where the healing journey must begin. But I fear if I dig up my past, the horror will be there waiting for me.

—Detective Alex Winterbone
From the novel *The Ghosts of Winterbone*
by Kyle Elkheart

Chapter One

"Fear wears many skins..." a raspy voice whispered into Kyle Elkheart's ear while he was sleeping. Cold fingers touched his cheek. *"Kyle, wake up..."*

He opened his eyes to the dark and saw the blurry outline of someone standing over him. Before Kyle could react, hands gripped his throat, choking. He jerked up in bed and swung blindly, but his fists struck nothing but air.

The hands released his neck. A shadowy shape backed away, merging with the darkness that concealed Kyle's bedroom.

"Who's there?" He pushed a set of buttons on the wall, hoping to turn on the lights. Instead, his TV flashed on a channel with white noise and the automatic curtains began to open. Gray light poured in through the high-rise apartment windows. Kyle's visitor retreated with the shadows to the far corner of the bedroom. Then, like so many mornings before, the ghost sank into the wall.

It's just another bad dream, Kyle tried to convince himself as he rubbed his aching neck. The feeling that someone's icy hands had gripped his throat wouldn't go away. More and more, his nightmares were crossing over into the waking world. Usually Kyle heard noises or saw movement out of the corner of his eye. This was the first time his haunter had tried to physically harm him. *What's happening to me?* Kyle lay back in bed, staring up at the ceiling.

At 6:00 a.m. the alarm radio blared and a DJ spoke like he was high on Starbucks. "Goooood morninggggg, Seattle! You're waking up with Rowdy Roscoe! Forecast for today is fog and rain! The weather may be gloomy, but you don't have to be—"

Kyle hit the off button, groaning. He started to call his shrink to tell her about the nightmare that had awakened him, but then hung up. He already knew what Dr. Norberg would say, "The ghost is a figment of your imagination, Kyle. Keep journaling and we'll talk about it on Tuesday."

He got up and went to the bathroom sink. A reflection with mussed brown hair and a three-day beard stared back at him. He couldn't believe that last night he had gone out onto the balcony, looked over the rail and imagined what it would be like to free fall out of his miserable life. He had two voices battling inside his head—one telling him to jump, the other urging him not to give up. After nearly teetering over from vertigo, he had stepped away from the edge and gone back inside. This morning the memory frightened him. Last night had been a turning point. Kyle was determined to get his life back on course before his shrink sent him to the nuthouse or his haunter convinced him death was the best option.

"You're not going to waste another day," Kyle said to the man in the mirror. "No more feeling sorry for yourself."

He started his wake-up routine with twenty minutes on the treadmill. Streamers of rain trickled down the floor-to-ceiling window. Living in a corner apartment on the fifteenth floor, he had a spectacular view of downtown Seattle and the main harbor, Elliot Bay. Another gray storm enshrouded the seaport city. "Great," Kyle muttered. He had planned to drive to Lake Union and go kayaking. "Another day trapped indoors."

As he was doing pushups, he heard a knock on the wall. Footsteps echoed from another part of the apartment. A door clicked shut. *What the hell was that?* No one lived in his three-bedroom apartment but him. Grabbing a baseball bat, Kyle hurried to the living room. The apartment was quiet now, except for a clock ticking on the wall. He checked the front door. The two deadbolts were still latched. No sign of a break-in. He searched his office and closet. Empty. As he stepped back into the hallway, another sound, like a book falling over, issued from behind the closed third bedroom door. He crept down the hallway, gripping the bat. He listened at the door. The thought of going in that room got his heart racing. This door had remained shut the past two years. He placed his fingers on the knob, then paused.

I'm imagining things again.

Swallowing hard, he turned the knob and pushed the door open with the bat. The smell of paint and turpentine brought back a flood of memories. He struggled to breathe. His trembling hand flipped on the light. The extra bedroom was an art studio with wall-to-wall oil paintings of seaside landscapes, harbors and Seattle skylines, all painted as if seen from a far distance. An unfinished painting of Mt. Rainier sat on an easel. The room was covered in layers of dust.

Venturing inside, he checked behind the door. Empty. Then he checked the walk-in closet. The walls were lined with canvasses and shelved painting supplies. Kyle sighed, shaking his head. Thunder rumbled outside and a heavy rain slapped the windows.

It's just the storm.

As he was leaving the room he glimpsed a shelf on the wall full of seashells, colored crystals and other knickknacks. In a silver frame was a photo of himself with his late wife Stephanie on a beach in Maui, holding up handfuls of shells. Her auburn hair blew sideways across her face. Her smile almost knocked him to his knees. God, he had loved her.

He rested the photo in a drawer, closed it and left the room.

Today was going to be different. Instead of moping around and watching TV, Kyle was going to get back to his writing. He stepped into his office and fired up the computer. The screen flashed to a desktop image from the movie *The Shining*: Jack Nicholson's crazed face peering through a broken door. "Here's Johnny!" the computer said as it completed its boot up.

He sat at his computer, eager to write the next chapter of his latest Detective Winterbone novel. Kyle's brain was electric with remnants from last night's dream: visions of shadowy woods and a village haunted by ghosts. His dark muse had finally returned from her silent crypt. His eyes locked on to the screen, and he typed as fast as his fingers would move.

More pounding startled him. At first Kyle thought his haunter was back, but he traced the pounding to the front door. Kyle peered out the peephole. It was Eric.

"Shit," Kyle whispered, debating whether to answer. The two hadn't spoken since their fallout a year ago.

"Kyle, I know you're home. Open the door." His brother knocked impatiently.

"Hold on." Kyle unlatched the deadbolts and opened the door. "What the hell? It's six thirty in the morning."

"I've left a dozen messages." Eric barged into the living room, his soaked shoes and umbrella dripping water onto the carpet. At six-three, he was taller than Kyle and built of solid muscle. Once a star high school quarterback, Eric had been blessed with looks and charisma, which he now used to his advantage as an M and A lawyer at Nelson, Fairbanks and Koch.

Eric had a suspicious gleam in his eyes. "How's my big brother?"

Kyle crossed his arms. "Writing. What's up?"

Eric removed his trench coat without being asked to stay. As usual, he was wearing a silver Brooks Brothers suit with a power tie perfectly knotted. "Can we sit?"

Kyle's heart plummeted as he recognized the somber tone in Eric's voice. "Shit, something's happened to Shawna." Kyle had visions of his sister's dead body on an ER gurney somewhere. Another OD, this one successful.

"Relax. Shawna's fine," Eric assured. "In fact, right now she and her latest freak boyfriend are crashing on my futon."

Kyle released his breath. Thank God their sister was all right. He couldn't go through another scare like last year.

Eric's face remained grim. "Listen, I received a strange call yesterday from Ray Roamingbear."

Kyle, Eric and their younger sister, Shawna, had been born on a Cree reservation in British Columbia. Their mother, who was white, left their alcoholic father, Jon Elkheart, and moved them to Seattle. It had been a turbulent time in Kyle's life because he had been close to his Cree father. In the past twenty years, Kyle had been back to the reservation to visit a number of times. Eric and Shawna, who were estranged from Elkheart, hadn't been back once. Whenever their cousin, Ray Roamingbear, called out of the blue, it usually was to share bad news about their father.

Kyle braced himself for the worst. "What's the news?"

"Last month Elkheart went on another drinking binge and disappeared. He didn't tell anyone he was leaving or where he was going."

"Shit." Kyle felt a mixture of fear and disappointment. Every couple years their father, an archaeologist and chronic myth chaser, called asking Kyle to wire money to help fund some expedition or, when his father went through a bad bender, bail him out of a drunk tank. "Does Ray have any clue where Dad went?"

"Nothing." Eric opened the fridge and helped himself to a bottle of Evian. "Ray thinks Elkheart took off to South America on another one of his treasure hunts. My bet is he's probably passed out again and doesn't know where the fuck he is."

Kyle stared out the window at the drizzling rain and the fog shrouding downtown Seattle. "The last time Dad and I spoke he said he had quit drinking and started going to AA."

"Elkheart called you?" Kyle thought he heard jealousy in Eric's voice. Talking about their father had always been a sensitive subject.

"Yeah, last summer." Kyle gazed at a bookshelf that had a framed photo of himself with his father on one of their camping trips. "I went to visit him for a weekend at the reservation. Dad looked great. Happy for once. He had a new university job and a steady girlfriend. He's been making an effort to turn his life around."

"Elkheart never asked me up for a visit," Eric grumbled.

An awkward silence fell between them. There had to be more to the story, because Eric wouldn't have bothered to visit otherwise. Eager to get back to writing, Kyle wished his brother would cut to the chase. "Any other news?"

"Yeah, Ray said that he and Grandfather Two Hawks are the last tribe members living on the reservation. And check this out…with Elkheart M.I.A. or whatever, you, me and Shawna are the last descendents of the tribe. Ray and Grandfather have something to pass on to us. Something our father was supposed to give us years ago."

"Did Ray say what it was?"

Eric shook his head. "He said we have to come up to Canada to find out. He invited us all to visit the reservation. Shawna and I have already agreed to go. She's bringing what's-his-face, and I'm taking Jessica."

"I thought you were dating Stella."

Eric laughed. "Man, you've been out of touch. I see Stella when I'm in Portland. There's Rachel in Vegas and Kristen in L.A. Jessica's the one I've been dating in Seattle."

Kyle shook his head. "I don't even bother to keep up anymore." He ushered his brother toward the door. "You guys have a great time in Canada. Send me a postcard."

"Actually…" Eric cleared his throat. "We were hoping you could break away for a few days and go with us. Maybe even fly us there in your plane."

And there it was—the sales pitch Kyle had been waiting for. "I can't. I've…" Kyle looked down at a stack of unedited chapters on the coffee table. "I need to focus on finishing my book. I've got a deadline to meet."

"What better place to write than a remote cabin?" Eric flashed the smile he used to win over clients. "The fresh mountain air could do wonders for your writing. Think about it. This is a chance for all three of us to travel back to our childhood home. Reconnect with our Cree heritage."

Or find out why we're all so screwed up. A week in the mountains with his brother and one of his bimbo girlfriends was not a selling point, but Kyle did miss his sister and was slightly curious as to what his native relatives had for them. There was also the off chance that their father might show up, assuming he wasn't rehabbing at a hacienda in the Mexican desert.

Kyle remained on the fence.

Eric switched his tone to begging. "Come on, it's been ages since the three of us did anything together. We've all had it pretty tough since Mom passed away. It would be good for all of us if we made this trip a family vacation."

Kyle gave his brother a sideways look. "Since when did you start caring so much about doing things with me and Shawna?"

"Since we almost lost her last year. If you won't go for me, at the very least go for Shawna. She needs her brothers to steer her in the right direction." Eric walked up and put a hand on Kyle's shoulder. "What do you say?"

Kyle looked around at the apartment that had grown tomblike since his wife's death two years ago. His shrink had diagnosed him as borderline agoraphobic. Except to buy groceries, go kayaking alone or maintaining currency on his pilot's license, he rarely ventured outside. He couldn't remember the last time he'd gotten together with his siblings. Lately, Kyle's only company had been the ghost that walked the apartment at night, whispering strange phrases into his ear. A vacation in the mountains might be just the thing. He sighed. "Okay, you win. When do you guys want to leave?"

His brother grinned. "Tomorrow at the crack of dawn."

Chapter Two

The next morning, Kyle arrived at Lake Union as the sun was stretching its golden fingers behind Mt. Rainier. He sat behind the wheel and stared at the lake. Fog drifted across the dark water. He felt a strong tug to go back to his apartment. *Why did I let Eric talk me into this?* Kyle picked up his phone and started to call his brother to back out, but then hung up. He needed this trip.

He got out and grabbed his backpack and bedroll. The dew was heavy on the grass, and a light haze floated around the marina. The weather report said the fog should dissipate within the hour, followed by clear skies and sunshine. A perfect day for flying. As Kyle walked down the dock to the hangar wharf, the sight of his pontoon plane was like seeing an old friend. Painted yellow and forest green, the single-prop de Havilland Turbo Otter seaplane had been his first major purchase after he'd gotten out of college.

He climbed onto a pontoon and ran his hand along the side of the plane. "Hey, girl. Did you miss me?"

The plane rocked on the water from the wake of a passing boat.

Kyle climbed up into the cockpit and was quickly reminded of the man he used to be: adventurous, confident, happy to be alive. As he went through his preflight procedures, he was taken back to a time when he used to work as a charter pilot, flying scenic tours over Seattle and Washington's beautiful forests and mountains. Occasionally, he had delivered supplies to Vancouver or Kodiak Island. He had taken the plane up a couple times in the past year, but it had been routine flights to stay up to code with his currency. The last flight that he had actually enjoyed had been with Stephanie on her birthday. The memory of his late wife threatened to shatter Kyle's mood. He quickly pushed thoughts of her away and focused on the checklist.

"Don't leave me, Kyle," a woman's voice whispered with the wind.

Startled, he looked around the harbor wharf at all the floating planes. There was no one here but him.

* * *

Eric parked his Lexus near a dock at the lake. He looked at his three sleeping passengers. Jessica, Shawna and Zack had slept the entire forty-minute ride from his house to the lake. "Wake up, everybody. Time to get moving." Eric patted his girlfriend's leg.

In the passenger seat, Jessica stretched and yawned. "Where's the airport?"

"You're looking at it." Eric motioned toward the vast lake, where a pontoon plane was already taking off. "Where we're going, they don't have runways."

"Sounds adventurous." Jessica said with a grin. "I'm looking forward to meeting your brother. Is that him?"

Eric spotted Kyle down at the end of the pier, pumping fuel into his plane. "Yeah, but don't expect him to be too friendly. He's a bit of a loner."

Jessica put her hand on Eric's. "I'm happy you're finally introducing me to your family."

Ever since his girlfriend had moved in with him last month, she had been asking about meeting his family. Well, she would get a heavy dose of his siblings this week.

In the backseat, Shawna and Zack were still snoozing head to shoulder. Eric snapped his fingers. "Guys, come on. Up and at 'em!" He stared at his twenty-two-year-old sister. Shawna's blonde hair had a few rebel streaks of blue—a look that all the members of her rock band, the Black Mollies, wore. Eric couldn't figure out what the hell had happened to his sister. In high school she had been an honor student and a cheerleader. Then, at age seventeen, Shawna had a blow-out with their stepfather, Blake, and ran away from home. For the past four years she had been running around with a bunch of coke-snorting Goth freaks. Eric figured all of Shawna's tattoos were a way to say "fuck you" to their born-again Christian stepfather.

Now, Shawna opened her sleepy eyes and stuck a cigarette in her mouth. Eric yanked it out. "No smoking in my car." He shoved the cigarette into the car's ashtray.

"Okay, that wasn't rude," Shawna said.

"You said you were going to quit."

"Why give up something I enjoy?" she challenged.

"Because cigarettes turn your lungs black," Eric said. "You want to die of cancer?"

"Whatever, *Dad*."

"Cut the 'Dad' crap. I'm just looking out for your ass."

"Well, I can look out for my own ass, thank you." Shawna stuck a fresh cigarette in her mouth and stepped out of the car. Zack quickly followed.

Eric wished he could relate to his sister, but Shawna was seven years younger and they had never been close. He looked at Jessica, who was still seated in the passenger seat, putting on her makeup. "You sure you want to spend a week with my family?"

She smiled. "Of course, love. I want to get to know everyone in your life."

"Well, don't say I didn't warn you."

* * *

As Kyle was opening the cargo area to store luggage, Shawna ambushed him with the video camera. "Well, I'll be damned. Kyle Elkheart, rich-and-famous author, has finally ventured out of his crypt."

"Hey, kid." Kyle hugged his sister. "It's good to see you."

He rarely saw Shawna ever since she had started living like a gypsy, shacking up with various boyfriends. Last year, she'd nearly died from an overdose of heroin and cocaine—a party concoction that a previous boyfriend, Razor, had given her. The guy had died that night. Shawna had gone into rehab for a couple months but then went back to running around with the same drugged-up crowd. She punched Kyle's shoulder. "You never come see me play."

"Sorry, sis, I haven't been out much. I've been under a lot of pressure to finish my next book."

"Writing another best seller?" she asked.

Kyle shrugged. "I'm hoping my readers don't crucify me for taking so damned long."

"Well, I'm glad you're going with us. You've been a recluse too long." She handed him her guitar case to stow. "Maybe I'll play some new songs for you."

"I would love that."

A skinny kid in a black *Dawn of the Dead* T-shirt walked up behind her. Tucked under one of his heavily tattooed arms was a bongo drum.

Shawna said, "Kyle, meet my boyfriend, Zack. He just joined our band. He's wicked on the drums."

"Dude, it's such an honor to meet you." Zack walked over and gripped Kyle's hand gang-style. "I totally wigged out when Shawna told me her brother was Kyle Elkheart. I've read every one of your novels. *Ghost Hunter* is my all-time favorite." He patted his backpack. "I hope you don't mind. I brought some books for you to autograph."

"Sure, when we get to the cabin." Kyle did his best not to judge Zack's demonic tattoos, skull earring, or the haircut that looked like it had been hacked by Freddy Krueger. As long as Shawna was staying off heroin and her boyfriend wasn't beating her or stealing her money, Kyle was happy for her. This guy at least read books.

Shawna squeezed her boyfriend's hand. They both seemed to be under the spell of new love.

"So how long have you two been dating?" Kyle asked.

"About a month," Shawna said, beaming. "How about you, big brother? Got any new women in your life?"

"No, I'm too busy."

"You have to eventually get back out there, you know."

Great, now my little sister's giving me advice. "I'll date again when I meet the right woman. Until then, I'm in no rush."

"How do you get by without having sex for so long?"

"Shawna!" Zack nudged her shoulder. "Show the man some respect."

"Hey, I'm curious," she said. "Are you like a monk or something?"

Kyle laughed. "Something like that. Why don't you get on board?"

As Kyle loaded their luggage and instruments into the cargo hold, Eric walked down the pier, toting several bags. He was wearing a bucket hat and tank top that showed off his muscles. "High mountain country, here we come!"

Kyle looked down at his brother's flip-flops. "Where we're going hiking boots would be more appropriate."

Eric patted one of his bags. "Don't worry. I'm prepared for everything. But first, Ray invited us to spend the day on the lake." His cell phone rang.

"Who would be calling you this early in the morning?" Kyle asked.

"Investors. I've got deals going in three time zones." He glanced at the caller ID. "Excuse me." Eric walked down one of the airplane docks to talk in private.

"His phone never stops ringing," spoke a feminine voice.

Kyle turned and saw a slender woman approaching. His brother normally dated tall blondes with large fake boobs and heavy makeup. Eric's latest girlfriend stood about five foot five. With long, dark brown hair and freckles on her nose, she was a natural beauty. She was decked out for the wilderness in cargo shorts, a fleece pullover, backpack and a sun hat with a daisy on it. When their eyes met, Kyle became momentarily speechless.

After an awkward silence, the pretty brunette offered her hand. "G'day. It's Kyle, right?"

"Uh, yes, and you must be…" He had already forgotten her name.

"Jessica. Pleased to finally meet you." Her accent sounded Australian. "I swear most of this luggage is Eric's, not mine." Her whole face lit up when she smiled.

"I believe it." Feeling oddly nervous around his brother's girlfriend, Kyle focused on loading the luggage. Suddenly he was all thumbs, and it took two attempts to fit one of his brother's large suitcases into the compartment. He hadn't been this clumsy around a woman since he met his wife back in college.

Jessica pulled out a Nikon camera and took photos of him and the plane. "I hope this is okay. I'm documenting our trip for my travel blog."

Eric returned, looking agitated. "You guys ready to go?"

Jessica put her palm on his chest. "Everything okay, love?"

"Yeah, ready to start this vacation. Does this flight serve alcohol?" Eric asked, half-smiling. "I could go for a Bloody Mary."

Kyle said, "Sorry, just sodas and bottled water. You'll have to wait 'til we get to Canada for the hard stuff." He picked up an oversized duffle bag that must have weighed sixty pounds. "Jesus, Eric, what do you have in here, a corpse?"

"My dumbbells."

Jessica rolled her eyes. "He doesn't leave home without them."

"Hey, as much as I travel, I have to take my gym with me." Eric put his arm around her. "Come on, babe. Let's let the pilot do his job and find our seats."

While Kyle loaded their luggage into the cargo hold, Eric ushered his girlfriend into the plane. A moment later, he returned as Kyle was closing the cargo door.

"Thanks for helping me load," Kyle needled.

Eric's face remained serious. "Can we take a walk before we go?"

"Sure." Kyle walked with his brother along the dock. "What's up?"

Eric glanced back at the plane and spoke in a hushed tone, "Don't mention anything about Stella or the other girls. Jessica doesn't know about them."

Kyle sighed. "If you're going to date multiple women, you should at least be upfront with them."

"Yeah, right. Women do crazy shit when they get jealous. I don't need the drama."

Back in high school, two of Eric's girlfriends had once shown up at the same party. They got into an ugly, drunken cat fight and then one of them rammed her car into Eric's Corvette. Ever since, his policy had been never to date two women in the same city.

"If you keep playing these women, someone's going to get hurt. You should try focusing on one for a change. You might actually like it."

"Appreciate the advice, bro, but all I'm asking is that you keep this our little secret." Eric gripped Kyle's shoulder. "Can I count on you?"

"Just don't expect me to lie for you."

As his brother boarded the seaplane, Kyle remained on the dock to untie the ropes. A chilly wind blew against his face, and for a split second he glimpsed a pale woman swimming beneath the plane. Kyle drew back, staring down at the dark water.

It was just a large fish.

He pushed the plane away from the dock and hopped on to the pontoon, suddenly fearful that a bloated hand would reach up and grab his leg. He climbed into the plane and slammed the door, getting a strange look from the four passengers.

"Everything okay?" Eric asked from the front row.

Kyle faked a smile. "Just eager to get up in the air." He climbed into the cockpit and fired up the single-prop engine. The Otter seaplane vibrated as he took hold of the yoke.

Eric, Jessica, Shawna and Zack chattered behind him as Kyle taxied the plane away from the dock. Gripping the yoke, he held his breath, watching the wind blow white caps across the water. Suddenly, the thought of leaving his home made his throat constrict. He sped across the lake and in seconds the seaplane was aloft over Lake Union. Thinking about the ghost he'd left behind, Kyle released his breath as the Seattle skyline faded behind him.

* * *

Kyle felt a rush of adrenaline as he flew the seaplane over a mountain ridge. The vibration of the plane's six hundred horsepower Pratt & Whitney engine surged through him. Due to the wind, the flight was a little bumpy at first, but then he found his groove and cruised northeast, keeping the speed at 120 knots, the altitude at 10,000 feet. This high up, the blue horizon went on forever.

Below, thousands of pine trees swayed in the wind. An occasional lake or river passed under them. As the four passengers stared out the windows, Kyle spoke through his intercom, "We've crossed into British Columbia now. Down below, you'll occasionally see ghost towns from the 1800s." He directed their attention to the ruins of several log structures nestled in the mountain valleys. "Many of these towns are located near copper and silver mines that have been abandoned. Some are even claimed to be haunted." Being an author of ghost stories, he had always enjoyed spooking his passengers with strange tales about the old mining towns that came and went. "In one mountain town named Eureka Canyon, all of the townspeople completely vanished and were never found."

Eric hummed the theme song to *The Twilight Zone*. Jessica took photos out the windows and Shawna and Zack shot video. Glancing back at their smiling faces reminded Kyle how much fun he used to have flying tourists on charter flights. "Hang on, everybody." He angled the plane, swooping above the pine-green ocean. The vast untamed wilderness reconnected Kyle with a part of himself that he had forgotten. Even though he had lived most his of life in Seattle, he had always felt a connection to the mountains and woods. Maybe it was because he had spent the first ten years of his life camping, fishing and hunting with his Cree father. Kyle often yearned to be surrounded by nature and escaped to the forest to go hiking, kayaking, or mountain biking at least once a week. The Canadian Rockies offered plenty of places to escape, and the Cree reservation was one of the most remote places in British Columbia. Kyle couldn't believe he had almost passed on this opportunity to return with his brother and sister to the place where they were born. Their enthusiasm lifted his spirits, and he was now looking forward to seeing Ray Roamingbear and Grandfather again.

* * *

Three hours into the flight, the group's excitement had waned. Shawna and Zack, each wearing headphones, leaned shoulder to shoulder and watched a movie on a video player. Eric slept soundly with his head nestled in a neck pillow. Jessica tried to read a new medical thriller, but couldn't concentrate. Maybe it was nerves. She had never flown in a small plane before. They hit some unexpected turbulence and she grabbed the armrests and gasped. Jessica wished Eric would wake up and keep her company, but she knew how much he liked to sleep during flights. She looked out the window at the blue sky. They seemed so high up now. Her mind kept replaying news videos of private planes that had crashed, killing all the passengers.

Stop it, she told herself. *We're going to arrive there safely.*

Jessica looked toward the cockpit at the man piloting the plane. Kyle wore a headset and mirrored sunglasses and stared out the front windshield. His hands seemed calm on the steering wheel, or whatever pilots called it.

What Jessica needed to do was occupy her mind. Grabbing her Nikon camera, she stepped up to the cockpit. The single-prop engine was so loud up here. She tapped Kyle on the shoulder. "Excuse me, do you mind if I ride in the copilot's seat?" She pointed to the empty seat next to him. "I'd like to take some pictures."

"Be my guest," he shouted over the noise from the propeller.

She strapped herself in as they hit another patch of turbulence. Gripping both armrests, she closed her eyes and took a long, deep breath.

Kyle steered the plane upward to an altitude where the ride became smooth again. He offered Jessica the extra headset. "If you'll put this on, we can hear each other better."

She put on the headset and his voice crackled in her ear. "First time in a seaplane?"

"Is it that obvious?"

"Don't worry. I've clocked hundreds of hours in this plane through all kinds of weather. You're in safe hands." He gave her an assuring smile. "Here, I find Chopin puts me at ease." He flipped a switch on the console and classical piano music played through her headphones. Her tension dissolved and she exhaled.

Kyle smiled. "I also have the Red Hot Chili Peppers, if that's more your flavor."

She laughed. "No, Chopin's great."

"You have an accent. Are you from Australia, by chance?"

Jessica nodded. "Queensland. I grew up in a small town on the coast, north of Sydney."

"One of my favorite cities."

"You've been there?"

He nodded. "After college, I spent a summer backpacking across Australia."

"Really..." She leaned toward him. "What all did you do?"

Kyle smiled, his whole face lighting up. "Well, my friends and I stayed in Sydney for a couple weeks and surfed Bondi Beach. Then we flew up to Cairns and did some scuba diving along the Great Barrier Reef."

"I love the Reef. My family used to vacation there every summer." Talking about helicopter rides over the reef, landing on Green Island and exploring the rainforest north of Cairns took Jessica back to her childhood days. "Did you visit the Outback?" she asked.

"Yeah, drove a Jeep to Ayers Rock, then circled back down to the Blue Mountains. Saw plenty of kangaroos and koala bears and drank God knows how many Tooeys and Fourex."

She touched a hand to her chest. "There are days I really miss my hometown. Everybody I know meets up at the pub and drinks Fourex and watches rugby. No one seems to hang out at neighborhood pubs in Seattle. Well, not anyone you'd want to know, anyway."

As Kyle focused on flying, Jessica snuck admiring glances at him. She was surprised that he still wore his wedding ring. Eric said his wife had passed away a couple of years ago. *He must have really loved her.*

Kyle pointed toward the windshield. "We're passing over Glacier National Park." He went on like a tour guide, sharing interesting facts about the region.

The aerial view of mountains and valleys took Jessica's breath away. She snapped several photos. She couldn't wait to post these on Facebook for all her friends to see. She turned the camera and snapped a few of her pilot.

Again, Kyle flashed his boyish grin. "Am I going to end up on your travel blog?"

"If that's okay," she said, suddenly feeling intrusive. "It's not every day I get to be a copilot."

"Would you like a quick flying lesson?"

"Seriously?"

"I used to work as a flight instructor. I could show you the basics."

Jessica shrugged. "Sure, why not?"

He explained the plane's many instruments and gauges. Then he pointed above their heads to the engine and flap controls on the ceiling and called the steering wheel thingies in front of each of their seats "yokes". He talked about flaps and rudders and finding tail winds. Jessica followed some of it, but mostly she found herself studying his face. He was handsome like Eric, but there was something gentle about Kyle that she really liked.

After a twenty-minute lesson, he said, "Okay, ready to help me fly?"

"No way. I don't want to crash the plane."

He laughed. "Don't worry. I won't let you."

Jessica took another deep breath. "What do I do?"

"Take hold of the yoke, like this."

Mimicking Kyle, she gripped the copilot's yoke. The exhilaration of flying sent a thrill through her whole body. "Oh, wow."

"Pretty wild, huh?" He held on to his yoke alongside her. For several minutes they flew the plane together, listening to one of Chopin's piano concertos and cruising over a mountain town. Below, a flock of white birds flew in a V-shaped pattern.

"This is surreal," she said.

"You're doing great," his soothing voice spoke through her headphones. "Hold her steady. Feel like you've got it under control?"

She nodded.

"Good," Kyle said. "I'm going to let go now."

"Oh, no you don't."

"Just for a second. Don't worry, you're safe. Keep holding her steady, like that." He took his hands off the yoke, holding them an inch above it.

Her heart rate soared. "Oh, my God."

Kyle laughed into the headset. "You're flying."

Jessica giggled with excitement. Kyle let her fly solo for several thrilling minutes before he gripped the yoke again. "Nice job, copilot. You just earned your wings."

"That was so amazing." She grinned and looked over her shoulder. Eric was glaring.

* * *

After Jessica returned to her seat, Kyle found a nice tailwind and flew high above the Canadian wilderness. The familiar Rocky Mountain vistas brought back memories of last summer's trip to visit his father. After nearly twenty years of being estranged, Kyle and Jon Elkheart had begun the process of getting to know one another again. At the time, his father had sobered up and was seeing a new woman, Wynona, one of the locals of the town that neighbored the reservation. This week, Kyle planned to visit her and see if she knew where his father had gone.

Shawna poked her head into the cockpit. "Hey, bro, how long 'til we land?"

"We'll be touching down within the hour. Why don't you keep me company?"

His sister climbed into the copilot's seat. They spent the next half hour catching up. She told him about her growing success as a singer for the Black Mollies, a rock band that played in the Seattle area. Shawna had so much potential, if she could just stop destroying herself with drugs.

Kyle studied his sister. With her arms covered in tattoos and her hair dyed blonde with blue streaks, she barely resembled the baby sister he'd grown up with. Since their mother's death, Shawna had more or less raised herself. Their stepfather certainly didn't deserve any credit. Blake Nelson had run their household like a tyrant, trying to discipline the three half-Cree kids into becoming good little Christians. He had whipped them with belts and hammered Jesus into their knuckles with a metal ruler. When that didn't work, he gave them a hard slap to the face. Blake had liked Eric best because he was obedient and did everything he could to please his stepfather. The old man didn't care much for Kyle or Shawna, who seemed to have "too much Indian in them" to follow the rules. Hating their home life, Kyle had escaped inward, writing horror novels, while Shawna rebelled through drug abuse and her angry music. Blake still invited them over for Christmas and Thanksgiving, but only Eric ever showed up. They were the picture-perfect dysfunctional family.

As if reading his mind, Shawna gave him a look that said, *We've been to hell and back together, big brother, but we're still here.*

Despite all the bad choices Shawna had made in the past few years, Kyle loved her deeply. Every so often she landed on his doorstep homeless and crashed on his couch. He'd give her some money and then she would disappear again. Maybe this trip would give Kyle an opportunity to be the big brother that he couldn't be in the past.

The plane glided over another ridge, and Kyle spotted a belt of thick forest surrounding an emerald-green lake. "Down below is Lake Akwâkopiy," he said over the intercom. "One of Canada's hidden treasures." As Kyle made the final descent, he circled the lake, checking the wind. The plane passed over a lumber mill where hundreds of logs floated on one section of the lake. Men in hardhats drove small motorboats and operated cranes that stacked logs onto the shore next to the mill. Several loggers looked up. "That's Thorpe Timber's lumber mill," Kyle explained. "Almost everyone who lives around Lake Akwâkopiy works there."

Flying into the wind now, Kyle powered back and added flaps. The seaplane's shadow glided across the placid lake. Sparkling with sequins of sunlight, the water along the cove was completely empty of boats. The plane descended with a dip that caused Shawna to laugh. The group cheered as the pontoons skidded across the water toward Hagen's Cove— a Danish logging town nestled in the pines and protected by a backdrop of granite bluffs. A white church with a high steeple loomed at the center of town. Along the water's edge stretched the docks of a marina packed with boats. Up the hill stood the Beowulf Lodge and Tavern, a rustic log-and-rock structure that overlooked the lake.

Kyle said over the intercom, "Welcome to paradise, everyone."

Below them on the dock, Ray Roamingbear walked with the aid of a wooden staff. He waved as the plane taxied up to the marina. A man in coveralls tossed a rope around one of the pontoons and pulled the plane to the dock. Kyle cut the engine and Eric opened the hatch. The group climbed out, stretching and taking in the scenery.

It was a hot summer day, and Shawna wasn't off the plane two seconds before she stripped down to her bikini top. Zack pulled out his video camera and chased her down the pier. Shawna vogued for the camera. Her antics captured the attention of a handful of locals climbing out of a fishing boat.

Ray Roamingbear approached wearing a broad smile. "It's about time you kids came back for a visit. It only took you twenty years. Kyle, it's been over a year since you last visited."

"Sorry," Kyle said, feeling guilty. "I intended to come back sooner, but life kept getting in the way."

Eric shook their cousin's hand. "We appreciate you inviting us."

"Anytime. You guys are family." Nearing fifty now, Ray had silver streaks in his long black hair. He stood well over six feet and was built strong from his years working as a logger. Most of his muscle had softened since he had retired from the mill. Now he managed the marina and the Beowulf Lodge and Tavern.

"How have you been, Ray?" Kyle asked.

"Pretty good, I guess. Can't complain." He tapped his bum leg. "Except when the weather gets moody." Ray eyed each of the Elkheart siblings. "Can't believe you kids are all grown up." He hobbled with his wooden staff toward Shawna. "When I last saw you, young lady, you were just a tyke in diapers. How old are you now?"

"Twenty-two," she said, suddenly bashful.

Kyle put an arm around his sister. "Shawna's the singer for a rock band. Zack here is the drummer. They just signed with a label."

Ray raised an eyebrow. "Is that so?"

Shawna nodded. "We start recording next month. I plan to write a couple songs while I'm here."

Ray grinned. "Well, you've come to the right place for inspiration. Your grandfather and I sing and play a bit ourselves."

Eric said, "I can't believe we're actually back in Hagen's Cove. Ray, you look the same as I remember."

"My hair's turning white and I've put on a few pounds." He let out a husky laugh and looked at Jessica. "Eric, you didn't say you were bringing such a pretty lady." Then to Jessica, he said, "The loggers may riot if they get a look at you."

She smiled. "I like you already." Then she gave the big man a hug.

Ray clapped his hands. "I want you kids to feel at home. You're welcome to have lunch at the tavern, and I've got boats and Seadoos if you want to spend the day out on the lake."

"Now, you're talking." Eric threw his arm around his girlfriend's shoulder. "It's time we got this vacation rolling. Let's get beer and snacks and take a boat out. What do you say, babe?"

"Whatever the gang wants to do," Jessica said.

"Let's hit the lake!" Shawna said.

"Hell yeah!" said Zack.

"All right, then," Ray said, grinning. As the group followed him down to the marina, Eric, still arm in arm with Jessica, looked back at Kyle. "You coming, bro?"

"Go on. I'll catch up." Kyle watched his brother and Jessica walk away, her head resting on Eric's shoulder, and tried not to think of his brother's roster of out-of-town girlfriends. This one was different, special. Kyle thought she deserved better, but it was none of his business.

After making sure his plane was securely tied to the docks, Kyle stood and inhaled the fresh pine air. The reeds along the banks were alive with croaking frogs and mating dragonflies. He took in the vista of forest and mountains that surrounded Hagen's Cove. The logging community neighbored their reservation. When Kyle and Eric were boys, they used to ride their bikes through town, checking out the latest comic books at the marina's general store while Elkheart and Ray put down a few beers at the tavern.

Hagen's Cove looked exactly the same as it did when Kyle was ten years old, before his whole world shattered. Since leaving the reservation, his life had been a series of tragedies—growing up with an abusive stepfather, losing his mother to cancer and then his wife to a car accident. Kyle was returning to his Cree roots with many wounds in need of healing. While he was thinking this, an eagle flew overhead. According to legend, eagles were divine messengers, able to commune with the gods. Kyle smiled as the creature's shadow passed over him. He could use a little divine intervention. Perhaps retreating to the land of his ancestors would help him in a way that psychotherapy could not.

Chapter Three

Kendra Meacham gripped her passenger door's armrest when the semi-truck she'd hitched a ride on turned off Trans-Canada Highway and onto a narrow backwoods road.

Goodbye civilization. Hello new life in the sticks.

Calgary was far behind and Kendra almost cried tears of relief that she was going somewhere Jake couldn't find her. She pulled down her sunglasses and examined her black eye in the side mirror. It hurt every time she blinked. She needed to touch it up with makeup, but didn't want the truck driver to start asking a bunch of questions.

Some country song was playing on the radio. Jorgen, the trucker who had been so generous to give her a lift, hummed along, his deep voice way off rhythm.

Kendra smiled to herself. She felt powerful riding so high up as the eighteen-wheeler carved a swath through a dense evergreen forest.

"So what takes you to Hagen's Cove?" Jorgen said with a thick Danish accent.

"A new job."

"Let me guess. Ray Roamingbear hired you to waitress at Beowulf Tavern."

"Yeah, how'd you know?"

"Most girls who move to Hagen's Cove start off at the tavern."

"Oh." The way he worded it made Kendra think of the last strip club she'd worked at. *Most girls start out as cocktail waitresses,* her oily-haired manager had said. *Then you work your way up to the stage where you can make some serious cash. And if you do special favors for me, I'll give you special treatment.* She had hoped to be done with working for slimeballs. The Beowulf Tavern that she'd found on the Internet wasn't a strip joint. An old-fashioned bar and grill that overlooked a lake. The photos had made it look like an oasis hidden away from the modern world. The man who ran the tavern had seemed nice enough on the phone, but Kendra had a pattern of gravitating toward the wrong men. For the first time, she felt apprehensive about leaving the city for some backwoods town. "How does Ray Roamingbear treat the waitresses?"

"Like his own kin," the truck driver said.

"Does he have a high turnover rate?"

"Only when the seasons change. Summer kids go back to college. Locals work the off season." Jorgen looked over at her. "You sure are starting late in the summer. Is this a permanent stop for you?"

"I don't know, maybe. Have any of the women ever complained about Ray?"

"Nah. Don't worry. He's a good man. A well-respected Cree First Nation. You'll see."

They rode in silence for a while. The eighteen-wheeler trundled along, the chains rattling on its long flatbed trailer. She was amazed how there was nothing for miles along this road except endless walls of trees broken up by the occasional rise of a rocky cliff. They passed a moose crossing sign, and then a few kilometers later, a bear crossing sign. *I'm not in Kansas anymore,* she mused. The road narrowed, as if the forest on either side were trying to twine back together. Overgrown branches scraped the tops and sides of the truck. Kendra caught herself squeezing her armrest.

"You got a place to live?" Jorgen asked.

"Not yet. Ray's putting me up at the lodge until I find a place to rent."

"I can ask around town for you. I know a good many folks."

"Thanks. That would be nice."

"Nothing to it. In these parts, we help our own. I scratch your back and you scratch mine, if you know what I mean."

Kendra slid over against the door and looked out her side window. "How much farther?"

"About fifteen kilometers." Jorgen hummed along with another country song.

She pulled out her cell phone. She had no bars, not that she had anyone to call. There were a dozen text messages from Jake. She didn't dare read them.

The truck suddenly came to a stop at a junction. The brakes made a hissing sound.

Kendra looked at the trucker with the heavy sideburns. "Something wrong?"

"I've reached my destination." Jorgen pointed to a sign: *Thorpe Timber Mill and Logging Company.* A dirt road led into another part of the forest. "I'm gonna have to let you off here."

Kendra's heart dropped. "But this is the middle of nowhere. Can't you take me all the way into town?"

"Sorry, miss, I got a shipment to pick up. Can't be late. You'll have to hitch another ride."

She hadn't seen any other cars since they turned off the highway. She stared at the narrow paved road that snaked into a dark patch of woods. "Please, I'll pay you to drive me into town. I can give you twenty bucks."

"I don't want your money. But I can think of another way you can pay me." Jorgen grinned at her. "How 'bout a ride for a ride?" He nodded toward the bed area behind their seats. The twisted sheets smelled of sweat and cigarettes.

"I'd rather walk." Kendra picked up her backpack and opened the passenger door.

Jorgen grabbed her wrist. "Then how 'bout a blow job, you little whore?" He forced her head down to the bulge of his crotch.

Kendra clawed his arm and ripped loose from his hold. She scrambled for the door.

"Oh, don't leave." Jorgen's hands grabbed her from behind, squeezing her breasts. "We're just getting started."

"Let go of me!" Kendra pulled a taser out of her purse and zapped his ribs with five thousand volts of don't fuck with me. His eyes rolled back. He flopped against the seat, gibbering.

She leaped out of the truck, landing hard on her ankle. "Damn it!" She limped down the road, backpack and purse slung over one shoulder, taser gripped in her fist. She reached the junction of the dirt road and considered walking toward the timber mill. Maybe a lumberjack would give her a ride into town. But there was no mill in sight, just a lonely dirt road that stretched about a hundred yards before the forest swallowed it.

Besides, that was the way *he* was going.

Looking back, she saw Jorgen sit up behind the wheel, grinning. "You want to play with me, bitch!" He gunned the Mack truck's engine. The dual exhaust pipes spat black smoke.

Kendra hurried up the paved road, favoring her right foot. There was no shoulder. Just the shadowy woods choked with pine needles and underbrush.

The truck growled as it lurched several feet then stopped. Jorgen spun the wheel and turned the big rig at the junction. He poked his head out the window. "Have a nice walk. Be careful when you pass the old Indian reservation. Those woods are haunted." Laughing, he drove the long flatbed down the dirt road, kicking up dust.

Kendra hobbled along the paved road, fighting back tears and losing the battle. No matter where she went, she seemed to always attract bad men.

* * *

As Shawna and Zack followed Ray into the marina's general store, Eric and Jessica stopped outside. He was eager to get down to the boat rental shack where he'd spotted a pretty young thing in a bikini top and shorts.

Eric handed Jessica a twenty. "Go inside and get us some snacks. I'll line up the boat."

"Okay." His girlfriend clung to his waist, gazing up at him. "Thank you, love."

"For what?"

"For bringing me here. For introducing me to your family. This is a big step for us."

"You mean you're not ready to run?"

She laughed. "No. Your family's quite nice, actually."

"Yeah, we'll see what you think after a whole week with them." He guided her toward the store's front door. "Now, go get us some snacks." He swatted her on the behind.

"Eric!" Jessica blushed and then entered the general store.

He hurried in the opposite direction toward the boat rental shack. Behind the counter stood a girl with a dark tan and an amazing body. Eric approached with a swagger. As soon as her eyes met his, he feigned stubbing his flip-flop on a dock board and hopped around on one foot. He gave the girl an embarrassed look. She smiled big.

Game on.

"Are you okay?" she asked.

"Let me start over." He walked away, turned around and walked back toward the girl at the counter. "Was that more graceful?"

"Much. You must be from the city."

"Yes. And you must be a local."

"Born and raised."

He offered his hand. "I'm Eric."

She placed her small hand in his. "Nadine." The feel of her skin against his was electric. She let go too soon. "What can I do for you?"

"Well, let's see, Nadine." He glanced back at the marina store to make sure no one was coming. Then he leaned against the counter, inches from Nadine's face. "Do you know anyplace around here where a man can rent a boat from a girl with beautiful brown eyes?" He knew the line was cheesy, but the small town girls ate it up.

She giggled. "I can do that for you."

He held her gaze for several seconds. She looked away and then back at him. Damn she was cute. No older than nineteen, maybe twenty. Her tan skin was so smooth and toned, and Eric imagined what her large breasts must look like underneath that bikini top. *She's probably a firecracker in the sack.* He should have come on this trip stag. Then he'd be free to roam the town and check out the local talent. Maybe he could break away from the group one evening.

The girl tucked a strand of hair behind her ear. "So, um, would you like to see our boats?"

"I'll take the fastest ride you've got." Eric gave her his most charming smile. "And then you can give me your phone number."

* * *

As Kyle and a dockworker stored everyone's luggage in a shed, the distant sound of a motorboat reverberated off the lake. A flock of ducks flew up as a red speedboat torpedoed across the water toward the marina. Eric stood behind the boat's wheel. He was shirtless now, wearing his swimsuit, bucket hat and sunglasses. He swerved the boat sideways, splashing water against the docks. Jessica, Shawna and Zack all sat on the boat in their bathing suits, drinking beers. Music blared, disturbing the serenity of this normally quiet haven.

Eric raised a beer can. "We're going for a spin around the lake. Come join us."

"You guys go ahead," Kyle said. "I'm going to hang back and get some writing done."

"Ah, come on," Shawna said. "Even Stephen King takes a vacation. Let's have some fun."

Getting drunk with his siblings was not high on his list of fun activities. Whenever any of them got wasted, the family demons surfaced. "I'll pass. Maybe later this week."

"Suit yourself, bro. We'll be back before sunset." Eric spun the boat around and sped off.

Kyle grabbed his backpack and retreated to a table on the deck of the Beowulf Tavern. A waitress dressed like a medieval wench took his order and then brought him a bottle of Coke and a bowl of venison stew. He pulled out some printed chapters of his manuscript, the fifth installment of his *Detective Winterbone Series*. Alex Winterbone was a private eye who solved mysteries for ghosts. Kyle's editor had been on his back all month to finish this book. "Kyle, you've got rabid fans hungry for your next *Winterbone* novel. Check out your Facebook fan page. They're getting restless."

His previous four novels had risen to the top of the best-seller lists and had been optioned by Hollywood. The first movie had been released last Halloween and was a cult hit with horror fans. Since his career had exploded, the pressure to write the next installment had intensified. His publisher and fans expected nothing less than a blockbuster. His publisher's blog reported that Kyle Elkheart was busy writing the final chapters of the fifth Winterbone novel, *Ghost Vengeance*. What the fans didn't know was that Kyle had been creatively blocked for two years.

He read his manuscript for an hour, striking out words and making notes. The chapters he'd written yesterday were a disjointed wreck. If his readers read this crap, they'd burn his books and "un-like" his Facebook page. His muse had not returned since he had been interrupted by his brother yesterday morning. Hopefully immersing himself in nature would inspire him again. All he needed was to free his mind from distractions.

"This town looks straight out of a postcard, don't you think?" spoke a woman's voice with a familiar Australian accent.

Kyle looked up, surprised to see Jessica. She had changed from her bikini to a T-shirt and cargo shorts. She looked beyond the marina toward the log structures of Hagen's Cove. "I love rustic towns like this one, don't you?"

"Yeah, it's much more peaceful than the city." They stared at one another for an awkward moment. "So…you didn't stay on the boat with the others?"

She shook her head. "If I'm out in the sun too long, I turn beet red. Besides, I don't really party like I did in my college days."

"Yeah, me neither."

Jessica was even cuter without her makeup. Freckles on her nose made her look young, but Kyle figured by the maturity in her eyes she was close to thirty like himself. Again, he became spellbound by her beauty. "Mind if I join you for lunch?" she asked.

"Sure." As he stood up to move his laptop and backpack, half his pages blew onto the deck. "Shit."

She helped him chase down the flying papers. As they scrambled after the same page, they bumped shoulders. "Oh, bugger." She touched his arm. "Sorry about that."

"No, I can be such a klutz."

"Me, too." She laughed and looked down at his jumbled pages. "So what's this you're reading?"

"Uh, just some work I brought with me." He stuffed his manuscript into his backpack and invited her to take a seat across from him. The waitress came over and Jessica ordered a bowl of freshwater mussels and a pint of ale from the local brewery. "Funny, they call the beer here 'mead.'"

"That's what the Vikings used to call it," Kyle said. "The Danish brewers ferment it with water, honey, malt and yeast. Careful though, you can get drunk off the stuff faster than beer."

As they made small talk, the waitress brought a bowl of steamed mussels and a stein of mead. Jessica clinked her drink against Kyle's Coke. "Cheers."

He felt alive in Jessica's presence. It had been too long since he'd had a stimulating conversation with an attractive woman. His leg wouldn't stop bouncing. *Chill out, she's Eric's girlfriend.* The more she talked, the more baffled Kyle became. How could an intelligent woman like this be dating a self-centered asshole like his brother? "So, how did you and Eric meet?"

"We met at a fundraiser for breast cancer. Eric donates a lot of pro bono work for the charity that I volunteer for."

Their mother had died of breast cancer. Maybe his brother wasn't always self-centered after all.

Jessica continued, "One of our fundraisers was to auction dates with Seattle's most eligible bachelors. When Eric got onstage, a bunch of my girlfriends dared me to bid on him and I won. He turned out to be quite charming."

In college, Eric could charm the panties off any sorority girl. Women were nothing more than a game to him. Poor Jessica didn't know her boyfriend had at least three other lovers on the side. "So how long have

BRIAN MORELAND

you two been dating?"

"Almost a year. This weekend will be our anniversary."

"Wow, sounds serious."

"It's getting that way. I moved in with him last month." She glanced down at her left hand. No engagement ring yet. She rubbed her ring finger as she looked back at the lake.

Kyle wanted to warn her that Eric would never propose. That he was going to date her until he got bored and then drop her like all the rest. But it wasn't his place. *Who knows? Maybe Eric will actually grow up and devote himself to her.* Kyle wasn't holding his breath.

The tavern's back door swung open, and a well-dressed man in a tan cowboy hat and alligator boots came out with a redheaded girl no taller than his knees. They walked hand in hand over to Kyle and Jessica's table. "Afternoon," the man said, speaking with a local Danish accent and tipping his hat. With distinguished features and silver hair, he looked to be in his mid-fifties. "I'm Mayor Jensen Thorpe and this is my daughter, Chloe."

"We're going to feed the ducks," the girl announced.

"How fun," Jessica said. "How old are you, Chloe?"

She held up four fingers.

"Well, you are just adorable. I love your dress."

"Thanks." The girl tugged at the hem of her skirt.

Mayor Thorpe picked Chloe up and perched her on his arm. "We saw your plane land and wanted to welcome you to our town. A lot of tourists visit Hagen's Cove for the summer, and we like to meet as many as we can." The girl nodded in agreement.

Jessica said, "Kyle and I were just talking about how lovely it is here."

"We have plenty of fun activities to offer: fishing, hunting, boating, you name it, and lots of great places to camp." Mayor Thorpe winked. "If you two lovebirds rent a boat, there's a romantic spot around the cove that's perfect for watching the sunset."

Kyle said, "Oh, we're not together."

"My apologies," the mayor said. "With the number of honeymooners who stay here at the lodge, I've gotten in the habit of talking like a travel brochure. Chloe, you want to give our guests your mother's card?" The girl reached into his breast pocket and handed each of them a business card. Mayor Thorpe said, "If there's anything you need, feel free to call my wife, Celeste. She'd be more than happy to book your activities."

"Thanks," Kyle said.

Thorpe looked proudly at Chloe. "You ready to go feed the ducks?"

The girl nodded.

He looked at Kyle and Jessica and tipped his hat. "Enjoy your afternoon."

As the mayor and his daughter walked down the hill toward the lake, Jessica said, "Wow, you don't get this kind of hospitality in a big city."

Kyle looked down at the marina. "The others still aren't back yet." He called his brother's cell phone, but it went to voicemail.

"They must be having a bloody good time," she said. "I guess we're on our own for a while."

It surprised Kyle how much he was enjoying Jessica's company. He grabbed his backpack. "Hey, come with me. I want to show you something."

* * *

Jessica felt a little guilty following Kyle, but who knew how long it would be before Eric and the others returned? Besides, Kyle had made her curious. "What are you going to show me?"

"You'll see." He led her inside the Beowulf Tavern. Jessica was greeted by the aroma of venison stew, beer and pinewood. She ran her hand across a log column adorned with intricate carvings that reflected Danish folklore. Mounted on every wall were dozens of game animals with jutting antlers—deer, elk, moose and mountain goats. Even a few wild boars with large tusks.

Kyle whispered into her ear. "Everybody hunts out here in the sticks."

"I can see that."

He pointed to a giant stuffed grizzly bear standing in one corner. "Ray Roamingbear brought that one down himself."

Above a rock fireplace hung a large tapestry of a Viking warrior swinging a sword toward a giant ogre. Kyle said, "That's Beowulf slaying the mythological monster, Grendel."

Jessica nodded. "The hero from the poem, *The Eddas*."

Kyle gave her a sideways glance. "You know Norse mythology?"

"I took a course in college that covered Scandinavian history. I found it so fascinating that a girlfriend and I traveled to Denmark and Norway during our summer break. The Beowulf tale was my favorite."

"You're full of surprises." He smiled and guided her through the dining hall. The tavern was packed with locals sitting in booths. Several old men sat around one long table, smoking pipes, playing dominoes and talking in Danish. Most of the patrons were thick-bearded loggers drinking beer. A few ogled Jessica like they hadn't seen a woman in ages. There were also a couple of Royal Canadian Mounted Policemen in red uniforms eating lunch. They stared at the new arrivals, nodding their heads with friendly hellos. In another section, men were shooting pool, and a jukebox in the corner played an old Willie Nelson song. The atmosphere reminded Jessica of her hometown in Australia. It was the tight-knit community that she missed most when she had moved to Seattle.

She followed Kyle down a hall to an alcove decorated like a museum.

He said, "This shows the history of Hagen's Cove."

The walls were covered in framed photos of several decades: men at the barber shop, Mounties on horseback, Mayor Thorpe in a suit and hardhat with a group of loggers at the mill. The color photos faded as Jessica walked backward along the timeline of the town's evolution. The back corner held the oldest pictures, grainy black-and-white photos of lumberjacks posing in front of felled trees.

"Absolutely charming," Jessica said. "I love towns full of history."

Kyle leaned in close to her. "Hagen's Cove started out as a logging town back in the 1880s, when a large number of Danish immigrants migrated from Denmark to Canada." He pointed to a photo of lumberjacks meeting with Indians. "These are my Cree ancestors who settled on the reservation right outside of town. Our people were here long before the Danes arrived."

Centered among the lumberjacks and Cree men stood a stout white man dressed in a three-piece suit and top hat. He had a bushy mustache and a strong jaw. He looked more educated than the others. A sign next to the man read, *Thorpe Timber Company. Estab. 1882.*

"Who's the tall man in the suit?" Jessica asked.

"Hagen Thorpe, the town's founder."

"A relative of the mayor's?"

Kyle nodded. "The Thorpe clan has governed this community since the mill first opened. They own this hunting lodge and tavern and practically every business in town." He put a hand on her shoulder. "If you'll excuse me, I need to go talk to Ray about renting a vehicle. Be right back." He went up a staircase.

Left alone, Jessica looked back at the wall of photos. Using her Nikon camera, she snapped pics of them for her blog. She heard footsteps. A tall woman had stepped into the alcove and was examining the color photos. The lady gave a friendly nod, then turned back toward the pictures. Jessica snapped a few more photos. When she lowered her camera, she noticed the tall woman had moved closer. Jessica said, "I was admiring the town's history."

"Oh, yes, Hagen's Cove's full of history."

"Are you from around here?" Jessica asked.

"Been living here the past thirty years. I saw your plane arrive. Are you with Kyle Elkheart's group, by chance?"

Jessica nodded. "You know him?"

"I knew his father." The woman's kind eyes darkened with concern. "When are you aiming to go the reservation?"

"When the others return from the lake, I guess." After an awkward pause, she offered her hand to the woman. "I'm Jessica, by the way."

"Where are my manners? Wynona Thorpe, pleased to meet you."

"Are you a descendent of Hagen Thorpe?" Jessica looked back at the black-and-white photo of the businessman standing among the lumberjacks.

"I married into the family." Wynona looked back toward the people eating in the restaurant and then lowered her voice. "Let me offer some advice. Tell Kyle to take you and your friends someplace else to spend your holiday. Vancouver or Banff. It doesn't matter where, just get far away from the reservation."

"Why? What's wrong with staying there?"

Wynona pressed closer. Her breath smelled of stale liquor. "I've been dreaming about you."

Jessica released a nervous laugh. "What?"

The woman pointed a shaky finger up toward the ceiling. "They've been speaking to me in my dreams. They told me you were coming and that you would be in danger out there in the woods."

Jessica looked up the staircase, hoping Kyle would return soon. "Uh, I need to go find my friend."

"Listen to me!" Wynona's hand lashed out and grabbed Jessica's wrist.

"Let me go." She tried to break loose, but the woman's grip was strong.

"Trust me, Jessica. The sins of the father shall fall upon the sons. Tell Kyle to go far away from the Devil's Woods as quick as you can."

As Wynona turned and hurried toward the exit, a crumpled piece of paper fell from her purse. Jessica picked up the paper and called out, "Ma'am?" but the woman rushed out of the tavern too quickly.

Confused, Jessica unfolded the paper. On it were sketches drawn in heavy charcoal. Demon faces bordered a collage of mutilated bodies, some disemboweled, some decapitated, others of nude women with their legs spread wide, like a teenage boy might draw, only these women were more realistic, sketched by someone with a talented hand and a demented mind.

* * *

Wynona Thorpe pounded the steering wheel as she left the tavern in her Buick. She glared at her reflection in the rearview mirror. "Wynona, you stupid, stupid fool. You've gone and done it this time." She shook her head and laughed. "Bet she thought I was crazy." She touched the ivory Jesus hanging from her mirror. "Lord, forgive me for my sins. And deliver the innocent from evil. In Christ's name, Amen."

Wynona pulled into the driveway of the Thorpe Funeral Home and Crematorium. She parked beside a maroon hearse. The front half of the building was where Wynona worked as the town's mortician. She walked through a parlor full of empty coffins. In the mortuary, her thirty-year-old son, Hugo, was sitting at a metal slab, listening to opera music and painting makeup onto the face of a naked woman's corpse.

Wynona yelled, "Hugo!"

Her son turned around on his stool. "What, Mother?"

"I…" She squeezed her fist. "I told you to dress them before you apply the makeup. Show the dead some decency."

Hugo looked back at the corpse's large gray breasts and grinned. "It's such a waste when they die so young. Especially the pretty ones." He caressed the sutures that stitched up the college girl's chest.

Wynona couldn't believe this man had once come out of her womb. Hugo had his father's gray eyes. Every time she looked at them she saw the bastard who had knocked her up thirty years ago.

Hugo grinned. "Now, if you'll excuse me, Mother, I've got a masterpiece to finish." Moving to the rhythm of the opera, he rolled lipstick across the dead girl's lips.

Wynona shook her head and walked down the hall to their home at the back half of the building. She went to the liquor cabinet in the den. Her hands trembled as she poured brandy into a tumbler. She gulped down the entire drink and then poured another.

She stepped into her art studio where the walls were covered in charcoal drawings of the twisted nightmares she'd been having lately. One of a black demon face with white pinpoints for eyes stared back at her. She went to a curio cabinet, opened a drawer and pulled out a photo of Jon Elkheart and herself taken at the reservation. They once had an affair that got too many people whispering in this town. Now, seeing Elkheart's face, the brandy absorbed Wynona's sorrow. Her eyes clouded with memories of a time when lying in Elkheart's arms was the only thing that made life worth living.

Wynona rubbed the scars on her wrists. *What was Kyle doing bringing people to the reservation? Hadn't Elkheart warned his kids to stay away? Obviously not, the stupid drunk.* She sipped her brandy. *Best not to worry about 'em. What happens to those kids is the devil's doing.*

Part Two

Ghost Village

I don't know why I have strange visions and can see ghosts or how I became cursed with this gift. Maybe it was falling through the ice and drowning when I was five, dying for three whole minutes before I was revived. Or perhaps it was after my God-fearing stepfather beat me so brutally that I crossed death's doorway once more. However it started, I can assure you there is a spirit world and it is all around us. And not all ghosts are friendly.

—Detective Alex Winterbone

Chapter Four

After Eric, Shawna and Zack returned from the boat ride around the lake, the group gathered with Ray in front of the marina's general store. Kyle was stunned that his dad's ex-girlfriend had threatened Jessica. He looked down at the twisted charcoal drawings of mutilated bodies, shaking his head. "I met Wynona last summer when I visited Dad. She seemed like a nice woman. Ray, what happened to her?"

"Their relationship ended badly, and Wynona never got over it. Every time your father comes into town, she shows up drunk and begs him to take her back."

Shawna said, "Wow, our dad has a stalker?"

Eric put an arm around his girlfriend. "Where does this bitch live? I'm going to have a word with her."

"I'll take care of it," Ray said. "Your threatening her would only make things worse. She once came at your dad with a knife. I'll let her doctor know she's had another episode."

Jessica said, "She warned us to stay away from a place called the Devil's Woods."

"That's just an old superstition among the townspeople," Ray said. "They have all kinds of stories about the woods around here. Campfire tales mostly. Pay no attention to anything Wynona told you."

Kyle looked at his watch. "Guys, we've only got a couple hours of sunlight left. Let's get some groceries and then hit the road."

While Eric and Jessica went to rent a second vehicle, Kyle, Shawna and Zack shopped at the general store and stocked up on enough food, beer and supplies to last a week. Kyle carried a box of groceries outside to a beat-up blue Jeep Cherokee that was already packed with their luggage.

Ray tossed the keys to Kyle. "It's gassed up and ready to go."

Kyle opened his wallet and pulled out some cash. "How much to rent your vehicle?"

Ray waved his hand. "Nothing. Use it for as long as you need it. I've got another one."

"Thanks." Now that Kyle had a moment alone with his cousin, he said, "Ray, I'm concerned about the drawings that Wynona left behind. Do you think she had anything to do with Elkheart's disappearance?"

"Nah, the most Wynona would have done is run him out of town for a while."

"I hate not knowing where Dad went."

"He'll come back after he sobers up. He always does."

Kyle nodded.

"Sure I can't talk you into staying here in town?" Ray asked. "Since the tribe left, the cabins at the reservation have gotten pretty run down. I keep meaning to go out there and fix the place up, but I'm too busy running the lodge and marina."

"I'd prefer to stay at my father's house. I also want to check on Grandfather."

"He's gotten more senile since you last saw him. He might not even recognize you. You'd be more comfortable staying at the lodge."

"I appreciate the offer, but I want Eric and Shawna to revisit our childhood home."

Ray nodded. "If you change your mind, you're welcome to stay here free of charge."

The sound of an engine growling turned into the gravel lot. Eric parked a shiny black Hummer next to the scratched-up Jeep Cherokee.

Kyle narrowed his eyes. "Seriously, Eric, do you always have to one-up me?"

His brother smirked and took a swig of beer.

Ray walked up to his window. "Ey, I'd hold off on drinking until you get to the reservation. The police around here are real sticklers about drinking and driving."

"You got it." Eric downed his beer and tossed it into a barrel. His eyes looked glassy after drinking on the boat.

Kyle said, "Why don't you let Jessica drive?"

From the passenger seat, she said, "I offered, but he won't let me."

"I can drive just fine," Eric said. "Let's get a move on."

There was no use trying to take Eric's keys away. Kyle had tried a few times before and ended up in a fistfight. His brother was taller, stockier and threw a mean punch.

"Just drive slowly," Kyle said. "It's only ten miles, but the roads are narrow."

Eric gave a salute.

Kyle went back to the Jeep. Now, Shawna and Zack had disappeared again. It seemed like every time Kyle turned his back, they were gallivanting off somewhere. Earlier they had locked themselves in the marina bathroom doing God knows what. This time he found them down by the lake.

Shawna saw him coming and hid whatever she was smoking. Giggling, she punched Zack's shoulder to get his attention. The air around them reeked of pot smoke.

Kyle glared at his sister and her boyfriend. "Okay, let's get one thing straight. What you do back in Seattle is your business. But we're in a foreign country. That means no drugs."

Zack lowered his face. "Sorry, Mr. Elkheart."

Shawna made a little girl face. "Ah, don't be like Eric."

"Seriously, Shawna, you can get into some serious shit if you're caught with that." Kyle held out his palm. "Hand it over."

"Fine." She gave him the joint.

Kyle walked over to the reeds and tossed it into the lake.

Still giggling, Shawna and Zack followed him back to the Jeep. Kyle sat behind the wheel and started the engine. His sister climbed into the front seat. "Sorry, bro. Still mad?"

"No, just use your head."

Ray walked up to Kyle's window and gave him a knowing look. "You kids stay out of trouble, you hear? This is a peaceful town, and we'd like to keep it that way."

"We will." Kyle felt ashamed of his siblings. "Can you make it over for dinner this evening? I'm making my mother's world famous stew."

Their cousin smiled. "I'll do my best. No promises though. The tavern keeps me busy on Friday night. Probably be after supper if I do."

"Swing by anytime," Kyle said.

Everyone waved goodbye to Ray as the Jeep and Hummer left the marina store. Kyle felt a surge of excitement as he drove down the paved road that led out of Hagen's Cove and into the backwoods where he was born.

* * *

Buzzards circled the blue sky, searching for road kill.

Kendra Meacham lost track of how long she'd been walking along the winding road. With her twisted ankle, she had to stop every few hundred yards. She kept looking back to see if any cars were coming, but none came. She wished she had driven her own car, but her ex-boyfriend Jake had taken her keys. She imagined him barreling around the curve in her Mustang, hell-bent on running her over. The thought caused her to quicken her step.

He can't find me here. I'm safe. I'm safe.

The late-afternoon sun bore down on her. Her clothes were sticking to her, her hair matted down with sweat. She drank the last of her water and stuffed the bottle back into her backpack. Everything Kendra owned was beginning to burden her shoulders. She couldn't wait to reach town.

Up ahead a green sign read, *Hagen's Cove 10 Kilometers.*

Her spirits deflated. At this pace it would be nightfall before she reached town. Someone had to come along soon. Eventually the mill workers would end their shift and drive into town. She just hoped Jorgen wasn't one of them. The thought of seeing that pig again made her nauseous. If he was a regular at the tavern, then she had no choice. At least she had shown him what happens when you mess with Kendra Meacham. Next time she'd zap his balls.

That brought a smile to her face.

She came upon another dirt road with some rusty mailboxes. A dilapidated sign with bullet holes in it read,

Lake Akwâkopiy
Cree First Nation Reserve
No Trespassing

Be careful when you pass the old Indian reservation. The woods are haunted. Remembering Jorgen's warning, Kendra hurried past the sign.

He was just trying to spook me. Nothing to be afraid of here. Move along, folks.

She heard a rustle somewhere in the woods. She hop-walked quickly, earning lots of complaints from her bad ankle. Once again the woods choked the road, the long pine branches reaching for her. A thick canopy of branches blocked out the sun, forming a natural tunnel. The forest along this stretch was darker, the maple, aspen and pines hovering close together. They didn't seem like normal trees. More like beings with old souls who had gathered close to the road to watch the plight of the gimp girl.

Keep going, keep going.

The story of her life. Always running.

This time she was going to plant some roots. Make long-time friends. Maybe even settle down with a man who knew how to treat her.

Kendra stopped for a rest. She was growing weak from exhaustion and thirst, and to top off her miseries, she had to pee wicked bad. She started to squat alongside the road, but felt too self-conscious. She hiked into the woods, having to push back branches. "Shit!" The ground sloped and she stumbled downhill several feet before it finally leveled off. She groaned, rubbing her ankle. It hurt so badly now that when she put any weight on her left foot, the ankle buckled.

"Christ!" Now she had to find a walking stick. But first she had to take care of business before her bladder burst. Kendra pulled down her shorts and panties. Pine needles scraped her ass as she squatted at the base of a spruce. Relief came instantly. She looked around. The vegetation was so overgrown in here that her eyes had to adjust to the gloom.

Again something rustled in the trees.

Kendra jerked her head. The tangle of pine needles distorted her view of anything beyond a few feet.

It's probably just a squirrel.

But the sounds persisted. Footsteps crunching over leaves, a body snapping branches. And then the air filled with a god-awful stench, like the smell of carrion.

Kendra willed her body to stop peeing and held her breath.

From the road came the sound of tires trundling over pavement. *Thank God. A ride out of here.*

"Hey!" Kendra yelled, rising to her feet. She pulled up her shorts and started to run up the hill. A lightning bolt of pain shot up her left leg. She collapsed.

The sound of the vehicle drew closer.

"Wait!" Kendra climbed, dragging her leg. "Wait!"

Up hill, a white RV passed.

"Down here! Stop! Stop!"

The motor home kept going.

Kendra lay on the side of the hill. "Damn it!"

A twig snapped.

Gasping, she glanced downhill. A dark shape hunched on the other side of the limbs. Some kind of animal was watching her.

"Oh, Christ!" Kendra scurried up the hill.

Behind her something exploded through the tree limbs.

She crawled onto the road, just as the RV disappeared around a curve. "Wait!"

Something grabbed Kendra's ankle, yanking her back down the hill. Her nails clawed the asphalt as the thing dragged her screaming into the forest.

* * *

Jessica rode in the Hummer's passenger seat while Eric drove and fiddled with his cell phone. "Christ, I can't get any signal out here."

"Can't you go a few hours without checking your messages?" Jessica asked.

"Just because I'm on vacation, doesn't mean everything stops back at the office."

"You're checking to see if your stepfather left any messages, aren't you?" She could tell, because Eric had a nervous look in his eyes like he was on the verge of an anxiety attack. His addiction to his cell phone was his one vice that drove Jessica bonkers. Well, that and the fact that Blake Nelson kept controlling their life. She rather liked that their cell phones didn't work out here. Maybe a few days without a phone would show Eric that his stepfather's law firm would run fine without him.

He tried to call again, and their SUV swerved into the other lane.

Jessica grabbed the wheel. "Watch the road."

Eric grumbled and tossed his phone in the backseat. He twisted the stereo volume. Guns 'N' Roses screeched, "Welcome to the Jungle". His fingers thrummed along the gear stick, and the Hummer edged so close to the rear of the Jeep, Jessica thought they were going to ram it.

"Eric, ease up, you're scaring me."

"Kyle drives like my grandmother." He honked repeatedly, swerving left and right.

* * *

As Kyle drove down the country road, watching the endless walls of trees pass by, he tried his best to enjoy the moment. But the Hummer kept creeping up on his bumper. His brother honked and poked his head out the window. "Speed up, Granny!"

Kyle honked and waved Eric to back off.

The black Hummer whipped out from behind them and raced up the opposite lane. The passenger window rolled down and Eric yelled, "How about we drag like old times?"

"No, get back behind me!" Kyle said, but the cocky motherfucker revved his engine, taunting him to race or wuss out.

Fucking great! Eric's drunk and wants to show everyone he's the alpha dog.

"Fine, pass!" Kyle let up on the gas.

Eric honked and drove ahead.

"Why did you let him take the lead?" Shawna asked from the passenger seat.

"Because he's being an idiot."

From the back seat, Zack asked, "Does Eric know where we're going?"

"Not a fucking clue," Kyle said.

The Hummer stayed on the left side of the road. Up ahead an RV came around a blind curve. A horn honked frantically. The Hummer veered left and the RV swerved into Kyle's lane.

He spun the Jeep onto the shoulder. The camper screeched past them.

The Jeep bucked and snaked along the side of the road, branches scraping across the windows. Kyle braced one arm across his sister's chest and slammed the brakes, tires shrieking to a halt.

Up ahead, Eric parked the Hummer and got out. Kyle wanted to kick his brother's ass, but right now there were more pressing matters. He took a quick inventory of his passengers. "Anybody hurt?"

"No," Shawna said. "But I peed my pants."

Zack was thrown sideways, but unscathed.

Glancing in his rearview mirror, Kyle saw that the RV had run off the side of the road. A dog barked and a man and girl stumbled out.

"Shit." Kyle backed the Jeep to the wounded camper and hopped out like a paramedic responding to an emergency. Eric and Jessica jogged behind him and assisted the shaken passengers of the RV.

"Are you guys okay?" Kyle asked.

A blonde teenage girl nodded, holding her hand against her chest. Jessica examined the girl. Kyle and Eric rounded the front end of the RV where a man in his mid-forties stood, shaking his head and staring down at a bent front bumper and mutilated tire. He glared at Kyle and Eric. "Which of you assholes was driving the Hummer?"

Eric said, "Sorry, sir. I was trying to pass my brother on a curve—"

"You've been drinking, haven't you?" the man said.

"No," Eric denied.

"Don't bullshit me! I'm a cop. Your breath reeks of beer."

Eric said, "Okay, I had a couple earlier out on the lake, but I swear I'm sober." Eric went into a melodramatic tirade that he often used in court to confuse the jury and draw sympathy. It was all an act, of course. Like their stepfather, Eric could steamroll anyone with his passionate rants. "I was just trying to pass on a curve and it was stupid, stupid, stupid!"

"Settle down, son," the man said with a calming hand. "My daughter's okay. She's my biggest concern. Luckily, I was only going thirty, which is the speed limit by the way."

Kyle said, "Sir, let us make things right. We'll pay for the damages and swap out your tire. Do you have a spare?"

"Yeah, it's at the back."

"I'll take care of it." Eric dashed behind the RV. He reappeared a minute later with a jack and lug wrench in hand and set about propping up the backside of the camper.

* * *

As Eric changed the RV's tire, Kyle and Jessica tended to the man, Carl Hanson, and his teenage daughter, Lindsey. She only had a bruise on her forearm. She was more shaken than anything.

Jessica fished into her first-aid kit. "Here take an aspirin."

"I'm fine," Lindsey said. "I'm just worried about my dog, Chaser."

Kyle looked around. He had briefly seen a black dog earlier when the Hansons first climbed out of their RV. "Where'd he run off to?"

"Through there." Lindsey pointed to a stand of blue spruce. "I'm afraid he might be hurt."

The last thing Kyle wanted was for this family to lose their dog. "I'll find him." He led Jessica and the girl into the woods. Thirty yards in they stopped at a steep incline.

Lindsey backed away, gulping. "I don't like heights." Remaining ten feet back, she cupped her hands around her mouth. "Chaser!"

The dog barked from somewhere deep in the pines.

Kyle and Jessica exchanged glances and then helped call the dog's name, but Chaser didn't return. The barking trailed off.

"Does he usually come back?" Kyle asked.

Lindsey said, "Sometimes, except when he's scared. I'm worried he's going to get lost in the woods."

Kyle peered down the near-vertical incline. It was a good twenty yards down to a creek full of sharp rocks. He looked across at Lindsey, who was biting her lip.

"I'll go find him."

"Are you sure?" Jessica looked over the ledge. "That drop looks pretty steep."

"You guys stay here." Kyle started climbing down, using exposed roots and rock ledges to keep from falling. The hill was only treacherous at the beginning and descended more gradually midway. He slid in a few places where there were a lot of leaves, but made it to the bottom in no time. Kyle looked up at the girls and gave a thumbs-up.

"Here, you'll need this." Lindsey tossed down a leash.

He crossed a stream, using a few mossy stones as a bridge. On the other side, the pines went on for miles. It suddenly occurred to him that he was about to go after a dog that was possibly scared. He imagined a wounded dog bearing its fangs. He looked back at Lindsey. "What kind of dog is Chaser?"

"A Rottweiler."

Great. "Does he bite?"

"No, he's a teddy bear. Please find him."

When Kyle was growing up in Seattle, the next-door neighbors had a Rottweiler that used to growl through the fence. It had sounded like a demon hound from hell that would have given anything to burst through that fence and rip Kyle's throat out. Thanks to that devil dog, he wasn't a big fan of Rottweilers.

He hiked deeper into the forest. "Chaser..." He whistled. "Here, boy!" Kyle worked his way through the branches until he reached a clearing where the pines began humming lightly, like organ pipes playing a single key.

He felt strange vibrations along the ground.

Kyle didn't like the feeling he got from these woods. He touched a tree and his mind filled with a vision of an animal's fangs. He heard a growl surge from the bark and jumped back. The echo trailed off. "What the...?"

He listened, but the surrounding trees were quiet now, except for the wind rustling the evergreen branches. A vibration still reverberated through his hiking boots. It was the same sensation he felt when he entered a cemetery, as if the dead were whispering inside their graves. Sometimes when he touched a tombstone, he saw fleeting visions of the person entombed there, a glimpse of a car accident, an argument, blood seeping from a chest wound. A series of quick flashes. A story that wished to be told.

So what was it about this patch of woods that triggered his psychic ability?

Kyle gripped the tree again. The forest suddenly chorused with cricket chants. His eyes closed, and something from the deepest shadows released a stretched-out, feline scream. Was Chaser stalking a wild cat? Kyle let go of the tree, and the cat cries and crickets ceased as if breaking contact with the tree muted the forest. He scanned the woods. No sign of any dog-and-cat chase. But the low hum persisted.

"Chaser!" Kyle kept searching, listening for a bark or a hiss. The pines beckoned him with ghostly whispers. He avoided touching them. He didn't like using those channels. The deeper he ventured, the louder the humming resonated, as if an Aboriginal tribe were playing didgeridoos. Why did this forest channel so strongly? The vibrations from the ground pulsed stronger now, tingling up his legs. A crying cat wailed through Kyle's head.

What the hell happened here?

The mysterious cat was crying and running. Kyle closed his eyes. It was now night inside his mind. Moonlight shone on the ground and what looked like large cat paws raced across it. Then a blur of a beast larger than a dog. Then shrieking. Huffing. Squealing. Growling.

Silence.

"Come on, Chaser. Where are you?" Keeping his eyes closed, he touched another tree. In his mind night turned back to daylight. He saw a brief glimpse of Chaser's wagging tail. The dog backed away from a deadwood thicket. The barking sounded nearby.

Kyle opened his eyes, felt dizzy for a second and then ran between the trees. "Chaser!" He reached a small clearing. The Rottweiler knocked him over. Chaser put his paws on Kyle's chest and licked his throat.

He saw the dog's red nose and jowls and backed away. "Chaser…oh, sick!" Wiping his own throat, Kyle felt the congealed blood on his neck. "What have you been into?"

The Rottweiler barked and ran to a thick pile of limbs that looked like a giant beaver hut. Kyle hurried to the brush. He froze at the sight of a headless carcass. The rotting remains of what looked like a mountain lion lay twisted and deformed. Hundreds of black flies peppered its wet Elena sinews. The air around the carcass made Kyle gag. The lion looked as if it had been dead at least a day or two. Maybe a bear roamed this area. He looked at the burrow inside the large wooden hut. It appeared empty, but Kyle wasn't about to wait around for the predator to return.

"Chaser, we better get back to the road." Kyle snapped the leash to the dog's collar. As he hurried back with the girl's dog, he wondered whether he should tell the others about the dead mountain lion and the strange vibrations the woods gave off. They wouldn't believe the visions he received. Kyle could try to explain, but then everybody would think he was a freak. When he reached a stream, he washed the blood off Chaser's nose and jowls and then cleaned his own face.

As he walked back with the dog, he said to Chaser, "Let's keep what we saw between you and me."

* * *

After returning with the Hansons' Rottweiler, Kyle visited with Carl Hanson, a homicide detective from Calgary. He was searching the area for his oldest daughter. Amy had gone missing six weeks earlier. He showed a photo of a pretty blonde, a couple years older than Lindsey.

Carl's brow furrowed with worry lines. "Amy's attending graduate school in Vancouver. She was out here working on some kind of archaeology expedition when she and a few others disappeared."

Kyle got a cold chill. "Who was leading the expedition?"

"Her professor, Dr. Elkheart."

"Jon Elkheart?"

The man nodded.

"That's my father. He disappeared around the same time."

Carl's eyes turned desperate. "Do you have any idea where they might have gone?"

Kyle shook his head. "We haven't spoken in months."

"It's not like Amy to stay out of touch this long. When I contacted her school, the head of the archaeology department hadn't heard from either one of the professors. He said they didn't usually report in while they were out in the field, but he thought they were somewhere up near Lake Akwâkopiy."

"I'm sure they're okay," Kyle said, feeling a knot in his stomach.

"I hope I'm just being a paranoid father and that Amy is working and hasn't checked in. But I've been doing some research on the area. Come with me. I want to show you something." Carl led Kyle into the RV where the two men sat opposite each other at the small built-in table. The detective opened a briefcase and pulled out a file.

Kyle read the label upside down. *Missing Persons*. He flipped through dozens of pages with photos of girls. Some of the disappearances dated as far back as the 1950s.

"Most were runaways," Carl said. "But there were a few who'd gone camping with groups and just vanished without a trace. The majority were teenage girls. A few young women in their twenties."

Kyle set the sheets down. "These disappearances can't be related to your daughter."

"I'm not so sure about that." Carl pointed to a map on the wall that was dotted with pins all around the lake. "I've talked to a lot of people living in this area. They call the forests around Lake Akwâkopiy 'Canada's Bermuda Triangle.'"

Before leaving, Kyle and Carl exchanged phone numbers. The cop from Calgary shook Kyle's hand. "Call me if you learn anything about your father and Amy's whereabouts, and I'll do the same. I'm going to find out where they are one way or another."

As Lindsey and her dog climbed back into the RV, Carl glared at Eric and spoke firmly to Kyle. "Normally, I would have your brother thrown in jail for drunk driving, but I'm going to let him off the hook this time. If you guys are going to be drinking, then stay off the road."

Kyle nodded, feeling ashamed. "We will, sir."

When the RV disappeared around a curve, Kyle walked over to his brother.

Eric held up his palms. "Ey, I fucked up, okay? Sorry."

"Give me your keys."

Eric handed them over without protest.

Kyle got in his face. "If I catch you drinking and driving again, I'll report you to the police myself."

* * *

As the two SUVs continued down the country road, Kyle spotted the familiar junction road up ahead. A faded sign marked the entrance to the Lake Akwâkopiy Cree First Nation Reserve. "Here we are, guys." He steered onto a winding dirt road. His stress seemed to dissipate as familiar pines, spruce and aspens formed a continuous wall on either side. The road, curving sharply, was mostly a stretch of sun-bleached dirt patched with bunchgrass. The weeds had grown high in several places, scraping against the bumper as the Jeep passed over them.

As Kyle drove, he shared the tribe's history with Shawna and Zack. "Our ancestors were issued this reservation by the Crown in late 1800s. It's just over five thousand acres. And most of the land is pure wilderness. Thanks to our grandfather, who's been an activist against the logging companies all his life, our land is one of the few places in the world left untouched." When they passed another dirt road, Kyle said, "That leads to Ray Roamingbear's cabin. He lives a half mile from Elkheart and Grandfather."

The main driveway declined down a steep hill between two small ponds. As Kyle rounded the last curve, the Cree village emerged from behind the branches. The sight stirred up memories from his childhood and previous visits: waking up to the smell of wet pine needles, fly-fishing in the ponds and streams, venturing into the woods with Elkheart and Grandfather to camp by an open fire. Kyle wished he had come back here more often.

At the center of the village stood the main cabin—a three-level log-and-rock structure. Behind the cabin smaller shacks stood decrepit and leaning. A couple had collapsed to piles of rotted timber. Scattered about the village were a few rusted cars and trucks that had been taken over by vegetation.

Shawna frowned. "You said we'd be staying in paradise."

Kyle said, "I meant the land. The cabins need some TLC."

"They look like they're about to topple over," Shawna said. "Are you sure it's safe to stay here?"

"Don't worry. Dad's cabin is built solid."

"Where are all the people?" Zack asked from the backseat.

"The tribe moved off the land years ago. Only our grandfather lives here fulltime." Kyle spotted Grandfather Two Hawks sitting in his favorite rocking chair on the front porch, smoking a pipe. He looked their way as the Jeep and Hummer parked. As everyone piled out, Kyle shouted, "Hello, Grandfather. It's your grandkids."

The old man stuck his pipe in his mouth and looked down at his crossword puzzle. Next to his rocker, a bin was stacked full of puzzle books and weathered copies of *TV Guide*.

Kyle leaned against the porch post. "It's good to see you again."

Grandfather had short silver hair and wore thick glasses. He was dressed in his usual buttoned-down shirt and jeans. He looked like he'd put on some weight since last summer. Grandfather had diabetes and Kyle wondered if he remembered to take his shots when no one was around to look after him. "Here, I brought you this." He placed a new crossword puzzle book and a pouch of tobacco on a table next to his grandfather. In the tribe's tradition, it was custom to bring tobacco whenever meeting with elders.

Grandfather only glanced at the gifts. Last time Kyle visited, his grandfather had been showing signs of senility. He was hard of hearing and half-blind from cataracts. These days he kept mostly to himself.

The others came up the porch steps and Kyle introduced them. Grandfather barely acknowledged them also. Kyle wondered if he could even see them. *We must be blurry images to him.*

Eric and Shawna gave Kyle a concerned look. He nodded for them to head into the cabin.

After everyone went inside, Kyle sat next to Grandfather. "I was wondering…can you tell me where our father went? Has he been here lately?"

The old chief stared straight ahead and mumbled something in Cree.

Kyle wished he had taken the time to learn his native language. "Can you say it in English? I can't understand you."

Grandfather looked confused. He sank back into his chair and smoked his pipe.

Kyle heard one of the girls yelp and ran inside the cabin. "What's wrong?"

Shawna was standing on a chair, waving her hands real fast.

Jessica said, "Eric just chased a raccoon out of the house." She pointed to a plate of food that had spilt on the floor. "The back door was left open."

Shawna climbed down and examined something on the floor. "Lovely, raccoon droppings."

Kyle put his hands on his hips. "What a mess." The den was a shambles. The air smelled stale and fetid. Flies swarmed the entire den, buzzing in his ears.

"The electricity doesn't work, either." Jessica flipped a light switch up and down.

"There's a generator out back," Kyle said. "I'll take a look. First, let's check the rest of the cabin for critters."

Zack and Shawna disappeared up the back stairway. Jessica wound up the spiral staircase to the third-story loft that overlooked the den and dining area. Kyle cleaned up the mess in the kitchen. He cursed Elkheart and Ray for leaving Grandfather unattended. Kyle's dad and uncle, both alcoholics, could be so irresponsible. Kyle never quite understood why, but the relationship between Ray, Elkheart and their father had always been strained.

At the dinner table, Eric and Zack unloaded beer from the coolers.

"Is it Miller time?" Shawna asked.

"No," Kyle said. "We have a few issues to work out first."

"Yeah," Eric said. "The fridge doesn't work, and it's full of rotten food."

"The entire cabin's been overrun by rodents and bugs," Jessica called down from the loft. "I found several spiders up here."

"Ew." Shawna grimaced. "I hate spiders."

Zack's fingers crawled up her arm. Shawna slapped his hand. "Quit it. I vote we go back into town and stay at the lodge."

"We're staying here," Kyle said. "This used to be our home."

"Kyle, seriously," Eric said. "This is not livable."

"We'll make it livable." Kyle slapped his hands together. "Gang, put your work clothes on. We've got some cleaning to do before we settle in."

* * *

In the Podunk town of Hagen's Cove, Lindsey Hanson listened to a Beyoncé song on her iPhone, while stapling a flyer of her missing sister onto a telephone pole. Lindsey's dad was across the street, showing two Mounties on horseback a photo of Amy. The two men in red uniforms shook their heads.

Lindsey walked down the main street, stapling flyers on every pole she passed. This was the fifth small town she and her dad had visited in the past two weeks. He was convinced that something bad had happened to Amy. That maybe some backwoods stalker had abducted her like so many girls before. Lindsey couldn't even go there. She had seen too many scary movies to bear the thought that something horrible could happen to her big sister. No, Dad was wrong. Amy was alive somewhere, working on an expedition with her anthropology professor. Lindsey's sister was a grad student at the University of Vancouver and had been so excited to finally get off campus and do research in the field. She couldn't talk about the location or what she was researching, because her professor was all secretive about it. The big secret Lindsey did know was that Amy was sleeping with her professor. She had emailed a photo of Dr. Elkheart. Lindsey had freaked. Her sister was seeing a man older than their father.

Just four years apart, Lindsey and Amy texted each other daily. As soon as Amy had gone on the expedition, the texting had stopped. Weeks had gone by and she hadn't responded to any of Lindsey's or her father's messages. Lindsey told herself that her sister was just off the grid, either because she wasn't near a decent satellite signal or she was working on a project so top secret that she couldn't talk to anyone until the expedition was over. Lindsey liked that scenario most. She just wished Amy would send some kind of message so their dad could finally chill. At this point Lindsey would settle for smoke signals.

On her iPhone, a Lady Gaga song ended and switched to Nickelback. Lindsey rocked her head to the music. She turned a corner off the main street and walked down the hill to a cemetery and stapled another flyer to a pole.

A maroon hearse pulled up to the curb beside her, and a man rolled down his window. "Hey, what you posting there?"

Lindsey handed him a flyer. "We're looking for my sister, Amy Hanson. Have you seen her by chance?"

He stared at the sheet for several seconds, reading all the stats below her photo. The guy, who was probably thirty-something, had an odd smell to him. Then again, he was driving a corpse wagon. He looked back at Lindsey. "No, don't believe I've seen this one. Is she a college girl?"

"She's a grad student from Vancouver," Lindsey said. "She was supposed to be somewhere around this lake before we lost touch with her."

"How long ago?"

"About six weeks. Her last contact was June first."

The guy nodded. "We get a lot of college girls this time of year. They come up for the summer and party on their boats. Do a lot of drugs and whatnot." He winked. "My name's Hugo. You must be Lindsey."

"How do you know my name?"

"Word travels fast in this town." Hugo grinned and stared at her breasts. "You like to party, Lindsey?"

"Excuse me?"

"I got a boat down at the marina and a couple hits of *X*." He nodded toward the backseat. "After I bury this casket, I'd be happy to take you for a ride."

"Fuck off, creep!" Lindsey started walking back toward Main Street. She could no longer see her father.

The man drove his maroon hearse alongside her. "Sunset's mighty pretty on the lake."

* * *

It took over two hours to get the cabin into a livable state. Every window and door was open, and a breeze blew through, airing out the dust and raccoon odors. Although the power still wasn't working, Kyle stocked the fridge and pantry full of groceries.

In the den, Jessica sprayed lemon-scented Lysol. "Can one of you strong men give me a hand moving the furniture?"

Kyle helped her slide the sofa, loveseat and two chairs around a coffee table.

"There that does it." She surveyed the spacious den. "The cabin's quite roomy now that we've tidied up a bit."

Above them, Eric leaned over the rail of the loft. "Hey, babe, can you get my laptop? I left it in the Hummer."

"Sure. Excuse me, Kyle, duty calls."

Kyle watched Jessica exit the front door, admiring how she looked just as good from the back as the front. When he turned, he noticed Eric staring down from the loft.

"Like what you see?"

Kyle smiled. "She's a great girl. You have my approval."

"Uh-huh. Just remember who she came here with." Eric stepped away from the railing.

His brother's words stung. Kyle *had* been staring at Jessica. He had felt such a rush hanging out with her today that he'd had to watch himself to keep from letting it show.

At least I know I can like someone new.

He stashed his backpack and bedroll in one corner of the den. The foldout couch was going to be his bed, since there were only enough bedrooms for the couples and Grandfather. Elkheart's upstairs bedroom would remain empty in case he returned. Kyle wasn't crazy about sleeping below the loft within earshot of Eric and Jessica.

She came back inside, carrying Eric's laptop case. She was wearing the biggest grin. "I just saw some deer run across the road."

"We usually put corn out and watch them eat in the backyard. Maybe later you can help me fill the feeder."

"I'd like that." She started up the stairs to the loft.

Kyle looked away. *Damn it, quit flirting.*

A half hour later, as he swept the floor, he got the strange sensation he was being watched. He looked out the back windows that offered a panoramic view of the forest. Just past a covered porch lay a backyard overgrown with weeds and high grass. Beyond, a path parted the trees. Kyle's throat constricted, just as it did every time he was about to leave his apartment. As if Death were waiting for him to step across the threshold. Kyle now wondered if he should venture out into the woods. Remaining within the safety of the cabin seemed like a perfectly fine vacation to him. *And what would Dr. Norberg say about that, Kyle?* He knew what she would say: that he was transferring his agoraphobia from his apartment to the reservation. That if he stayed inside, he wasn't taking any positive steps toward facing his fear of the outside world.

Great, now I'm being my own shrink.

Kyle stared at the desolate village and woods beyond. Why was he feeling so paranoid? He had lived here the first ten years of his life, when his mom and Elkheart were still married. Kyle had fond memories of playing with his brother and cousins, while the tribe grilled the catch of the day and sat around a fire. Grandfather Two Hawks, who had spoken English then, told story after story about the trials of their ancestors. Kyle remembered Grandfather leaning over, pointing a bony finger at him, staring with piercing brown eyes. "The forest on our land is sacred and alive. So be careful how far you wander. The trees have eyes, and they are always watching." Later one night, at the age of nine, Kyle swore he saw something creeping through the moonlit woods—a scarecrow-shaped shadow with eyes of white fire.

Now, staring at the same forest at dusk, Kyle felt the hairs on the back of his neck standing. To the naked eye, the forest appeared serene, a benign place straight out of a nature film, with singing birds, chirping cicadas and yellow butterflies fluttering in a field of wildflowers. But he had a bad feeling this was just a façade.

"Um, Mr. Elkheart?"

Kyle turned around to see Zack standing there, holding a stack of Alex Winterbone novels. "I was wondering if you'd autograph my books."

"Sure." Kyle was thankful for the distraction. "Got a pen?"

"Yes, sir." He dug one out of a long, black wallet that was chained to his jeans.

Kyle set the hardback books on the dining table and signed all four of them.

Zack hovered next to him like an eager fan at one of his signings. "If you don't mind my asking, how do you come up with such wild ghost stories?"

Kyle thought about all his real encounters with ghosts—the specter that walked the halls of his apartment, the murmurings at the cemetery whenever he visited the graves of his mother and his wife. "I've always had an active imagination." He once told an audience that he was clairvoyant and could see beyond the veil of the physical world, but they all laughed, thinking he was kidding. *Better to let them think it's all just fiction.*

"I can't wait to read what happens to Winterbone in *Ghost Vengeance,*" Zack said. "Your last book ended with such a mind-fucking cliffhanger. Any idea when it's going to come out?"

"As soon as I finish writing and deliver it to my editor. Maybe while we're here you could read the first few chapters and let me know what you think."

Zack's eyes widened. "Dude, that'd be a total honor."

Kyle handed him the books. "Here you go."

"Thanks, Mr. Elkheart."

"Please, call me Kyle."

"Yes, sir." Zack went back up the stairs with an armload of books.

Shaking his head, Kyle returned to the back windows. The forest had darkened with shadows as the sun went behind the clouds. Again, he felt eyes watching him.

"Is that the path that leads to the swimming hole?" his sister said.

Kyle turned to see Shawna and Jessica were standing behind him, wearing shorts and bathing suits. Towels hung across their shoulders.

"Yeah, it's a couple hundred yards down the hill."

"Good," Shawna said. "Jessica and I are going for a swim before it gets dark."

Kyle glanced at his watch. "You only have about an hour of sunlight left."

"That's all we need," Shawna said.

"Care to join us for a dip?" Jessica asked.

"Uh…" Kyle looked out at the forest. Was that a face peering through the branches? He didn't want to leave the cabin. But he knew how stubborn Shawna could be when she set her mind to something. She would go with or without him. "Yeah, sure, I'll join you guys."

"Not so fast." Eric's hand gripped his shoulder. "We need to fix the generator."

Shawna grinned at Jessica. "All right then, I guess it's just us girls."

Kyle said, "Don't stray too far from the village. The bears are out this time of year."

"Bears?" Jessica shuddered.

"Yeah, brown bears," Kyle said. "They won't bother you if you make a lot of noise. If you see one, wave your arms and make loud whooping sounds. That should run it off."

Eric pulled Jessica into his arms and kissed her. "See you in an hour, babe."

"Okay."

As the two women disappeared into the mouth of the woods, Kyle had the urge to run after them. He felt frustrated. No one else seemed to sense the forest the way he did. How the shadows moved behind the trees when no one was watching. How the trees themselves formed hateful, twisted faces. This wasn't the same reservation he had loved so fondly. Something had changed.

The trees have eyes, and they are always watching.

Feeling like he'd made a bad decision coming here, Kyle wished he were back in Seattle. His apartment might have been haunted, but at least the ghost was familiar.

* * *

As Jessica hiked down the forest path, she realized this was her first time alone with Eric's sister. Jessica normally swam laps by herself, but she had invited Shawna along, so she could get to know her better. It felt awkward. They had nothing but Eric in common. When Shawna and Zack had shown up on their doorstep three days ago, both were dressed in all-black Goth outfits with matching spiked collars. The first couple nights, Jessica had feared Shawna and Zack were going to steal from her purse or freebase heroin in the guest bathroom, but so far they'd behaved themselves.

"Have you ever ventured this far out in the wilderness?" Jessica asked as they hiked down the trail.

"Not since I was tiny," Shawna said. "I don't remember what it was like living here. We moved away when I was two. Do you think we'll come across any bears?"

"Are you wanting us to?"

Shawna laughed. "Might be kinda cool. A baby cub, that is."

"Where there's a cub, there's usually a mama nearby. And you don't want to get between them. That's when a bear is most likely to attack."

Jessica studied the trees. Luckily, the pines were spaced several feet apart, so she could see quite a ways into the forest. The trail was wide and clear up and down nearly the whole way, except for a few sharp turns. So far, the only wildlife she'd seen were lots of chirping birds, a couple squirrels and a woodpecker.

Shawna let out a "Whoop! Whoop! Whoop!" waving her hand over her head like she was swinging a lasso. "This feels really silly."

"Looks silly too."

After a ten-minute hike, they finally reached a large pond that glowed like polished copper. Upside-down conifers and mountains reflected across its glassy mirror. The sun was a gold medallion that illuminated from its depths. In the center of the pond, a huge boulder protruded the surface like a partly submerged skull.

Eager to feel the water's embrace, Jessica hurried down the hill to a grassy bank. On the trail she had worked up a sweat, and now, out from under the branch canopy, she felt the heat of the sun that was approaching the horizon. An occasional breeze cooled her skin, which offered some relief.

The width of the pond stretched about fifty yards. The water around the banks was shallow, and Jessica could see rocks and small fish. The center looked dark, murky and deep. It constantly rippled with fish kisses.

Jessica stepped across the grass and plunged her right foot beneath the surface. Unlike the lukewarm swimming pool back at the campus where she swam laps, this was invigorating.

"This place is so private," Shawna said. "Just us and no guys. It's perfect for a skinny dip."

To Jessica's surprise Shawna removed her bikini. Both her nipples were pierced with silver rods, and she had tattoos covering half her body. On Shawna's back were large purple fairy wings. And there was an orange butterfly on her shaved pubic area and a piercing that went right through her…

"All righty," Jessica said, looking for the nearest rock to crawl under.

Shawna dove into the water and swam backwards. "Water feels awesome! Let's be one with nature. Strip down and join me."

"No, thanks, I'm good." Jessica kept her two-piece on. She dove forward and swam. Within seconds, her body acclimated to the cool water. They swam alongside one another. "Shawna, if you don't mind me asking, what compelled you to get so many tattoos?"

"I used to date a tattoo artist," she said, floating on her back. "A guy named Lex. He saw my body as a canvas."

"You couldn't stop at just one or two?"

"I know I probably look like a freak to you, but every tattoo has a special meaning for me."

"I don't think you're a freak. I'm sorry if I gave that impression."

"Don't worry, I'm used to it. I *am* a bit of a freak." Shawna swam out to the boulder and climbed on top. She looked like a mythical siren, laid out in the sun, her long hair fanning across the rock like golden seaweed.

Jessica swam laps the width of the pond for several minutes. When she was done with her first set, she treaded water. Tiny waves circled her legs and waist, caressing her body. Feeling at home, she dipped her head back. Gentle currents trickled through her hair as she stared up at the broad sky. "This is heaven."

Shawna, who was sitting naked on the boulder and meditating, opened her eyes and stretched. "How do you have so much stamina?"

"I've been swimming competitively since I was a kid. I normally swim an hour, but I've gotten out of shape."

"Well, you've got me beat by about fifty laps. I'd kill to have your grace in the water."

Jessica thought maybe Eric's sister wasn't so bad after all.

* * *

Getting out of L.A. and back to nature was the best decision Shawna ever made. The guys in her band had been getting on her nerves lately. Onstage, the Black Mollies rocked the house. At home, all they did was get stoned and play Xbox games, while Shawna paid the bills waiting tables at a coffee shop. During her off time, she wrote music for their upcoming album. Traveling with her brothers to Canada was a chance to clear her mind and get back in touch with her music. As she meditated on the boulder, the breeze caressing her bare skin, a rustling off in the woods broke her tranquil state. Opening her eyes, Shawna looked across the water at the trees. Dragon flies buzzed, frogs croaked and birds twittered off in the distance. Just a random forest noise. Nothing to be alarmed about. The sun began sinking behind the mountains, casting long shadows across the pond.

Jessica said, "It'll be dark soon. Let's head back."

"Fine by me." Shawna dove into the water and followed Jessica back to the grassy bank. As Shawna bent over, drying her legs with the towel, she heard another noise. The trees around the pond were tangled with brush and provided infinite hiding places for anyone who wanted to peep. She suddenly got an image of a deformed hillbilly creeping through woods, ogling her body. Shawna covered herself with the towel.

She heard the slightest slapping of branches and then again the forest sounds: birds, frogs, dragonflies. Then faintly, something else. A *shuff-shuff-shuff* that didn't seem to belong to the normal sounds of the forest. It was subtle, but definitely out there.

Shawna pulled up her bikini bottoms and looked at Jessica. "Did you hear something?"

"No, what?"

"I thought I heard footsteps." Shawna scrutinized every tree as far as she could see, which was only about twenty yards or so. After that, the hill inclined and the trees meshed together. She shivered, her body covered in goose bumps. "I can't believe I'm getting so spooked. It's probably just a rabbit."

The *shuff-shuff-shuff* came again.

"That was no rabbit," Jessica said, quickly pulling up her shorts.

Shawna tried to think of all the big animals that lived in the wilderness: bears, wolves, wild boar, moose, mountain lions. She couldn't think of one that she wanted to come across, especially when the forest was getting dark. "Let's head back."

Jessica slid on her tennis shoes. "Whatever it is, don't panic."

"Right." Shawna's legs wouldn't stop trembling. The woods were getting darker by the second. "I wish we'd brought a flashlight." As the breeze died down, she heard the sounds again, like feet shuffling over a pine-needle floor, legs pushing through clinging branches. "I bet that's the guys." Shawna yelled, "Eric, Kyle, is that you?"

About twenty-five yards into the trees the footsteps ceased.

"Why aren't they answering?" Jessica asked.

"Because they're trying to scare us. They used to scare me all the time when we were kids, especially Kyle."

"Maybe it isn't them. Maybe it's a bear."

"Oh, that's reassuring." Shawna wondered if she could race up the hill fast enough.

Damn it, why did we hike down here without the guys?

She remembered Kyle's advice and started waving her arms. "Whoop! Whoop! Whoop!"

Jessica joined in. "Go away bear, if you're in there! Whoop! Whoop!"

The footsteps moved toward them.

* * *

In a shed behind the main cabin, Kyle examined a Coleman generator that was covered in soot and spider webs. "No wonder the power is out. Fuel monitor reads empty."

"Where does Elkheart keep the gas cans?" Eric asked.

"Should be some in the garage."

As they walked down the hill, leaves and pine cones blew along the dirt road. The dark, hollow shacks bordering the main road looked like a ghost town. When they had lived on the reservation as children, there had been over a hundred people living in the village.

Eric asked, "What happened to the others?"

"They migrated to a Cree res up in northern Canada."

"I know that, but why did they leave?"

Kyle shrugged. "Dad never told me. Poverty, I guess. Infighting. Alcoholism. We should be thankful Mom moved us away from here." As they walked a chilly wind blew through, causing one of the abandoned cabins to moan. "Do you get any bad vibes from this place?"

"Vibes?" Eric laughed and patted Kyle's shoulder. "Writing horror novels is making you paranoid, bro."

Kyle chuckled. "Yeah, you're probably right."

A narrow driveway forked off the main road and led down to the garage. Embedded into a hill, its entrance bordered with pine logs. The two-car garage looked like a mine shaft. Kyle slid open the wide garage door and saw something he hadn't expected: his father's red 4x4 Bronco.

"What's Big Red doing here?"

Eric turned on his flashlight and poked around the garage. "Something wrong?"

"Yeah. I figured since Dad left the reservation, he would've taken his Bronco." The scratched-up Ford faced them, its windshield caked in dust. "This is so unlike him to leave his truck. He loves this hunk of junk."

Eric said, "Remember when Elkheart and Mom used to take us to the lake in it?"

"Yeah, those were some good times." Turning on a flashlight, Kyle opened the driver's side door. More dust covered the dashboard and seats inside. The backseat was down and the cargo area packed with something under a tarp. He opened the Bronco's back door and lifted the covering. Underneath were tents, bedrolls, kerosene lamps, several boxes of food, digging tools, containers of plaster and a dozen vodka bottles.

"Why would they leave all this behind?" Kyle said.

"Yeah, especially Elkheart's case of Stoli."

Kyle glared at his brother. "I mean the camping gear. They should be using all this for their expedition."

"Maybe they finished already and came back, and then Elkheart left with his crew."

"Then Amy Hanson would have called her father by now. Something's not right."

Eric shrugged. "Then maybe Elkheart and Amy ran off together. I bet they're down in Cozumel, drinking margaritas."

"Get real."

"I am. Remember, he got fired from Berkley for sleeping with one of his students?"

"I'm not buying that's the case here. Carl Hanson checked with the university. They said Dad came to Lake Akwâkopiy with a crew of archaeologists six weeks ago. They were on an expedition out here, but I have no idea where." Kyle looked back at the equipment in the Bronco. "It's like they came to the reservation but never left."

"Well, there's no use worrying about Elkheart. He'll show up when he wants to."

Kyle found three red gasoline cans on a metal shelf. He grabbed a full one. "Let's get the generator running before the sun goes down. It can get really dark out here at night."

* * *

Shawna backtracked toward the pond next to Jessica. The *shuff-shuff-shuff* and snapping twigs drew closer. The chin-high grass parted straight in front of them.

They let out a "Whoop-whoop-whoop-whoop!" and then bolted up the path.

Jessica scaled the hill faster. Shawna slipped and grabbed a branch, her feet sliding back down. She didn't dare look back. Instead, she got her footing and barreled up the path. Tears welled in her eyes.

"Jessica, wait up!"

Jessica slowed down, waving her arms. "Hurry! Hurry!"

* * *

Shawna felt eyes penetrating her back and sensed that the animal was now on the path behind her. She ran harder, not looking back. Afraid if she saw it, she would freeze. She caught up with Jessica. "Let's get the hell back."

Shawna did her best to keep up, but Jessica broke away.

More noises echoed to Shawna's left. In the high grass, she saw two places where the tops of the brush were swaying. Unseen predators raced parallel with her. And behind her, the galloping footfalls were gaining.

Do bears hunt in packs? No, but wild boar do.

Shawna sped up. Her thighs and calves tightened so taut she thought the muscles would snap.

Just keep moving.

She raced around another curve. Jessica was nowhere in sight. Neither was the cabin.

I can't keep this up.

The high grass to Shawna's left ended, and the forest opened up with trees spaced farther apart. She glanced back. Nothing rushed from the tall bunchgrass. Had they given up?

From the trail behind her, she heard pounding footfalls and heavy breathing, followed by a series of grunts. She wasn't going to make it. She could feel the air of the beast's motion as it moved inches behind her.

Sobbing, Shawna took a blind curve at a full sprint. A body leaped from behind a tree and grabbed her, growling.

She broke free in fitful screams, stumbled backward.

Zack laughed like a goddamned hyena.

"You fucking asshole!" Shawna slapped his arms and chest. "That wasn't the least bit funny."

"Ah, come on, sunshine. It was just a prank."

"You could have given me a heart attack. I thought I was dead." She shoved him.

"Don't be mad." Zack gave her his wounded puppy face.

"That's not going to work this time. You know I hate it when you scare me, and you always do it."

"That's because you bite every time."

"For once, I'd like to go a week without you pulling your stunts."

"I'm sorry. I'll try to behave." He stroked her arm. "Still mad at me?"

Shawna stared into his boyish eyes and tried to stay angry. "You can tell Kyle and Eric they can come out now."

"Huh?"

"Don't play dumb. They were chasing me through the grass while you were waiting to pounce." She turned back to where the high grass ended. "Okay, guys. Game's over. Zack caught me. Ha-ha. Score one for the boys."

Shawna paced and looked down the hill. She called for her brothers to come out of hiding.

"Kyle and Eric aren't out there," Zack insisted. "I snuck down here alone. Your brothers are back at the village."

"I saw the grass moving in two places," the girl said in a shaky voice. "If it wasn't you, and it wasn't them, then who was moving through the grass?"

Zack tickled her ribs and made a ghostly sound. "Wooooo, Shawna, maybe you were being stalked by a pack of hungry wolves."

"Fuck off, Zack!" She punched his chest and then stomped up the hill.

* * *

Behind the cabin, the generator fired up.

"Hallelujah!" Eric said, as one of the lights came on inside the cabin. The last thing he wanted was to stay the night out here without any power. He and Kyle went inside and turned on lights in the den and kitchen. Eric was putting beer in the fridge when Jessica came in, covered in sweat and breathing heavily. Her dark hair was wet. Damn, she was looking sexy.

"Hey, babe. Have a good workout?"

She nodded and leaned against a wall to catch her breath. "Swimming in the pond was wonderful. Then Zack spooked us and I got in a nice run I wasn't expecting."

Kyle flipped on the porch light. "Where are Shawna and Zack?"

"On the trail," Jessica said. "They got into a bit of a lover's quarrel."

Eric said, "Good. Maybe they'll break up and we can send his ass home."

"He's not so bad," Kyle said.

"He's a fucking freak show."

Jessica said, "Eric, be nice. Your sister really likes Zack."

"Trust me, Jess. She's got a habit of picking losers."

"He has to fly back with us," Kyle said. "So we're better off if they kiss and make up."

As Kyle went down the hall and switched on a light in the study, Jessica looked around the den. "Hey, the lights make this place look quite cozy."

"It still smells like raccoon, though." Eric surveyed all the worn-out furniture, the dust-covered antlers, faded paintings that had been hanging on the walls since his childhood. Staying in his father's cabin only dredged up bad memories. "You and I can stay in town, if you want." Eric hugged Jessica from behind and kissed her neck. "We'd have a lot more privacy."

"This will be fine. The cabin's growing on me." She was still in her shorts and that sexy bikini top that covered her small breasts. Her exposed skin glistened with sweat, and Eric felt himself getting aroused.

"Whew, I'm ready for a shower," she said, wiping her forehead.

Eric pulled her against him. "How about I join you?"

"No, I feel gross. How about opening a beer for me? We can sit out on the porch and have a cold one when I get out." She kissed his cheek and then went into the bathroom.

Frustrated, Eric went to the fridge and opened a can of Moosehead. Chugging it, he walked into the back study where his brother was sitting behind Elkheart's desk.

Kyle opened a box of cigars. "Hey remember when Dad used to smoke these?"

Eric picked up one of the Cubans and smelled it, flashing back to a time when all his father did was smoke cigars and get drunk. Eric hated cigars for that reason. He looked around their father's office. It was much neater than expected. On the wall hung a few framed diplomas from the University of Vancouver and plaques of Dr. Jon Elkheart's scientific achievements. Another wall had photos of him working around the globe on expeditions—standing on a pyramid, posing with children from an African tribe and with a group of elderly Mayan women at a village. Their father had aged quite a bit, his black hair now partly silver. Wearing wire-framed glasses, he looked more scholarly than Eric remembered. He perused a bookshelf full of science books and noticed one titled *Mysteries of the Sumerian People* with his father's name on the spine.

"Elkheart's a published author?" He showed Kyle the book. "You never told me that."

"Actually, I did. You just tune me out whenever I talk about Dad. He's written half a dozen books."

Eric flipped through the pages, observing photos of his father on a dig in Iraq. "I always thought he was just a drifter."

"That's what Mom and Blake want you to think. But Dad has traveled the world as an archaeologist. That's how he collected most of this stuff." Kyle pointed to two shelves full of statues, pottery and tribal masks.

"So why did he settle back here?"

"To retire, I had hoped. Grandfather's too old to manage the reservation by himself, so Dad returned to take over. He was supposed to live here and write fulltime."

"Yeah, well, I don't think he's capable of staying in one place too long." Eric thumbed along the spines of a row of books that ranged from archaeology and quantum physics to the occult. Several were authored by their father.

Kyle said, "Most of his books died a quick death and ended up buried in libraries. He never got a lot of respect for his theories."

"What kind of theories?" Eric opened a book called *Spiritual Vortexes and Other Sacred Places.*

"He's got a lot of wild ideas about the evolution of civilization. He believes the Aztecs, Mayans and Pharaohs built pyramids with sacred geometry and somehow they were all linked by ancient races. That kind of stuff. Dad puts a lot of faith in the mystical." Kyle closed the drawer of the filing cabinet and sighed. "There's nothing in his files but old articles and unpaid credit card bills. I can already hear him calling, asking for more money."

"How come Elkheart always calls you, but never me or Shawna?" Eric asked.

"Because I call *him*. My coming out here brought us closer together."

"You were always his favorite."

"I made an effort, that's all."

"If Elkheart had ever invited me, I might've come."

"Listen, Eric, I discovered with Dad you have to take the initiative."

"Fuck that. A father should want to be with his kids. We just got a raw deal." Eric opened a gun cabinet that was full of rifles and shotguns. He pulled out a Remington 30.06. He loved the power he felt when holding a rifle. "Remember when Grandfather and Elkheart used to take us deer hunting?"

"Yeah, those were some good times."

Eric peered through the scope. "There was nothing more kick ass than bringing down a buck." He sighed. "Wish it were deer season."

Kyle stepped up beside him. "Maybe this winter we can come back and go hunting with Ray and Dad. Start a new family tradition."

"Yeah, maybe." Eric put the rifle back.

Kyle peered into the cabinet. "This is strange. One of Dad's rifles is missing."

Eric saw two rifles and two shotguns lined in a row and one dust-covered slot that was empty. "Is this supposed to mean something, Sherlock?"

"Yes, Watson. If Dad took his rifle with him, then it kills your theory that he and his assistant ran off to Cozumel together."

"I was just tossing out ideas. Hell, for all we know he and Amy could be camping somewhere on the reservation, roasting hotdogs and drinking vodka tonics."

"I hadn't thought of that." Kyle's eyes lit up. "Dad's been known to go off camping without telling anyone."

"Seems like that's all he did when we were kids—disappear for days at a time." Eric had always resented Elkheart for abandoning their mother, leaving her with two young boys and a screaming baby. He remembered staying up nights with his mother, holding her hand while she cried and got shitfaced on vodka. She cursed Elkheart's name, calling him a useless husband. One day she got fed up and took a trip to her sister's in Seattle. While there, his mother found Jesus and met Blake Nelson, a successful man, the exact opposite of their father.

Kyle placed a hand on Eric's shoulder, snapping him back to the present. "I say tomorrow we go looking for Dad and his crew."

"I was just kidding. They're probably long gone."

"If there's even the slightest chance that Dad's here somewhere, then we should search for him." Kyle grinned. "How cool would it be to have us all reunited again?"

Eric hated it when his brother got his heart set on a mission. "Exactly how big is our land, anyway?"

"Five thousand acres. But I know all the places Dad likes to camp."

Eric looked out the window. A full moon had risen over the pines and outlined the nocturnal world with silvery light. He concentrated on the dark trees, trying to imagine where his father might be. *Do I even want to find him?*

When Eric had accepted Ray's offer to visit their reservation for old time's sake, he never imagined he might reunite with his father. If they did find Elkheart out there on the land, would he even be happy to see his kids? Eric remembered the belligerent drunk screaming at their mother as she and Blake and some child protection officers took Kyle, Eric and Shawna away from the tribe.

Twenty years was a long time, and the only evidence that Eric even had a father was a stack of postcards he kept in a shoebox. Now, if he came face-to-face with Elkheart, Eric didn't know if he'd hug his father or punch the bastard in the face.

Chapter Five

That evening Kyle cooked dinner while the others gathered in the den around a fire burning in a fireplace. Everyone was in good cheer tonight, drinking beers and listening to music. Zack beat his bongo drum while Shawna played guitar and sang some of her new songs. Even Grandfather Two Hawks was tapping his knee to the rhythm. The soulful way Shawna sang reminded Kyle of Sheryl Crow.

In the kitchen, he sliced a knife through an onion and chopped it up. Eyes watering, he put diced onions and bell peppers into a large pot. Chicken broth boiled as he added sliced potatoes, garlic and sausage.

"Something smells marvelous." Jessica peeked under the lid. "Is it some kind of stew?"

Kyle grinned. "Hey, you're not supposed to be in here until dinner's ready."

She folded her arms and leaned against the counter. "Well, if you won't let me help, at least let me watch. I may pick up a few tips."

"Suit yourself." Kyle felt nervous in Jessica's presence. He knocked over a roll of paper towels. She smiled and righted it. *What was it about this girl's presence that made his heart beat faster?* He returned his attention to the stove, adding a pat of butter to the boiling rice. The kitchen suddenly felt hotter. "I'm going to crack the window," he said. "This old stove really heats up the kitchen." When she didn't answer, he ventured a look her way. And there it was again—the connection that ran between them was so strong he thought it should be visible. *Does she feel the same?* The question was wrong and he knew it. *Man, ease up. She's Eric's.*

"So what's your secret?" Jessica asked.

For a moment Kyle feared his feelings had been exposed, but then she tipped her head toward the pot. "Secret recipe, I mean."

I'm dangerously attracted to you, that's my secret. "It's chicken and sausage gumbo with rice. I tossed in some of the local freshwater mussels."

"Sounds delicious. How'd you come up with the recipe?"

Kyle stirred the pot, adding some paprika and cayenne pepper. "It's an old family recipe on my mother's side. They're full-blood Cajun."

"So you're half Cree and half Cajun?" she asked. "Sounds like a spicy combination."

"I guess," Kyle chuckled. *Is she flirting with me?* He set the timer on the stove and leaned against the sink.

As they chatted about cooking, he admired the delicate features of her face, her crystal-blue eyes. She had the cutest dimples when she smiled.

Their conversation was effortless. It roamed from cooking to her attending med school at Washington State, volunteering for Doctor's Without Borders for the upcoming fall semester, and her ambitions after she graduated. Once she became a pediatrician, Jessica planned to open her own health center for children. Aside from interning, she was working to finish a double major in alternative medicine and business. Her ambition and deep passion for helping children only drew him in more. *What is she doing with Eric?* The answer was none of his business.

He noticed Eric watching from the den, the veins tightening around his temples. Jessica hadn't noticed. In fact she hadn't once looked into the den. Instead, her attention remained fixed on Kyle as she turned the subject back on to him. "So, if I may ask, what happened to your wife?"

The question took him by surprise. "My wife?"

"Oh, uh, I saw the wedding band and just assumed..."

"I'd rather not talk about it." Turning away, he lowered the chopping block into the sink and let the faucet water run over it. But the question had already worked its black magic. Thoughts of Stephanie blotted out everything light and warm in the moment and left him leaning against the kitchen sink, trying to loosen the tightness in his chest. For a second, he thought he saw his wife's angry visage in the dark window over the sink, but then she was gone.

Why did Jessica bring up Stephanie? Had Eric mentioned something?

"I'm sorry, I didn't mean to pry..." she said. "I mean, it's none of my business—"

Eric entered the kitchen. "Jess, I thought you just came in here to get another beer."

"You're speaking to me again?"

"Of course. Why wouldn't I?" Eric opened the fridge and pulled out a can of the local brew.

Jessica folded her arms across her chest. "I thought you were mad at me."

"Nah." Eric put his arm around her shoulder. "Come back in here, babe. You've got to come hear this story Shawna's telling. It's damned hilarious." As Eric pulled his girlfriend into the den, he looked back over his shoulder, shooting Kyle a look that was unmistakable. *She's mine,* it said.

* * *

After dinner, Jessica cleared the table while Eric washed dishes. Kyle tried to help, but Eric shooed him out, insisting that the chef was done with his kitchen duties. Kyle smirked at the sight of his brother in an apron and rubber dish gloves.

"What?" Eric said.

"Nothing." Normally Kyle would have ribbed his brother for going overboard to impress a woman, but since Jessica was in earshot, he let it slide. He went into the den where Shawna was on the couch, softly strumming her guitar.

Kyle took a seat on the hearth. The logs in the fireplace had burned down to warm cinders. He allowed himself to relax for the first time today. He admired the melody Shawna was playing. It was softer than her usual anger jams. This piece sounded like the beginning of a soul-searching ballad. "Is that new?"

"Nah, I've been working on this song off and on since high school."

"What's the name of it?" Kyle asked.

Shawna shook her head. "You'll make fun."

"No I won't. Come on."

"It's called 'My Heart Burns for You'. I know, totally cheesy."

"I like it. You should put that on your new album."

"That's what I keep telling her," Zack said from the dining room.

"I don't know." Shawna shrugged. "The band might think it's too mushy."

Kyle said, "Hey, every great rock band has released at least one love song."

"You really like it? You're not just pulling my chain?"

Kyle held up three fingers. "Scout's honor. It's the best music I've ever heard you play."

Shawna shrugged but Kyle noticed a hint of a smile.

The wind shook the windowpanes. A cold draft swept through the cabin. Kyle rubbed his arms. "Is there any more firewood around here?"

"There's more stacked out back near the trail," Eric said from the kitchen. Pulling off his dish gloves, he started toward the back door.

"No, finish the dishes. I'll get it," Kyle said, standing.

Eric barked, "Zack, make yourself useful and go with him."

"All right, I need a smoke anyway." He unrolled a pack of Camels out of his sleeve.

Eric said, "Don't throw any butts on the ground. I found one earlier."

"That was mine," Shawna said, defending her boyfriend.

Eric gave them both a hard look. "Well, it'd only take a spark to start a grass fire out there, so respect our tribe's land."

Zack nodded and followed Kyle onto the covered back porch.

Looking hurt, Zack lit a cigarette. "Why is your brother always riding my ass?"

"Eric does that to all of Shawna's boyfriends. He's testing you to see if you'll bail."

"I'm not going anywhere. Shawna stuck by me when my father died. I know she's your sister and all, but I'm in love with her."

Kyle looked at the guy. Beyond the angry tattoos, rebel haircut and Goth costume was a sensitive kid who had feelings like anybody else. Kyle put a firm hand on his shoulder. "I tell you little a secret, Zack. If you want our approval, then all you have to do is love our sister and treat her with respect."

"I will. I want nothing but the best for her."

"If you ever lay a hand on her, you're dead."

"I won't hurt her, sir. Promise." Zack held eye contact long enough to show he meant it.

Kyle nodded. "Good. Then we're on the same page. Now, let's find that firewood before we freeze our asses off." Stepping off the porch, he felt the cold breath of the boreal wind on his face. The dark complexion of the moon dimly lit the sky as bloated clouds drifted across it, dropping shadowed veils upon the forest. A congregation of timbers huddled around the cabin. A couple hours had passed since Kyle had thought about the surrounding woods. He tried to pinpoint the moment when the trees stopped bothering him and decided it was when he started talking with Jessica in the kitchen. Kyle had been too entranced by her beauty to be worried about the woods.

What was it about her that made him forget his fears?

He studied the pines, which were now cloaked in darkness. With no walls to protect him, with only the scattered moonbeams to reveal their mysteries, he sensed watchful eyes. Tiny spiders of fear scurried up his back. His throat tightened. Then a sound echoed off in the distance. "Do you hear that?"

"What?" Zack asked.

"Sounds like something's moving out there."

"All I hear is the wind, my friend." Zack stamped the cigarette against his boot and stuffed the butt into his pocket. "You coming?"

Kyle challenged the trees with a bold stare.

Zack marched ten feet ahead along the timberline. Nothing attacked him. The branches shook with the wind but stayed their distance. Feeling foolish for being frightened, Kyle hiked through the patches of dead grass that made up the backyard, moving away from the light that glowed through the windows. One porch light illuminated only half the yard, so they had to search for the firewood in the darkness.

"Over there." Zack pointed, hiking toward a woodpile.

Squinting, Kyle observed eight logs on a platform. "This won't last another day. Guess we'll have to chop some more tomorrow."

Zack held up his arms while Kyle stacked logs on top of them.

From behind the woodpile, amid the swaying trees, Kyle heard branches snap. "Okay, you had to hear that."

"What?"

Kyle studied the gloom beyond the woodpile. Silence. "Thought I heard movement again. Just my imagination, I guess."

Zack chuckled. "Yeah, I've read plenty of your imagination. I'd hate to see any of it roaming the dark woods at night."

Chapter Six

Ten miles away, the full moon glowed through the forest canopy in slanted, scattered beams. Beyond the gloom that surrounded the RV, nocturnal creatures crooned at the moon.

Lindsey Hanson hiked with her dog through the woods to a campfire and sat down on a log next to her dad. The glow flickered orange flames in his glasses. He was humming to himself and roasting hotdogs, which Chaser eyed, licking his chops.

Lindsey rubbed her hands over the fire. "Whew, it gets nippy real fast up here."

"Why don't you put on your coat?" her dad said, glancing at her sweatshirt. "You could catch pneumonia."

She rolled her eyes. "Dadddddd, I'm a big girl, now, practically a woman."

"Am I being a worry wart again?"

"Yes."

"Sorry, ladybug. Old habits die hard."

Ever since Lindsey's mother passed away, her dad was constantly fussing over her like she was still five years old. She looked down at the dark lake. All the boats had gone in for the night. It was quiet now, except for the frogs. They sure were croaking it up out there in the reeds. Her dad used to say when the frogs croaked louder it meant a storm was coming. The wind did seem to be picking up a bit, shaking the pine branches.

She glanced back at the RV, half hidden by the trees about twenty yards away. There was no one else camping out here but them. It wasn't a typical campground. More like a dirt road that ended at a small clearing by the water. There were no picnic tables or barbecue grills. The only sign that anyone had ever camped here was a small pit that had once been a campfire. It had been littered with beer cans and a Trojan wrapper.

"Hungry?" Her dad pulled the sizzling franks out of the fire. "These are about as charred as I can get them."

"Guess so." Lindsey fixed herself a hotdog. She wasn't real hungry, but anxious to get something warm in her stomach. The chill wasn't the only thing bothering her. She couldn't shake the slimy feeling she'd gotten from that hearse driver back in Hagen's Cove. Hugo's face kept popping into her head, leering at her breasts with those dull gray eyes. *You like to party?*

Unable to eat more than two bites, Lindsey gave the rest of her hotdog to Chaser, who chomped it down.

Her dad frowned. "That's all you're eating?"

Lindsey faked a smile. "Saving room for s'mores."

"Good idea. I'll get the marshmallows." He walked toward the camper.

To take her mind off things, Lindsey tried to text her friend, Megan, but couldn't find a signal. She wanted to tell her about the cute guy who had rescued her dog earlier. Kyle was hot. But each time she tried to focus on his face, that creep, Hugo, appeared instead.

After I bury this casket, I'd be happy to take you for a ride.

Lindsey shuddered. Her dad returned with a bag of marshmallows, chocolate bars and a box of graham crackers. "How about after dessert, we hit the hay? We've got an early rise tomorrow."

Staring into the crackling flames, she rubbed her hands together for warmth. "I want to go home."

"Soon, ladybug. But tomorrow we've got one more town. Then we'll head back."

Lindsey began tearing up. She tried to hide it, looking back over her shoulder, but her dad, a homicide detective, noticed everything.

"Hey…" He put his arm around her. "I miss Amy too. Don't worry. We'll find her."

Lindsey leaned her head against his shoulder.

Somewhere out in the darkness of the pines, branches snapped.

Chaser rose to his feet, barking.

An animal growled back with a deep guttural sound.

Carl Hanson rose at the sound.

"What was that?" Lindsey gripped his arm.

"I don't know. A wolf, maybe. Stay behind me." Carl pulled out his .38 pistol from a holster on his hip. "Chaser, get back here!"

The Rottweiler backed up to the edge of the fire's glow but continued barking.

The wolf or whatever it was remained in the trees that bordered the campfire. In between growls it made wheezing-hacking sounds.

Her dad stood. "It might have rabies. Let's get inside the camper." He doused the fire with a cooler of water and the campsite went dark.

Lindsey turned on her flashlight and trained it on the woods. The pine branches were moving. Her beam reflected in a pair of eyes.

At the lake, terror hit Carl Hanson when he saw glowing eyes high up in the trees. Through thirty-odd years of bear hunting he had faced many a grizzly, but never anything as horrifying as this. Although the beast stood at least eight feet, it wasn't shaped like any bear.

Carl wished he had his rifle. He fired his pistol, hoping to scare the thing off.

It wailed and tore through the branches.

"Run, Lindsey!"

His daughter bolted for the RV.

Carl jerked his legs and started to turn, but moved like a man submerged in quicksand.

The thing snarled. An arm too long for its body swooped from the darkness and slammed into Carl's jaw. White sparks burst behind his eyes. Trees spun. The forest flipped upside down.

His back plunged into a mound of cindering ash, clouds of white dust puffing up around him.

Lindsey's screams echoed from somewhere. Chaser barked.

Gasping, Carl smelled steak burning, and then felt a hundred wasp stings searing his back. Beneath him, charred logs were burning through his flannel shirt. Screaming, Carl rolled out of the biting embers, rolling his body through the grass to extinguish his scalding back.

The giant shadow blocked out the moon. It reached down for Carl's leg, but Chaser leaped for the beast's throat. With quicksilver swiftness, a massive hand whacked across the dog's neck, sending the Rottweiler's body flying into the underbrush. Chaser didn't return.

Then the beast, outlined in the luminance of the moon, glared down at Carl. His hands sprawled over a pile of wood, grabbing a log he hadn't burned. He jumped up and smacked the log against its skull, knocking it sideways.

Carl sprinted through the woods. Toward the camper.

The beast, roaring, charged from behind with earth-shaking footfalls.

Twenty yards away Lindsey held out her arm. "Daddy!"

"Get inside!"

Ten more yards to the door.

Behind, heavy footsteps pounded closer. Steaming breath heaved above him.

Carl's heart felt as if it would burst. He reached the open camper door, fingers touching Lindsey's outstretched hand. Five talons dug into Carl's back, gripped around his spine and catapulted him back. Blood flooded up his throat, spurted over his lips.

Carl's arms and legs flailed. The night spun like a carnival ride, with the ground above and the moon below. As novas of fiery pain incinerated every lobe of his brain, he pictured Amy and Lindsey, two little girls smiling and waving.

* * *

Lindsey stood helpless at the RV's doorway as the nightmare hurled her father. His body spun through the air, end over end, smacking against the trees with an explosion of blood and broken body limbs.

"Daddy!"

The thing turned and charged at Lindsey.

She tried to push the door closed.

Like a blur, the shadow covered the stretch between the camp and RV in a blink. An elongated arm speared forward. Lindsey slammed the door against it. Black fingers clawed the air above her head.

Lindsey pulled the door tighter against the arm.

Dark blood splattered along the cabinets and across her cheeks. She slammed the camper door several more times against the arm until it pulled away.

She locked the side door as a shoulder impression protruded through the metal with a crashing sound, testing the hinges. They held, but the impact rattled the motor home. Lindsey tumbled against the dining table and then recoiled to the center aisle.

Something took hold of the camper's back bumper. The rear section began shaking, the tires and shocks squeaking.

Fighting to maintain her balance, Lindsey tottered back against the stove as the RV rocked. Then, as quickly as it had started, the violent rocking ceased. The night became silent. Moments passed like hours, without a sound, and then the wind picked up, scraping branches against the metal.

Lindsey flattened against the bathroom door, away from the windows.

Her body trembled.

The front doors aren't locked!

She burst down the narrow hall and slammed down the lock on the passenger's side. Then she turned around to hit the lock on the driver's side, only to see a hideous face lurking in the window.

As Lindsey slammed her fist down on the driver's door lock, a sudden blur burst through the glass. A hand with long black fingers gripped her wrist. Screaming, she clung to the steering wheel, struggling to keep from being pulled out the jagged window.

Lindsey braced her leg against the door and pulled with every ounce of strength she could muster. The beast's arm raked across the serrated teeth of the broken window, drenching the door an oily black.

The thing released its grip in an animal cry of pain.

Lindsey fell back against the passenger's seat. She spotted her dad's keys on the console.

Sucking in a hard breath, she grabbed the keys and jumped behind the wheel. She jammed the key into the ignition. The night pressed pitch-black against the windshield. She could see the moon and a few conifers spearing through it. She turned the key. The engine roared. She found the reverse gear, and blind to what was behind her, started backing the motor home down the narrow road. Branches scraped overhead, slapped at her window. Tires trundled over rocks.

Running feet pounded the road in front of her.

The beast's grunts grew louder.

Lindsey slammed down on the accelerator. Rolling backward, the motor home lurched. Branches screeched across the outside walls. She watched the side mirror as the rear end of the RV swayed from side to side, bumping trees. She fought the wheel to stay on course. The darkness made it impossible to maneuver along such a narrow path. To make matters worse, a tree tore off the side mirror with a metallic shriek.

In a sudden jolt, the camper crashed ass-end into a tree, and Lindsey fell against the steering wheel. She shifted into drive, stomped on the accelerator, spinning the wheels madly.

"Come on! Come on!" The RV refused to budge, its bumper hung up on something.

"Shit!" She fled to the back of the camper.

Something rammed the side wall with the force of a Mack truck, rocking the RV back on its wheels. Lindsey hit the floor, landing on her elbow. Hot needles stitched up her arm. Panicking from the snarling outside, Lindsey crawled along the floor. The trailer lifted off the ground on one side. Pots and pans clattered to the floor around her. The TV tipped off its console and smashed against the floor a foot away.

The RV tilted farther back, the metal supports grating. Lindsey rolled sideways over the cabinets, then across the kitchen sink as she felt her world turning off its axis. Then with a crash that shuddered throughout the interior, the camper upended on its side. Shards of glass exploded upward from all the windows, showering down upon her. The ceiling light popped out, tossing elongated shadows through the corridor.

When the falling debris finally settled, Lindsey found herself lying flat against the window that had been over the sink. It was broken and she could feel grass poking through. Shaking her bruised head, she sat up and opened her eyes to a new dark world. Only the faint wash of moon glow, spilling down through the side windows that were now above her, illuminated the corridor. The RV's interior had been invaded by the forest, with pine branches and shrubs jutting up through all the windows. To Lindsey, who was still dizzy, everything bloomed at the edges with hazy features.

She sat up in a cone of moonlight, wiped her tear-drenched face.

The thing outside jumped on top of the RV. The metal above groaned with every footstep. An elongated arm burst through a window and swooped down, tearing Lindsey's sweatshirt. She recoiled, curling into a fetal position beneath a mattress. She heard a door wrench open. The camper shook from feet crunching along the aisle. The footsteps stopped when they reached the mattress under which she hid.

Heavy breathing.

The mattress lifted off of her. She kept her eyes clamped tight, like a child willing the bogeyman to go away. But the nightmare continued as leathery hands draped around her limp body, snatching her up from the floor.

Chapter Seven

Alone behind the cabin, Kyle collected the last of the firewood. Again he heard a noise just beyond the trees. Clouds drifted away from the bright moon, pushing shadows back. Something moved back with them.

Shuff, shuff, shuff.

Strange shapes roamed through the forest beyond the woodpile.

Kyle flinched, trying to focus through the dark maze of pines. A few yards down the hill a tall figure was moving through the gloom. A person? Or just the wind blowing a tree?

Definitely not a tree, because it was advancing toward Kyle, climbing the hill. A rush of adrenaline flooded his body as he thought maybe his father was returning. "Dad? Is that you?"

Smaller silhouettes ran ahead of the larger one.

The forest grew alive with grunts and huffs, and the shuffling of several feet over thick, dry grass. Kyle dropped the pile of logs and grabbed an axe that was stuck blade down into a stump. He had been right. The forest was alive. One of the creatures made clicking sounds.

Gripping the axe, Kyle backed away from the trees, heading toward the cabin. A shadow shape charged with a rising growl and lurched from the blackness. It knocked Kyle flat against the ground. Sharp fangs tore into his wrist as he fought with the axe to hold back the four-legged beast. Arching its furry humped back, it growled and ripped at the sleeve of his shirt, cutting into his forearm.

Kyle yelled as blood trickled down his arm. Holding the axe with both hands, he slammed the handle against the thing's muzzle, and the shadow released its painful grip, only to snap back, snarling. Before jagged teeth could rip into his throat, he dropped the axe and caught the beast with both hands by its thick-muscled nape. Saliva spattered onto Kyle's cheeks. Fangs snapped inches from his face. Its neck twisted and jerked in his hands. The full moon reflected in its silvery eyes. Kyle tried to flip it off his chest, but the wolf-beast's paws scraped and jabbed into his chest and stomach.

Pinned beneath one beast, Kyle felt two more hungry muzzles tear at the cuffs of his jeans. Twisting snouts stretched and pulled at the denim as their growls tore through the blackness.

He was going to die. Eaten alive by wolves.

His back and buttocks began sliding over grass and rocks toward the tree line. The pines loomed over him, like hellish gods waiting for their minions to bring them prey.

With one hand, Kyle kept the fangs above his throat at bay, while his other hand clawed at the pine-needled earth to keep the creatures from dragging him into the forest.

Above, thorny branches shredded the moon as they swiftly raked across the sky. Three snarling beasts dragged him deeper into the woods. Swallowed by hovering trees and gloom, kicking and yelling as tree limbs and underbrush slapped past him, Kyle grabbed a rock with one free hand. Growling with his own preternatural rage, he struck the wolf on his chest square in the head. The animal yelped and ran off. Kyle clung to a tree to keep himself from being dragged any farther. The two wolves at his ankles tore at the cuffs of his jeans. Raising the rock, he was about to smack another beast, when the third wolf pounced on his chest again, its dripping fangs growling inches from Kyle's face.

A man's voice called from the shadows, "Arok! Get off him! Now!"

The dog-wolf crushing Kyle's chest scuttled back into the gloom.

"Kiche! Maskwa! Get!"

The two snouts released the jeans at Kyle's ankles. A shadowy mask eclipsed the moon and trees. "Are you all right?"

Choking, Kyle gripped his bruised chest.

Someone's hand kept patting his shoulder. "You okay?"

Kyle's mind drifted into blackness.

Again someone was tapping his shoulder. "Hey, Kyle, you still alive?"

Dazed, he tried sitting up to stop the earth from shaking, but the ghoul-like mask above was spinning, and the trees were spinning, and Kyle's stomach was tossing, and bile was rising in his throat. Pitching forward, he wretched onto the grass.

"I'm so sorry," a familiar deep voice reached Kyle. "I let my dogs get too far ahead of me."

Kyle finally recognized the voice. "Ray?"

"Yeah, bud, it's me." His cousin's large hand pulled Kyle up with ease, and a new pain, like barbwire being dragged along the bone beneath his skin, spiked up to his shoulder. He staggered, leaning against Ray. It took Kyle a moment to catch his wits. His arm was bleeding. His shirt and pants were damp and hung in tatters. His entire skull ached where his head had bumped across the rocky ground, and he could feel blood swelling in a scrape on his forehead where pine branches had slapped him.

From behind, voices called his name.

Several shadows rushed from the trees.

Zack arrived first. "We heard screaming. You okay?"

"I don't know."

Shawna said, "Holy shit, look at your hand!"

Kyle raised a red wet glove that dripped from his fingertips. The pain had finally stopped, but so had any feeling in his arm.

Jessica examined his wounds. "My God, what happened?"

"It's my fault." Ray Roamingbear stepped forward, leaning on his staff. "I hiked up here to see how you kids were doing. My dogs got away from me and jumped him. I feel terrible."

"Don't worry about it," Kyle said, trying to look brave for Jessica. He forced a grin. "It's just a few scrapes." A fiery pain pulsated through his forearm, reminding him that it was still attached. He heard the fear of rabies ripple through the group, but Ray assured them his dogs had been vaccinated. Three wolflike dogs slipped from the trees and herded around the tall Indian.

Kyle's body trembled as if the chilly night had turned subzero.

Jessica's soft fingers gently touched his arm as she examined the bites. "It's not as bad as it looks." She smiled. "Let's get you back to the house and cleaned up."

She escorted Kyle to the kitchen sink and ran cool tap water over his bleeding arm. He cringed as it stung, but took the pain in stride. The water washed blood, saliva, dirt and pine needles out of the multiple gashes in his forearm. After wiping his filthy face with a damp washcloth, Jessica said, "Now leave your arm under the water while I go get my bag."

"Okay, Doc." As Kyle watched her climb up the spiral stairs to the loft, he realized that Eric was sitting at the dinner table. The muscles in his jaw tightened, his eyes glassy and bloodshot. Beer cans littered the table. His fist crumpled one as if it were a Dixie cup. He then rose, staggering, and lumbered toward Kyle. "What the fuck are you trying to pull?"

"I was attacked by Ray's dogs. Go outside and see for yourself."

Eric pointed a finger. "I know what you're up to."

Kyle felt defenseless with a numb, bleeding arm pinned under the running tap. His head still felt woozy. Half-expecting a punch in the nose, Kyle raised his good arm, ready to block a blow if necessary. But Eric stopped midway. Then changing directions, he headed for the cabinets where with visible effort he retrieved a bottle of Dad's Stoli.

"Eric, don't you think you've had enough?"

"Fuck off." He headed out the front door. It slammed on its hinges.

"Shit," Kyle whispered, shaking his head.

A moment later, Jessica returned with a handbag. She didn't seem to notice Eric had left.

"You really come prepared, don't you?" Kyle said, as she zipped open the small black bag on the counter.

"I never leave home without my bag of tricks." After emptying half the contents onto the counter, she gave him Advil for his headache and then began dressing his wounds. His heart rate rocketed when she touched him. Not since his wife, Stephanie, had anyone caressed him. Blushing, he tried to shake the warm fuzziness in his chest, but Jessica's hands touched him with such tenderness he couldn't help but enjoy it. As she swabbed the scrape on his forehead, her face drifted inches from his, her blue eyes concentrating on her work. Her lips drifted so close, he could feel her breath on his cheek. Then an even stranger feeling swept through Kyle—a magnetic urge to kiss her. A desire he thought he'd never feel again.

He jerked away.

"I'm sorry, did I hurt you?" Her eyes blinked with concern.

"No, I just…" Kyle moved away from her, needing cool air. He opened the fridge and leaned inside as if looking for a drink. Frosty air relieved his burning chest.

"Are you okay?"

He grabbed a bottle of water. "Yeah, just thirsty." He took a swig. "Ahh, hits the spot. I guess we're done. Thanks. I feel much better."

"Don't run off. I still need to bandage your arm."

He looked down at his gnarled arm that was now clean but starting to bleed again where canine teeth had cut the deepest. "Oh, yeah." He sat down at the table, letting Jessica swab some kind of oil on the wounds. It had a strong, but pleasant odor.

"What is that?" he asked.

"Melalueca oil. It's a natural remedy for healing wounds and fighting off infections."

Kyle noticed that, other than Advil and bandages, most of her first-aid supplies were brown bottles of oil and bags of herbs. "Are you some kind of witch doctor or something?"

She smiled. "No, but I learned a lot about healing from studying with the aborigines. They taught me that natural medicine is far more holistic for our bodies than traditional Western medicine."

Kyle tried to avoid Jessica's eyes, so she wouldn't see that he was falling for her. The closeness of her face, her hair, the smell of her perfume nearly drove him to forget the pact he had made with himself. He glanced down at the gold band on his wedding finger. He could barely breathe. He tried to lower his face. Too late. She looked up. "Are you all right?" She touched his cheek. "You're trembling."

"Just nerves from the attack."

"Poor thing." She left her hand on his face.

"It'll pass. This used to happen a lot when I was a kid." He tried to smile like it was nothing, but then his upper lip trembled, so he clamped his mouth shut.

After wrapping his arm with gauze, Jessica pulled away and smiled. "All done."

"Am I going to live, Doc?" he asked, trying to make light of the situation.

"Oh, I think you'll make it. You're a lucky one, you are. The wound on your wrist just broke the skin. No major arteries severed." She grinned and brushed some pine needles out of his hair. "And I don't see any signs of brain damage."

* * *

"Sure you're okay?" Ray said as Kyle and Jessica stepped back outside. "I feel terrible."

"I'll be fine, thanks to Doc here." Kyle stared at the three dogs that watched the group with suspicious eyes. Two of the dogs were charcoal gray and one was a solid, shiny black. All stood waist high to Kyle, with thick torsos, monstrous jowls and sharp pointed ears that always stood alert. The black one that featured more wolf than dog was the largest of the pack, with a thick spiky coat and an odd hump that rose along its spine. Its stare made Kyle wary. "I don't remember you having guard dogs."

"I got 'em a year ago. Sometimes we get poachers out here. When my dogs saw you roaming outside the cabin, they must've thought you were a trespasser. I'm afraid I've trained 'em too well."

The three dogs packed around Ray, tightly coiled and ready to spring at any sudden move. As Ray talked, nobody so much as flinched. Kyle wished Shawna and Jessica were safe inside, unsure of how much control his cousin had over his killer pets.

"You guys can relax," Ray assured the group. "Really, they won't harm you now that they see you're family." He spoke Cree to the dogs in a commanding voice. The pack relaxed in unison, lying sphinx-like on their bellies, tongues panting.

Ray smiled proudly. "They're the best trained guard dogs I've ever owned. Part German shepherd, part mountain wolf. When I'm around, they don't do anything unless I command it. Watch." He clicked his tongue, and all three dogs stood up in attention like a disciplined platoon. Ray's mouth did a single cluck and the black wolf lumbered forward and licked his palm. "This one's Arok. He's the meanest. Doesn't like many folks, but don't worry. He's a puppy dog when I'm around. And when he gets to know you, he's your best friend."

Ray made squirrel sounds with his tongue then snapped his fingers over his head. Arok returned to his position and the two dark gray dogs padded forward, flanking Ray on either side. "Kiche and Maskwa. They're my twins. Kiche here is a female, and Maskwa, he's the charmer."

Another chilly wind whistled from the forest, and Shawna hugged her shoulders. "Guys, let's go inside and build that fire."

"Good idea," Kyle said. "Ray, come join us. We've got plenty of beer and leftover gumbo."

"I don't know," Ray said. "I should probably head home."

Kyle said, "Nonsense, you walked all this way to visit. Besides, I was hoping this week you would share some campfire stories." To the group Kyle said, "Ray is a master storyteller."

Shawna said, "Ooh, yeah, the scarier, the better."

Their cousin grinned broadly. "Well, all right, I never turn down an opportunity to share stories." Looking down at his dogs, Ray made clicking and clucking noises, and the pack danced about his legs like well-trained circus animals. "Arok, you're in charge. Keep the twins in line."

* * *

On the front side of the cabin, an icy wraith of wind embraced Eric as he sat on an old tire swing. He welcomed the cold, for it cooled his anger.

All night Jessica had flirted with Kyle in the kitchen, giggled with him during dinner, going on and on about his cooking, and then finally playing doctor with him at the sink. And that fucking grin Kyle wore as he watched Jessica wiggling her ass up the stairs.

"There you are," Jessica said from the front porch. "I was wondering what happened to you."

"I went for a walk."

She came over and caressed Eric's shoulder. "Come join us inside. Ray's going to tell us some stories."

"I'm fine out here."

"Don't you want to snuggle up on the couch with me?"

"Not in the mood." He drank straight from a vodka bottle.

"What has gotten into you tonight? You never drink like this."

"Not in the mood to talk either."

"Fine, get bloody drunk for all I care." Jessica went back inside.

Clutching the half-empty bottle of vodka, he walked over and peered in the through the front window. The group had gathered in the den with Grandfather and Ray Roamingbear. Jessica sat down on the loveseat next to Kyle. Watching his brother and girlfriend with one another caused an unfamiliar tightness in Eric's chest. He wanted to put his fist through something, preferably Kyle's face.

Eric took another swig. The sting of the vodka made his eyes water. As he wiped his face on his sleeve, he heard a lone wolf howling somewhere in the distance. *I hear you, my friend.*

* * *

In the cozy warmth of the cabin's den, the group sat around Ray Roamingbear and Grandfather. Sitting on the loveseat, Kyle relaxed, enjoying the reunion with his relatives. Across from him, Shawna looked at peace as she held hands with Zack. Her eyes met Kyle's and she grinned. He couldn't remember the last time the two of them had been happy at the same time. All they had needed was to make the journey home.

Kyle's heart rose when Jessica joined him on the loveseat. She looked bothered by something.

"Eric's not coming in?" Kyle asked.

"He's being a butt."

No, he's just being Eric, Kyle wanted to say, but it wasn't his place.

Jessica leaned back, and as her arm brushed his, Kyle felt a rush like he was in junior high again. He imagined what it would feel like to put his arm around her shoulder and pull her closer. That, unfortunately, could never happen. He took it as a good sign that he was ready to date again. Maybe when he got home, he'd join a matchmaker site.

As the group listened, Ray told stories of growing up on the reservation with their father. "Elkheart and I were always getting into something. When I was a tyke, we found a lone brown bear cub in the woods and I thought it would make a great pet." Ray chuckled. "So like a couple of nitwits, we tied a rope around its neck and guided it back to the village. As you can imagine, this caused quite a panic as the mama grizzly came roaring after her baby. Everyone scattered. We had to hide indoors all day, because mama and baby bear decided to stick around and eat the lunch we'd laid out on a picnic table. No one got hurt, but I think that's when Grandfather's hair started turning silver." He grinned at the old man. "Anyhow, that's how I got my name, Roamingbear."

As Ray told humorous stories, Kyle laughed harder than he had in a long time. "Tell us a story about the history of our tribe."

Ray cocked his head. "Let me see if I can think of one."

Grandfather said, "*Macâya Sakâw!*" His cataract eyes were intense and his face animated with emotion.

Ray looked startled, as if Grandfather had asked him to pull a rattlesnake out of thin air.

"What's he saying?" Kyle asked.

"He wants me to tell you the legend of Macâya Forest."

Kyle remembered hearing the legend when he was a boy. "That's an old campfire tale, isn't it?"

"It's been passed down for generations," Ray said. "Mainly to scare the kids and keep them from wandering too far from the village."

Kyle said, "We were warned not to go past Kakaskitewak Swamp or the woods would snatch us."

Grandfather spoke in Cree again, his ancient voice uttering words Kyle wished he could comprehend.

Ray translated, "He says the warnings were for the tribe's protection. Grandfather had been warned when he was a child. And his father before him, and so on. This legend still gives me the willies, because Macâya Forest lies on the edge of this reservation. And is considered haunted."

"All right, a ghost story!" Shawna leaped up and turned off the kitchen light. Shadows curtained down the walls, draping them in a gloomy orange-gray glow. The fire in the hearth popped and crackled. Dim light undulated around the den, shadows dancing like goblins along the walls and ceiling. Everyone's faces were half in light, half in shadow as they waited for the speaker of legends.

Firelight reflected off Ray's reddish-brown face. He spoke just above a whisper, "My momma told me this one when I was nine, just before she went to the spirit world. 'Macâya Forest,' she had said in a raspy voice, 'got its name from Cree lore and has remained forbidden for centuries. The forest was known for devouring any man or animal that ventured into it. Our ancestors respected its boundaries. But then came wagons carrying lumberjacks who had dreams of turning the woods around Lake Akwâkopiy into money. They moved in with our people. Offered promises of a better life. The white men, speaking Danish, called this dream Hagen's Cove. Together the tribe and the settlers cut down the forest and built crude roads, a square of shops and houses and a timber mill owned by the Thorpe family."

"Founded by Hagen Thorpe," Jessica said.

Ray nodded. "That's right. In the 1880s, Hagen's Cove flourished as lumberjacks scalped the mountain and the mill guzzled logs. Soon they reached a valley of woods that our ancestors held sacred. *Macâya Sakâw*, they called it. The Devil's Woods. The Cree elders warned the lumberjacks not to cut those trees, but the white men were too stubborn and had no respect for the land or our beliefs."

Ray stood and, leaning on his staff, walked with a limp to the atrium doors and peered out at the dark woods. "This is the part I've always refused to believe. See, my momma was a sick old woman and very superstitious. A strong believer that spirits inhabit these woods. But I'll tell you anyway because this legend is like a parasite that burrows in the back of the minds of everyone who lives in Hagen's Cove. They fear that even mentioning Macâya Forest will summon the devil to your door."

Kyle felt Jessica inching closer. Damn, he wanted to put his arm around her.

Ray turned around and reflections of the fire flickered in his eyes. "According to legend, a heavy storm formed over these mountains and hovered there for several weeks. Inside Macâya Forest an iridescent green mist spread across the woods all the way to Hagen's Cove. The inhabitants bolted their doors. But the strange glowing mist remained. People heard moaning and saw ghosts inside that green fog. Having a mill to keep fed, Hagen Thorpe and his lumberjacks set out into the mist, wielding axes. But something was waiting for them. The screams of those men echoed across the land, heard by the Cree tribe and the white people back in town. Only Hagen returned with a haunted expression on his face. He swore he saw the devil himself. The next day, when the mist dissolved, a few Cree warriors ventured into the woods and found the remains of the lumberjacks torn and twisted and covered in flies… Scattered all around them were large footprints and trees slashed with claw marks…"

Jessica gasped and grabbed Kyle's thigh.

Ray leaned forward on his staff, gazing at everyone with an expression that was dead serious. "And to this day, it is believed if you go anywhere near Macâya Forest, you can still hear the cries of the men who were slaughtered and the ferocious howl of the Macâya."

Zack growled and grabbed Shawna's shoulder. She screamed and leapt from her seat. Zack laughed uncontrollably.

"You bastard!" Shawna punched his shoulder.

"That's twice today."

Shawna's face turned red. "Just for that, dipshit, you can sleep alone tonight."

"Hey now!" Zack chuckled. "You gotta admit it was funny. You practically jumped out of your skin."

"Good night, everybody." Shawna stomped up the stairs.

Zack looked at the group, holding up his hands. "What? It was a joke."

Jessica said, "Seriously, Zack, scaring your girlfriend's not going to win you any points."

Kyle said, "If you want to sleep in a bed tonight, you better go patch things up."

Zack hit himself and said, "Idiot," and then ran up the stairs after his girlfriend.

* * *

"Ray, do you believe the legend?" Kyle asked.

"Not hardly." His cousin chuckled, shaking his head. "Our elders were always coming up with supernatural myths. Some were to explain the phenomena of nature. Others to scare the children. As for Macâya Forest, the forbidden woods do exist, but I don't believe there was ever any green fog. But there's one part of the story I can't deny…the mysterious slaughter of a dozen lumberjacks is docked in Hagen's Cove's history."

"So then there was something out there that night," Kyle said. "The Macâya."

"That's what the locals believe, but nobody ever found an animal that could kill a dozen men armed with axes. My guess is they pissed off the wrong grizzly bear."

A strange animal sound echoed from the woods.

"What was that?" Jessica asked.

Kyle turned to face the back windows. Ray's dogs stood on the back porch with their fur bristled, barking at the forest.

Ray lunged out of his seat. "Something's got them spooked."

The three dogs dashed off the porch.

* * *

Eric sat on the hood of the Hummer out front, his head floating in a watery world, a near-empty vodka bottle clutched in his fingers. His anger was gone now, diluted by the liquor he'd drunk.

The howling suddenly seemed too close for comfort. And there was more than one wolf now.

Shit, time to head inside. But first he had to take one hell of a piss. He hopped down from the Hummer. The ground spun as he stumbled to the edge of the front yard where tall pines bordered the clearing. As he relieved himself, he vaguely remembered Jessica coming out and looking for him. He didn't remember the conversation, but she had left pissed off.

Hell, she was so sensitive it could have been any goddamn little thing. What Eric needed to do was man-up and apologize for whatever he said and then take Jessica upstairs and have sex with her. That always put things right between them.

He zipped his jeans and started back toward the cabin when he heard something moving through the trees. "Who's there?"

No one. Just the wind.

Then something in the gloom released a guttural snarl, and Eric kicked backward.

An animal burst through the branches.

Eric backed into the Hummer and fell to the ground. From the pines a four-legged beast rushed into the moonlight, lips curled back over what looked like a rack of sharp fangs. It slowed to a prowl, lowering its head, growling.

Eric eased up the side of the Hummer and glanced toward the house. Between him and the front door stood three wolves, barking and growling. *Fuck!* Eric froze, feeling cornered. Shaking, he looked behind him. Toward the fourth beast that had rushed from the forest.

When it nearly reached him, Eric yelled. He shielded his face. Through the cracks of his fingers he could see a snarling mouth, angry eyes. The beast came within a yard, but didn't attack. Instead, what up close looked like a black-and-brown dog, advanced past him, toward the three wolves. They stooped their heads and snarled. The black wolf crept from behind, surrounding the dog that Eric finally recognized: the Rottweiler with that family who owned the RV.

Chaser.

All at once the three wolves pounced the dog, snapping at its back and nape. Chaser fought them off, biting and barking and twisting.

The front door opened and Ray Roamingbear hobbled out, yelling and breaking up the fight with his staff. "Get! Get!" The three wolves split from the scene, leaving Chaser to lick his wounds.

Jessica rushed out when she saw the battered Rottweiler. "Oh, my God, Chaser!" She raced to its aid. "Ah, boy, you're bleeding."

The dog whimpered and licked her chin.

Eric remained on the ground in front of the Hummer, trying to calm his fast-beating heart.

Kyle came out into the front yard. "What happened this time?"

"I'm afraid it's my damned dogs again," Ray said, shaking his head. "They got into a scuff with this fellow."

Kyle looked down at Chaser. "What's Carl's dog doing here?"

"I don't know." Jessica brushed pine needles out of its gnarled fur. "He must've run away again. But how'd you ever find us, you little mongrel?" She flapped his ears.

Eric's fury returned as Kyle bent down beside Jessica, helping her keep the dog from running away.

Ray said, "Eric, you all right?"

He stood up. "Yeah, fine." He couldn't believe he was nearly killed, and Jessica ran to help a stupid dog. "Don't worry about me, Jess. I was nearly attacked, but I'm all right now."

Jessica stood. "I only ran to Chaser because he was bleeding. I'm a doctor. That's what I do."

Eric snarled, "You're a student doctor back home at the hospital. On vacation, you're supposed to be my girlfriend." He brushed past her and Kyle on his way inside.

Kyle surveyed the wounded dog. "Chaser, looks like you need the same treatment as me. But don't worry. Doc here will fix you up."

The battered Rottweiler moaned and staggered as Kyle and Jessica guided him into the cabin.

Kyle closed the door and remained outside to say good night to Ray. He was obviously embarrassed about the evening catastrophes with his dogs. "I better get my dogs home."

Kyle said, "Before you go, I've been meaning to ask you something about Dad."

He raised an eyebrow. "What do you want to know?"

Kyle explained how they came across Detective Carl Hanson, searching the area for his missing daughter. And how later they found Elkheart's red Bronco packed with camping gear. "Do you think it's possible Dad and his crew might be camping somewhere on the land?"

"I doubt it. Your grandfather and I would've seen him by now if he'd stuck around."

"Detective Hanson suspects they were working on some kind of top-secret expedition in the area and that none of the crew has reported back yet. I've decided to hike to some of our old campsites tomorrow and see if I can locate him."

"We're on the edge of untamed wilderness," Ray said. "It wouldn't take much to get yourself lost out there."

"If Dad taught me anything, it's how to navigate the woods."

"All right," Ray said. "If you want, I'll hike with you. I know every trail on this reservation. If Elkheart's camping on the property, I have a few ideas where he'd be."

"Thanks, I'd appreciate the help." There was hope yet.

They agreed to meet at sunrise. Then, saying good night, Ray walked up the driveway, clicking his tongue. His three wolf dogs came out of the woods and walked with him into the night.

Chapter Eight

Back inside the cabin, all was quiet now. Grandfather had retired to the downstairs bedroom, while Zack and Shawna remained upstairs. Eric was passed out in a seated position on the loveseat.

Leaning against the kitchen counter, Kyle watched Jessica bandage the wounded Rottweiler. The smooth fur of Chaser's back was covered with welts and lacerations and an ugly three-clawed scrape across his neck. Those cuts bothered Kyle most, because they had run deep enough valleys to show dark red tissue. But the dog was in good hands.

Jessica coddled Chaser as if he were a child.

Kyle said, "You know, if being a doctor doesn't pan out, you'd make a great veterinarian. You have a way with animals."

"When I was a girl, I actually wanted to become a vet." She petted Chaser's forehead. "At our ranch back in Australia, we had horses, goats, sheep and a couple of blue heelers. I looked after the animals, feeding and watering them, patching up their cuts. Whenever the vet paid us a visit, I always tagged along and helped him. But as I grew older, I felt more called to help people, but I miss these guys."

She swabbed the last cut, covered it with a bandage then let the Rottweiler loose to roam. Limping, Chaser padded into the kitchen and licked Kyle's hand.

Jessica smiled and tilted her head in a way that made her dark hair fall across one shoulder. "He likes you."

"You think?" Kyle scratched Chaser behind the ears.

"You did rescue him from the woods today."

The dog returned to her, and Kyle said, "Maybe so, but he clearly has chosen his favorite. Just don't get too attached. We have to return him tomorrow."

She stroked the Rottweiler's fur. "Ahh, and we were just starting to become good mates."

Kyle placed another log on the fire. On the loveseat, Eric snored like a buzz saw. Kyle shook his brother's shoulder. "Hey, wake up. I need to set up my bed."

Eric moaned and rolled over.

Jessica laughed. "A fog horn between his ears won't wake him. No worries. Just push his couch back."

Kyle shoved the loveseat back and then unfolded the sleeper sofa and unrolled his goose-down bag. When he was done, he realized Jessica was watching him.

After a moment of awkward silence, she said, "Um, before we turn in, there's something I'd love to show you."

Jessica's surprise was that she had brought her telescope. Kyle joined her on the cabin's balcony for a little stargazing. Up here, Kyle had a view of the shadowy village. Several cabins creaked in the wind and a door slammed against its frame at the stables. He focused on the sky. Away from the light pollution of the city, the stars sparkled like diamonds on black velvet. The night was clear, the moon a bright pearl.

"There," Jessica panned the telescope and pointed to the sky. "See the constellation that's shaped like a Y?"

Kyle peered into the scope and found the grouping of Y-shaped stars.

"That's Aries," Jessica said. "Over there's the Big Dipper. And the brightest star with a red hue, that's Mars."

As they took turns peering into the lens, she named off constellations like a well-studied astronomer. "My first big dream—do you want to know what it was?"

"Yes."

"To be an astronaut and travel into space."

Kyle said, "Seriously? I thought you wanted to be a vet and then a doctor."

"I did. But before that, until the age of nine, I wanted to be an astronaut more than anything. I had the entire universe on my bedroom ceiling. I could name any of the constellations and planets."

Kyle peered into the scope. "So why didn't you pursue that dream?"

"My dad told me that being an astronaut was a man's profession, that I'd be better off practicing medicine like him. I named all the women who'd become astronauts before me."

"And?"

"He was unmoved, said he wouldn't pay for college if I studied anything but medicine." Jessica looked away from the stars to glance at Kyle. "I've grown to love med school. It's funny, with all the micro medical technology now exploring the human body it's a lot like traveling in outer space. So you see, I got my wish after all." The smile she gave him was irresistible.

Kyle had never paid much attention to the sky. Now it had greater depths. Some of the stars were bright and closer to the Earth, others dim, submerged deeper in the vast pool of the universe. He felt inspired to encourage her. "You know, it's not unheard of for medical specialists to go on space missions."

"I've thought of that." There was that smile again, her eyes gleaming. "Who knows? Maybe one day I'll be the first doctor on Mars."

"I'd go there with you." The words escaped his mouth before he could stop them.

She laughed. "Absolutely. We'll need a writer too, I suppose." But the moment was awkward and she looked away. "So tell me. What's your next dream, Mr. Famous Author?"

Kyle hesitated, not sure how to answer. "I don't dream much."

"Sure you do. Everybody dreams."

He shrugged.

"You must have goals as a writer, hopes for future projects and so forth." When he didn't answer, she said, "Shall I gaze into my crystal ball then?" Jessica mimed conjuring a ball on the handrail between them.

"Please do."

"All right. I see you publishing your next book to massive critical acclaim, talk shows, ticker-tape parades, and later being the first artist-in-residence on Mars."

Kyle laughed. It felt so good that it frightened him. "That all seems perfectly reasonable."

She smiled. "Seriously, don't you think about your future?"

"Not really. Not since…well, the last couple years I've lived pretty much day by day." Kyle watched the woods in silence for a while. He didn't want her to know this lifeless part of him. The part that had given up caring after Stephanie died.

Jessica gave him a half smile. Her eyes looked bothered that he was being so closed off.

Kyle wanted to share more about himself, but felt like he'd be dishonoring Stephanie. "I guess I better call it a night."

"Okay." Jessica sounded disappointed.

There was an awkward silence between them as they descended the stairs.

The den was dark except for a faint glow from the fireplace. As Kyle approached his bedroll, he saw a hand stretched across his pillow. "Oh, great!" Eric had crawled onto Kyle's double bed and was lying beside the sleeping bag.

Jessica shook her boyfriend's shoulder. "Eric, wake up. It's time to go upstairs."

He didn't respond.

"Looks like he's dead to the world," Kyle said.

She made a sound of exasperation, then saying good night, disappeared upstairs.

Part Three
Ghost Detective

When one can see into the spirit realm and speak to ghosts, it opens up a whole new world of opportunities the average man cannot attain. You see, ghosts come to me for services. They want to understand their deaths. They want closure. And most of all they want to be released from their limbo states before the Hollowers come to claim their souls. As a ghost detective, I help them find their way home and in return, they watch over me.

—Detective Alex Winterbone

Chapter Nine

Lying zipped up in his bedroll, Kyle looked up at the loft, which was dark now.

Jessica's up there, sleeping alone.

He fantasized about climbing the stairs and crawling into bed with her. How good it would feel to make love to a woman again. To feel the warmth of Jessica's naked skin against his own. Feeling restless, Kyle climbed out of bed. He went into the kitchen and made a cup of chamomile tea. As he was leaning against the counter, sipping from the mug, he saw a twinkling of small lights out in the woods. He turned off the light above the sink and watched out the window. Two fireflies moved along the edge of the trees. They paused, side by side, like two silver buttons floating in blackness. Like glowing eyes. Kyle's face got the familiar tingling sensations he felt whenever he peered into the spirit realm. He hid behind the wall, heart racing. Catching his breath, he ventured another look out the window.

The lights were gone.

Kyle released a nervous laugh. *What is it about these woods?* He had witnessed strange phenomena like this many times in his life. Often, ghosts passed through a space, barely visible, and were gone in a blink. Only rarely did they make eye contact or notice that he was watching. When they did, he always got spooked.

Kyle had never known what to do with this extraordinary gift—or curse, however you wanted to look at it—so he invented a character for his novel series. Unlike Kyle, Detective Winterbone had the ability to talk to ghosts and could peer into the spirit realm at will. Kyle's ability was more sporadic and often he had to touch objects to connect with the spirit world. Some objects held visions. Others didn't. Many sightings were random and too short to make much sense. But in some places, the vibrations of the dead were stronger, like his wife's art studio in his apartment, like these woods, where the souls remained in limbo, haunting the place. Those he feared because they were malcontent spirits and could harm him. Detective Winterbone had a gift for helping ghosts find their way to the next world. Kyle could only live among them as a helpless onlooker.

Outside, the silver buttons returned to the edge of the forest. Kyle's face tingled again, but this time he didn't break eye contact. The glowing orbs moved closer. A head took shape in the moonlight, a pale oval face, dark braids hanging past the shoulders. A teenage girl wearing a sundress. She was so faint, barely an outline, and Kyle could see the trees through her. As she walked, the wind blew the hem of her dress.

He held her gaze, not wanting this amazing vision to slip away. She crossed the back lawn, moving toward the cabin, disappearing and reappearing every five feet. When she reached the porch, her head craned toward Kyle, peering at him with those blazing silver orbs. He moved away from the window and snapped his eyes shut.

Footsteps creaked on the porch steps.

Oh, shit. He held his breath. *How would Winterbone handle this situation?*

He'd confront the ghost instead of hiding like a coward.

The back atrium door opened. Wind rustled magazines on the coffee table. The footsteps entered the den, the sound of bare feet on the wood floor. The cabin suddenly felt colder. The door closed gently, the moaning wind shaking the windowpanes.

From the kitchen, Kyle peered around the wall.

The specter of the Indian girl was standing by the door, her head turned sideways, facing him. She was barely visible. Only her silver eyes, alight like beacons, were in sharp detail. She opened her mouth and uttered a hollow sound, like damp wind blowing through a pipe, but no words formed. Her eyes narrowed, as if frustrated. The girl motioned with her arm, gesturing for Kyle to follow. She moved toward the hallway. Again, she flickered in and out, a stuttering projection of a girl, advancing five feet at a time. She opened the door to Elkheart's study and disappeared around the wall.

Kyle moved slowly into the den, unsure of whether to follow her. He could hear Detective Winterbone at the back of his mind calling him a chickenshit.

At the far end of the cabin, another door opened and then came a crash.

Shit. He ran into the study and flipped on the light.

The closet door was open and a box of files had fallen to the floor.

The girl was gone.

Kyle turned over the box and put the files back in. From one folder, a yellow newspaper clipping fell to the floor. He picked it up and saw a familiar high school portrait of a teenage girl with black braids. Kyle's heart nearly stopped. The headline read, *Missing Cree Girl's Body Found Floating in Lake Akwâkopiy.* The file was full of clippings of articles about sixteen-year-old Nina Whitefeather, who had been murdered over twenty years ago.

"Holy shit." Nina used to babysit him, Eric and Shawna. Nina cooked meals with their mother and read bedtime stories to the kids. Then came the dark period after Nina went missing. Their babysitter had been found dead months later, but Kyle never knew the details because the adults had kept silent. Even in Hagen's Cove, where rumors spread like wildfire, no one had talked about Nina Whitefeather's death.

Kyle opened the folder and read one of the articles. Nina had been raped and lacerated with multiple knife wounds. A riot between the Cree tribe and the loggers had followed, as the two opposing sides blamed the other for the girl's death. A photo depicted Cree men and women picketing Thorpe's Lumber Mill. Inspector Zano, an RCMP detective working the case, said that he would question every male living within fifty miles of Lake Akwâkopiy until he found Nina's killer. The articles about her in later newspapers got smaller and smaller, and Inspector Zano's quotes lacked the conviction of the first month. Eventually, the picketing stopped. A final article, dated two years after the murder, stated that the Whitefeather case had finally gone cold. Zano believed Nina's killer was a drifter who had passed through Hagen's Cove, and kept going.

According to Carl Hanson, dozens of women had vanished in the woods around this lake since the 1950s. Carl had suspected a serial killer. *Canada's Bermuda Triangle.*

Was Nina's death related?

Kyle suddenly had a disturbing thought. What if his father killed Nina?

No way.

Winterbone was in Kyle's head again. *Are you sure?* the detective challenged. *How well do you know him really? You've only seen him a few times in twenty years.*

Kyle had to admit, Professor Jon Elkheart was an enigma—a heavy drinker, notorious for disappearing for months at a time, but he was also a dedicated archaeologist, author of a number of related books, and wildly popular with his students, who followed his doings on social media like he was the second coming. When he was posting, anyway, which he hadn't in a while. He'd gotten fired a few years back for sleeping with one of his students, who was nineteen—not his finest hour. Now a more recent student, Amy Hanson, had vanished along with Elkheart and possibly an entire expedition team.

If Elkheart wasn't guilty, why had Nina Whitefeather's ghost led Kyle to this box in his father's closet? *There has to be another explanation.*

Kyle thought it was odd that his father had held on to the clippings about Nina's murder for so many years, but then not really. *Nina was practically family.* Elkheart had never gotten over her death.

Kyle had almost convinced himself of his father's innocence when he remembered something Jessica had said earlier. It was after Wynona Thorpe had accosted her at the tavern. His father's ex-girlfriend had warned Jessica to stay away from the reservation. Then Wynona said something that had stuck at the back of Kyle's mind.

The sins of the father shall fall upon the sons.

Chapter Ten

Kyle woke to a strange noise. He sat up in his bedroll. Still dark outside, the forest black against the pale moonlight. The den was a sepulcher of shadows. The logs in the fireplace had burned to ash. The room was cold now. A chill passed across his bare back like the stroke of icy fingers. Kyle shivered. Rubbed his face.

He thought of Nina Whitefeather's ghost. Had he imagined her?

Clump-scraaaape.

He started at the sound. It came from his father's study. A door creaked open.

Clump-scraaaape. The noise echoed down the dark hallway.

"Who's there?" he whispered, hoping Shawna or Zack would respond.

Nails dragged across a wall.

"Nina?"

The scraping stopped at the edge of the hallway. An outline of a jagged head formed out of the darkness and slowly turned toward him, twisting at an impossible angle. Bones cracked. A shaft of moonlight from a window slashed across a mouth with shredded lips. The pale face split into a glistening red grimace. "Kyyyllle," a woman's raspy voice gurgled.

His wife's hunched silhouette scurried across the room, reaching for Kyle. He snapped his eyes shut. *Christ, she's followed me here.*

Are you sure it wasn't just another nightmare? asked Detective Winterbone. Kyle had a vision of the private eye sitting behind his desk in an office filled with antique books.

No, I can feel Stephanie's presence, just like at my apartment. She's come back for revenge.

A vengeful ghost is the worst kind. Winterbone scribbled on a notepad. *We'll have to take extreme measures to protect you.*

Can you stop her?

I'll do my best. But we'll have to work this case from the inside out.

How so?

Detective Winterbone leaned forward. *Your wife's spirit has somehow gotten inside you, like a virus. She's haunting the halls of your psyche. Where you go, she goes.*

The image of Detective Winterbone evaporated and Kyle woke up in the cabin's den. He lay in his sleeping bag, staring at the dark ceiling. He rubbed his face. Another crazy dream.

From the hall bathroom came the sound of spraying water. A few moments later, it stopped and somebody stepped out of the shower.

Chaser stirred in the corner when he heard that people were finally moving about. The wounded Rottweiler padded over to the sofa bed, licked Kyle's palm.

"Morning, fur face." He scratched the dog behind the ears. "I bet you miss Lindsey and Carl."

Chaser whimpered.

"Don't worry. We'll get you back to them."

Beside Kyle, Eric grumbled and rolled flat on his back. His mouth open, he continued his drunken slumber with one elbow across his forehead.

Still groggy, Kyle zipped up his bedroll and tried to sleep a little longer.

Kyle heard the bathroom door open and feet tramp across the wood floor. Wearing only a towel, Jessica came into the den.

Chaser limped toward her, and she stopped and petted him. "Good morning, boy," she said with a voice too cheery for morning. "You've been scratching at your bandages, haven't you? No worries, I'll patch you up." Jessica sauntered past Kyle's bed. "Aren't we the late sleeper? Plan to snooze all day?"

He looked at his watch. "It's five thirty."

"I know. I love getting up before dawn." Jessica looked over her shoulder at him. Her wet hair appeared almost black. The wavy strands hung freely down her back. Her towel barely covered her slender legs.

Kyle had a vision of what the rest of her might look like beneath that towel and felt himself getting an erection. Thankfully, he was sealed up in his sleeping bag. He looked away, concentrating on anything that would hold fantasies at bay. He tried hard not to watch as Jessica walked around the room with only a towel concealing her slender frame. She stopped at the loft's circular stairway, held the towel in a knot at her chest. "Care to join me on the balcony to watch the sunrise?"

"I would, uh…but Ray and I are headed out this morning."

"Maybe tomorrow then." Jessica smiled and then climbed up to the loft to get dressed.

Fully awake now, Kyle jumped down and did thirty pushups. It wasn't enough to work down his arousal, though. He considered a cold shower, but Grandfather got to the bathroom first. Kyle put on a pair of cargo shorts, a T-shirt and hiking shoes. In the kitchen, he made a banana protein smoothie with a dash of wheat grass and raw chocolate, packing it in a canister for the hike. He peered out the window above the sink. Outside, the dark of night was starting to shift into a gray-green morning haze. He searched the forest for Nina Whitefeather's ghost, but saw only birds.

Kyle fried up sausage and eggs for the early risers. Chaser followed him everywhere he went. He tossed the dog a few strips of sausage. On the floor beside the fridge were a couple of dog bowls. Kyle's father had a German Shepherd named Scout. *Dad must have taken the dog with him.*

"Chaser, let's see if we can find you something to eat." Kyle searched the pantry and found a bag of Dog Chow. "Ah, you're in luck, boy." He filled the dog bowls with food and water and let Chaser take it from there.

As Kyle was setting the table, Ray came up the back steps and entered the cabin through the den. "Top of the morning. Mmm, something smells delish."

"The usual grub." Kyle poured Ray a cup of coffee. "Are your dogs going with us?"

"Nah, I left 'em back at the house where they'll stay out of trouble. How's your arm?"

"Feeling better. Thanks to Doc, here."

Jessica came down fully dressed. "G'day, Ray."

He gave her a sideways hug. "Mornin'."

Even in the early morning, Jessica looked radiant. Kyle poured her some coffee. "Want some *brekkie*?" he asked, using the Australian word for breakfast.

"What've you got?"

"Bangers and eggs."

"Definitely save me some," she said. "I want to catch the sunrise over the mountains." Taking her coffee mug, Jessica hurried up the back staircase.

Ray watched her, shaking his head. "She sure is a pretty little thing.

Your brother's a lucky man."

My brother's an idiot. Kyle unfolded a topography map of the five thousand acres that made up the Cree reservation. "I found this in Dad's study."

Ray sat down with a plate of fried eggs and sausage. "That's a lot of territory to cover. It'd take years to walk the whole property."

"We're only going to hike to a few campsites where Dad and I used to camp. Most are within a two-mile radius of the compound." He circled four *Xs* along a network of trails. "If Dad's still on Cree land, there's a good chance he'll be at one of these spots."

"Then we'll search each of them. I'd like to find your father myself. He owes me two hundred dollars."

Kyle looked across the table at his cousin. "Do you remember Nina Whitefeather's murder several years ago?"

"Of course." His eyes went somber as he chewed. "It was a damned tragedy what happened to that poor girl. Why do you ask?"

Kyle gave him the file of newspaper clippings. "Last night I found this in Dad's closet."

Ray opened the folder and skimmed the top article. "Man, I haven't thought about this in ages."

"Why would Dad collect these articles?"

"I wasn't aware that he had. Your father and I were close, but he kept a lot of things to himself."

"What do you remember about his relationship with Nina?"

Ray stopped chewing and wiped his mouth with a napkin. "I remember she used to spend a lot of time at your house, babysitting you kids. Your father treated her like his own daughter. He was crushed when she was murdered. As a tribe, we were all outraged. We followed the news, hoping her killer would be found. Months passed, then a year. The rest of us gave up, but not your father. He grew obsessed with trying to find answers that would solve the Whitefeather case. He visited the lake cove where her body was found. He badgered the police, read every report he could get his hands on. It took him a few years to get over Nina's death, but he finally let it go."

Kyle nodded, feeling guilty for thinking that his father could have been her killer. He folded the topography map. "Come on. Let's get a move on before the day gets too hot."

* * *

As the sun rose over the mountains, Kyle and Ray hiked in silence through the woods along twin trails that had been made by tires. When he was a boy, the Cree men and their sons used to pile into Jeeps and trucks and drive down this dirt road to go deer hunting. While Elkheart drove Big Red, Kyle and his brother and a couple cousins would sit crammed together in the back, holding their deer rifles. No one spoke the whole ride. Kyle remembered the grind of the Ford Bronco's engine and the sound of tires rolling over rocks. His father's eyes would always peer into the rearview mirror and give Kyle a look that he interpreted as pride. Being back here in the woods where they had connected through hunting and camping made Kyle want to find his father all the more.

He and Ray checked out three campsites, but found each of them empty. The fourth campsite they hiked to marked the final X on the map. Kyle had been almost certain his father's team would be camping at this one, but there were no tents. No archaeologists sitting around a campfire. No Elkheart.

"Damn it." Kyle took off his cap and rubbed a hand through his hair.

Using his staff, Ray limped to an area where log benches circled a fire pit. He knelt over a circle of rocks and ran his fingers through weeds growing inside the pit. "I'd say it's been several months since anyone camped here. Sure this was the spot?"

"This was his favorite." Staring across a creek, Kyle felt his faith waning.

Ray stood. "I don't know what to say, except maybe we should head back west toward my neck of the woods."

But Kyle had stopped listening. Something at the far side of the site had caught his eye. A swatch of beige fabric was caught on a thorny bush. Kyle removed it, examining the fabric. It was made of smooth nylon. "This came from Dad's tent. I recognize the camouflage pattern." Kyle shook his head. "I told him it was dog-shit brown. He said he didn't care. He'd gotten it on sale. You know how Elkheart likes to buy things cheap." Kyle rubbed the swatch between his fingers, trying to pick up an imprint, but no visions came. His intuition felt strong, though. "Dad was here." He scanned the forest that ran alongside the road. "Maybe he's still in these woods, at a site that's not on the map."

Ray examined the scrap of cloth. "It's pretty faded. This could have been left from a year ago."

Kyle pulled out a compass, stared at the direction of the rising sun, then pointed to where an even lesser traveled road seemed to continue northeast. The tire tracks were almost overgrown with grass, but Kyle had a strong gut feeling. "Let's follow this road awhile."

"I doubt he would've gone that way," Ray said. "The reservation ends not far past this point. Let's head west."

"We can turn around once we hit the border." Kyle started down the grassy road.

Sighing, Ray hobbled after him. "Walk slower then."

They hiked through a field of giant ferns. Kyle's heart beat wildly at the thought of finding his father. Around a second bend the tire tracks ended at a wall of dense brush.

"I told you, dead end," Ray said. "Time to turn back."

"I think he's here." Kyle pushed back prickly branches and squeezed through the thicket. For several yards, he could see nothing in the maze of crisscrossing limbs but blue sky above. His boots splashed through shallow water, stirring up a sulfur stench. Then the briars opened to a dark, murky swamp. "This must be Kakaskitewak Swamp," he said as Ray caught up.

All around, thick vegetation pressed against the stagnant water's edge.

Ray whispered, "We shouldn't be here."

But Kyle wasn't listening. He hurried out of the sucking mud and stepped onto the wooden boards of a dock. Tied at the end of it was a canoe. Muddy water, leaves, and mosquito larvae collected in the bottom of the canoe. A steady wind bumped it against the pier.

Ray hobbled onto the dock behind him. "Kyle, we need to get away from this place."

"Why?"

"This swamp borders the forbidden section of the reservation. See?" Ray pointed. Fifty yards across the tar-colored water, a wall of black pines pressed up to the edge. Several pines had bone-white animal skulls nailed to the bark. Some with antlers, some with tusks. There were at least three per tree. Like totem poles.

Kyle looked at Ray. "What's with the skulls?"

"Our ancestors hung them there long before you or I were born. The totems serve as a warning to stay away from these woods."

* * *

When Eric finally drifted out of his slumber and into the blinding-bright den, the ceiling was spinning like a top, and a circus of people were chattering around him. Something wet and sticky brushed against his cheek. Eric got a whiff of stale canine breath. His face twisted away in disgust. "Get this mutt off me." Instead the Rottweiler licked his face. "Dog, go the hell away."

"He's just showing you a little affection." Jessica sat beside Eric, running her fingers through his hair. "Wake up, sleepy head. You're the last one still in bed."

He rubbed his face. "I have a screaming headache."

"Well, that's what you get for drinking too much," she said with her motherly gaze. "You need to learn when to stop."

"Excellent, this hangover comes with a lecture." As his eyes fully focused, Eric realized where he lay. "Why am I on the couch?"

"This is where you passed out. So you got to sleep with Kyle."

"What!" Eric felt his anger rising, but then gritted his teeth. *No, keep your cool.* He was going to start this day on Jessica's good side. The first step was not to say anything bad about his brother. Eric forced a grin and stroked her arm. "You mean you had to sleep alone?"

"That's right. Drink that much again, and you'll sleep down here tonight, as well."

Man was she being cold. Eric wasn't worried. His charm always warmed her up. She started to stand, but he held her arm. "Don't go yet. How about a good-morning kiss?"

"I'd rather kiss Chaser. Brush your teeth, and we'll see."

"We'll see? How about a kiss on the forehead?"

Jessica sighed, glanced at the others in the kitchen, then leaned over the bed and kissed his forehead. Eric bear hugged her, pulling her small body on top of his and gripping her ass. He kissed her neck and was surprised when she pulled away, hitting his shoulder. "Eric, don't. Not in front of your family." Jessica climbed off of him. "Now get up. You're wasting the day."

"Fine, I'm up."

"Want some breakfast? Kyle made a batch of scrambled eggs and sausage."

"No thanks." Eric sagged back against his pillow, too sick to his stomach to have an appetite. He should never have mixed beer and vodka. He watched Jessica prepare herself a plate and sit at the table with Shawna and Zack. They said something to her and Jessica laughed.

Eric sensed something different about his girlfriend today. She seemed friendly to everyone but him. He didn't like it.

Shawna gave him a look that was full of attitude. "Bro, you look like the walking dead."

"Yeah, Yeah." While the others ate breakfast, Eric staggered into the downstairs bathroom and washed his face with cold water. He stared into the mirror at his dripping reflection. His hair stood up in corkscrews. His eyes were puffy and bloodshot. No wonder his girlfriend hadn't wanted to kiss him.

Eric added Visine drops to clear his red eyes. He then took a shower, then shaved his face and styled his hair with gel. After toweling off, he sprayed on cologne, brushed his teeth and rinsed his mouth with mint-flavored mouthwash.

When Eric looked back in the mirror, he smiled. A face no woman could resist winked back at him. Let the games begin.

* * *

At Kakaskitewak Swamp, Kyle felt a knot in his stomach as he stared across the black water at the pines covered with animal skulls. These trees gave off the same humming vibration as the forest yesterday where he'd rescued Chaser. Kyle wondered if he were to touch those totem poles what secrets they would tell. He reached down and grabbed the canoe's rope. "I'm going to paddle over."

Ray grabbed his arm. "It's forbidden."

"Why?"

"It's sacred Cree law."

Kyle remembered the warnings the elders used to say to the kids, *If you go past Kakaskitewak Swamp, the woods will snatch you.* "Why has our tribe always been afraid of this place?"

Ray stared across the swamp. "Macâya Forest is like a living thing that feeds on whoever enters it. It happened to Hagen Thorpe's lumberjacks over a century ago. And it's happened to a few members of our tribe since. Grandfather lost his brother to those woods. He says it was the Macâya that got him."

"Some kind of devil creature?"

"I don't know what it is." Ray stared at the black pines. "But it's not an animal."

At the opposite bank, Kyle thought he saw something move behind the trees, a flash of gray, but when he blinked it was gone. He looked back at his cousin. "Wait a minute, you told me that you didn't believe in the Macâya legend."

"I didn't, until a year ago. I decided to explore the woods and see why everybody around here fears Macâya Forest so much."

"What did you find?"

"A dark rainforest, thick as a jungle. The vegetation conceals numerous sinkholes. I nearly fell into one that I couldn't see the bottom of. As I wandered deeper, I started to think of the legend. Pictured a dozen stout men with axes slung over their shoulders, hiking through a green mist into these woods. And then something going horribly wrong, as if the forest itself had turned against them, tearing the men to pieces."

Ray looked at Kyle with eyes full of fear. "Well, those images got to me, so I headed back. But then something happened in there that I can't explain. A creature roared from the tunnels beneath the forest. Somewhat like an angered grizzly, but worse. And then the ground attacked my leg, and I was being dragged toward a dark pit. I gripped some roots and hung on for dear life. But the beast grabbing me was damned strong, and I felt the tendons in my leg tearing as the thing and I played tug-of-war. I kicked myself loose, then raced like hell, dragging my limp leg behind me. I've never gone back."

"So why not just tell me the whole story from the beginning?" Kyle asked.

"Because I was afraid you kids might get curious and go exploring in there."

"So you believe the Macâya really does exist."

Ray rubbed his bum leg. "Some underground creature clawed my leg and crippled me. I paid the price for breaking sacred law. And that's reason enough to stay away from this area. I suggest you do the same."

* * *

Eric exited the downstairs bathroom, wrapped in his towel, allowing Jessica a glimpse of his tanned pecks.

He climbed up to the loft to get dressed. As he was sifting through his suitcase, he noticed Jessica's journal on the air mattress beside her pillow. He glanced over the rail. She was still seated at the breakfast table. He grabbed the journal and opened it. He had read sections of her diary before. Most of it was musings about what she did that day or venting about the stress of med school. Eric flipped to the back page. Each day was a different colored ink, which reflected her mood. Today's page was purple.

Saturday morning. I'm sitting on the cabin's balcony with a fresh cup of coffee. Birds are singing in the trees. The sunrise over the Canadian mountains is so beautiful. Eric skimmed through all the boring description until he got to a paragraph where he saw his name. *I don't know what's going on with me and Eric. Our one-year anniversary is tomorrow and we aren't getting along. He seems different now. Or maybe I'm different. Are my feelings changing? Can I really be sure he's the one for me? If so, then why am I so drawn to Kyle?*

Angry, Eric tossed the journal across the room.

He heard footsteps coming up the winding staircase and Jessica stepped onto the loft. "There you are."

Turning his back to her, Eric pretended to look busy, digging through his suitcase. He felt knots of jealousy and sadness in his chest. He dropped his towel to see if she would respond to his nakedness. He expected her to hug him from behind, but she didn't. Instead, she stood at her dresser with her back to him, searching through that damn medicine kit.

"What patient are you treating now?"

Jessica held up a bottle of Advil. "You, silly. You said you had a headache." She gave him the bottle, but didn't hold eye contact or even so much as glance at his body. She started to turn. He grabbed her wrist. "Jess, wait."

"Yes?" She looked more beautiful than ever.

Eric's anger dissolved into a sudden fear of losing her. As he stared into her eyes, he was overcome by a strange tingling sensation in his chest that he had never felt before. "I…uh…uh…"

Her eyebrows raised and she looked impatient to get somewhere. "Yes?"

"Uh…thanks."

She pinched his chin then put the aspirin bottle back in her bag.

Eric released a breath. He'd almost said the words "I love you". Yet they hung at the back of his throat. He wanted to say them. But expressing his feelings didn't come as easily for him as it did for her. He dressed and tried to think of a way to get Jessica's attention away from Kyle.

Eric stepped behind her at the window and caressed her shoulder. She was busy going through their stuff and didn't stop when he touched her. He massaged her tense muscles. "Hey, slow down, babe. What's the hurry?"

"I'm trying to get organized. Everything up here's a mess."

Eric looked at his stuff scattered across the loft. True, it was a little messy, but in a comfortable way. "Don't worry about that. I'll clean it up in a minute. Babe, relax. How about we—"

Jessica moved away from him and crossed the room to where her journal was turned upside down. "Why is my diary all the way over here?" Her face was taut, her brows pinched.

"I don't know."

"You've been reading my diary, haven't you?"

"What? No, no."

"Don't lie to me, Eric."

"Okay, I may have glanced—"

"These are my private thoughts. You have no right—"

"Well, I can't believe you're doubting our relationship after all I've done for you!"

"Maybe I wouldn't be doubting if I thought I could trust you. I saw you flirting with that girl at the marina yesterday."

"That? That was innocent. You're thinking about cheating with my brother. That's fucked up. I can't believe you would even consider such a thing."

Her eyes sparked with fire. "I was only processing my feelings. You're blowing this all out of proportion. Don't *ever* read my diary again!" She stormed down the stairs, leaving him standing alone in the loft.

* * *

Kyle and Ray returned to the village later that afternoon. Kyle felt about as hollow as the rundown shacks that lined the dirt road. He was nowhere closer to finding his father than before. He couldn't get Macâya Forest out of his mind. Would Elkheart have gone in there? He would have been breaking the tribe's sacred law. According to Ray, the woods beyond Kakaskitewak Swamp harbored a mythical creature, like the Jersey Devil in the backwoods of New Jersey. As much as Kyle was a fan of horror films and novels, he didn't believe that legendary monsters really existed. He saw them as reflections of man's dark psyche. Ray had probably been attacked by a bear or wild boar and out of sheer superstition believed it was the Macâya.

When Kyle entered the main cabin, he heard Jimmy Buffet singing

"Margaritaville". Zack, Eric and Grandfather were seated around the dining table, playing dominoes. The girls were in the kitchen, making sandwiches. Shawna looked up. "Hey, guys, you hungry?"

Ray sat on a barstool at the counter. "Famished."

Kyle stood in the den, watching everyone having fun. No one seemed to care that Elkheart was missing but him.

Ray munched on a potato chip. "Kyle, your father will return when he wants to and not a moment sooner. If you spend your whole week worrying about him, you're going to spoil your vacation."

Shawna said, "Yeah, bro, kick back and have a beer." She popped open a can of Moosehead and passed it to him.

Kyle drank the cold brew.

"You guys see anything interesting out there?" Jessica asked.

Ray shot Kyle a conspiratorial glance. "Nothing but trees."

Kyle debated on whether to let the others in on what he and Ray had discovered. Eric didn't seem to have any interest in finding their father, and Shawna, who had never known John Elkheart, only cared about partying. Kyle reminded himself that they had come here to reunite with their cousin and grandfather and enjoy being on the land. "So, Ray, Eric said that you and Grandfather have something you wanted to pass down to us."

"That's right," Eric said. "Did we inherit something?"

Ray smiled. "You'll find out soon enough."

"When? When?" Shawna asked, bouncing up and down.

"Tonight." Ray laughed. "You kids will have to be patient."

Chapter Eleven

Sitting on the balcony overlooking the backyard, Kyle found a quiet place to write. Up here, he had a stunning view of the conifers and snow-capped mountains.

He fired up his laptop and opened the last chapter that he had written back in Seattle. In the fifth installment of the Winterbone series, *Ghost Vengeance*, Detective Alex Winterbone was trying to help a ghost named Elena solve her own murder. In the mortal world, he was coming dangerously close to a backwoods serial killer. Winterbone was falling deeply in love with Elena. A sensual ghost, she could turn her body solid for an hour at a time. In that short window her body heated up and she could feel pleasure from his touch. And Alex could feel her flesh and the warmth of her lips. Their union, which broke the laws between spirits and mortals, angered a coven of soul snatchers called the Hollowers. These beings of the underworld scoured the earth, collecting souls who lingered too long.

It wasn't long before Kyle's solitude was disrupted. In the backyard below, Jessica and Shawna came off the porch steps, talking and laughing. Kyle watched as they draped beach towels over two lawn chairs and then stripped down to their bikinis. The sight of Jessica in a bathing suit made Kyle feel distracted and, for the second time today, aroused. Two years was a long time to be a monk.

Jessica looked up at him and waved. He waved back then looked away before she could see the hunger in his eyes.

I've got to get my mind off of her.

He started reading his manuscript. When Winterbone met up with his ghostly lover in a realm that lay between the living and the dead, their souls were at risk of being taken by the Hollowers. But Alex and Elena could not control their passions for one another.

Alex awoke to the caress of a warm hand touching his chest. Elena was above him, her face radiant in the twilight hour. Their eyes met and held.

He pulled her closer. "You shouldn't be here." Her scent of rose petals and honeysuckle enveloped him, calling up other times when they had lain together.

"But I've missed you," she said between kisses.

Reading the love scene stirred Kyle's own needs for touch and warmth. He stole glances at Jessica stretched out on the lawn chair below him, one slender leg bent at the knee. She was reading a paperback novel and absentmindedly curling a strand of hair around her finger, stopping only to turn the page. Again their eyes met, and Kyle focused back on his computer screen.

"This is too risky." Alex leaned away, attempting to put some distance *between them.*

Elena was beside him again. She sighed and ran her fingers through his hair. Her breath was warm on his skin. That her hunger matched his never failed to surprise him. "Do you not miss me?" she whispered.

"What do you think?" With that, he entered her and in their union *life became death and death became life. "I've been lost without you." His breathing was ragged. "But they'll track us."*

Elena stared into his eyes, even as she moved against the rhythm of his body. "We have one hour. Then I'll be gone."

This time Shawna caught him staring at Jessica. His sister cocked her head and gave him a suspicious look.

Kyle tried again to focus on the manuscript. As he reread the final passage, his eyes caught and held on the last lines. The strange phrase that his wife's ghost had whispered two days ago had appeared in his novel, typed over and over, like a mantra.

Fear wears many skins. Fear wears many skins. Fear wears many skins. Fear wears many skins...

Kyle had no memory of his fingers striking those keys. What the hell? Maybe his mind really was slipping. He tried to decipher its significance. Again any logical meaning evaded him. He deleted the repeated sentences. *There.* Now he could move on. He had to remind himself that as creator of a fictional world, he always had the power to edit.

Feeling like a burden had been lifted, he continued to write where he'd left off. Before he knew it, new paragraphs filled the computer screen. And then he typed another page. His mind had again tapped into the

Infinite Creative. That was how Kyle liked to think of those moments when words flowed easily. As he read over the new passages, he found the phrase again.

In the shapes of man's sins, fear wears many skins.

He started to delete it, but his hand stopped short. There was a reason Elena had spoken those words. A hidden meaning in the phrase somehow. So he left the new sentence untouched. Frustrated, he closed his laptop.

Kyyyle... A girl's voice echoed in a raspy whisper.

He saw a flash of movement in the forest, but it was gone too quickly. He listened, studying the trees beyond the backyard. Another hint of silvery white. A girl moved wraithlike through the trees, appearing then disappearing.

Kyle looked down at Jessica and Shawna. Lost in their conversation, they seemed oblivious to the female specter that meandered through the trees toward them.

I'm the only one who can see her.

A teenage Indian girl stepped into the yard. Her image flickered like a hologram that couldn't quite maintain its signal. He recognized her face and black braids.

Nina Whitefeather.

Her transparent hand beckoned Kyle.

His body tensed. What did she want?

Nina pointed toward the woods, indicating she had something to show him.

What would Winterbone do? He thought about that a moment, then Winterbone, himself, spoke, *"Hell, I'd get off my ass and follow her."*

Kyle walked downstairs, out the back door, and past Jessica and Shawna, who looked at him quizzically.

"Going for a hike?" Jessica asked.

"Yeah, be back later." Taking a deep breath, he stepped into the woods and followed the flickering apparition, doing his best to keep up. Nina's wraith moved effortlessly through the forest. Kyle, on the other hand, had to weave around the trees and dense brush. Branches choked a trail that looked like it hadn't been used in ages.

As he ventured after Nina, he felt both excited and chilled to be interacting with the spirit world. Despite the fact that he had witnessed ghosts before, he had never had this close of an encounter. There were moments that the girl's body turned almost solid. Other times he had to strain to make out her form among the pine needles. He lost her a few times. But she always stopped and waited for him to catch up, her eyes glowing like silver coins.

Nina, now forever sixteen, was still as pretty as when Kyle was a boy. Seeing her again brought back a rush of memories—her reading books to him and his brother on the back porch…playing hide and seek in the village…then their parents telling them that Nina had disappeared…the whole family crying the day they learned she'd been found dead in the lake.

Now, she turned almost fully visible. Was that a sign of trust?

Kyle reached out to touch her, but Nina backed away and continued walking.

"Where are you taking me?"

She didn't answer. Just kept moving along the trail.

As he followed, Kyle began to feel vibrations in his feet and tingles along his spine. He passed through a few cold spots, yet there was no breeze on this hot August day.

The path ended at a campsite that was different from the others. This one had a large fire pit in the ground and an old shed with double doors that were closed. The gray wooden building was long and narrow, as if designed to store a boat, yet this patch of woods was nowhere near the water or even a road.

"What is this place?"

She stopped where the trees bordered the campsite but gestured for Kyle to keep going. The wraith watched him closely but didn't follow. Instead, she remained hidden behind a tree.

Kyle walked around the campfire pit. It was full of ash and a few charred logs. The vibrations along the ground grew stronger as he eased toward the shed. He touched one of the doors. Behind him, Nina released a high-pitched scream.

He walked toward her. "What is it?"

She tried to speak, but her voice sounded like water coughing through a clogged faucet. It was then Kyle saw the bruises across her throat. Her dress suddenly tore in several places. Bloody scratches appeared on her arms. Nina cried out and fell to the ground, kicking and screaming, as something unseen dragged her into the shed.

* * *

Kendra Meacham wandered through the thick and unforgiving woods in a daze. Endless trees with spiky pine needles filled her vision. She leaned against a crutch made from a dead branch. Her ankle was purple and swollen. Probably broken. She kept it raised above the ground, half-hopping as she walked. Her clothes hung on her in bloody tatters. Her exposed skin was covered in scratches. With every step fiery pain erupted between her thighs. *What happened to me?*

Memories flashed through Kendra's mind in horrid fragments… riding in a semi with a truck driver…the asshole trying to rape her, then abandoning her on the side of the road…some kind of animal dragging her into the woods, carrying her off to its den.

She remembered nothing from last night, having blacked out. This morning she had woken in cold darkness, alone and shivering. She blindly found her way back to sunlight. Back to the woods. She had been walking aimlessly for hours. She was hungry, dehydrated, and terrified she was going to die out here in the sticks.

All Kendra had wanted was to make a clean break from Calgary, from her ex-boyfriend, Jake, and her slimy manager at the dance club. She had thought hitching a ride to Hagen's Cove was the answer. There she could start a new life. Kendra always made the worst choices. *One day you'll pay hell for it, her mother used to say.* And now Kendra saw that she was right.

She didn't want to think about what that rotten-smelling creature was that took her deep into the forest and somewhere underground. She just wanted to get out of these godforsaken woods before it discovered she had escaped its den.

* * *

Standing before the strange shed, Kyle froze, his mind in shock of what he'd just witnessed. Nina's screams now echoed from inside that wooden tomb.

His heart felt like a bird flapping inside his rib cage. He wanted to run, flee up the trail and never look back. But something kept his feet rooted to the spot.

She brought you here for a reason! Winterbone yelled inside his head. *Save her!*

Kyle yanked open the double doors and the screaming stopped.

The only sound now came from a swarm of buzzing flies.

"Nina?"

The shed was a single room with a dirt floor covered in dead leaves. There were no windows. Only bare walls with a few holes where the sunlight lanced the gloom. Nina was nowhere in sight.

Kyle stepped inside. He moved toward the shadows in back. The flies swirled in front of his face. They dotted the walls like spores of black mold and landed on a stained mattress in the far corner. Kyle crept closer. The vibrations along the ground now felt as if a freight train were passing on some nearby railroad, yet there was no sound but the maddening buzz of the flies. The storage building reeked of damp soil and leaves and a stench like a rotten carcass. He noticed chains on the floor on either side of the mattress. The links were bolted to the back wall, which was mostly hidden in shadow. On the opposite ends were shackles.

He held a hand across his mouth and nose. *What the hell happened here?*

Use your gift, Winterbone whispered in his head. *These walls can speak.*

Taking a deep breath, Kyle pressed his palm against a wall.

The top of the mattress started *moving*. He heard crying coming from that spot. Nina appeared, barely visible. "Please. Don't…" Her cries turned to screams.

Another figure took form, a red wraith kneeling over her, its arm coming down in a hacking motion. Blood spread across the mattress.

"Nina!" Kyle swung his fist, but it passed right through her killer.

The girl's screams ended with a gurgling cough.

The red ghost rose from the mattress, taller than Kyle. He backed away. It walked right through him with a cold shock that iced his bones. The killer stepped outside, leaving Nina's body splayed out on the mattress. Her blood was everywhere. Her eyes stared wide open, lifeless.

Kyle's knees buckled. He had to use the wall for support. "Dear God…"

She shifted her head and looked up at him, reaching with a blood-soaked arm, and screamed.

He ran out of the shed.

He didn't stop running until he reached the Cree village. His lungs hurt. He couldn't get Nina's violent death out of his mind. The dark shed. The stained mattress. Her screams. The red ghost of her killer.

Kyle's gut twisted with guilt. He wished he'd been able to save her. His rational mind knew that the vision was an imprint of a murder that happened twenty years ago. Her killer could have been someone from the reservation, but who? Back then there were over a hundred tribe members living in the village. No, the Cree people that Kyle had lived with the first ten years of his life had treated one another like one big family.

Nina's killer had to have been someone outside the tribe. A poacher? The reservation bordered the land that was owned by the Thorpe Timber mill. Kyle remembered years ago the elders complaining that the loggers had been seen deer hunting on the reservation. It had caused a feud between the tribe and the lumberjacks. Some of Kyle's older cousins had gotten into a gang fight with the white kids at the high school. One of the loggers' sons had ended up in the hospital not long after Nina Whitefeather disappeared.

Kyle considered telling the others what he had seen, but decided against it. Who would believe him?

He entered the cabin out of breath. The others were still hanging out, oblivious to the atrocity he'd witnessed. Kyle paced the den, his mind buzzing like the end of a live wire. He had to do something.

The Hansons' Rottweiler lay curled up on a blanket. Jessica had applied fresh bandages across his back. Kyle pulled out his cell phone and dialed Carl Hanson's number, but the call didn't go through. He tried again. Same result. *There's no signal.*

"Anybody's phone work out here?" he asked.

"It's hopeless," Eric said. "No texting, no internet. The whole village is a dead zone."

Kyle tried an old phone mounted on the wall, but the landline was also dead.

Ray chuckled. "That phone hasn't worked in ages."

"Then I'm driving into town," Kyle said. "We have to return Chaser before Carl and his daughter leave the area."

Eric stood from the table. "I'll go with you. I've probably got a hundred messages by now." He looked at his girlfriend, who was fawning over the dog. "Jess, how about you and I hit the tavern for some pool?"

"Shawna and I already made plans. She's going to do a Tarot reading for me. You guys go on without us."

Eric's eyes flashed with anger, but his tone was even. "You girls have fun."

Kyle grabbed the keys to the Jeep and looked down at the Rottweiler. "Chaser, let's get you back to your family."

* * *

The endless maze of trees finally opened up to a paved road.

Kendra cried tears of relief. She'd made it. Her body was so exhausted and weak she felt the urge to collapse.

Buzzards circled overhead.

No, she had hiked too far to become road kill. Moving as fast as her battered body could go, she limped down the road. She felt déjà vu as she passed a green sign: *Hagen's Cove 10 Kilometers.*

She needed a ride out of this forest and prayed God would send her one. It wasn't long before she heard an engine and tires rolling over asphalt. She turned and spotted a car coming around a curve.

Kendra cried out and stepped into the middle of the road, waving her arms.

The vehicle stopped in front of her. A man climbed out and rushed to her aid. "Dear Lord, what's happened?"

Kendra fell against him. She could barely speak through all the tears. "P-please…take me to a hospital."

"Sure, sure." He walked her around to the passenger side. The elongated car had an odd shape to it and a dark crimson paint job. Then she realized it was a hearse. A limousine for the dead. The man eased her into the front seat. "We'll get you to town. Don't you worry, sugar," he said with a Danish accent. Then he rounded the side and disappeared for a moment. She heard the hearse's rear door open and him rustling back there.

Kendra suddenly felt nervous. Why weren't they driving the hell out of here? Her mind had a vision of the predator charging from the woods and snatching him. She turned around in her seat to see what he was doing, but maroon velvet curtains blocked her view. "Can we please leave?"

"Be just a minute," the man answered.

She faced forward, staring at the narrow wooded road that led toward town. Hanging from the rearview mirror were a pair of fuzzy pink dice and a tree-shaped air freshener that smelled like moth balls. Kendra released a laugh and shook her head at the absurdity. This was all just one endless fucking nightmare.

The driver's side door opened and the man climbed behind the wheel. "Thought you might be thirsty." He offered her a cold bottle of water.

She gulped it down.

He sat there watching her. "Wow, you were thirsty. I've got more bottles in the fridge back there. Beer too, if you'd like a cold one."

"No, let's just get out of here."

He drove down the road and Kendra breathed a sigh of relief as the pines moved quickly past her side window.

"What you doing all the way out here?" the man asked.

"Long story."

"Not every day you find a pretty girl hitching on the side of the road."

She leaned against the passenger door. "How far to the hospital?"

"We don't have one out here. But Doc Thorpe can see to you." He constantly glanced at her with a strange grin. "I'm Hugo, by the way."

His face started to go blurry.

Kendra pressed a hand to her forehead. "Can you step on it? I feel like I'm going to faint."

"That's 'cause I spiked your water with Ketamine," he said matter-of-factly. "Won't be long now before you're off to dreamland." Hugo's face warped as his smile widened. His hand stroked her thigh. "Do you like to party?"

Part Four

Warnings

Chapter Twelve

In Hagen's Cove, Kyle pulled the Jeep Cherokee into the gravel parking lot of the Beowulf Tavern. "This is the best spot to catch a signal," he told Eric. They both whipped out their cell phones, and Kyle frowned at how technology had changed their lives. Even out here in the wilderness they couldn't go a day without connecting electronically with the outside world.

Eric scrolled through his Blackberry. "Shit, I've got a dozen texts from Blake."

He worked for their stepfather's Seattle law firm. After Blake Nelson married their mother, he tried his damndest to mold Kyle and Eric after himself. When Kyle was twelve and Eric ten, Blake took them on a tour through the firm's law library. High up on the dark-paneled walls hung portraits of all the attorneys who had reached partner. There were two empty slots next to a long line of Nelson men. *See those two slots up there?* Their stepfather had pointed. *Those are for you two. Just imagine it, boys. Your portraits up there next to mine.*

Both boys worked for the firm during high school, first as couriers, then clerks. Kyle had hated working for his overbearing stepfather and quit once he got his pilot's license. Eric, always wanting to please Blake, went to law school and eventually joined the firm as an associate.

"I don't know how you stand working for him," Kyle said.

Eric shrugged. "It's not so bad."

"But you have no life."

"I make good money, travel a lot, and when I make partner, I'll be set."

"Partner?" Kyle chuckled. "He's been dangling that carrot in front of you for years. I think he enjoys controlling you."

Eric looked offended. "At least I didn't fucking quit on him."

"I had no interest in becoming one of Blake's minions."

"No, you'd rather stay home, wallow in self-pity and pretend to write."

Kyle glared. "That was uncalled for."

"Well, you've got no business judging me."

"I just think you'd be happier doing something else."

"Like what?"

"Don't you have any interests beyond law?"

Eric grinned. "Women."

"I'm serious. If Blake hadn't pressured you into working for his firm, what would you be doing?"

"Living in Napa. Running a winery."

"Seriously?"

He nodded. "I've been thinking it'd be fun to own one after I retire."

"Why wait? You've got some money."

"You're kidding, right? Do you have any idea the amount of capital required to open a winery?"

"Then go work for an existing one. Learn the business."

Eric shook his head. "I'm too close to making partner."

"Is that the real reason? Or are you just afraid you'll disappoint Blake?"

"What, now you're my shrink?"

"Just your brother."

"Don't you have a call to make?"

Chaser, who was riding in back, stuck his head between the two front seats and licked Kyle's cheek.

"Don't worry, boy. I haven't forgotten you." He dialed Carl Hanson's cell but the call went straight to voicemail. He left a brief message about having found Chaser. "Sorry, boy. It looks like you're stuck with us awhile longer."

The Rottweiler paced in the backseat, whimpering.

"How about we hang here at the tavern?" Eric said. "First round's on me."

"First, let's go to the police station. See if Carl filed a report about his missing daughter. The police might be able to tell us where Dad and Amy went."

"I thought you were going to drop the goose chase."

"I just want to ask around a little. Maybe one of the locals knows something."

Eric opened his door. "When you're done playing detective, join me at the bar."

* * *

The Jeep Cherokee drove up the road toward the center of town. Eric remained in the gravel parking lot with his Blackberry out. In addition to text messages, his stepfather had left several voice messages, asking how Eric was coming along on the corporate merger he was going to represent in three weeks. Eric's paralegals—two brunettes and a blonde— were preparing the case in his absence. The girls also had questions that needed his immediate response. He and the blonde named Kristin usually exchanged sexual innuendos, but today he wasn't in the mood, keeping his texts short and all business.

Feeling bored, he looked around the sleepy town of Hagen's Cove. Not a soul in sight. *Wonder what little Nadine is up to?* Downhill at the marina, the boat rental shack was closed. Imagining Nadine in her bikini, he started to dial her number, but then an image of Jessica flashed in his mind and he remembered his dating code: *Never have sex with two women in the same zip code. Unless it's a threesome, of course.*

Unfortunately, Jessica wasn't into that. Remembering how cold his girlfriend had acted all day, he thought he needed a new code: *Never bring a date on a trip, especially around Kyle.* His brother was the tragic sensitive type. For some reason, which Eric would never understand, girls ate that shit up. After reading Jessica's diary that morning, Eric knew he had to play it cool this week and focus his attention on her. He sighed. *Sorry, Nadine, we could've had fun.* He filed her number into a hidden folder titled *Future Prospects.* Between women issues and his badgering stepfather, Eric needed a hard drink. As he started for the tavern, his cell phone vibrated with Blake Nelson's caller ID.

Speak of the devil.

Eric answered. "Yes, sir."

"Finally!" his stepdad said. "You've been hell to reach."

"Sorry, there's hardly any signal out—"

"Climb a mountain if you have to. I need you to stay close to your phone."

Eric rolled his eyes as his stepfather rambled on. The firm was deep in a beauty contest. The prize was a large corporate client intent on what would surely be a hostile and heavily litigated takeover. "I don't have to tell you this case is big money. High publicity too. If we land Marston-Bauer, you and I will be working together for the next six to nine months. In fact I may need you back a few days early to jumpstart the due diligence."

Eric's throat constricted. He started to tell Blake to give the case to one of the other attorneys, but they were all competing to make partner. Blake's choosing Eric for the Marston-Bauer work was a good sign. It meant he was the front-runner for the partner slot.

Six months working eighty-plus hours a week with his workaholic stepfather; the thought was like grim death. There'd be no time to party. No traveling for weekend flings. Eric reminded himself of the perks of making partner: the seven-figure income, the company jet, and the women. God, he'd need two dicks after his name went up on the masthead.

"You're my boy, Eric. I can count on you with Marston-Bauer, yes?"

"Absolutely. Does this mean I'll make partner?"

"That's up to you, son. Are you ready to stop chasing tail, settle down, and get married?"

Blake and his cronies had a rule. Attorneys weren't promoted to partner until they were married. They believed that wives made for more stable partners, less likely to de-camp to pursue other options.

"Jessica's nice," Blake said. "She'd make a fine addition to the family."

Blake had been dropping not-so-subtle hints for a few months now.

"We're celebrating our one-year anniversary tomorrow. I've been thinking about marriage too."

"Well, I wouldn't waste time if I were you. Women like her are good for business."

After Blake hung up, Eric remained in the parking lot, thinking about his future. If he married, the firm would promote him within the year. Eric would get the windowed office, the astronomical salary and all the other perks. All he needed was a wife. He ran through the list of women he'd slept with in the past year. Blake was right. Of all of them, Jessica was the winner—beautiful, smart, sophisticated, great bod and best of all she was low maintenance. Busy with her med school classes, she gave him a lot of space. That was definitely how they'd lasted a whole year together. She'd hinted about marriage more than once recently. And a proposal would put an end to this crap with Kyle. So what was he waiting for?

Eric got a flash of inspiration. He left the tavern and walked down the main street. With the backdrop of cliffs and rustic log buildings, Hagen's Cove reminded him of small ski towns in Colorado, like Durango or Telluride. Several tourist shops lined the road. He entered one called Celeste's Boutique and Jewelry Shop. He weaved between faceless mannequins dressed in women's clothing.

A stunning redhead stood behind the counter. She wore a red dress that showed off her bare shoulders and ample cleavage. Tucking a strand of auburn hair behind one ear, she smiled as Eric approached. "Well, hello," she said with the local accent.

"Hey there." He flashed her his most charming smile. "It seems like everywhere I go in this town, I see a beautiful lady."

She blushed. "Well, it's not every day a handsome man walks into my store."

Man, these small town women were easy. He thought about escalating the banter with some sexual innuendo, but then reined himself in. Today was about Jessica. "I'm looking for an engagement ring for my girlfriend."

The redhead looked disappointed but recovered quickly at the prospect of a sizable commission. "I have some beautiful rings." She led him to a glass case with a dozen rings. "Most are vintage. Sebastian picks them up at estate sales." The shop girl treated Eric to another view of her cleavage. "See anything you like?"

Most of the rings had colored stones.

"Do you have any diamonds?" he asked. "I think Jessica mentioned something about a princess cut."

The shop girl laughed. "In Hagen's Cove?" She shook her head. "This is the best you're going to find here."

He pointed to a heart-shaped ruby in a gold setting. "Let me see that one." Jessica was big into hearts. She had a heart-shaped necklace and earrings and even wore pajamas covered in hearts. Probably couldn't go wrong keeping with the heart theme.

The girl removed the ring from the case and passed it to Eric.

"Would you try it on for me?" he asked.

"Sure." She slid the ruby on her ring finger and held it out for him to see. "Beautiful, isn't it?"

Eric took her hand in his, pretending to look at the ring. "Exquisite. I'll take it."

She gave him a half-smile that faded quickly. "You girlfriend's a lucky woman." She boxed up the ring and ran his credit card. "I carry lingerie too. You know, for the wedding night." She gazed at him with her big green eyes. "I'd be happy to model some for you." She tipped her head toward the back of the store. "We could see what works."

She wants it. It would be so easy to follow her into the dressing room. It was the thought of his brother sniffing around Jessica that made up his mind. "No, thanks. Just the ring."

* * *

Chaser remained in the Jeep, while Kyle climbed the steps of the police station. The two-story building, made of natural rock and log beams, blended in with the tall pines and aspen behind it. Out front stood a sign with the Royal Canadian Mounted Police insignia: a bison head surrounded by gold maple leaves, topped with a red and gold crown. When Kyle was ten, he'd dreamed of growing up to become a Mountie. That dream ended the day his mother moved him to Seattle to live with Blake Nelson.

Inside the foyer the elderly receptionist stood to greet him. "Well, well, look who the wind blew in."

"Hello, Ruby." Kyle hugged the heavy-set woman. Ruby Zano was the inspector's sister and a fixture at the police station's front desk since Kyle was a kid. She squeezed his forearm. "Dear boy, you look like you've lost weight since I last saw you. If I had known you were coming, I'd have saved you some brownies." Ruby made the best chocolate-and-peanut-butter brownies Kyle had ever tasted. "I brought a batch this morning, but they're long gone."

Kyle smiled. "Maybe I can get some before I fly home. Is Sam in?"

"Just got back from lunch." She called the inspector's office and announced Kyle's arrival. "He says to tell you come on up."

Kyle hurried up the stairs to the second floor. The common area was furnished like a large den with leather couches, a rock fireplace and a bison head that hung above the mantle. The far wall was lined with offices. Kyle knocked on Sam Zano's door.

"Come in." Sam stood and shook his hand. "Kyle Elkheart, what brings you to my office?"

"I need to discuss a few matters with you."

Sam stroked his white mustache and gestured for Kyle to have a seat in the chair in front of his desk.

Kyle noticed a framed photograph of Inspector Zano standing on the banks of a stream, fishing rod in hand. Mayor Thorpe was in the picture, too, along with a number of other town elders. "Do you guys still go fly-fishing?"

"Every Saturday." Sam pulled out a pipe. "Mind if I smoke?"

Kyle shook his head. As a kid he had loved the smell of pipe tobacco. It reminded him of all the times the native elders sat in a circle and told stories.

The old inspector lit his pipe, puffing. "Ruby says it's a bad habit, but when you get to my age, you grow fond of your bad habits." He leaned back in his chair. "So what brings you in?"

"Yesterday I met a Calgary detective named Carl Hanson. He's in the area, searching for his missing daughter, Amy."

Sam nodded. "He filed a report with us."

"Well, Carl and I talked and discovered that Amy came here with my father and a crew of archeologists about a month ago. Dad's also missing."

"Now that's nothing unusual, knowing your father."

"There were at least five people on his expedition team and, according to Carl, none of them have reported back. Any idea where they all went?"

Inspector Zano shook his head. "Sorry, no."

"Would it be possible to check the flight logs to see if Dad's crew came in on a plane?"

"They didn't."

"How can you be so sure?"

Zano looked insulted by the question. "It's my job to know who comes in and out of this town. Did you ask Ray? Maybe they're out on the reservation."

Kyle shook his head. "He hasn't seen them either."

Zano leaned back in his chair. "Well then, I wouldn't worry about it. Knowing your father, he'll turn up when the mood strikes him and not a minute sooner."

"I'd like to believe that. But we've tramped all over the rez and haven't found so much as a recent campfire. And another thing, last night Carl Hanson's dog ended up at the reservation." Kyle showed him a photo of the Rottweiler taken with his cell phone. "He goes by Chaser. I've left Carl messages on his cell, but so far no response. Any chance he reported his dog missing?"

"Haven't heard a word about it, but we typically don't handle missing pets." Sam picked up his phone and dialed. "I'll check the pound." He spoke with someone on the line, nodded, puffing his pipe, then hung up. "Sorry, the Hansons haven't called there either. They're probably camping in some spot where cell phones don't work."

Kyle frowned. "Maybe, but I saw them with Chaser. He's a member of the family. If he went missing, they would be asking around."

Sam shrugged. "Tell you what, you make me a poster with that picture and I'll put it on the bulletin board downstairs. How's that?"

"All right. And what should we do with their dog?"

"You've got two choices. Keep him until Carl calls you back or drop him off at the pound. If the owners fail to retrieve the dog though…"

"I'll take him with me. I'm sure Carl will call back soon."

Sam picked up some files. "Son, that's about all I can tell you. If you don't mind, I need to get back to my reports."

"Actually, sir, there's one other thing. You remember a case about fifteen years ago involving the murder of Nina Whitefeather?"

The mention of her name seemed to deflate the inspector. Zano nodded. "Of course. I spent years trying to solve that one. Why?"

"Just curious. My dad had saved a few newspaper clippings about the case." *Oh, and last night I was visited by her ghost.* "Did you ever find her killer?"

Sam sagged in his chair as his gaze turned inward. "No. Not long after you kids moved away, your tribe disbanded. Once the tribe was gone, the investigation stalled. Off the record?"

"Sure."

"I always thought the killer was a fellow tribe member, who left with the rest. I couldn't prove it though, so the case went cold." He shook his head. "It still haunts me—finding her body in the lake."

* * *

Eric sat on a stool at the tavern's bar. The idea that he would be taking himself off the market was starting to sink in. He needed a drink.

A stout bartender with slicked-back hair and a handlebar mustache tossed a napkin onto the bar. "What'll it be?"

"Crown and Coke," Eric said. "Heavy on the Crown."

"All I got is beer. Moosehead, Kokanee, or the local mead."

"Okay, you pick it then."

The bartender popped open a bottle of Kokanee and slid it into Eric's hand. He took a sip and looked around at the tavern. All the booths and pool tables were empty and the jukebox was dead.

"Where is everybody?"

"Out on the lake or working at the mill." The bartender wiped mugs with a rag. "Joint doesn't get hoppin' 'til happy hour."

Eric sipped his beer, unable to get Jessica off his mind. What was with her today? She had never acted distant before. And the things she'd written in her journal, what the hell was that about? Eric shook his head. *Women. They're so confusing sometimes. Especially mine.* Until this weekend, Jessica had been easy to seduce. Deep down she was needy, and Eric knew how to push her buttons. With the thrill of the chase gone, the last few months he'd found himself getting bored in bed with her. But this morning in the loft, her feisty attitude had really been a turn-on. He had wanted to throw her down right there. And what did she do? Reject his advances. Just when she was becoming the fiery creature he had wanted her to be, Jessica was pushing him away. Eric remembered her blue eyes, ablaze with anger. The image both turned him on and made him feel uneasy. Would she say yes if he proposed? For the first time in their relationship, he feared losing her. What Jessica needed was a firm commitment and reassurance that he loved her.

As he drank the cold beer, he began to work out a plan to win her back. His thoughts were interrupted when the jukebox turned on with slow country music. Patsy Cline crooned "Sweet Dreams of You". Glancing up from his beer, Eric grinned as the redhead from the shop stepped up to the bar and smiled his way.

* * *

Kyle let Chaser ride in the passenger seat with his head out the window, as they took a scenic route through Hagen's Cove. Not much had changed since he rode his bike along these streets as a kid. Olaf's Bakery still advertised *wienerbrød* pastries and *smørrebrød* sandwiches in the window. And the wooden lumberjack statue remained a timeless fixture in front of Gamel's Drugstore, where Kyle used to buy comic books and chocolate malts with his brother and cousins.

"It's like we've traveled back in time, huh, Chaser?"

The Rottweiler panted as he enjoyed the wind against his face.

Kyle smiled. "Coming back here sure stirs up a lot of memories."

They passed the ancient white church which stood prominently at the center of town. That was where Kyle and Eric got caught spying through the windows. Kyle, sitting on Eric's shoulders, had witnessed naked people wearing strange masks and dancing around a wicker statue. Some angry men grabbed Kyle and Eric and drove them back to the reservation, where they were punished. That was when Kyle had learned that his tribe and the people of Hagen's Cove had different spiritual beliefs. And the church was off limits. The memories of Kyle's youth leaped from his childhood to his troubled adult years, when he returned here a few times as a young man.

His last visit a year ago, he'd dined with his father and Wynona at her home, meeting his dad's new girlfriend for the first time. She had seemed normal then, an attractive woman in her fifties who was friendly and clearly in love with his father. She had gone out of her way to make a good impression on Kyle. He had been surprised to learn that Wynona and her son were the town's morticians. They gave Kyle and his father a tour of the mortuary and cremation room. Her son, Hugo, had fired up the oven with a sadistic look in his eyes, like a kid who loved to play with fire. Or in Hugo's case, burn boxes of dead people. Instinctively, Kyle had disliked the guy, but he'd tried to get along that evening for his father's sake.

Wynona had seemed too feminine and demure to be an undertaker. He couldn't imagine her embalming corpses and hosting funerals. But Kyle had liked Wynona. She was an avid reader, a talented artist and an amazing cook. Her *hakkebøf, brændende kærlighed* and *rødkål* (a dish of ground beef steak with caramelized onions, mashed potatoes and red cabbage) was one of the best meals Kyle had ever eaten. The only faults he'd noticed were that she drank too much brandy and that she had a strange relationship with her grown son. Several times during dinner Kyle had caught a look on Wynona's face that made him think she feared Hugo.

Now, Kyle was eager to talk with Wynona. She had approached Jessica yesterday and pleaded with her to convince Kyle and the others to leave the reservation. And to keep far away from the Devil's Woods, the townspeople's name for Macâya Forest. Why? Kyle hoped she knew something about his father.

The sins of the father shall fall upon the sons, Wynona had warned Jessica. But what did it mean? What sins had Elkheart committed? And what was it about the Devil's Woods that made the townspeople so afraid?

Kyle hoped Wynona was sober enough to explain some things. He turned down a residential street lined with old houses on one side and a cemetery on the other. Chaser moaned like he needed to relieve himself, so Kyle pulled over. He hooked a leash onto the dog's collar and took him for a walk in a grassy meadow next to the graveyard. The Rottweiler eagerly sniffed the ground and marked a wrought-iron fence that bordered the burial grounds. Weathered tombstones dotted the hill. Many of them tilted sideways. The grass was overgrown, and some stones had been taken over by ivy. As he walked Chaser up to the gate's brick archway, the gravestones began to whisper.

The fur on the dog's back spiked.

Kyle petted his back. "Can you hear them too?"

Chaser whimpered and tugged at the leash, urging Kyle to return to the Jeep.

After putting the dog in the car, Kyle stared at the cemetery.

You know you want to go in there, said Detective Winterbone.

Curiosity prodding him, Kyle stepped through the archway entering the cemetery. The ground vibrated through his hiking boots, same as the forest had. He walked between the whispering tombstones. The dead buried here were restless souls. Many wanted to communicate with him. The murmurings grew louder the farther he walked. None of the headstones were engraved with names or epitaphs. At first he'd thought the names and dates had been removed by time. But even the most recent grave markers bore no inscriptions. The blank headstones horrified him. There were hundreds of them, each one identical with a circular symbol near the top of the stone. The symbol reminded Kyle of Druid seals he'd researched for one of his Winterbone novels, although he figured this emblem was Scandinavian in origin rather than British.

Hoping to get an imprint, he pressed his palm to one of the tombstones. He heard a man's wailing cries but saw only darkness. Kyle touched other stones, but they were all the same—tortured voices screaming from pits of darkness. Oddly, they were all male. Where were the women buried? Perhaps they had their own section on the opposite side of the cemetery.

At the center of the graveyard, beneath a pair of tall oak trees, a gray-stoned mausoleum stood. Unlike the nameless headstones, the crypt had the name *THORPE* engraved above the door along with a Danish epitaph.

I mørke dyb,
evige søvn,
hvile i hæder på Store Fader.

Kyle pulled out his cell phone and logged on to a website that translated foreign languages to English. He typed in the phrase. The translation came back:

In darkness deep,
eternal sleep,
rest in the glory of Great Father.

As Kyle walked up the steps, the entire cemetery hushed to an eerie silence. He tried to open the stone door, but it was sealed shut. He pressed his palm against the door and felt a chill as if he had touched a slab of ice. Inside the mausoleum, he sensed an infinite darkness, a space that stretched farther than the physical borders of the granite walls and deeper than the floor. He felt the darkness within pulling at him, as if trying to leech his soul through the stone. Kyle yanked his hand loose and stumbled down the steps, his heart racing. The whispering voices returned as he hurried back to the Jeep. He sat behind the wheel and locked the doors, as if that were enough to keep the spirits out.

Chaser licked Kyle's face.

"Yeah, yeah, you were right. I shouldn't have gone in there."

* * *

At the tavern, Eric felt a twitch in his crotch as the woman in red stood at the bar, ordering a pack of Marlboro Lights. Her face was angled with high cheekbones. Her lips were thick and luscious. Eric imagined all the wonderful tricks she could do with them.

Ease up there, he warned himself. *You came here to drink and nothing else.*

But thoughts of the redhead's lips filled his mind with fantasies. He tried concentrating on Jessica, but that didn't help matters. Every girl he'd ever dated had done whatever he wanted. Jessica refused to dress up for him or wear handcuffs. Besides lacking sexual adventure, she didn't know how to let go herself. He liked to make a woman come. He'd made sort of a sport out of it, but Jessica couldn't orgasm worth a damn.

Is that the kind of woman you want to spend the rest of your life having sex with?

Getting married didn't mean he had to stop seeing other women.

Down the bar, the redhead looked his way again. The bartender went into the back storage room, leaving Eric alone with her.

As he watched, her hand slid up her bare thigh, disappearing into the folds of her skirt.

Eric felt himself swelling in his shorts.

The woman's hand moved higher, lifting her skirt. He saw red panties and her slender fingers toying beneath the lace.

Damn, he was going to bust a nut.

Little miss devil in a red dress looked his way with a flirtatious smile.

Then with the grace of an exotic dancer, she slid her panties down her legs and stepped out of them. Walking over, she put the panties in his pocket, her fingers grazing his erection. "A wedding gift for your bride-to-be."

To his relief, the bartender returned with a pack of cigarettes. The redhead released her hand from his pocket and paid for the smokes. She lit one and sauntered over to the billiard area. She bent over a pool table, showing off a hint of bare ass, and racked the balls.

Eric grinned at the challenge. *So she wants to play.*

* * *

Kendra Meacham awakened from a heavy slumber, feeling disoriented and afraid. She was lying in pitch darkness. She tried sitting up but her head hit a low ceiling. She felt around her. Cramped walls, padded, smooth as silk. She was inside a coffin. Had she been buried alive?

Claustrophobia kicked in. Her throat clenched. She couldn't breathe. She banged on the wooden ceiling and the top part of the casket gave a little. She pressed against it and the lid opened upward. Kendra sat up, gasping. The shadowy room was lined with displayed coffins. A funeral parlor.

"What the fuck?"

The last thing she remembered was hiking out of the forest and being picked up by a man in a maroon hearse. Hugo, that was his name. Why had he brought her here?

Faint light filtered in through a crack in the crimson curtains. Kendra searched the shadows, but there was no one else in the room.

She climbed out of the casket, her sprained ankle shooting spikes of pain up her leg as she landed on the carpeted floor. She cursed under her breath. Limping, she stepped into a hallway. Opera music was playing from somewhere within the funeral home. She moved down the hall, using the walls for support. They were covered in vintage wallpaper and framed black-and-white photos of families posing with dead people lying inside coffins.

The female opera singer's voice grew louder as Kendra searched for a way out. She tried the windows, but they were nailed shut. Halfway down the hall she reached a doorway that opened into a brightly lit room with a tiled floor. The man who had brought her here was sitting at a metal slab, stitching up a dead woman's chest. Hugo's head moved with the rhythm of the opera.

Warm urine trickled down Kendra's leg. She hobbled past the door, fumbling down the wall. A framed photo fell to the floor, the glass breaking. The hallway led into some type of den with antique furniture and a ticking grandfather clock. Over the fireplace mantle was a portrait of a mother and her son.

"Did sleeping beauty finally wake?" Hugo stood in the hallway, holding a rag over a jar.

Kendra bolted, half-running, half-hopping across the den. She entered a kitchen. Frantically searching the drawers, she found a butcher's knife. She whirled around, holding the blade out in front of her. She stood alone in the gloomy kitchen.

The volume of the opera music turned up until it was maddening.

She tried a back door, but it was dead-bolted. She needed a key. She had to find another door. A dark opening in the wall led to a crooked hallway that disappeared into uncertain darkness. Christ, was there no end to this place?

Swinging the knife, Kendra backed her way through the kitchen, into a dining room. Arms grabbed her from behind. A strong hand squeezed her wrist and the knife dropped to the floor. Hugging her from behind, Hugo pressed his cheek to hers. "Where do you think you're going, pretty girl? You and I are just getting started."

She felt his erection swelling against her back. A soaked rag covered her nose. Kendra inhaled chloroform and the walls started spinning. The last thing she heard was Hugo saying, "You're mine now."

* * *

Continuing his drive down the cemetery road, Kyle passed the *Thorpe Funeral Home and Crematorium* sign and turned onto a long driveway lined with trees. It ended before a rambling, two-story house. The left side was made up of white clapboards covered in ivy. The right side had been cobbled with dark brown bricks, and the front windows were uneven, giving the funeral home a Jekyll and Hyde appearance.

As Kyle got out, Chaser started barking. The dog's eyes were fixed on a maroon hearse parked in the driveway.

"Calm down, boy." But nothing Kyle said had any effect. Leaving the dog barking in the Jeep, Kyle peered into the hearse's back windows, but they were too tinted for him see anything.

Hoping Wynona was home alone, Kyle walked a path to the front of the house. A weed-infested garden centered around a moss-covered statue of a woman with a cracked face. Kyle rang the doorbell. To his disappointment, Hugo answered, holding a bag of pretzels.

Christ, thirty years old and still living with his mother.

Hugo's heavy-lidded eyes widened with recognition. "Kyle? Hey, what's up?"

"I'm here to see your mother. Is she home?"

"Sorry, man, she left."

"Any idea when she'll be back?"

"Soon, I'm sure. Probably just stepped out for some cigarettes." Hugo opened the door wider. "Want to come in and wait for her? I got beer and snacks. We could shoot some pool."

The smell of formaldehyde wafted from the doorway. Opera music played from the depths of funeral home.

"No, thanks." Kyle pulled out a business card. "Please tell Wynona to call me."

"What do you want with her?"

"It's a personal matter."

Hugo nodded and stuffed the card in the chest pocket of his lab coat. "Sure, you don't want a beer? A cold one's just the thing for a day like this."

"Maybe another time. If you'll just pass along the message to your mother, I'd appreciate it." Kyle started down the porch steps, then stopped and turned around. He tipped his head toward the cemetery next to the funeral home. "Those tombstones are all blank. No names engraved on them. Why?"

"What were you doing in there?" Hugo asked, his brow furrowing. He was the groundskeeper.

"Just taking a stroll and seeing the sites." Kyle tried to sound offhand. "I found it peculiar though—grave markers without names—and every tombstone had the same round symbol."

"We bury our dead in the old way." Hugo said, his face suddenly unreadable.

"Like they did back in Denmark?"

Hugo nodded, his mouth a tight line.

Kyle nodded. "The symbol looks pre-Christian. What does it mean?"

Hugo was getting more annoyed with each question. He shrugged. "Hell if I know. I don't make the headstones. I just put 'em in the ground." Then he smiled. "Good seeing you again, Kyle. I'll let Mother know you called."

Hugo remained at the door, watching as Kyle walked back to the Jeep and drove away. Chaser didn't stop barking until the funeral home was out of sight.

* * *

As Eric watched the redhead teasing him at the pool table, he tried his best to resist her temptations. But as he drank his beer, he kept thinking of Jessica in the kitchen giggling with Kyle and rejecting Eric's invitation to come with him into town. Had she accepted his offer, he wouldn't be in this predicament.

This is her fault.

The image of her flirting with Kyle pissed him off.

Fuck it. Grabbing his long-neck beer, Eric walked up beside the redhead. Up close, she radiated high-voltage electricity. "Excuse me, mind if I bum a smoke?"

"You can't afford your own?" she said with a teasing eyebrow.

"Sure, I just thought one of yours might be more satisfying."

"Well, then." She lit a cigarette against the one clamped between her lips, handed it to Eric.

He took a drag, released a stream of smoke. He gazed into her jade-green eyes. "That was quite a show you put on over there."

"You liked it?" She blew out a long puff.

"I did."

She leaned closer and whispered in his ear. "Well, there's plenty more where that came from."

Eric's crotch swelled so much it hurt. He wanted to pin this woman right here against the pool table. Forget Jessica. This firecracker knew how to push his buttons.

"Wait right here." She ran a finger across his chest then walked over to the jukebox. She chose another slow country song. "Shameless", an old Garth Brooks tune.

"Care to dance?" She put her arms around his neck and pressed her body against his.

Eric swayed with her to the music, feeling her grinding against his erection. "So what's your name?" he asked.

"Celeste." Then she whispered in his ear, "It's a great name for poetry."

"Oh?" As a general rule, Eric liked his women doing anything with their mouths but talking.

"Rhymes with all my favorite things." Her voice was teasing, seductive.

"I'm listening." And he was.

"Let's see, there's 'obsessed', 'caressed'." Her voice was driving him crazy. "And 'acquiesced', one of my personal favorites. 'Pressed.' That one doesn't sound like much but…" Her hand slipped over his erection and squeezed him gently until his knees started to buckle. "See? I can tell you like it too. There's 'quest', which sounds like a challenge. I always like a challenge. How bout you?"

"Definitely."

"Undressed." She was playing with his zipper now, running a fingernail over the metal teeth until he thought he might come right there. And finally 'guest' as in won't you be my…" She guided his hand underneath her skirt. He moaned softly at the feel of her.

"Damn, girl, you are something."

Next thing Eric knew they were kissing, locked in an embrace that was all business when the front door banged open, filling the room with sunlight.

An older man in a cowboy hat, flanked by a pair of loggers, entered the tavern.

The bartender pointed to Eric. "That's him, Mayor Thorpe."

"What do you think you're doing?" The mayor started for Eric. "Get your fucking hands off my wife!"

* * *

Kyle walked into the tavern to find two giant loggers beating the crap out of Eric. They were taking turns slugging him.

"Stop it!" Kyle rushed to the billiard area, grabbed a pool cue and struck one man in the back of the neck. The big man wobbled for a moment and then hit the floor. Kyle stepped between Eric and the second bully. He held the pool cue like a bat. "Back off, you son of a bitch!"

The bear-sized lumberjack raised his fist. "Out of my way or I'll knock your fucking teeth in."

"That's enough, Brody," ordered Mayor Thorpe. He was seated against a pool table with his arms crossed. "Boys, go help yourselves to a pitcher of beer on me."

The two ruffians walked to the bar, chuckling.

Kyle helped Eric to his feet. His face was bruised and bleeding. Kyle glared at Jensen Thorpe. "Mayor, what the hell's going on here?"

Thorpe stood, straightening his tweed jacket. "You know this piece of shit?"

"He's my brother."

"Well, your brother needs to learn some fucking manners. He had his hands up my wife's skirt just now. Came in and caught him myself."

Kyle noticed the young Mrs. Thorpe sitting at the bar, smoking a cigarette. She looked half the mayor's age. Kyle looked at his brother. "Is that true?"

Eric spat blood onto the floor. "She came on to me. She never said she was married."

Thorpe said, "Didn't her wedding ring give you a goddamned clue?"

"She wasn't wearing it. I swear."

"Bullshit." The mayor rubbed his knuckles as if he wanted to get in a few shots of his own. "I don't like cheaters and I sure as hell don't like being lied to."

The front door opened and a large group of loggers entered the tavern and headed for the bar, chattering about Happy Hour.

Mayor Thorpe pointed at Eric. "Kyle, get this son of a bitch out of my sight. I better not see him in my town again. Have you got that?"

"Yes, sir."

Thorpe walked to the door and held it open. "Let's go, Celeste." As the redhead sauntered past, the mayor glared at Kyle and Eric. "He'd better be gone in two minutes or I'll let my men get right back at him."

Chapter Thirteen

At the reservation, Jessica and Shawna sat on lawn chairs behind the cabin and drank margaritas, both still in their bikinis. Jessica rubbed sun block on her shoulders so she didn't burn.

Shawna, whose natural tan had already turned to a beautiful golden brown, shuffled her Tarot cards. "Let's see what your future holds."

Jessica had never received a tarot reading and was more than a little curious. She noticed in the colorful vines and flowers that covered Shawna's left arm was a tattoo of the High Priestess card.

"What does the High Priestess mean?"

Shawna's brown eyes gleamed. "She represents the divine feminine, intuition and wisdom. She is always a mystery to be discovered." She held up the deck. "Okay, focus on an area of your life you'd like to gain insight on and then touch the cards."

Jessica thought of Eric and Kyle and all the mixed feelings that they stirred up inside her. She placed her hand upon the deck. *Who is my one true love?*

As soon as she asked the question, she regretted it. What if it wasn't Eric? Could she truly leave him for his brother? Could she deal with the pain of breaking his heart? But then what if her true love was Eric? Would he ever fill her chest with butterflies?

Will I ever truly feel safe?

She wanted to tell Shawna to stop, but she flipped over the first card.

"The Lovers."

"That's good, right?"

"Unfortunately it's upside down. This means infidelity and deception."

Jessica thought of the flirting she had done with Kyle, her desire to hike with him in the woods, and felt a pang of guilt.

The next card was the three of swords stabbing into a heart. "Uh-oh." Shawna frowned. "Pain and sorrow. You're about to go through a period of great conflict. It isn't clear what the outcome will be, but your heart is torn."

* * *

Around the side of the cabin, Zack chopped wood with an axe. A lit Camel hung between his lips as he split his log in two. He couldn't believe Eric had assigned him the chore of replenishing the woodpile. This was supposed to be a vacation.

Working beside him, Ray Roamingbear slammed a second axe into a log, sending bark sky high. "Whew, I think this is the hottest day yet," he said, wiping his sweaty brow. "What do you think?"

"I'd rather be doing anything other than chopping wood." Ray was really working on his last nerve. Not only did he talk too much and drive him crazy with endless questions, but he constantly gave advice, sounding like Eric. Zack caught Ray staring at him. "What?"

"I was looking at all your tattoos. What made you choose so many skulls and demons?"

Zack shrugged. "I don't know. That's what appealed to me when I got them."

"Don't you know the symbols you ink on your skin call in those spirits?"

"Yeah, whatever." He split another log.

Ray stood, hands resting on his axe. "You ever have nightmares?"

Zack had suffered night terrors for years, but he wasn't about to talk to Ray like he was his shrink. "Everybody has bad dreams."

"I don't. You know why?" Ray tapped his skull. "Because I keep my thoughts pure. If you want later, I'll bring my medicine bag over and clear you of any demons."

"Uh, that's okay, Ray. I'm good."

"I can help cure you of any addictions."

"Wait a minute." Zack stopped chopping. "Did Eric put you up to this?"

"He asked me to have a talk with you, yes, see if you might be open to my services."

"Thanks, Ray, but I don't need an exorcism." Biting down on his cigarette, Zack gripped his axe, imagined the log on the chopping block was Eric's head and split it in two.

* * *

Wynona sped down the reservation dirt road like God's fury on wheels. On her AM radio a preacher spoke the Lord's Prayer, "...forgive us our debts, as we also have forgiven our debtors. And lead us not into temptation, but deliver us from evil..."

"Amen." She smiled at the ivory Jesus hanging from her rearview mirror. "This is a good thing I'm doing, right? Somebody's got to warn those kids that Satan walks their woods."

Wynona sipped from her flask, trying to settle her nerves. *I am a servant of light. I am God's holy messenger. Deliver me from evil.*

As she approached the Cree village, the locusts seemed to buzz louder at her arrival. Jon Elkheart's cabin appeared from behind the pines. Seeing the upstairs bedroom window, she remembered all the mornings waking up in Elkheart's arms, feeling safe and protected. They used to sit out on the balcony, talking at sunrise and sunset, about love, life, his travels. Elkheart had opened her mind and spirit to so many things.

Feeling a hole inside her chest, Wynona washed those memories away with another quick swig from her flask. Her Buick skidded in front of the house, nearly hitting one of the giant Ponderosa pines. Throwing open her door, she ran up the porch steps and knocked several times. No one answered. A black Hummer was parked out front. Someone had to be home. Wynona hurried around back where she found two women in bikinis lying out on the back lawn.

* * *

Jessica dropped the tarot book and gasped when a woman charged around the corner of the cabin. It was *her*. That crazy woman from the tavern. Wiry black hair with silver streaks hung past her shoulders. Deep crow's feet marked the corners of her brown eyes. She looked so like a witch that Jessica half expected her to throw her head back and let out a cackle.

"Thank God, you're still alive," the woman said.

Shawna turned around. "Oh...can we help you?"

"Where's Kyle?" Wynona rasped. "I need to speak with him."

"He went into town," Jessica said, standing, ready to run if necessary.

Shana also stood. The woman was taller than both of them.

"Damn it!" Wynona's hand went to her mouth and for a moment it looked like she might cry.

Jessica thought her eyes appeared glassy and wondered if she'd been drinking. Looking around for Ray and Zack, Jessica couldn't see them anywhere.

Shawna held up her palms. "Ma'am, please calm down. Is there some kind of emergency?"

"You girls must listen to me. You can't stay here. These woods are dangerous. There are demons out here that want to hurt you. You must leave this place at once." Wynona's trembling hands dug into her breast pocket.

Jessica and Shawna remained frozen for an awkward moment, as the woman lit a cigarette and smoked. Her eyes teary, she glanced into the windows of the cabin. "You wouldn't happen to have any brandy here, would you? I could use a drink."

Shawna slid a nervous glance to Jessica. "We have vodka."

"Okay…" The woman's mouth froze and her eyes widened.

Jessica turned to see Ray Roamingbear and Zack coming around the corner. Ray frowned at Wynona. "What are you doing on our land?"

She bolted away, rounded the corner and was gone.

Jessica said, "Ray, what's wrong with her?"

"She's crazy as a loon. I'll make sure she leaves." He walked around to the front.

Jessica released a breath when she heard Ray yelling and a car peeling away.

"That was some crazy shit." Shawna's gaze remained locked on the corner of the house.

Zack gave her his cigarette. "What the hell was that about?"

"I don't know." Shawna took a drag and blew out smoke. "She just showed up talking like a freak."

Jessica pulled a T-shirt over her bathing suit. "That's the same lady who grabbed me at the restaurant yesterday. She bloody scares me."

Ray returned. "Sorry, girls. Wynona has some demons. Fine on her meds but when she starts drinking, all bets are off. After Elkheart broke up with her, she stalked him until he had to file a restraining order against her. She's not supposed to come anywhere near here. Are you two okay?"

"We are now," Shawna said.

"What did she mean?" Jessica asked. "About demons and the forest being dangerous?"

"Like I said last night, some of the townspeople are superstitious about the reservation because it backs up to Macâya Forest. Wynona's always popping up places and warning tourists that the woods are full of demon spirits. That's why she has to be kept under watch. You can imagine what that does for the tourist business."

"Well, I've had enough sun for the day." With her book and towel under one arm, Jessica headed into the cabin. Still shaken, she half expected the crazy witch to come charging through the front door.

* * *

"What the hell were you thinking, Eric?" Kyle shook his head in disgust as he drove the country road toward the reservation.

His brother sat in the passenger seat, holding a blood-soaked T-shirt to his battered face. "She seduced me. I was minding my own business."

"It's bad enough that you cheat on business trips. But you're on vacation with her. Jesus!"

"Don't mention this," Eric pleaded. "It was a slip. It won't happen again."

"Just show her some respect." He hated that Eric was cheating, but Kyle also honored the guy code: *You don't rat on your brother or your friends, no matter what stupid shit they get themselves into.*

Up ahead, a gray Buick was speeding toward them. The woman driver honked as they passed.

"That was Wynona." In his rearview mirror he saw her brake lights brighten. Her car screeched to a halt. Kyle stopped and hit reverse, backing down the road.

Wynona climbed out of her car, marching toward him, waving her hands. "Kyle!"

He jumped out and met up with her in the middle of the road. She was crying and stuttering, unable to get any words out.

He gripped her forearms. "Wynona, calm down. What is it?"

"You're…all in danger…the demons are coming for you."

"What?"

She pointed to the sky. "They warned me…you should leave." Her breath stank of liquor.

"You're not making any sense."

"I have to get home." She ripped loose, stumbling back to her car. "Leave, Kyle. Get far away from here." She climbed into her car and tore down the road toward Hagen's Cove.

* * *

Inspector Sam Zano felt the acids roiling in his stomach as he climbed out of his SUV and walked to where four Mounties stood examining the ground around a camper. The motor home that had belonged to Detective Carl Hanson lay on its side like a large slain animal. All the windows had been shattered and the roof was scratched up.

Zano peered into the camper through a missing skylight. White stuffing from a shredded mattress covered everything like dandelion. Pots and pans and clothing were scattered everywhere.

The inspector sighed. "Bjorn, what's the report?"

The Mountie who had been first on the scene flipped open his notepad. "Sir, it appears that Carl Hanson and his daughter, Lindsey, were attacked sometime last night. We've found plenty of blood but no bodies. Just a man's severed arm."

Zano nodded. "Show me."

The site of the attack was about fifty meters down the road at a campsite by the lake. A couple of Mounties stood near a large patch of crimson grass at the base of a tree that looked as if someone had splattered dark red paint on the bark. High above their heads some of the branches were broken. A piece of torn clothing clung to the pine needles.

"Somebody climb up there and get that," Zano ordered.

"Inspector, we found this in the bushes near the water." One of the men held up a baggie that contained Carl's arm. By the deep scratches on the arm it was clear this had been an attack by a large predator. And Inspector Zano, having lived around Lake Akwâkopiy all his life, had a pretty good idea what that was. He got his confirmation when he saw what the thing had left behind in the ashes of the campfire—a monstrous footprint with pointed lines that speared from each toe print.

Shaking his head, Zano popped a few Tums into his mouth. "All right, men, let's get to work."

* * *

"I have to get out of this godforsaken town," Wynona said as she drove down her driveway. On the frantic ride home, she'd come up with a plan of escape. First, fix a double brandy to calm her nerves. Next, pack clothes and her .38 Special. She hated guns, but she might need it. Her tank had plenty of gas, so she could drive right out of here, not stopping to say goodbye to anyone, leaving Hagen's Cove and all its horrible memories behind her.

Wynona parked beside the hearse and left the engine running. She hurried past the caskets in the funeral parlor, past the mortuary, and walked the long hallway to the living quarters behind the funeral home. Dozens of black-and-white photos of lumberjacks and elders lined the walls. Their eyes followed Wynona as if they knew she was about to betray the town. She headed straight for the liquor cabinet, turned on the lamp, poured a heavy dose of Napoleon brandy into her flask, then took several large gulps. Turning around, she dropped the flask and yelped.

Hugo was leaning against a wall in the kitchen. "Hello, Mother. We've been waiting for you."

Several men entered the room. All of them she'd known for thirty years. On the couch sat Mayor Thorpe, his hand patting the armrest. "We were wondering when you'd get home."

"I…uh…" Wynona glanced toward the back door.

Mayor Thorpe stood. "Hugo says you've been gone all day."

Her mind raced. "I-I was feeling under the weather, so I went for a drive." She tried to smile. "I feel much better now."

"Well, I don't want to take any chances on you falling ill. I'm giving Hugo the evening off, so he can take care of you."

Her son grinned. "Looks like it's just you and me tonight, Mother."

Wynona faked a smile. "That really isn't necessary. I feel okay, really. You need to earn your money."

"I'm letting him stay on the clock," the mayor said. "It's important that my head mortician keep in good health. Call it insurance."

The group of men chuckled.

Mayor Thorpe gave her a stern look. "We want you to sleep well tonight. Doc has brought a tranquilizer to help you relax."

The old doctor held up a syringe. He moved toward her, needle stabbing the air, yellow liquid squirting upward.

Wynona made a break for the back door. Hugo cut her off and pinned her against the wall, while Doc jammed the needle into her arm.

The faces of all the men went fuzzy.

She felt them lifting her, carrying her down the hallway like pallbearers. *They're going to cremate me in the oven. Make me disappear.* Wynona panicked, giving the men one last fight, but then the drug took over, pulling down a drape of shadows over her awareness, their ominous voices her last sounds as she escaped into darkness.

Part Five

Lust and Lucidity

*I felt guilty for desiring her, this new woman in my life. Part of
me felt like it was time to move on, that I was young and could
still create a happy life with someone. But an angry voice spoke
cold whispers in my head, "You deserve no such happiness."
And that's when my late wife's ghost started haunting me.*

—Detective Alex Winterbone

Chapter Fourteen

At twilight, the forest began to turn gray as the sun dipped behind the mountains. On the back porch Jessica swabbed a cut above Eric's swollen eye. He sat in a chair with his shirt off. She frowned at the bruises that covered his face and upper body. He looked like a boxer who had taken a beating for twelve rounds.

"How did this happen?" Jessica asked.

"Kyle dropped me off at the tavern to have a drink. I was just sitting at the bar, minding my own business, when a couple of lumberjacks picked a fight with me. It hurts like fucking hell."

"I'm sorry, love. I should have gone with you today."

"I wish you had. This might not have happened." He gave her his wounded puppy face.

"Are you feeling neglected?"

"I'm wondering where my girlfriend went. The last couple of days you've been a different person."

"I'm sorry." Jessica stroked his hair. "Next time I'll go with you."

"Tonight the others are going off to do a ceremony with Ray and Grandfather." Eric rubbed her leg. "I thought maybe you and I'd hang back here. I've got a surprise for you that I think you're going to like."

* * *

Kyle and Shawna followed Ray Roamingbear down the road that wound through the Cree village. Tonight they were going to receive the gift that Ray had promised them before coming on the trip. Whatever their elders had in store, it required them bringing backpacks and bedrolls for a sleepover.

"Are we camping out in the woods?" Shawna asked.

Ray grinned. "You'll see."

A continuous *pum-pum-pum* of drumbeats echoed in the distance.

The wind made the vacated cabins creak. A large bird that might have been an owl flew into a hole in one of the rooftops. The stars were visible tonight, which made Kyle imagine Jessica on the balcony looking through her telescope. He hated that she would probably be stargazing with Eric tonight. The moon was full again, a bright cratered face reflecting silvery-blue light onto the surrounding forest. The silhouetted pines seemed to watch him as he walked. Kyle tightened his grip on the straps of his backpack. He hoped Ray wasn't taking them into the woods.

At the center of the village, they entered a long rectangular building called the Great House. It was made up of one large room where the tribe used to gather for meetings, talk story and celebrations. The community building felt hollow now without all the tables and chairs and other tribe members. Several windows were broken and sections of the roof were missing, letting in scattered moonbeams. A gray gloom shrouded most of the room, except for the center, where a campfire glowed in a circular pit. Smoke billowed up to an opening in the ceiling.

Grandfather Two Hawks was seated on the floor, beating a tom-tom and singing an ancient Cree song. The old chief wore a headband full of colorful feathers. In front of him was a rabbit-fur blanket topped with numerous ceremonial objects: bowls of herbs, fur pouches, a crow's wing and a small animal skull. An oyster shell of smoking incense filled the sacred area with the scent of burning sage.

Kyle and Shawna sat down with their elders and placed tobacco offerings in a bowl.

Ray joined in on the drumming and singing.

Kyle had forgotten how much he used to enjoy the tribe's drum circles. As children they had danced around a campfire while the grownups drummed and sang. Afterward, Grandfather told stories that held all the children captivated. Those nights were always filled with the smells of tobacco and barbecued meat and corn cobs cooking on a grill. In one memory he saw himself and Eric as innocent boys not yet jaded by life and loss...Shawna as a toddler in diapers crawling around and playing with bugs...Elkheart sitting with his arms around their mother, moving with the music—happier times that were long gone.

Tonight, Grandfather sang with a mix of fiery passion and haunting sadness. The drumming and singing rose to a crescendo then abruptly stopped. The Great House fell silent except for the sounds of insects chirping in the forest. The flames flickered in Grandfather's thick glasses. Kyle and Shawna watched as the old medicine man spoke in Cree.

Ray translated. "The ceremonies of our people are becoming lost.

It is up to younger generations to carry on our traditions or our culture will die out."

Grandfather directed his piercing stare toward the two initiates, speaking with a power that Kyle felt resonating in his chest.

"Kyle, Shawna," Ray said, looking at both of them intently. "You two and Eric are the last descendants of the Lake Akwâkopiy Cree Band. Grandfather hopes that you will take an interest in your heritage and keep our traditions alive. He has much to teach. Since you all grew up in the city, you missed out on the opportunity to do a rite of passage from childhood into adulthood. Tonight we offer you a chance to do a vision quest to connect with our ancestors and the power of *Kisemanito*, Great Spirit." Ray put his hands on his knees, smiling. "I did my first vision quest with your father when I turned sixteen. It was a pivotal moment. I've done several since."

Kyle felt a surge of adrenaline, unsure of what trials they were going to put him through.

Grandfather picked up two halves of a peace pipe adorned with feathers and held them above his head.

Ray said, "The sacred pipe symbolizes the joining of the masculine and feminine energies. It is only when these two parts of ourselves are bonded that we are whole."

Speaking another blessing, Grandfather joined the two halves of the pipe. He tapped one end of it on an animal skull then circled the pipe over his head. He said something in Cree.

Ray translated, "We call in the spirits of the four directions."

Grandfather stuffed tobacco into the buffalo head bowl, lit a flame over it, and puffed. The tobacco glowed orange and gray tendrils drifted up toward the ceiling.

Ray said, "The smoke represents our prayers that we send to the spirit world. So as the pipe comes around be thinking about an issue you'd like to give away and a dream you'd like to manifest. Call on the guidance of Great Spirit."

Grandfather drew on the pipe, blew out circular rings, then passed it to Ray. As the pipe made its way around the circle, Kyle tried to think of something to wish for. He had all the money he could ever want, a successful career, good health, yet for the past two years he had felt hollow, lonely and depressed. His most intimate relationship had been with his shrink. What could he wish for that could bring joy back to his life? When Shawna's turn was done, Kyle held the pipe to his chest and closed his eyes.

Great Spirit, what I give away is my loneliness and depression. What I wish for is to be able to love a woman again. If not Jessica, then someone just as special.

He inhaled the tobacco-flavored smoke, felt his throat tingle and then blew it back out. As Kyle thought of his third wish, he was struck with a pang of guilt, remembering the pact he had made with himself at his wife's grave. And now as the smoke swirled above, he thought it formed into her angry face.

* * *

Up in the loft, Eric lay on the air mattress with an icepack on his face. Tonight wasn't going as good as he'd hoped. He hadn't planned on being in so much pain. He felt jealous that his brother and sister were receiving their gift without him, but then decided with Kyle away for the night, maybe this was a blessing in disguise.

Jessica came upstairs with a glass of water and some vitamin capsules. "Here, take some Valerian root. This'll help you sleep."

Eric sat up halfway and she put the herbal capsules into his mouth and tilted the glass of water for him to sip. "Thanks." He had more strength than he let on, but he loved it when she nursed him. He sank back into the mattress. She turned off the lamp.

"Is there anything I can do to make you feel better?" she asked.

"I'd love one of your famous foot massages."

"Coming right up." She lit a lavender candle and turned on some soft music. She got on her knees the way Eric liked and began rubbing his feet. "How does that feel?"

"Good, babe. Keep doing what you're doing."

Eric thought of the strange turn of events that had gotten his face and stomach beaten. He felt like an idiot for allowing that redheaded slut to seduce him. Kissing Celeste Thorpe had been stupid and reckless. If there was a way to erase his mistake he would, but his brief infidelity was in the past and as long as Kyle kept his mouth shut, Jessica never had to know about it.

Despite the attention Eric was getting on his feet, Jessica still seemed distant, which made her a challenge suddenly.

"Babe, you're making me horny." He patted his hips. "Climb on top."

Jessica laughed. "You're in no condition for that tonight. Your lips are so swollen I can't even kiss you."

"The lower half of my body still works. See?" He pointed to the bulge in his boxers.

"Maybe tomorrow. Besides, Zack's downstairs."

Eric sighed. He had to come up with a better plan. Jessica was in a volatile place and Eric didn't want to lose her to Kyle. "Hey, can you bring me my duffle bag?"

"Sure." She brought it over and set it on the bed beside him.

"I know it's not our anniversary until tomorrow, but I wanted to go ahead and give you this." He pulled out a small white box with a red ribbon.

She lit up. "You got me a present?"

"Of course. I know how much our anniversary means to you."

"Let's wait until tomorrow."

"No, open it now."

"Okay, just a minute." Jessica hopped up and dug into her bag. She came back to the bed holding a present with a card taped to the top of it.

Eric hadn't thought to get her a card. *I'll give her something better.* He sat up, lightning bolts of pain searing across his ribs. He nodded toward the presents. "Ladies first."

"No, you first," she said with a girlish grin. Good, she was warming up. He'd finally gotten something right.

Eric read the card. It was a bunch of flowery words that rhymed. He skipped down to the handwriting beneath the poem.

Eric,
I am so glad to have you in my life and hope this is the first of many anniversaries.
All my love, Jessica.

"Babe…" Eric placed his hand on her leg.

"Now open your present," she said.

He unwrapped a framed photo of the two of them.

"It's for your office. I noticed you didn't have one of us there."

"Thanks. It'll go right on my desk. Okay, now open yours."

Jessica tore off the ribbon and lifted the box's lid. Her eyes widened when she saw the gold ring with the ruby heart. She put her hand to her chest. "Oh, my God."

"I know it's not a diamond, but…" Eric got down on one knee and took her hand. "Jessica, will you marry me?"

She took a step back. "Wow, I had no idea you were planning… Seriously?"

"You're living with me now. We might as well make it official. What do you say? Marry me, Jess."

"I've still got school to finish, my residency."

"You can do all that as my wife. This is what you've been wanting, isn't it?"

"Someday."

"How about now, babe?" He gave her his most charming smile. "Say yes. Be my wife."

"Okay."

"That's a yes?"

"Yes." She nodded and kissed him.

"Careful, not on the lips." He pointed to the side of his face that wasn't bruised and she kissed it.

The Valerian root pills started to kick in, making him drowsy. He yawned. She stroked the back of his head. "You should get to bed."

"Wait." He grabbed her hands. "I know I don't say it much, but I want you to know that I…I love you."

"Ah, Eric. You're full of surprises tonight." She started to hug him and he winced, feeling pain jag through his ribs. "Sorry, love, I forgot. Get some sleep. We'll celebrate more tomorrow."

Eric yawned again, his eyelids growing heavy. She turned off the music and blew out the candle. She said good night then went downstairs. Eric drifted off with a smile on his face. He couldn't wait to call Blake tomorrow and share the big news.

* * *

As Grandfather chanted to the spirit world, Shawna was surprised by how much she was enjoying the ceremony. Growing up with a God-fearing mother and fire-and-brimstone stepfather, Shawna had never connected with anything spiritual. Instead, she had raged against it. Goth had become her religion and recreational drugs her escape from hell. But tonight, after smoking the sacred pipe, she was feeling as if a heavy burden had been lifted from her heart. Her head felt light, like being stoned, but energized instead of relaxed.

"What exactly are we smoking?" Shawna asked.

"Tobacco," Ray answered. "When blessed in a ceremony, it has magical properties. Now to aid you with your vision quest we have something for you to eat."

Grandfather lifted a bowl of purple mushrooms.

Shawna grinned. "Shrooms?"

Ray nodded. "These will put you into an altered state and open your awareness to parts of yourself that have been dormant. All it takes is one of these to feel connected to everything."

"All right, I'm game." Shawna felt giddy. The last time she'd done shrooms was the night she met Zack.

Kyle didn't look so thrilled. "I don't feel comfortable eating those."

Ray said, "There's nothing to be afraid of. They're natural."

"But they're illegal."

"Only if we take them off the reservation." Ray winked. "Don't worry. We're miles from civilization." He grabbed one out of the bowl first.

"How long will it last?" Kyle asked.

Ray said, "It's different for everybody, but typically around eight hours."

"Just go for it, Kyle." Shawna bit into a mushroom. "You'll have the best time, I promise."

Ray said, "This is not to party, kids. A vision quest is to help you step outside of your conscious mind so you can get directions from the spirit world. It will also help you call in your animal spirit guides. So pay attention to what shows up."

* * *

Kyle gazed at the purple mushroom in his hand. It had a long stem and small cap that glittered with crystals. He was afraid to eat it, terrified of what doors might open if he did. He had spent most of his days trapped indoors by his own paralyzing fears. A prisoner looking out at the city from his high-rise apartment. No parties, no family dinners, no dating. Just living in a comfortable box. But his home had become a coffin. A purgatory he shared with the ghost of his dead wife. He had taken a quantum leap coming here with his siblings. Now Kyle had a chance to face his fears and step back into the world of the living. And, God willing, know how it feels to touch a woman again.

He bit into the mushroom's cap. It was dry and crunchy and had a strong earthy flavor. It took him a couple of minutes and a few gulps of water to get the whole mushroom down. He sat back and watched the fire as Grandfather continued drumming and chanting.

Kyle didn't feel anything at first, just centered. He became acutely aware of his surroundings…the fire crackling…the *pum-pum* of sticks against the tom-tom drums…Ray moving his arms like serpents… Shawna feverishly writing passages in a journal, the pen's black ink pouring across the page like her soul bleeding into words.

Shawna journaled?

Kyle knew so little about his sister. They had never been ones to share what was going on inside. Other than his late wife, Stephanie, who was the only person Kyle had ever let in, he had barely gotten to know anyone outside of his own mind. His private world had been his sanctuary, the characters of his novels his family and friends. *What a pathetic life I've been living.*

"That's all about to change," Grandfather spoke in their ancient language and somehow Kyle understood the words. The old man's eyes were fully alert and focused on Kyle. "Your life doesn't have to be pathetic."

"How did you read my thoughts?"

"We're all connected. Do you see it yet?"

"See what?"

"The cosmic field." Grandfather waved his hand across the air. It rippled like the surface of a pool.

Kyle scooted back. "Holy shit!"

Grandfather said, "Everything we see with our conscious minds is just an illusion. A material world made up of moving particles. See?" He held up his drumstick. It broke apart into a thousand tiny flying insects.

"You're freaking me out," Kyle said.

Shawna said, "There's nothing to be afraid of. Enjoy the magic carpet ride." She got up and walked over to a wall and did a tribal dance with her shadow, only her shadow was moving at a faster rhythm. Ray's and Grandfather's heads seemed to be shaking a hundred miles per hour.

Kyle closed his eyes and pressed his fingers against his temples. Kaleidoscopes of colored lights swirled in the darkness. A head shape-shifted into a dozen faces—Alex Winterbone, Dr. Norberg, Kyle, Shawna, Ray, Grandfather, Elkheart screaming a warrior's battle cry, the face of a demon…

BRIAN MORELAND

Kyle opened his eyes to discover he was sitting against the wall several feet away from the others. The walls warped. The floor seemed to undulate. Everything rippled outward as if he had plunged into a pool.

Shawna sat down in front of him. "Are you seeing visions yet?"

"Shit, yeah, everything looks distorted. Like I'm underwater." Kyle waved his arms through the liquid air. "I feel like I'm scuba diving."

"Fucking cool, isn't it?"

As the drumbeats softened, the watery ripples slowed down and the room stabilized.

"Your reality is going to shift and morph," Shawna said. "Everything is a message trying to tell you something. Think of it as feedback. If you don't like what you see, you have the power to shift your perception and watch how life changes."

"You make it sound simple."

"It is when you can get over your fears and start going for what you want."

"How did you become so wise?" Kyle asked.

Shawna laughed. "You think of me as wise?"

"Yes, I've always admired the way you see the world."

"What I've always loved about you, Kyle, is that you're successful working a career that you love. When we were kids you always talked about being a published author. I thought you were crazy because you'd rather stay up in your room writing than play outside with the rest of us, but you went after your dream and achieved it."

Kyle had never heard praise from his kid sister. He got a little misty-eyed and looked away.

She put a hand on his arm. "Hey, it's okay if we show a little emotion every now and then. We're family. I'm always going to love you know matter what, bro."

"Me too, Shawna. From now on, I'm going to be more present in your life. I love you, sis. Always have."

Now it was Shawna whose eyes filled with tears. "Thanks, it's good to hear that every once in a while. Okay, enough mushiness. Go have fun on your vision quest. Think of this land as a magic dream world. Play with it. Dance with it. Talk to the animals. Sing to the trees. Everything is your mirror."

"Okay, I will." Kyle blinked and Shawna was suddenly across the room, dancing again.

At the fire pit, Grandfather Two Hawks said, "We are all dream walkers. Souls searching to find our path home. The waking world is only a pinpoint of our true reality. These woods reflect our deepest desire and darkest fears. Whatever you see out here, keep your thoughts positive. Focus on someone you love." Grandfather opened a pouch and a swarm of bats flew up to the ceiling. "Take off your shirt, Kyle."

Grandfather dipped his fingers into a bowl of red paint and drew symbols on Kyle's chest and biceps. "These will call in your animal guides. Now, go to the forest and seek them."

Kyle stepped outside. The warm night embraced him. He gazed at the moonlit forest, trying to remember why it scared him. The tree limbs were perfectly still now and made him think of wise old men—the elders of the land watching over the village.

"What are my animal guides?" Kyle asked the trees.

The pine branches rustled. Thundering hooves echoed through the woods. He turned as a herd of elk entered the village. At least two dozen stout beasts. Several had broad antlers. As they surrounded Kyle, brushing up against him, he petted their fur. His intuition told him another time, hundreds of years ago, they had been his kin.

* * *

After Eric fell asleep, Jessica poured herself a glass of red wine and retreated to the cabin's balcony and peered through her telescope, but her mind was too distracted to search for constellations.

She stared at the engagement ring on her finger. A red ruby heart. The ring was a little too tight and constricted her finger. *Eric and I are engaged.* It all happened so fast. She had hoped that Eric would propose one day. And for the past year she had longed to hear him say that he loved her. Now that her two wishes had come true, Jessica felt like something wasn't right. She should be floating on air right now, giddy as the first time they kissed. What was wrong with her?

She sighed and sipped her wine.

The sound of running hooves disrupted her thoughts. She noticed deer gathering on the road at the center of the village. Her heart soared at the chance to see wildlife. She turned her telescope and peered into it. There was enough moonlight to make out the shapes of elk. And then she spotted Kyle standing in the center of the herd.

Jessica gasped. He was shirtless, petting the elk. Then the herd ran off into the forest, and Kyle vanished along with them.

* * *

Kyle raced among the elk, feeling alive and fearless. He weaved in between the pines, running at an impossible speed. The bulls bellowed and snorted. The many cows rubbed their furry flanks against him as they passed. Their heavy musk filled Kyle's nostrils. The herd led him down to the pond and stopped to drink. The surface was dark and glassy, reflecting the moon and stars. Frogs croaked. The forest sang with the chorus of cicadas and crickets.

The elk faced Kyle. He sensed that his father had run with this very herd on his vision quest. They shared the same animal spirit. The lead elk walked over and snorted. Kyle petted its forehead, staring into the eyes of a soul that he intuitively knew had once belonged to a great chief. As Kyle touched its massive antlers, he felt energy transferring into him, making him stronger, connecting him with his lineage. Images flashed through his mind of Cree warriors battling a beast in these woods over a century ago. Their death cries echoed inside his head, as their bodies were torn apart. Kyle pulled his hand away from the antler and the visions stopped.

The chief elk turned its head, snorted and stomped its hoof.

Animal grunts, like a pack of wild hogs, resonated from the forest. The elk scattered.

Tree branches cracked. Something was coming.

Kyle dove into the pond, plunging into cold water. He swam to the large boulder in the center and climbed to the top, shaking.

At the shadowy edges of the pines, a dozen dark figures surrounded the pond. They were too far away to make out much detail. Their faces were pitch-black. A strange hum resonated from their throats. Kyle felt them probing his mind, digging up memories long buried. He remembered seeing one of them before, when he was six. He had been walking along the village road by himself on a summer night. A thing that looked like a tall black scarecrow with stalk-like arms and legs had stood outside the village. Its long, claw-tipped finger had beckoned him to step into the woods. He had screamed and run all the way home. None of his family had believed what he'd seen. His mother had scorned him for speaking of such evils. He wouldn't go into the woods alone after that. Whether the beast had been real or not, it had shown up in his nightmares, compelling him to write his horrors into books.

Now several of those creatures were moving through the trees like wolves circling their prey. A malignant hatred radiated from them. Kyle got a sense that if the things could reach him, they would tear him apart. But for some reason they didn't come into the pond. One of them came to the water's edge. Its face rippled into his stepfather's, but with dark skin. It spoke in Blake Nelson's voice, "You think you can hide from me, you little sinner? I'll tan your hide if I ever catch you drawing demons again."

Kyle felt like a ten-year-old child again, hiding in the closet as Blake searched the house with a belt in his hand.

Another of the creatures spoke in Eric's voice, "I found him, Dad," and Kyle remembered the terror of seeing Eric holding open the closet door as Blake ripped Kyle from his hiding place. The creatures mimicked the sounds of a belt whipping and a child crying.

They're just hallucinations. Demons from my twisted imagination. "You're not real!" he yelled at them. He remembered Grandfather's words. *Whatever you see out here, keep your thoughts positive. Focus on someone you love.*

He closed his eyes and focused on his late wife. The time he felt most in love was on their honeymoon on Maui. He saw Stephanie talking and laughing as they drove the winding, curving road to Hana. But the memory wasn't working, because now the things were scratching at his brain, pulling up the tragic times. From across the pond Stephanie's voice said, "You should have died with me."

Don't let them get to you. Keep your thoughts positive.

He pictured Jessica's face—her blue eyes, the freckles on her nose, her Australian accent, the way her cheeks crinkled when she laughed. Stephanie was nothing but an angry ghost from his past, but Jessica was real. He imagined dating her, kissing her, making love to her. The feelings in his heart expanded outward like a cosmic wave.

When Kyle opened his eyes the beasts from his nightmares were gone. He felt invincible after facing his darkest fears. He had become one with everything—the earth, the trees, the rocks, the nocturnal animals that looked up as he passed. A night hawk fluttered up into the sky and his soul flew with it. His awareness soared over the evergreen canopy, the ponds, the mountains. In one bowl-shaped valley he saw a thick rainforest cloaked by clouds, the tips of pine conifers spearing upward. An iridescent-green luminance pulsed beneath the mist, resonating a heartbeat of a force that was older than old.

The hawk changed course, flying over the vast stretches of woods and fields that made up the reservation. Kyle saw the village below, Jessica alone on the balcony with her telescope. He laughed as his winged companion swooped downward into the forest behind the village. His awareness returned to his body. Now Kyle was charging between the trees. The spirit of elk flowed through his legs. His body tingled as he thought of the woman who had awakened every fiber of his being.

* * *

When Jessica came back downstairs, the cabin was dark and quiet. She could hear Eric snoring up in the loft. She still wasn't ready to go to bed. She poured herself another glass of wine.

Chaser whimpered at the back door, so she took him outside. As the dog sniffed the grass and relieved himself, Jessica sat on the back porch. Her fingers played with her new ring. Maybe she should have had sex with Eric tonight. That always made her feel more connected to him. So why did she turn him down? The problem was she couldn't imagine making love without kissing. That was the part she loved most, and Eric's poor lips were swollen and split. The two of them needed to do something romantic for their anniversary tomorrow because she feared her heart was drifting away. *All we need is some alone time. Tomorrow I'll spend the entire day with Eric.* And she would find a way to get in the mood to make love to him, even without kissing.

The Rottweiler perked up his ears and woofed.

"What is it, Chaser?"

The dog started barking and then dashed off into the forest.

Jessica ran into the grassy area. "Chaser!" She waited several minutes but the dog didn't return. Then she heard movement in the trees. The branches parted and Kyle stepped into the clearing.

Startled, Jessica took a step back. "Oh, my."

The moonlight illuminated the contours of his muscular body. He looked like some kind of Indian warrior with symbols painted on his chest and biceps. His hair was wild. He stared at Jessica with a lustful look in his eyes.

* * *

Kyle felt a primal lust when he spotted Jessica standing in the backyard. He didn't care that he she had come here with Eric. Kyle wanted her and felt no shame about it. He walked straight up to Jessica and kissed her on the lips, his mouth hungry to consume her. She breathed his name then kissed him back. There was hunger in her kiss, as well. A tremble in her hands as she touched his face. Their bodies embraced, tumbled to the ground. He lay on top of her, kissing her lips, her face, her throat.

His hands explored her body, squeezed her thighs. She kissed the side of his face, nibbled his ear. A fireball of heat built between them. The animal in Kyle had to have her. As he started to unbutton her shirt, Jessica grabbed his hands. "No, I can't. Stop, please, stop, I can't do this."

"Why not?"

"I'm with Eric."

"Do you love him?"

She paused. "He's your brother."

"I don't care. All I know is that I'm mad about you." He kissed her lips again and she succumbed for several seconds before pulling away again.

"No, this is wrong." She backed away from him. "I'm sorry. I can't do this. I'm engaged to Eric." She hurried into the cabin.

Engaged? Kyle grabbed his chest, feeling as if Jessica had ripped out his heart.

* * *

Jessica ran into the bathroom. Breathless, she flattened against the door as if trying to keep something from getting in. What had she done? She had lost all control. Never in her life had a man kissed her so ferociously. Part of her wanted to go back out there, let Kyle take her fully. Surrender to his rapture. She reached for the knob.

No, this is wrong! She thought of Eric sleeping upstairs, oblivious to his cheating girlfriend. *I promised to marry him.*

She looked at herself in the mirror. Her hair was speckled with grass. Her shirt unbuttoned, her bra exposed. She pulled her shirt closed. The ruby ring sparkled on her finger, mocking her. She held it to her chest and cried.

Chapter Fifteen

So far Shawna's vision quest had been the wildest trip of her life. She'd done acid, coke, heroin, shrooms and weed, but never with a medicine man. The entire night had been mind blowing. Grandfather had spoken Cree words that made her brain fizz like a shaken can of Red Bull. Then he'd done some kind of healing on her that made her body levitate.

Now, she was running up the road, giggling. She climbed the main cabin's porch steps and peered through a window. Zack was lying on the couch, reading a novel. Shawna looked around the room to make sure he was alone, then tapped on the glass.

Zack looked up from his book. He gave her a funny look and came out onto the porch. "Hey, sunshine, what are you doing here?"

She pulled him against her and kissed him. "I am so hot for you right now."

He pulled back. "Whoa, are you on X?"

"Something even better." She held up a bag of shrooms. "Ready to have some fun?"

Zack looked back into the den. "Not with your brothers around. They'll kill me."

"Then go get your sleeping bag," she said, kissing him seductively. "We're sleeping under the stars tonight."

* * *

Kyle walked alone down the village road. Every part of his body felt as if it were caving in, his bones compressing his insides. The tree branches scraped against the hollow cabins. He heard rattling, like the sound of a mystic shaking a can of bones. He saw a black scarecrow-shaped creature standing at the edge of the road, a long curved finger summoning him into the woods. It was there and then it wasn't.

There are many tricksters here that draw power from your fears, Grandfather had once told him.

Kyle tried to think positive but there was too much pain in his heart.

He was such a fool to believe that Jessica would leave Eric for him.

You belong only to me, whispered the wind. *You promised, remember?*

The vision shifted. Kyle saw himself standing at a tombstone, promising he'd never love anyone else. That eventually he'd find a way to meet his wife on the other side. A pact with a ghost who couldn't let go.

Or was it Kyle who couldn't let go?

He remembered the lonely nights spent in his apartment, contemplating suicide.

We can be together again, spoke Stephanie's voice.

He looked at the edge of the road. Now it was his wife's hunched specter that stood there, the trees visible through her head and body. *We can journey through these woods forever.*

"Leave me alone." He walked faster.

Don't turn your back on me, Kyle.

The pines began to pop and stretch, branches curving over his head. Vines snaked along the road. Long limbs with wooden claws reached for him. He sprinted into the Great House. It was empty now, except for sleeping bags and backpacks. Where were the others? The fire at the center had dwindled to glowing embers.

I've got to get back to the cabin. Kyle dressed and grabbed his backpack. He could come back for the sleeping bags tomorrow. He started for the door.

Branches and vines came in through all the windows, breaking glass. More foliage clotted the skylight. The long room darkened. Kyle ran to the far corner, hiding in the shadows. Twisted roots and creeping vines slithered toward him along the floor and walls, protruding like sickly veins across a junkie's skin.

"Stop! Stop!" he yelled.

The roots stopped within feet of him.

Clump-scraaaape echoed from the darkness.

Kyle dumped out the contents of his backpack. Flipped on his flashlight.

Clump-scraaaape...

He aimed the beam.

Moving toward him was the hunched corpse of his wife, dragging her broken leg.

* * *

At a campsite in the woods, Zack sat on his sleeping bag, feeling like he'd found Nirvana after eating a mushroom. He smiled as Shawna danced naked by a campfire. She moved with the fluidity of a belly dancer. The tattooed vines on her arms spread leafy tendrils across her body. Her purple fairy wings flapped on her back as she teased Zack with her pixie charms. Feeling as horny as the goat-legged god Pan, he pulled his little wood nymph onto the sleeping bag. He sucked her pierced nipples and kissed his way down to the fiery sun that circled her navel.

"Zack?" She tapped his back.

"Yes, sunshine?"

"What's that shed for?"

He looked across the campfire at the long gray shack. "How would I know?" He returned to kissing her belly.

"Does anybody live in there?"

"I doubt it. There aren't any windows."

"Will you please check? It's freaking me out."

Zack stood and walked around the fire pit, feeling pine needles pricking the bottoms of his feet. He opened the double doors. A god-awful smell of a wet dead animal smacked his senses. He pinched his nose and peered inside. The campfire only lit up the front half. He could hear flies buzzing toward the back, probably nesting in a dead raccoon.

"It's an empty shed." He closed the doors, not wanting the reek to reach Shawna. She was already edgy about camping outdoors.

Zack hopped back over and landed on his side next to her. "Now where were we?"

She smiled. "I believe you were heading south."

* * *

As Zack's mouth pleasured Shawna, her moans rippled through the forest. And then her whole body shuddered. When she felt the next wave coming, she said, "Hurry. I want you inside me."

They merged like wild animals in heat. Shawna cried out as Zack penetrated the deepest part of her. She ran her fingers through his hair, kissed his face, hugged him tight against her. Their bodies moved together, faster and faster. As she yelled out in ecstasy, she felt a hard impact against her shoulder and wetness splatter her face. Shawna opened her eyes and screamed. Blood dribbled down Zack's face.

An axe blade had split the top of his head.

Chapter Sixteen

At the Great House, Kyle hunkered in the corner. "Stay away from me!"

Stephanie looked the same as the night she had flown through the windshield of their car. Her face was full of glass. A flap of skin hung over her head, exposing her bloody cranium. A sharp bone stabbed upward through her broken leg.

Kyle snapped his eyes shut. Her nails grazed his cheek. When he opened his eyes, his wife was still standing several feet away.

"You should have died with me."

"I know."

"We made a pact to stay together forever."

"I know."

"You promised to love no other woman but me."

Kyle nodded, spinning the wedding ring around his finger.

"You can cross over to me right here, right now."

"How?"

"The answer is at your feet."

He looked down at a bottle of sleeping pills that had fallen out of his backpack. He twisted the cap open. At least forty pills.

"You can escape into a new dream with me." Stephanie was whole again, as beautiful as the day they had collected seashells together on the Maui beach. "You can wake up in my arms."

More than anything he wanted to return to the sanctuary she had provided.

He stared into the darkness of his mind. Stephanie, lying on a bed, was hooked to a life-support system. Tubes entered her nose and mouth. An IV fed into her wrist. An EKG monitor beeped. Kyle was sitting beside her, watching Steph sleep. Her face was bruised and swollen. Bandages covered her head where they had stitched her scalp back together. Kyle held his wife's slender wrist, feeling its weakening pulse.

Stephanie's eyes had opened slowly. "Ky..."

"Don't," he had said. "You need your strength."

A tear rolled down her cheek. "Kyle...keep going."

"No, stay with me."

She managed a small smile. "Keep going." Then his wife's eyes closed for the last time.

Now Kyle's eyes snapped open, tears streaming down his face. He studied the pills in his hand.

"What are you waiting for, Kyle?"

Keep going. He had said those words to her when they were hiking and she was too tired to go any farther. Whenever publishers and agents had rejected his books over and over, Stephanie had said those two magical words. *Keep going.*

He looked up at the specter standing across from him. "You're not her."

"What?" Her face began to darken.

Kyle smiled. "You're not Stephanie."

Her ghost shape-shifted back to a disfigured face. "Of course I am." Her eyes were evil, not like Stephanie's eyes at all.

"My Steph would have never wanted me to give up."

"I am your wife! You made a pact to stay with me forever."

"You're nothing but a figment of my own guilt!" Kyle hurled the bottle of sleeping pills across the room. The ghost that had been impersonating his wife wailed like a banshee as it was sucked back into the darkness.

* * *

Shawna woke to a horrible stench. She was lying on a damp mattress. The stink of it made her gag. Flies landed on her naked body. *Where am I?*

Her eyes slowly came back into focus. A ceiling and walls made of gray wood.

The shed...

One of the double doors was open and she could see half of the campfire crackling outside. On the other side of the closed door a man was humming and making scraping sounds.

Shawna sat up and felt metal biting into her wrists. She was chained to the walls. She screamed, shaking the chains, trying to rip them loose.

Three wolf dogs ran into the shed, growling.

She froze and held her breath.

The other door opened and Ray Roamingbear stuck his head in. "Ah, sunshine's finally awake." He looked down at his dogs. "Arok, Kiche,

Maskwa." They wagged their tails. He made clicking sounds with his tongue and then threw out some scraps of meat. The three wolf dogs ran outside, eating and growling.

"Arok, share." Ray looked back at Shawna. "Sometimes they have such bad manners." The tall Indian stepped into the shed, ducking his head. He carried a large blood-stained knife.

Shawna recoiled to the back wall, trembling.

Ray approached her without his usual limp. He sat down on a small stool at the foot of the mattress, scraping the blade against a flat stone and humming.

Crying and quivering, Shawna lost control of her bladder and urinated on the red-stained mattress.

Ray cocked his head. "Ah, now look at the mess you made." He grinned and waved it off. "It's not like it's the first time that's happened. I keep meaning to swap that old thing out, but it's a mighty long way to drag a mattress and the trees just tear it up anyway."

Shawna had to be hallucinating from a bad shroom trip. Zack couldn't be dead. But her mind couldn't get rid of the image of the axe splitting his skull. Tears streamed down her cheeks. "Please, Ray...don't hurt me."

"Don't worry, sunshine, you're worth more to me alive."

She covered her nude body as best she could.

"I'm not going to fuck you either. I have somebody else in mind to be my plaything." He scraped the blade. "That's the arrangement, you see. I bring girls to them, and they let me pick out the cherries for myself."

They?

His dark eyes traced her body. "Now I do I like your skin. All those pretty tattoos. So I'm hoping one day they'll let me have it for my collection. Your boyfriend sure has some nice tats." He reached into a fur pouch tied to his hip and pulled out a long bloody flap of skin. It was covered in skull tattoos.

Shawna bent over the side of the mattress and vomited. Then she buried her face in her hands and cried until she was numb.

The wolf dogs began barking outside. Distant howls echoed in the forest.

Ray turned on his stool. "They're getting close now. Should be here any minute." He stood. "Well, I best be going. I'm sure I'll see you around one way or another." He stepped outside and bird-whistled his dogs. "Get away from there. You know better." They yipped and circled Ray as he pulled a chain over a branch. Zack's naked body swung into view. His back and arms had been skinned, the red muscle beneath glistening in the firelight. Blood dribbled down his bare buttocks and legs.

Shawna screamed then started balling.

"Your boyfriend's nothing but meat now, sunshine." Outside, Ray poured water over the campfire. Soon he and the dogs were just silhouettes in the moonlight. His tall form walked out of view and the three smaller shapes followed. Their footsteps crunched over dried leaves. Ray's humming voice trailed off.

Shawna jerked at her chains. One of the wall brackets hung by a loose bolt, but the other held tight. The shackles cut into her wrists. She stretched for a shovel that was against the wall, but her fingers barely touched it. "Goddamn it!" She collapsed in defeat.

Sounds in the distance, like crows cackling. And then came laughs that sounded like hyenas.

Shawna watched the doorway for several minutes.

The ground rumbled with a stampede of running feet.

No...

Claws raked the shed's outside walls. She yelped.

Some kind of animal leaped onto the roof. There was a *thump-thump-thump* as the thing's weight caused the wood planks above her head to buckle.

Shawna swallowed her urge to scream. And then she saw shadow shapes of things with long stalk-like legs and arms moving outside the doorway. They attacked Zack's hanging body in a frenzy. Shawna clamped her ears at the feasting sounds. Other creatures fought one another at the shed's entrance. One of them pushed back the others, shrieking. And then it stooped. A monstrous head peered in at her with luminous white eyes.

She screamed as its long arm stretched out and touched her.

* * *

In the Great House, Kyle sat on his bedroll by the fire, twirling the gold band around his finger. The lucid, dreamlike effects of the purple mushroom he'd eaten were finally wearing down, his senses returning to normal. The roots and vines that had invaded the building were gone. So was the ghost of his late wife. Kyle knew by the lightness in his chest that he was forever changed.

He couldn't believe that he had kissed Jessica. He smiled just thinking about it. He had to admit that for a few magical moments she had kissed him back with equal passion. He relished the memory of it, but didn't know how he was going to face her tomorrow. She must have thought he was a lunatic, grabbing her and kissing her like that.

And then he thought of Stephanie. The shroom journey just brought her to the surface so he could finally deal with her and move on. He slid his wedding ring halfway off his finger and then stopped. He wasn't ready. A part of him still loved her. He slid the ring back on.

Part Six

The Killing Ground

There are many challenges I face being in love with a ghost, my limited ability to touch her being the least of them. The hardest part is that my beloved experienced a brutal death, in a darkened wood off Old Blevins Road, an offshoot of a desolate highway that runs through the Smokey Mountains of Kentucky. What Elena experienced there shattered her soul and left her with a rage so fierce, she is compelled to haunt her killer and walk his killing ground among the sticks.

—Detective Alex Winterbone

Chapter Seventeen

The next morning, Kyle retreated to the back porch with his computer and a chocolate banana smoothie. Chaser came out with him and ran after a squirrel. Kyle smiled. There was a lightness in his chest that he hadn't felt in years. The sun was peeking over the mountains. White butterflies swooped and swirled over the grass and wildflowers. Birds were singing in the trees. For the first time since he arrived, Kyle understood why he had sensed the woods were watching. The reservation land held the spirits of his ancestors. He remembered running with the herd of elk, his legs moving faster than humanly possible. Had that really happened? He had faced his darkest childhood nightmares and confronted his guilt over Stephanie's death. And somewhere in the middle of last night's wild journey, he and Jessica had kissed passionately. He was curious to see how she was going to behave around him this morning.

Kyle noticed Grandfather sitting in his rocker at the far end of the porch, staring at the forest. His lips were moving as if in conversation with a ghost, but Kyle saw no one there. "Good morning, Grandfather."

The old man looked his way.

Kyle walked over to him and touched his frail hand. "Thank you for last night's ceremony. It was the most amazing thing I've ever experienced."

Grandfather spoke in Cree and Kyle remembered how while under the influence of the purple mushroom he had been able to understand the ancient language.

We are all dream walkers. Souls searching to find our path home. The waking world is only a pinpoint of our true reality.

Kyle wished he could understand his grandfather. He had so many questions, like were last night's visions real or hallucinations? Did the truth even matter? Everything he saw and touched was real enough and today he felt like a new man.

He sat down at a table and opened his laptop. He couldn't wait to start writing again. He typed fast, the words flowing across the screen. He finished a chapter and started another. The story was taking shape and he could begin to see now how the book would end. In an attempt to save Elena, Alex Winterbone was going to cross over into the spirit realm and battle the Hollowers.

The back door opened, disrupting Kyle's concentration. Jessica and Eric stepped out.

"'Morning, Stephen King," Eric said in a condescending tone. "Writing another ghost story?"

"Yeah." Part of Kyle wanted to make a crack about Eric's swollen black eye and busted lip, but he held back. He made brief eye contact with Jessica. She looked away. Her sudden shyness told him that last night's kiss had really happened.

Eric grinned, putting his arm around her shoulder. "Today Jess and I are celebrating our one-year anniversary. We also have a big announcement. Babe, show Kyle your engagement ring."

She held out her hand, but wouldn't meet Kyle's eyes.

He barely gave the ring a glance. "Congratulations," he said bitterly. "You two are perfect for each other."

Eric took Jessica's hand, and the two walked down the village road with Chaser running alongside them.

Feeling angry, Kyle watched them. What had he expected? That Jessica would break up with Eric to be with him? That his brother would go along with Kyle dating her? He cursed himself for crossing a line last night. No matter how strongly he felt about Jessica, she would never be his.

Kyle tried to focus back on his novel. As much as Winterbone loved the Elena character, he was going to lose her by the end of the story. That was the fate of Kyle's ghost detective. He always walked alone.

Unable to concentrate on writing, Kyle went back inside the cabin and headed to his father's study. He needed to get his mind on something other than Jessica and the hole he now felt in his heart. He continued to search for clues as to what might have happened to his father. The study had the atmosphere of a long-forgotten museum storage room. A wall of bookshelves was crowded with books and relics Elkheart had collected over the years. A career of leading expeditions around the world had brought his father full circle back to the reservation. What kind of research had Elkheart been doing?

On the desk sat the old IBM typewriter his father used to write books. Kyle sat in the duck-taped roller chair and went through all the desk drawers again. Leaning back in the chair, he spotted a wadded-up piece of paper on the floor underneath a curio cabinet. He had to get down on his hands and knees to reach it. He opened the paper. The heading read, *Macâya Forest Expedition*. A typed checklist followed of camping supplies, guns and ammo. Another column listed the names of the research team, including Amy Hanson. Four of the names were identified as mercenaries. *That's strange.* Elkheart had hired guides for his expositions, drivers, even bodyguards a time or two, but mercenaries? And why exploring Macâya Forest had he thought he needed hired guns?

Kyle made a quick decision and began filling his backpack full of gear and provisions. He also grabbed one of his father's deer rifles and a box of ammo. Wearing a pack and rifle slung over one shoulder, he stepped outside just as Eric and Jessica were returning from their walk.

"Where are you off to?" Eric asked.

Kyle told them about finding Elkheart's expedition supply list. "I believe there's a chance he and his team are camping in Macâya Forest. I'm hiking there to see if I can find them."

Eric said, "I'm going with you."

Jessica said, "Me too."

"Have either of you seen Zack and Shawna?"

"They're probably still in bed." Eric went into the cabin to check, leaving Kyle and Jessica alone together.

After a moment of awkward silence, she said, "We need to talk about last night."

"There's nothing to talk about. I was totally out of integrity. You're Eric's fiancée. From now on, I'm going to respect that."

"Kyle, I just want you to understand—"

The back door opened and Eric stepped onto the porch. "They're not up in their room or anywhere in the cabin."

"Have either of you seen them since last night?" Kyle asked.

Jessica shook her head. "They never came back."

Eric said, "I bet they spent the night in one of the other cabins."

Kyle walked to the village road and called for Shawna and Zack but got no response. He checked his watch. Already nine a.m. "I really want to get an early start."

"Well, leave it to Shawna…" Eric muttered. "They're probably getting stoned or something."

Kyle said, "You two pack some lunches. I'll go look for them." He walked around the perimeter of the village and called their names over and over. He searched for thirty minutes, checking the Great House, the barn and every run-down cabin, but neither Shawna nor Zack were in them.

Worried now, Kyle met up with Eric and Jessica at the main cabin's back porch. They both had on backpacks, and Eric carried a second deer rifle strapped over his shoulder.

"They must have camped out in the woods," Kyle said, annoyed that his sister had wandered off without telling anyone or leaving a note. Angry at himself for going to bed last night without checking to make sure they had returned safely.

Jessica looked concerned, as well. "Should I stay back and wait for them?"

Eric tugged her elbow. "No, we're spending the day together, remember?"

Kyle said, "Let's just start hiking. Hopefully, we'll run into them."

* * *

They reached Kakaskitewak Swamp by midmorning. Kyle and Eric paddled a canoe across the black water, while Jessica and Chaser sat between them. As the canoe reached the opposite bank, the Rottweiler hopped out and started sniffing and marking his territory. Kyle studied the strange animal skulls that lined the trees like macabre totem poles.

Jessica raised her Nikon and snapped photos. "What are those?"

Kyle said, "Warnings from our ancestors not to venture past this point."

"Lovely." She looked back at Eric. "Are you guys sure about this?"

"Hell yeah," Eric said. "I've been curious about this place since I was a kid."

"But what about Ray's warning?" she asked.

Kyle said, "I'm not afraid of superstitions." He helped his brother pull the canoe onto the shore. They grabbed their backpacks and rifles. Kyle slung one over his shoulder. Slapping at mosquitoes biting his neck, he sloshed through black mud to the row of totem poles. The vibe they gave off was a steady hum inside his head. One pine was decorated with a dozen small, bleached-white animal skulls. Each had tiny sharp teeth, possibly raccoons or possums. At the top of the column was an elk skull with long antlers.

Use your gift, spoke Winterbone's voice.

Kyle touched the elk skull and concentrated on his father. In his mind flashed images of an expedition team climbing out of two canoes and observing these totems. A couple of videographers stood at the shore, filming their arrival. A pretty young blonde, who must have been Amy Hanson, walked at Elkheart's side. They looked at one another in a way that suggested their relationship was more than professor and student. His father was armed with a black assault rifle. There was an older man with glasses whom Kyle figured was the other professor who had gone missing. The expedition team wore heavy backpacks with tents and bedrolls. A squad of four soldiers, each one toting an automatic rifle, escorted the scientists and cameramen as they disappeared into the thorny pines.

Kyle released his hand, wondering what had happened to his father's team. Had they paid dearly for crossing the sacred border? A few feet from the shore, he spotted a second canoe hidden away in the foliage. He began to get a bad vibe about what they might encounter beyond the pines. "Maybe you guys should wait at the dock. I can go the rest of the way on my own."

"Forget that." Eric aimed his rifle at the forest as if targeting a deer. "We came all this way. We're going in."

Kyle gripped his rifle and stepped past the totem poles. Jessica followed, swatting at mosquitoes. Eric brought up the rear as they wove between the trees, the mud sucking at their boots. Chaser ran ahead of them. They hiked in silence for a hundred yards and then the swamp ended and a hill descended into a vine-choked rainforest. Climbing down beside a waterfall, Kyle's adrenaline surged at the thought of finding his father.

* * *

Rocks tumbled down as Jessica descended the hill. Kyle reached up and helped her the last few feet. She hopped to the ground and stumbled, falling against his chest. The feel of him against her caused her heart to sputter.

"You okay?" he asked her.

"Fine." She looked away so he wouldn't see she was nervous, more from his presence than the forest. The entire journey here Kyle had not made eye contact or spoken directly to her once. She wished she could talk with him about last night, explain that Eric had sprung this proposal on to her suddenly, and that she was still processing it all. Deep down, she wasn't sure if she could follow through with marrying Eric. If she had had doubts before, kissing Kyle last night had thrown her into a state of utter confusion. She had tossed and turned all night. She needed time to think, to journal her feelings, but now she felt pressure from both brothers, and she was afraid of hurting either one of them.

Eric stepped between Jessica and Kyle. "Let's take a break. I'm getting one bitch of a blister." He plopped down on a log and pulled off his boot.

Kyle leaned against a tree, looking off into the woods. He drank from his water bottle.

Jessica sat next to Eric and munched on a granola bar. She caught Kyle staring at her engagement ring. He looked into her eyes and she saw they were filled with disappointment and questions.

Eric stuck out his bare foot. "Babe, you got something for that?"

She dug into her pack and pulled out a small first-aid kit. She swabbed Melalueca cream on the blister and then wrapped a Band-Aid around his toe.

"Thanks, Jess." When they stood up, Eric pulled her to him and gave her a firm kiss.

"What was that for?" she asked.

"For being such an amazing fiancée."

"Let's keep moving." Kyle pulled out a machete and entered the forest first, whacking at hanging branches.

Jessica followed. As the sunny day darkened, she had the sense they had just stepped through a time portal where the morning turned quickly to dusk. Underneath the canopy there were more shadows than patches of light. A drifting fog hid some of the trees. Jessica hovered close to Kyle, occasionally touching his back. When she glanced back to make sure Eric was keeping up, she could barely see him in the gloom. Those new boots were really giving him problems.

It got so dark they had to turn on their flashlights. But it was only eleven a.m.

Chaser kept venturing off and Jessica called him back. "Stay with us, boy." She wished they had put him on a leash.

Ahead of her, using his light and machete, Kyle followed the overgrown trail through the rainforest. The damp shirt that clung to his back was already stained with green smudges. Jessica shined her own light back and forth. Creeper vines spiraled up the trees like leafy veins.

The giant pines—several over a hundred feet tall—towered above them like ancient gods. Much of the forest floor was covered in damp ferns and mossy-green rocks and logs.

Kyle stopped. "Guys, hold up."

"What is it?" Jessica asked.

He looked around. His flashlight beam probed the thick vegetation. "Do you guys hear that?"

"What?" Eric asked.

"Dead silence," Kyle said. "No insects buzzing. No birds singing. This forest doesn't seem to have any animal life."

Eric snorted. "You're letting your imagination run away again."

"He's got a point," Jessica said. "The mosquitoes stopped biting the moment we came in here." She shone her light across wet leaves. "You'd think this place would be croaking with tree frogs."

Kyle kicked over a log. "No creepy crawlies either."

Jessica turned over another stone. "Bloody weird, is what it is."

Eric said, "I'm sure we'll come across plenty of animals. In fact, be on the lookout for bears and wild boar."

"Oh, that makes me want to keep going." Jessica groaned.

"Don't worry, babe. I've hunted just about every kind of animal. Most run away before you even see them."

Kyle pulled the rifle off his shoulder and continued down the winding trail. As they hiked another ten minutes, not once did Jessica hear a bird, see an animal, or get bit by a mosquito. Nothing but plants and fungus seemed to thrive inside this forest.

* * *

A light rain began to fall on the leaves and branches. Kyle put on his windbreaker and pulled the hood over his head. Macâya Forest reminded him of a rainforest he had explored in Costa Rica. While that jungle had teemed with exotic wildlife—giant blue butterflies, monkeys, sloths, toucans and poison frogs of every color—this forest teemed with spirits. He sensed them watching from the shadows, even saw a few ghostly faces before they vanished into the mist. Some had Cree features. Others were white men from an earlier time. Kyle remembered the legend about Hagen Thorpe and the dozen lumberjacks who had come into these woods over a hundred and thirty years ago. All but Hagen had been slain by a beast hiding in a glowing green fog.

The Macâya is just a legend, Kyle reminded himself. Still his imagination conjured a creature with enormous claws. As if to heighten his fear, the ghost of a man whose face had been slashed off crossed the path in front of Kyle. He fought back the urge to run.

Just stay calm, Winterbone said. *You're walking through a death pocket.*

What the hell's a death pocket? Kyle asked, grateful to hear the voice of his old friend.

A vortex where lost souls get trapped, like poltergeists haunting a house.

Kyle swallowed. *Are these spirits dangerous?*

Only if you fear them. Fear is like a doorway into your mind.

Kyle did his best to ignore the specters that moved just outside his flashlight beam. Eric and Jessica were oblivious, of course. When he asked them if they had seen anything strange, they both confirmed that all they saw were endless trees and plants. Kyle envied them for being blind to the spirit world.

A strong vibration pulsed up ahead. *We're getting close to the heart of the forest.* Kyle thought of his father leading his expedition team along this path. What had they been after? Elkheart had traveled the world to nearly every mysterious site imaginable—the pyramids of Central and South America, Egypt, and the ancient temples of Cambodia. What mystery did Macâya Forest hide that caused Elkheart to explore this long-forgotten place?

The trail ended at a cave at the base of a mountain. The strange vibration that sent pulses across Kyle's skin resonated from somewhere deep within that black chasm. All three huddled at the cave's entrance and shined their lights into its maw. Green lichen covered the walls and ivy grew over what appeared to be man-made crossbeams. A metal track ran down the center of the tunnel's dirt floor, disappearing into darkness.

"Well, I'll be damned," Kyle said. "An old mine shaft."

Jessica said, "Like the copper mines we saw on the flight over."

"Yeah. This one was probably abandoned in the 1800s."

Eric looked disappointed. "Dad hiked all this way on a top-secret expedition for this?"

"What were you expecting?" Kyle asked.

"Something more exotic, like an undiscovered pyramid."

Kyle laughed. "In Canada?" He shook his head.

His brother ducked under the dangling ivy and peered into the shaft.

"Hey, what are you doing?" Kyle asked.

"What does it look like? I'm going to see where it leads." Eric ventured into the cave. "You guys coming?"

Jessica shook her head. "I don't do caves. You boys have at it, but please stay where I can see you." Chaser stayed beside her.

Kyle hated any kind of tight spaces, especially dark ones. The thought of entering the mine shaft caused his throat to close up. But he didn't want to look like a coward in front of Jessica, so he stepped into the tunnel's dark mouth and hurried to catch up with his brother. They walked side by side, probing the glistening green walls with the beams of their flashlights.

Purple mushrooms with sparkling crystals grew on either side of the railcar tracks.

The ceremonial shrooms. Kyle suspected that Ray Roamingbear ventured in here more than he let on. Perhaps Grandfather, too, in his younger days. Kyle wondered what other secrets his elders were keeping. Something compelling enough for his father to bring an expedition team into these forbidden woods. One question nagged at Kyle. Why had the team brought along mercenaries with heavy assault rifles? Did his father believe that the legendary Macâya existed? Many of the mushrooms had been crushed by boots. Elkheart's team had explored this shaft. After twenty yards the tunnel curved. The muddy ground sloped downward into what seemed an infinite abyss.

Kyle glanced back at the entrance. It looked far away now. "I think we've gone far enough."

Eric kept exploring, testing the ground and crossbeams every few feet. "It's still pretty sturdy."

"You know those stories you read about people who get lost in caves? I'd really prefer that not be us."

"Kyle, don't be such a chicken shit."

"This is no time to bust my balls. Seriously, without caving equipment this is dangerous."

"Check this out." Eric pulled a torch off the wall. It smelled of fresh kerosene.

"Someone's been here recently." He lit the end of the torch with a lighter. The flame pushed back the shadows.

"I think Dad was here," Kyle said.

Eric cupped a hand around his mouth and yelled, "Elkheart!" His voice echoed in the hollow passage. They waited for a response. The vibration down below intensified.

Kyle got a gnawing feeling in his stomach. And then he heard distant cries, like tortured souls screaming up from hell. He grabbed his brother's arm. "We need to get out of here."

"Why?" Eric hadn't heard the voices.

The malevolent cries sounded like they were moving closer.

"Come on, Eric!"

"Just a little farther." He walked a few more feet, challenging the darkness with his torch. "Elkheart, are you down there?"

Kyle heard the echoes of running boots approaching. "Do you hear *that*?"

Eric turned around. "Hear what?" And then a specter passed right through him and dashed past Kyle, grazing him with frosty air.

Eric doubled over, gripping his chest and coughing. "What the fuck was that?"

Kyle rushed over to him. "You okay?"

"Yeah, just freezing. Fuck." Eric was shaking violently as if he'd just been pulled out of icy water.

"Let's get out of here." Kyle threw his brother's arm over his shoulder and walked him toward the exit. As they rounded the curve, Kyle nearly choked on his own breath. At the mouth of the mine shaft, standing in the limelight, was the ghost of a man from his father's expedition.

* * *

Shawna woke in a silent scream. She could still see fragments of her nightmare as they fluttered back into reality like a swarm of bats. She had dreamed she was drifting in total darkness, her body naked and open, while unseen claws and appendages ravaged every inch of her. The beast's hideous mouth had drooled onto her face, and she had screamed as saliva oozed down her cheeks like slimy tears.

Fully conscious now, Shawna searched for the nightmare that had brought her here. Was it finally gone? The stone chamber was dark except for one corner where flames crackled on a torch. Water constantly dripped down mossy walls.

She lay on her side in a muddy puddle, half her hair and face soaked. Filthy liquid seeped into her mouth. She spat, coughing. She felt her body. She was naked and shivering. Pain spiraled through her pelvis and legs as she tried to raise herself. She managed to half-sit, half-lie against a mossy wall. Her body was covered in cuts and bruises. The worst pain burned between her legs. The area felt raw and full of fire. She folded her legs against her chest, arms clinging around her knees, her buttocks submerged in a cold puddle.

Images of last night flashed through her mind. She couldn't believe Zack was dead. Torn apart and eaten by those things. And then one of them chose her. She sobbed. All she wished for now was an instant death. There was no point in living. No sanity to go home to. She searched for something sharp to cut her wrists, but there was nothing.

What now then? Wait until the beast returned? *I've got to get away.* She crawled toward a doorway that opened into a passage.

A groaning sound, like a sleeping bear, issued from above.

She froze.

Across the chamber, she spotted several dark crevices in the wall, like catacombs. In one of them something stirred. A head lifted. The thing glared down at her with glowing white eyes.

Shawna retreated back to her corner, pulling her legs tight against her body. She buried her face in her hands and muffled her sobs. *Fuck, I'm going to die down here.* And then she heard a distant voice echoing from some far off chamber. Shawna looked up. A man's voice was calling down. Someone to rescue her! Her hope was shattered by an angry growl. The beast climbed down from the catacombs and loped past her, shrieking down the tunnel.

* * *

In Macâya Forest, Kyle hurried back up the path with Eric and Jessica following.

"Where are you going?" Eric yelled.

"Just follow me." Kyle could see the ghost walking up ahead. It was the old professor, his father's partner. Kyle recognized him from his visions of the expedition team hiking into this forest. One of the lenses of his glasses was cracked and he had claw marks on his forehead. He veered off the path, waving for Kyle to follow him into the jungle.

As Kyle ventured into the dense foliage, Eric grabbed his shoulder and spun him around. "What's gotten into you? Are you nuts?"

Kyle squared off against Eric. "Do you want to know what happened to Dad? Then shut up and follow me." He pulled out the machete and kept walking.

"You've really lost it this time!"

Not looking back, Kyle whacked at branches, carving a new path with the machete. A moment later, he heard leaves slapping as his brother and Jessica followed. Chaser ran ahead, barking, as if he also saw the ghost. Another strange vibration pulsed from somewhere in the thicket. The rainforest brightened somewhat as the clouds above the treetops parted. Ten feet ahead, the ghost of the professor passed effortlessly through the brush. He was wearing a green parka that had wide slashes across the back of it. Kyle could see deep gashes in his flesh, and part of his spine. He wished the man would speak, but like Nina Whitefeather, the professor remained mute. He moved swiftly through the forest, urging Kyle to keep up. Kyle chopped his way through crisscrossing branches. He waded knee-deep across a stream to a wide clearing. He climbed the grassy bank and halted at the base of a campground that had been ravaged—shredded tents and backpacks, scattered pots and pans and clothing. Spatters of blood stained everything.

Kyle stumbled at the sight of the mutilated camp. His heart clenched.

Jessica said, "Oh, my God."

A garbled sound was all Kyle's throat could summon. He was tearing up, assuming the worst. He searched the refuse. An old campfire was nothing but damp ash. Dozens of empty brass cartridges covered the ground. There weren't any bodies. Just the violent aftermath of what must have been an animal attack.

"Shit, they're all dead," Eric said. "Every one of them."

"He's gone," was all Kyle could say as he collapsed to his knees.

* * *

Eric placed his hand on Kyle's shoulder. They had traveled all the way from Seattle only to discover that their father had been killed. Eric didn't know what to feel. His father had been dead to him for twenty years.

He rummaged through the campsite for any research that might have been left behind. Oddly, there were no journals or computers. No notes of any kind. No video cameras either. Who would have taken them? The attack appeared to have been by a large savage animal. Or perhaps a pack of them. Wild boars? Hungry wolves? Or some kind of anomaly that all the other animals feared? Where were the bodies? He looked under the torn nylon tents. All he found were shredded sleeping bags.

Eric stood and concentrated on a wall of foliage. Seeing a trail of bloody clothes, he stepped a few feet into the jungle and the ground fell out from under him.

He dropped several feet and landed in the mud at the bottom of a dark hole.

Up above, Kyle and Jessica called his name.

"Down here!"

Their heads peered over the edge about twelve feet up. Kyle said, "Holy shit! Are you okay?"

"I think so." He sat up. "It's dark as hell down here."

"You've fallen into a sink hole," Kyle said. "Don't panic. We're gonna get you out."

"Did you break any bones?" Jessica asked.

He rubbed his ankles and legs. "No. I'm okay. Fortunately I landed on a mound of mud." It was then that he noticed the odor. He put a hand over his nose. "God, it stinks down here."

Kyle lay on his stomach, reaching down his hands. "See if you can climb."

Eric stood, examining the mud walls. Water trickled from above, making tiny waterfalls. He grabbed a few twisted roots and started climbing, but they snapped and he slid back down. He kept trying, the tips of his fingers almost touching Kyle's, and then the last of the big roots broke and Eric landed on his ass in the mud. "Shit!"

"Hold tight," Kyle said. "We'll look for some rope."

Eric sat back against the earth wall. He turned on his flashlight and probed the darkness with his beam. The sink hole was actually a tunnel that ran in two directions. This one was different than the mine shaft. There were no metal tracks, just a muddy floor. The tunnel looked like something a giant mole would have burrowed. He walked in the direction of the foul odor, holding his forearm over his mouth and nose. His beam spotlighted several deep impressions in the mud as if someone had been exploring down here. He came across someone's boot. Then a bloody shirt. Then another boot with a shard of bone sticking out of it. "Oh, fuck." Swallowing hard, he raised the flashlight. His beam shone across a large pile of bloody bones.

Eric backpedaled, slipping and falling against the mud wall. He jerked the flashlight left then right then back to the death heap. Several human skulls sat atop the bone pile. They had been arranged in a circle, facing outward.

* * *

Kyle tossed a backpack and growled in frustration. "What kind of expedition team goes into the jungle without rope?"

Jessica searched one of the fallen tents. "There has to be some around here."

"We've checked everywhere." He scanned the campsite. So many empty brass cartridges littered the dirt floor like an insane battlefield. "And where are all the guns?"

"I don't see any."

"Precisely. Someone's taken all the weapons. And probably the rope, as well."

"How are we going to get Eric out?" Jessica asked.

"We'll have to improvise." Kyle grabbed his machete and started separating the tent nylon from the poles. "Help me tie these tents together."

They nearly had a makeshift rope made, when Chaser started growling at the forest. Kyle felt a strange vibration resonating from the ground. A sudden crashing came through the branches. He grabbed Jessica's hand and ran for cover.

* * *

Terrified of what kind of predator's den he'd fallen into, Eric ran back to the circle of light. He looked up at the hole. Kyle and Jessica were out of sight.

Where were they?

Heavy footfalls thundered above, followed by gunshots.

"Kyle!" Eric dug his hands into the dirt wall and tried to scale it, but the soil crumbled and he slid back down.

Chaser barked. Jessica screamed. More gunshots. Then an ungodly shriek.

"Oh, God, Jess—" Hands wrapped around Eric's mouth and chest and snatched him into the darkness.

* * *

Kyle and Jessica took refuge in the thick mangroves that grew along the banks of the stream. He sat half-submerged in water with her hiding behind him. She was shaking badly and looked as if she might take off running at any second. Kyle squeezed her thigh and signaled her not to make a sound.

Chaser stood in the center of the campground, barking at the shaking branches.

Kyle wanted to call the dog back, but to do so would give away their hiding place. With his rifle resting on a branch, he peered through the scope and followed a tall shadow moving through the jungle. It made one hell of a racket, grunting and cracking tree limbs. Kyle's rational mind identified the predator as a grizzly, but its roar sounded nothing like a bear. Occasionally it released an odd, high-pitched laugh like a jackal. From what Kyle could tell by the height of the moving branches it was seven to eight feet tall. He had shot it once, but all that did was piss it off.

The predator disappeared behind a wall of ivy-covered trees.

Chaser ran to the edge of the vines and growled.

Kyle held his breath. He felt Jessica's hand slide up his back and rest on his shoulder. He looked back at her. Her blue eyes were full of terror, yet fierce. She nodded that she was still with him. She was braver than he had given her credit for. Kyle heard a yelp and when he looked back, Chaser was gone.

Jessica gasped. Kyle peered through the scope, searching for the beast.

The forest turned silent. They waited several minutes and still no sound.

Kyle whispered, "I think it's gone. Stay here, while I go help Eric."

"No way," she whispered back. "We stay together."

He nodded. They crawled out of the mangroves and back onto the grassy bank. There was a spatter of blood on the ground where Chaser had stood. Kyle felt bad for the Hansons' dog, but there was no time to search for it. He watched the dense trees and bushes. The clouds moved back over the canopy, turning the jungle three shades darker. The fog returned as well, creeping through the branches and forming a smoky web around the campsite. Kyle and Jessica hurried to the coil of tents they had tied together. As they gathered it up in their arms, a giant shadow shape tore through the foliage. Kyle raised his rifle and fired at the fog. In the scope, he saw a dark blur moving toward him. A long arm shot out and struck Kyle in the shoulder. He skidded across the ground, dazed.

Heavy footfalls pounded the earth.

Jessica screamed and jumped behind him.

Kyle sat up, felt for his rifle, but it was too far away. He pulled out a knife and challenged the fog. The shadow shape charged again. And then rapid-fire gunshots exploded. Two mud-faced men wearing branches ran out of the jungle, yelling and firing automatic rifles. They pummeled the beast with bullets. It cried out then lumbered off into the mist.

"Get out of here!" One of the men yelled and unleashed a few more rapid shots. When the crazed gunman turned around, Kyle's fast-beating heart surged as his father offered him a hand. "You okay, son?"

* * *

In the subterranean darkness, Eric struggled against strong arms and legs that grappled his body and held him in a vise grip. A hand clamped his mouth. A man with a strange accent whispered in his ear, "Stay quiet or you'll get us both killed."

A machete blade pressed against Eric's crotch. He peed his pants. He closed his eyes, not wanting to die. Everything aboveground remained silent for some time. Then screams and rapid gunfire sent horrible images through Eric's mind. His brother and Jessica could be dead and there was nothing he could do.

The painful cries of the beast trailed off. Then someone bird-whistled.

The man behind Eric released his arms and legs. Eric backed away, staring at the darkness. "Who the fuck are you?"

"One of the good guys." A flame lit up a mud-covered face with large brown eyes and jet-black skin. He wore green camouflage and carried an assault rifle. "You must be one of Elkheart's boys."

Eric nodded, still in shock.

The man slid his machete into a sheath on his hip. "No hard feelings, friend."

Voices sounded from above. Eric ran back to the circle of light. He smiled at the sight of Kyle and Jessica peering over the hole. "Thank God, you're alive!"

Kyle grinned. "Barely, thanks to this guy."

A second mud-faced mercenary stood over the hole. "Everybody okay down there?"

Eric looked up at his father. "Fuck me."

Elkheart lowered down a rope. "Madu, let's get these kids out of here."

The black soldier stepped up beside Eric and offered him the rope. "After you."

* * *

No one said a word as Kyle, Jessica and Eric followed Elkheart and two mercenaries out of Macâya Forest. They stopped to rest at the waterfall where the rocky hill ascended. Kyle was still stunned to see his father alive. Elkheart kneeled down and splashed water on his face, washing off the mud. The black soldier did the same, cleaning his bald head.

When Elkheart was done, he stood and frowned at his sons and Jessica. "What in the hell are you kids doing here?"

Eric said, "It's great to see you, too, *Dad*."

"We were looking for you," Kyle said. "Ray told us you had gone missing, so I flew us up here."

"That bastard." Their father shouldered his rifle. "You've got no business being here."

"Why not?" Kyle asked.

"I'll tell you later." Dressed in camo and heavily armed, their father barely resembled the man Kyle had visited a year ago. Elkheart's eyes had hardened, his face lean and chiseled.

Eric nodded toward the two soldiers. "Who're your sidekicks?"

Elkheart said, "That's Madu. He's from South Africa."

Madu stared at them without expression.

"He's not much for words," Elkheart added. "And this is Scarpetti. He's ex-Delta Force."

The mercenary wearing a blue bandana around his head nodded and winked at Jessica. He had a thick black beard. Scarpetti met Kyle's eyes and stared him down with a half-cocked grin.

They all continued hiking until they reached the muddy banks at Kakaskitewak Swamp. Kyle peered back at the forest. "Will that thing follow us out here?"

"Probably not during the day." Scarpetti stuffed some tobacco in his cheek. "They mostly travel at night."

"There's more than one?" Jessica asked.

"Oh, yeah," Scarpetti said. His wild eyes made Kyle nervous.

"What are they?" Eric asked.

Elkheart dragged the canoe to the water. "No more talking. We need get back to the village. And then you three are leaving."

Kyle said, "First we have to find Shawna and Zack."

* * *

Shawna had to escape before the beast returned.

She used the mossy wall to help her walk. She felt wasp stings all through her hips, but her legs still had some strength. She crept down a damp narrow passage. Torches lit up part of the tunnel, with long stretches of blackness in between. Water dripped on her shoulders, dribbling cold streams down her back. The rocky ground was hell on her bare feet. In some places she squished through mud, which gave her relief.

Moans echoed up ahead. They didn't sound like the animal cries she'd heard last night. These moans sounded human. Then she heard a sob that was definitely from a girl.

Shawna blindly felt her way along the wall between the torches. She came upon two intersecting tunnels, but they were so dark she hurried past them. She reached the next torch and pulled it off the wall. She stabbed it at the blackness in front of her as she walked. The passage opened up to another stone chamber.

A girl's voice whispered over and over, "We're gonna be okay. We're gonna be okay."

Shawna entered the room, holding out the torch. It illuminated a pit where two mud-stained girls were huddled together. They were naked like she was and being held captive like caged pigs. A thatch-work of thin pine logs and evergreen branches covered the pit. One of girls stuck her hands through the open squares. "Help us."

Shawna put the torch in a groove on the wall. Then she kneeled and gripped the girl's hands, feeling relief that she was not alone down here. She recognized the girl from the RV they had assisted two days ago. They had chatted briefly about music and boys. "Oh, my God, Lindsey?"

"My sister's real sick. You have to get us out of here."

Her sister sat against a wall, rocking and sobbing.

Shawna walked around the pit, searching for an opening. She found what looked like a door to the wicker mesh. There was a padlock on it. "Shit," she whispered. She tried pushing the covering, but it wouldn't budge. She collapsed in frustration.

"Please hurry," Lindsey kept pleading.

"I can't get it open." Shawna yanked at the wicker covering, but the logs were fastened together by metal bindings. What she needed was an axe.

Humming echoed down the passage. Orange firelight moved this way.

Lindsey whispered, "Hide! Hide! Quick! He's coming."

Shawna crawled into a shadowy crevice. She stifled a scream as Ray Roamingbear entered the chamber carrying a torch and a bucket. "Hello, girls. Brought you some din-din and a fresh shit bucket." Ray's three wolf dogs came in with him, sniffing at the edges of the pit.

In the shadows between two boulders, Shawna shivered, her teeth clicking together.

Ray pulled off a backpack and tossed a couple of water bottles down to the girls. "Drink up. No use dying of thirst. We've got a big day tomorrow. Lindsey, make sure Amy eats. She needs more meat on those bones."

Ray Roamingbear was shirtless except for a tan vest that looked to be made from patches of human skin. He had sewn a few of Zack's tattoos into the design.

Tears rolled down Shawna's cheeks. She tried to muffle a sob, but it was too late. One of the dogs ran over to where she was hiding and growled inches from her face.

Ray stabbed his torch in her direction. "Well hello, sunshine."

Chapter Eighteen

Kyle, his father and Madu searched the woods surrounding the village. As soon as Kyle found his sister and Zack, the plan was to pack up and fly out tonight. Elkheart wouldn't explain what was happening in Macâya Forest. He had been cryptic all afternoon. Spending several weeks inside the Devil's Woods had changed Kyle's father. His hair looked more silver. The usual humor in his eyes had left. Elkheart and Madu now moved through the forest with urgency. Kyle, carrying a deer rifle, did his best to keep up. He clung to the hope that they'd find Shawna and Zack camping.

The searchers checked the pond to see if the two had gone swimming. The sinking sun cast long shadows across the placid water. The closer it got to dusk, the more Kyle feared for his sister. "I should have never left them last night."

"It wasn't your fault," his father said. "Those mushrooms Ray gave you are real mind fucks. You were under the influence of a trickster."

Kyle's head was full of questions. "Why would he trick us into coming here?"

"I don't know. Your cousin isn't the man I thought he was. Don't believe anything he's told you."

"Grandfather was at the ceremony too. Is he also a trickster?"

"No, your grandfather is so senile now, he's not all there. Only during vision quests, when he's taking mushrooms, has he been lucid enough to talk directly to me."

"That's the only time he spoke to me too, in perfect English," Kyle said, remembering his vision quest vividly. "Grandfather led me to my animal guides. I ran with the elks."

Elkheart nodded as if he understood. "Your grandfather is a good man, but he's no longer living in the reality that you and I see."

"He needs someone looking after him," Kyle said. "Or to be put in a nursing home."

"Believe me, I've tried, but your grandfather is stubborn and refuses to leave our land. And like me, he thought Ray was someone who could be trusted to look after him. Turns out, Ray's a pathological liar and a goddamned traitor." His face tight with anger, Elkheart returned his attention to the woods around them.

"You're holding something back, Dad. What is it?"

Elkheart and Madu shared a look that was filled with mutual hate. "Ray pretended to be helping us with our research. He led us into Macâya Forest to explore the old copper mine. But it was a trap and most of my crew was killed. Next time I see Ray, I'm going to put a bullet in his fucking brain."

Kyle watched curiously as Madu crept toward the edge of the woods. The South African pulled out his long machete and poked the pine branches with it. Kyle looked back at his father.

"What were you searching for in Macâya Forest?"

Elkheart spoke in a hushed tone, "Not out here. Later, I'll show you some things. Let's keep searching."

Madu issued a bird call and waved them over. He pulled a knot of bluish-blonde hair from the branches.

"That's Shawna's," Kyle said.

His father's eyes turned from anger to worry.

Kyle felt his heart sink. "What is it?"

Elkheart looked away. "It's almost sundown. We have to keep searching."

Kyle caught a flicker of movement in the bushes and spotted Nina Whitefeather's ghost, waving him to follow. A cold wave of dread coursed through him. He looked at his father and Madu. "I know of one place we haven't looked."

Kyle led them through the pines and aspen until he spotted the long gray shed that had no windows. His father put a hand on his shoulder. "Careful, son."

Kyle slowed his pace. "Have you been here before?"

"Not since I was a teenager. The tribe used that shed for butchering animals. Later, we discovered that poachers were using it too."

"I think it's where Nina Whitefeather was murdered."

Elkheart stopped walking. "What makes you bring up her?"

Kyle hesitated. "This is going to sound crazy but…" He pointed to where Nina stood behind a tree. "I can see her ghost."

His father looked in her direction.

"I can also touch things and pick up glimpses of the past," Kyle said. "I've been able to do this as far back as I can remember." He held his breath. He had never shared his ability with anyone.

"I always suspected," was all his father said. "Tell me about Nina."

Kyle felt relief. "I came here yesterday and saw an imprint of the day she was murdered. There's a bloody mattress in there and some chains."

Elkheart nodded. "Let's have a look."

They entered the camp with their guns ready. Kyle was shocked to find fresh blood stained the ground beside a large tree. A bloody rope dangled from the branch. "This wasn't here yesterday."

Elkheart said, "Madu, search the perimeter."

The South African mercenary moved through the forest as silent as a jungle cat.

Kyle couldn't stop shaking at the sight of all the blood. He prayed some poachers had skinned a deer here.

Elkheart turned on a flashlight and went inside the shed. Kyle remained outside. If Shawna had been taken in there, he didn't want to see the imprint. After a moment, his father came back out, holding an arm over his mouth and nose. His eyes were watery. "Kyle, go back to the cabin and pack your stuff." Elkheart bird-whistled Madu to return.

"Where are you going?" Kyle asked.

"To find your sister."

* * *

At the cabin, Scarpetti smoked a cigarette on the back porch.

Up in the loft, Jessica grabbed clothes and threw them into her suitcase. She couldn't wait to leave this place. Between Wynona's crazy warnings and nearly being killed by some strange animal, she was done with this vacation. Thankfully, Kyle had agreed to fly them back to Seattle tonight. All she could think of now was home.

She looked over the loft's railing. "Eric, you need to come pack."

"In a minute, babe." He was downstairs making a vodka tonic.

Jessica sighed. "How can you drink?"

"After what happened today, I need something stiff to calm my nerves."

"Fine. I'll pack for you." She grabbed his clothes, which had been flung everywhere. She folded his shorts and saw something red and lacy sticking out of a pocket. She pulled out a pair of French-cut panties. Her heart started beating fast followed by a rush of anger. "Eric, can you come upstairs please?"

When Eric climbed to the loft, she held up the red panties. "I found these in the shorts you wore yesterday."

He froze a moment, clearly busted. "They're yours."

"Who is she?"

"What the fuck are you talking about?"

"When I cleaned your cuts last night, you reeked of perfume. I told myself it was nothing, but then I find these. The truth, Eric. What's the real reason those guys punched you?"

He tried to give her his innocent grin. "Babe, you're blowing this all out—"

"Don't lie to me!"

"Okay, okay, yeah, I kissed a woman at the bar, big deal." He got into her face. "You've been flirting with my brother all weekend. Had you come into town with me, none of this would have happened." He pointed at his cuts and bruises as if they were all her fault.

"So you got mad and made out with some stranger?"

"She was coming on to me really strong. What can I say, Jess? I had a moment of weakness. You're going to get all bent over—"

"I kissed Kyle," she heard herself say.

"What!" He blinked several times. "You what?"

"Last night, while you were asleep, Kyle and I kissed."

"You slut. Did you fuck him too?"

"No, we just kissed."

"Fuck!" Eric raised his fist, as if he was going to hit her, but then pulled it back. "Goddamn it, I saw this coming! You told me I had nothing to be jealous about!"

"I didn't mean for it to happen but it did, just like you and red panties here." She threw them at him.

"She wasn't your fucking sister. Christ, Jessica. How could you do this?"

She started to tear up. "I don't know."

"How can I trust you after this?" He jabbed a finger at her, poking her chest hard. "Have there been other guys?"

"No, of course not." Jessica pushed his hand away. "And don't you fucking lay a hand on me."

Eric backed off, surprised to hear her swearing. The confusion wore off quickly though and he glared like he was angry enough to hit her. Again, he pointed his finger. "I don't want you ever around my brother again."

"That's impossible. He's your family."

"Not anymore."

They stared at one another for a long moment. Even though Jessica was on the brink of tears, she wouldn't allow herself to cry. She wasn't about to show Eric any emotional weakness. Not after he had so blatantly cheated on her and then tried to accuse her of seeing other men.

After an unbearable silence, he finally sighed. "Let's just put this all behind us. Forgive and forget." He tried to put his hand on her shoulder but she backed away. "Come on, babe. Now that we're getting married, we'll focus on each other. I'll make sure Kyle doesn't try and come between us."

Jessica shook her head. "Eric, I can't do this."

"Sure you can. We'll get through this."

She pulled his ring off her finger and gave it back to him. "I'm sorry."

"Fuck you!" Eric hurled the ring across the room. Then he grabbed his keys, thundered down the stairs and left out the front door. Seconds later, she heard the Hummer peel away.

"Man, what an asshole," Scarpetti said from the first floor. He looked up at Jessica, grinning. "Miss, is there anything I can help you with?"

Jessica turned away and buried her face in her hands.

* * *

Please let Shawna be alive. Although Elkheart hadn't seen or spoken to his daughter since she was two, he had always loved her. He had watched her grow up through the photos that Kyle had sent. Elkheart had even secretly gone to Seattle to see one of her concerts, hiding in the crowd, watching with pride as she sang onstage. Despite her rebel hair and clothes, Shawna looked as beautiful as her mother. Elkheart had always hoped that Shawna would one day accept him back into her life. Now, if what he feared were true, he would never forgive himself for trusting Ray Roamingbear.

With rifles aimed, Elkheart and Madu approached Ray's cabin. The yard was littered with broken-down cars, a few trailers with busted windows, and a rusty old school bus. Multiple sheds surrounded the main house. All the lights were off. Elkheart flattened against the wall of a tool shed and listened. No dogs barking. Good, Ray wasn't home.

Elkheart gave Madu hand signals, then together they crept to the back screen door and entered. They switched on their flashlights. The interior of the house was cluttered with more junk. Feathers covered everything. His cousin, who was the bastard son of an abusive alcoholic mother, always felt more at home living in squalor.

Dozens of mounted deer heads covered the walls, their broad antlers jutting outward. The flashlight beams caused spiked shadows to stretch across the walls. Marble eyes watched as the two gunmen searched the den and kitchen, which smelled of rot and mildew. Madu found a basement door. Elkheart clicked on a single bulb. He drew a semi-automatic pistol and went down the stairs first, ready to shoot anything that moved.

The basement was a multi-room maze of gray cinderblock walls. Human skins hung on hooks, the dry, hollow faces still attached like Halloween masks.

"Jesus Christ," Elkheart whispered.

The smell of rot got worse the farther they explored. A back room was full of large cages, the kind used for catching hogs. Elkheart panned his light across the metal frames, searching for Shawna, dreading what he might find. All the cages were empty, except one. The naked woman curled up inside it looked as if she had been dead for weeks. Elkheart had once worked an expedition in Cambodia where they dug up a mummified man from the mud. He had shriveled up, hugging himself in a fetal position. This woman looked like that, as if during her last breath, she had embraced death.

When Ray was a boy his mother had kept him down here in a cage whenever he disobeyed her. Then one day she drank herself to death while watching TV upstairs. Grandfather Two Hawks had found Ray locked in his cage, nearly starved to death.

Looking down at the dead girl, Elkheart felt horrified and relieved all at once. He sighed and looked at his comrade. "Shawna's not here."

Madu gave him a knowing look.

There was another place Elkheart's daughter could be, and if that were the case, getting her back in time was going to be damned near impossible.

* * *

Eric raced the Hummer down the reservation road, stirring up dust. "How dare that bitch!" He would have given her everything. "Fucking Kyle!" The thought of Jessica kissing his brother only fueled Eric's rage.

"I'll show them."

He had to get far away from here or he was afraid of what he might do. He had almost hit Jessica. Eric had never struck a woman. Had never cared enough to get worked up over a chick. If a woman got out of line, he dumped her and moved on.

But Eric had invested a year with Jessica. Now, he had to start all over and his dream of making partner would have to wait. "Fucking bitch!" He pounded the steering wheel.

He stopped at the T-section where the dirt road met the paved road. He hopped out and walked along the fence line until he found a signal. He got two bars. Good enough.

He scrolled through his saved numbers and found the one he was looking for. "There you are."

The phone rang and then a young, sexy voice answered, "Hello?"

"Hello, hot stuff."

* * *

Alone with Scarpetti at the cabin, Jessica stood on the porch, hugging herself. Her face was still damp from crying. How could she have been so blind not to see Eric for who he was? She had sensed for a while that he might be cheating on her, especially when he returned from his business trips, but she had ignored her instincts. *What a fool I've been.*

She felt hands rubbing her shoulders.

"There, there," spoke a man's voice.

She turned around to see Scarpetti grinning. His fingers kept massaging her. "You look tense."

Jessica backed away from him. The Italian soldier had a thick shaggy beard after living six weeks in the jungle. He smelled ripe, like an ape. And he had the look in his eyes of man who hadn't seen a woman in a very long time. A rapist's gaze. His dark eyes kept scanning her body, and she had the feeling he was mentally undressing her.

"Do you mind?" Jessica said, crossing her arms.

Scarpetti leaned against a post. "You know...you can do *so* much better than that jerk. A man who runs away from a woman as hot as you...he's an idiot."

"Please, just leave me alone." Jessica crossed the backyard to the edge of the tree line. She wished Kyle were here. She needed to talk to him. She called out to the woods, "Kyle?!"

The men had headed through the trees directly behind the cabin. She prayed they were still in earshot. She called for them again.

"They won't be back for a while," Scarpetti said. "Come back to the cabin."

"I prefer to stay right here," she said defiantly. She called again, "Kyle?!"

"Miss, you can yell till your throat hurts, but they're probably a mile away by now. Let's go inside. I need to drain the lizard."

"Go ahead. No one's stopping you."

"You and I need to stick together. If you won't go inside with me, then you leave me no choice." He walked to the end of the porch and unzipped his pants and started to pee on the ground. He did it an angle that left nothing to the imagination. "Ah, I've been holding that in too damn long."

Jessica was suddenly reminded of a time when she was young girl at elementary school and a janitor lured her into a bathroom. He had pulled out his member to pee and asked her to hold it for him. She had run out of the bathroom in terror. Now, watching Scarpetti with revulsion, panic took over her once again and she ran into the forest, pushing back branches.

"Hey, come back here!" Scarpetti yelled.

Her feet wouldn't stop running and she didn't look back until she was deep in the woods. She had either lost the soldier or he hadn't followed. She released a breath of relief. Kyle, his father, and Madu had to be somewhere around here.

"Kyle?!"

The path was overgrown, and she had to weave between trees and underbrush. No matter how much she concentrated on the maze of pines, aspen and spruce, her mind wandered back to Kyle. She envisioned his light blue eyes; the way they beamed when he smiled, his expression polite, easy going. She liked his strong, quiet confidence. She always felt safe with Kyle. And then she remembered how angry he'd seemed seeing Eric's engagement ring on her finger. How would Kyle respond after he found out that she and Eric were over?

Jessica began to worry. She had trekked a good distance and still hadn't found any of the men. How far did they go anyway?

Stopping to get her bearings, she scanned the forest. The vastness of the reservation overwhelmed her. She could search all day and never find Kyle or her way back to the cabin. It was getting dark anyway. And then she remembered the strange creature they had faced on the other side of the swamp. Elkheart had said there are more of them and sometimes at night they roam the forest. The thought of that stirred up childhood fears far more frightening than confronting a rapist. The shadows between the trees seemed to grow by the second, as the sunlight was quickly fading.

She suddenly felt stupid for leaving the safety of the cabin. Scarpetti may have been a horny soldier, but he wouldn't have really raped her, would he? She had probably overreacted, letting her fear get the best of her. She decided to head back. If Scarpetti continued to come onto her, she would lock herself in the bathroom until Kyle and the others returned.

Frustrated, she hiked back toward the cabin. To her right, there was a rustling sound as something moved from one clump of trees to another. Jessica froze. She slowly gazed back to the right again, building courage to face what animal might be roaming the trees. Nothing moved. The only sounds now were from the birds settling in the trees for the evening.

Relax, Jess, it's gone.

She continued walking. The pine-bristled floor inclined sharply. She had to work her legs with greater effort as the terrain grew rocky.

Again, something moved off to her right. A bushy tail vanished behind the pines.

Jessica's heart quickened.

From somewhere she heard *clicking*, and a black wolf dog stepped from the underbrush. Seeing its humped back, she remembered its name. Arok.

Her throat knotted and she struggled to breathe.

"Hey, boy." She eased down the path, hoping the dog wouldn't follow.

Up the hill a dark gray dog appeared from the thicket, licking its chops. Kiche or Maskwa?

Snapping echoed and both dogs rushed her.

Whirling, Jessica sprinted back down the hill. Paws trampled the ground behind her, gaining.

Click. Click. Click.

To her right a third wolf dog moved in to head her off.

Crying, Jessica veered left. The barking beast advanced.

Her lungs strained as she held her breath.

Two dogs snarled behind her.

She swung her staff, hitting trees.

A gray wolf leaped a log in front of her, moving in for the kill.

Jessica screamed as the beast opened its jaws at her knees. Then, loud *click-clicking* by her ears saved her legs, as Jessica crashed into the arms of Ray Roamingbear.

* * *

After his father and Madu disappeared into the forest, Kyle headed back up the path toward the cabin.

You just going to give up the search? Detective Winterbone spoke in his head.

I've got my orders.

Christ, Kyle, Shawna needs you!

This reservation was too vast for his father and Madu to search by themselves. Besides, Kyle had a special gift. If it meant combing these woods all night, he would do whatever it took to find her. He checked his rifle and made sure he had a round in the chamber.

He returned to the woodshed, once again sensing vibrations along the ground. The pines hummed like organ pipes. Nina was still hiding behind a tree, her spirit forever haunting this campground, being dragged into the shed by some unseen entity, replaying her death, over and over.

It's just a twenty-year imprint, Kyle thought to boost his courage. *Her killer is long gone.*

He entered the dark shed. Flies swarmed inside, landing on his face and neck. He swatted them away. The stained mattress was still against the back wall, the chains lying across it. *You can do this, Kyle.* He touched a wall and glimpsed a girl fighting for her life on the mattress, but this time it wasn't Nina. This was a heavyset girl with auburn hair. She was maybe twenty. Her mutilation was even more severe than Nina's. When Kyle released his hand from the wall, the redheaded girl vanished.

Two murders?

He heard a drumbeat and native chanting, the way the elders used to sing around the fire. He turned around and saw the red wraith again, sitting between him and the way out.

Kyle felt trapped, afraid the thing might suddenly close the doors.

It's just an imprint.

The red wraith raised its arms, as if performing some kind of ceremony. Then it got up and left.

Kyle walked back outside, but the wraith was gone.

Now, the recent kill. Taking a deep breath, Kyle touched the tree with the bloody rope. He saw flashes of a man's naked body hanging from the branch. A knife carving off tattooed skin from Zack's back and arms. And then a frenzy of black shadows tore him apart.

"No…" Kyle stumbled backward, the trees spinning. Hot bile rose up his throat and he vomited.

Kyyyyllle…

When he looked up he saw Zack's half-eaten ghost standing at the edge of the forest. Blood tears ran out of the empty eye sockets. Only tatters of flesh hung from his skeleton. Zack made a hollow sound and then walked behind the shed.

Follow him, Detective Winterbone urged.

"Hell no. I can't do this."

You can, Kyle. He's trying to help you.

Kyle gripped his rifle as he followed Zack's skeleton through a field of ferns. He kept looking back with those dark pits where his eyes should have been. Zack walked to a clearing with several scattered mounds. A graveyard. Only there were no tombstones. A shovel stuck out from a mound of fresh dirt, and Kyle had no doubt he'd find Zack's remains buried there. Kyle grabbed the shovel and got a vision of red hands digging. A bare foot kicked bloody bones into a grave. Then like a fast-cutting film, Kyle saw girl after girl being raped and murdered in the shed and then buried out here. Their screams filled his head with madness.

Kyle dropped the shovel. When he looked up, he saw the ghosts of more than twenty murdered girls standing around him and Zack.

Don't be afraid of them, Winterbone said. *You can save them.*

How?

By killing the monster who murdered them.

* * *

Inside a circle of thorny pines, Ray grabbed Jessica's arms. She screamed and tried to jerk free.

"Calm down, calm down, you're safe now." He yelled at his dogs, "Go on, get!" He made clucking sounds with his tongue and the three wolf dogs ran off into the forest. Ray shook his head. "Sorry, about that, Jessica. They thought you were a poacher."

She couldn't stop trembling. "Are they going to come back?"

"No, I sent them home." Ray was shirtless, except for a vest made from a strange hide. It was open, exposing his sweat-covered belly. "What are you doing wandering out here by yourself?"

"Searching for Kyle."

"Well, you could get yourself lost this far from the village. Let's get you back."

She followed him through the gloomy woods, wary of every tree and bush, afraid that his dogs might attack again. Ray led her into a clearing where there was a fire pit and an old woodshed. She got a weird feeling about the place. "I thought you were taking me to the cabin."

"I need to check my shed first."

Something about Ray's demeanor frightened her. A coldness in his eyes that wasn't there before. "Please, I really want to head back, if that's okay."

"This'll just take a minute. Stick close to me." He opened the double doors and a swarm of flies and a god-awful stink escaped the shed.

Jessica backed away.

Ray lunged and grabbed her arm. "Get back here!"

"Let go. You're hurting me."

"If you play nice, I won't hurt you." He pulled her into his arms. "No, no, no, I don't want to bruise such a pretty face." Ray pinned Jessica against the shed door. He petted her hair as if she were an animal. "They like the pretty ones." His mouth mashed against her clamped lips. His free hand reached under her shirt and bra.

Jessica twisted her head to the side. "Help!"

His bear paw of a hand muzzled her mouth. She mumbled hysterically under his sweaty palm. She kicked his shin and then clawed his face. She made a run for it, but Ray grabbed her wrist and spun her around. He backhanded her and she fell to the ground. He took hold of her ankles and dragged her into the shed. She kicked and clawed the earth. He pulled her into a dark corner. Threw her onto a damp mattress.

Jessica cried as Ray loomed over her, humming. He shackled one of her wrists.

She wailed.

"They'll be coming for you soon. But first, you and I get to have a little fun."

Ray cried out as something smacked him in the back of the head with a loud *thunk*.

He dropped to his knees. Kyle was standing behind him, holding a shovel.

* * *

Kyle swung again, striking Ray in the side of the face. He toppled over and Kyle pounded him again and again until his cousin's face was a bloody pulp. Out of breath, his arms shaking, Kyle unshackled Jessica and pulled her out of the shed. He closed the double doors and stuck the shovel through the metal handles, locking the sick bastard inside.

When Kyle turned to face Jessica, she buried herself in his arms, clinging to him, crying against his chest. He tried to persuade her to move, but she wouldn't budge. She was shaking severely, possibly going into shock. He held her, watching the double doors of the shed. He caressed her head. "It's okay. You're safe now, but we've got to get away from here. I'm not sure how long that door will hold."

A madman growled inside the shed. "I'm gonna skin you alive, Kyle!" The doors rattled from the impact of a body slamming into them, over and over.

Kyle aimed his rifle and fired a shot at the door.

The forest erupted with the sounds of barking dogs.

Kyle grabbed Jessica's hand and together they bolted up the trail.

"It's too far to the cabin," she panted. "We'll never make it."

He pushed her up the hill. "We will. Keep running." Glancing back, he saw two gray wolf dogs running behind them. Thirty yards away, and gaining.

Kyle stopped and raised the rifle's scope, lined up the cross hairs, and pulled the trigger. One of the dogs rolled backward. The other disappeared into the brush.

Kyle brought the rifle down. Off to his left, the black wolf snarled as it leaped, knocking him down. World spinning, pine-needled earth racing toward him, his face smacked solid ground. Somewhere in the maelstrom, he heard Jessica scream.

The black wolf dog climbed on top of him. Arok's teeth snapped at his neck, but Kyle pressed the rifle against its chest, keeping its fangs at bay. He rolled backwards, sending the wolf's momentum forward. Then Kyle swung the rifle like a bat, striking its back legs. Bones snapped. The black wolf squealed and hobbled down the hill. Gunshots brought it down.

In the delirium, Kyle stood on his knees, swaggered, heard barking and screaming. He spotted Jessica standing flat against a tree. She shielded her face as a gray wolf dog charged and leaped for her throat. Kyle raised his rifle and fired. The bullet tore open the dog's neck in a bloody spray. The beast catapulted back and skidded across the ground, dead.

"Kyle!" Elkheart and Madu hurried up the hill.

Jessica collapsed against Kyle. Both gasped for air.

Kyle, Elkheart and Madu listened as Jessica told her story of being caught by Ray and dragged into the shed. Moments later they all went back down to the shed to finish off Ray.

The doors stood wide open. The madman had escaped.

Part Seven

Shifters

Chapter Nineteen

After Jessica took a shower, Kyle tucked her into bed up in the loft. She was still shaken after the incident with Ray and his dogs. She told Kyle about her fight with Eric and the breakup. Now, as if things weren't bad enough with Shawna missing, Kyle's brother was M.I.A. Apparently, Eric had driven off to God knew where. Kyle tried calling his brother, but got no answer.

"Did you know about the other women?" she asked.

"Yes, but it wasn't my business. Is that why you broke up?"

"That was part of it."

Kyle froze. He hadn't dared to hope after he'd seen the engagement ring on her finger that morning.

"The rest was you." She gave him a shy smile. "I realized the first day that I had feelings for you, but I hoped they'd go away."

Kyle smiled. "And?"

"Well, they just keep getting stronger. The timing is a disaster, and I'm sorry I hurt Eric, regardless of what he's done. But I wouldn't change what happened between us last night. Would you?"

Kyle pulled her covers up, leaned over and kissed her lips. "No."

She grasped his hand. "Lie next to me." It wasn't an order, but a soft request, with a hint of vulnerability that he might say no.

He climbed onto her bed and lay on his side. She backed up against him, her body fitting perfectly within his. She wore only a terry cloth robe. Her damp hair smelled of honeysuckle. He put his arm around her. God, she felt good in his arms. Two years was too long to not feel the touch of a woman. She took his hand and held it against her chest. They lay like that for a long while, holding one another. He needed comforting as much as she did. She was still tense. Kyle stroked her hair and whispered, "You're safe now. I won't let anything happen to you. I promise."

She relaxed. Holding her, he drifted off to sleep.

When Kyle awoke some time later, it was growing dark outside, the sky charcoal gray. He felt Jessica's fingers stroking his hair. In the gloom, he could see her eyes watching him.

"Hey you," he said.

"Hey."

"Feeling better?"

She nodded. "Now that you're here."

Kyle stretched and yawned, rolling onto his back.

"Bored with me already?" she asked in a teasing voice.

He laughed. "With you? Never. I'm just getting started." He sat up, leaning on an elbow. He held her gaze for a moment. Even in the half-light her eyes seemed to sparkle. *I'm in bed with an angel.* He touched her face.

"Mmmm…" she sighed at the touch of his fingers.

Before he knew it they were kissing. The attraction between them was as strong as Kyle had thought. Jessica opened her robe and put his hand against her warm skin. Her rapid heartbeat thumped against his palm. She looked so delicate in his embrace, so ready to surrender her body and her heart. It was such an unexpected miracle that Kyle began to have doubts. "Are you sure about getting involved with me?"

"I've never been more sure about a bloke," she said in that sexy Aussie accent.

As he kissed her neck, she pulled her robe off her shoulders. There was just enough light coming through the windows to see the outline of her breasts. He took in her beauty, unsure of how far she wanted him to take this. He decided for them, closing her robe and kissing her lips.

"As much as I'd love to make love to you right now, Jessica, we should wait."

She frowned. "Why? Is it because you're not over *her*?" She touched the gold band on his wedding finger.

"No, I'm over Steph."

"Then why do you still wear it?"

"I don't know. It just hasn't felt like the right time to take it off."

Why couldn't he make love to Jessica right now? Was Stephanie's ghost still inside his head? He looked around the room to see if his wife might be lurking off in a corner, but she was nowhere to be seen. No, his inhibition wasn't about betraying his vow to Stephanie, but the speed in which Kyle and Jessica were moving. Just this morning, she had been his brother's fiancée.

Jessica held up her hand. "I took my ring off the moment I was done with Eric. I did it because I knew without a shadow of a doubt that you're the man I want to be with."

"And I want to be with you, too, Jess. God knows how much I want that. But you and Eric just broke up a couple hours ago."

Jessica nodded, her face not hiding her disappointment.

Kyle caressed her hair. "I want to do this right. After we get back to Seattle and some time has passed, I'd like to take you out on a date. Dinner, a movie, a kiss at the top of the Space Needle, the whole bit."

"I'd very much love that."

Her eyes, her smile got the better of Kyle. He kissed her more urgently, as if this moment might slip away and he found himself awakened from a dream. He clung to the fantasy, following the nape of her neck with his lips. Their moans filled the air of the loft. Kyle's erection pressed against the zipper of his shorts. As his animal urges started taking over again, he wanted nothing more than to rip open Jessica's robe and plunge inside her. After a moment of heavy kissing and petting, Kyle pulled the reins on his lust.

"I should get up now."

"Okay…" Jessica breathed, her face intoxicated with arousal.

He kissed her again and then climbed off the bed. "I'm going to check on the others. You should sleep."

"I don't think that's possible now." She sighed. "I'll get up and finish packing."

"Good idea." Kyle stopped at the windows on his way out of the room. The cloud cover was low and the woods looked angry beneath it. The spell from his desire for Jessica was broken by a harsh and sobering reality. They were stuck here at the reservation until Shawna was found and Eric returned.

* * *

In Hagen's Cove, Inspector Sam Zano chewed on a Tums as he rang the doorbell of the Thorpe Funeral Home. It had been a hell of a busy day handling all the details of the attack on the Hansons' RV. Zano's job of keeping the peace around Lake Akwâkopiy was getting more difficult by the day. The latest death had been a Calgary homicide detective. Talk about red tape. The last thing Zano needed was a bunch of city cops up here combing the woods and complicating matters. Another girl, Lindsey, had gone missing.

Zano had a remedy for days like this. As soon he finished with this last stop he was headed straight to Olaf's Bakery for a slice of strawberry pie and a scoop of vanilla ice cream.

He rang the bell again and the chime echoed throughout the funeral home.

Hugo finally answered the door. "Evening, Sam." Part of his mouth was smeared with red lipstick.

"Got a hot date tonight?"

"Huh?"

"You got a little lipstick on your face."

"Oh, yeah." Hugo wiped a hand across his mouth. "What can I do you for?"

Zano handed him a couple of trash bags. "You know what to do."

"I'll get right on it." Hugo started to close the door.

Zano grabbed it. "On second thought, I want to make sure you take care of it right away."

He followed the mortician through the parlor and down a long hallway. The mortuary smelled especially ripe tonight. There was a nude female corpse on the slab. An unfortunate hitchhiker, Kendra Meacham. A fresh kill. She looked and smelled like she might have been dead for less than ten hours. Her red lips were as smeared as Hugo's. Her legs were spread and semen speckled her bloated pubic area.

Zano shook his head in disgust. "You have no self-control, do you?" If it weren't for the fact that Hugo was the mayor's misfit son, Zano would discipline the sick bastard.

Hugo opened the trash bag and pulled out one of Carl Hanson's severed arms. He smirked and waved the fingers at Zano.

"Just get on with it."

Hugo threw the arm and bags into the cremation oven and set them on fire.

When all the evidence was burned, Zano nodded to the defiled corpse. "Your girlfriend, too, lover boy."

Zano headed back to his vehicle, thinking about Olaf's strawberry pie. His thoughts were interrupted by his cell phone ringing. He looked at the caller ID: Ray Roamingbear.

* * *

With a deer rifle strapped to his shoulder, Kyle stepped onto the second-story balcony just in time to see the sun make its final descent behind the mountains. As the last vestiges of daylight winked out, crickets and tree frogs played their nocturnal symphonies. It was a calming sound. The twilight hours had always been a peaceful time for Kyle to gather his thoughts. But tonight there would be no peace.

He was surprised to feel a woman's arms slip around him. "Hey."

He turned back to see Jessica. "I thought you were packing."

"I didn't like being alone." She kissed him, long and tender. He pulled away and was amazed to see her gazing at him with such loving eyes. Kyle wanted to enjoy the fact that Jessica was finally free to explore their amazing connection. But with Zack dead and Shawna still missing, those feelings would have to wait. Kyle was afraid for his sister. And with Ray Roamingbear on the loose, none of them would be safe tonight.

"I'm sure they're okay," Jessica said, as if reading the concern on his face.

He felt like he should tell her the truth about Zack—that Kyle had seen his ghost in the woods. But he couldn't bring himself to tell her. Not now at least. She had finally calmed down after what had happened with Ray, and Kyle didn't want to alarm her again.

As he held her, he watched the dark woods for any movement. There were no lurking ghosts. Just the branches moving in the wind as the gray between the pines faded deeper and deeper into black. Soon the only details were the spiky trees that bordered the village.

Flames flared up as Elkheart, Madu and Grandfather Two Hawks lit torches that stood every ten feet. Moments later, a ring of fire surrounded the cabin. Grandfather walked around the circle with a smoking bowl. With an owl feather, he smudged the smoke, speaking in Cree, occasionally singing.

"What are they doing?" Jessica asked.

"I don't know. Let's find out." Kyle led her downstairs.

Scarpetti stood on the back porch with his rifle. The orange dot of a cigarette glowed in his dark face. The mercenary nodded to Kyle and Jessica as they walked down the steps.

Elkheart and Madu stood in the backyard, surveying their handiwork. They turned when Kyle and Jessica approached.

"Where's your brother?" Elkheart asked.

Kyle shrugged. "I don't know. He took the Hummer and drove off somewhere."

"We got into a fight," Jessica added.

"Christ almighty. We need him here." His father paced.

Kyle felt guilty for not thinking about his brother's safety. "He probably drove to the tavern for a drink. Do you want me to go looking for him?"

"No. Stay put." The flames flickered in the reflection of his father's glasses.

"What are all the torches for?" Kyle asked.

"Protection."

"Against what?"

His father loaded bullets into a clip. "You two should stay inside."

Kyle looked off to the woods. "Have you seen any sign of Ray?"

"No, but I imagine he'll be angry that we killed his dogs."

"I found several graves behind the shed," Kyle said. "Did you know that Ray was murdering girls out here?"

Elkheart shook his head. "I had no idea Ray was capable of this."

Jessica looked shocked to hear this. "Murders?"

Kyle nodded. "You weren't the first woman Ray has chained up in that shed." He didn't explain how he knew this, that he had seen their ghosts. To his father, Kyle said, "We should go into town and notify the Mounties."

"No," Elkheart said with a sharp tone. "I don't want them involved."

"All we have to do is show Inspector Zano the shed and those graves. The Mounties can hunt down Ray and help us search for Shawna."

"I don't trust the police, especially Zano."

Jessica said, "Aren't you worried about Ray coming here tonight?"

"He's the least of our problems."

Kyle thought about the creature that attacked them earlier. His father had said there were more roaming Macâya Forest, mostly at night. They had killed his crew and abducted Amy, possibly Shawna as well. By the haunted look on his father's face, Kyle wondered if a part of Jon Elkheart had died in that forest. "Dad, tell me what's going on. What were you and your team searching for?"

His father snapped the clip into his assault rifle. He looked across at Scarpetti standing watch and then at Grandfather and Madu painting trees with a dark red liquid. Elkheart looked back at Kyle and Jessica. "It's better I show you."

They followed Elkheart into the cabin's study. He stepped up to a tall bookshelf. "Once you know the truth, you can never go back." His father reached high up on the top shelf and pulled on one of the books. The bookshelf rotated sideways, revealing a secret room.

* * *

Inspector Zano drove to the center of town where the old church stood. Made of pine lumber and painted white, the house of worship had been built back in 1890 by the hands of Hagen Thorpe and his sons. The bell tower with the high steeple made the church the tallest building in town. Zano pulled into the full parking lot. Several of his Mounties had already gathered out front.

"What do you want us to do, sir?" Sgt. Larson asked, his voice edgy.

The inspector could see nervous looks in the eyes of his men. "Everyone hang tight for now." Zano entered the church and stood at the back. The pews were packed tonight with every man, woman and child of Hagen's Cove. They cheered and clapped as Mayor Thorpe gave his sermon up onstage. With fire in his eyes, he spoke in the old language, "Are we not children of Lord Father?"

"Yes!" the congregation shouted.

"Do we not deserve our place in this world?"

"Yes!"

"Do we not want our children to have a future?"

"Yes!"

Thorpe paced the stage. "Then, brothers and sisters, we must not live in fear. No. We must stand *strong* in the presence of evil!"

Zano walked down the side aisle, passing pews. Men and women glanced his way. The mayor met eyes with the inspector but never lost a beat. "Chloe, could you come up onstage to Papa?" Thorpe kneeled as his four-year-old daughter climbed the steps. He picked her up and smiled proudly. "The love of my life. *This*, brothers and sisters, is what they will try to take from us. Our children."

The energy in the room rose. The townspeople in the pews hugged their children as if to keep them from being snatched away.

Thorpe pointed over their heads, toward the front door. "*They* will try to destroy our community. Our families." He paused to let the weight of his words sink in. "But they cannot and *will not* break our spirits."

"No!" the congregation shouted in unison.

Zano went up onstage and handed Mayor Thorpe a note.

Thorpe nodded and turned back to his followers. "Please take each other's hands."

The men, women and children gripped hands, their faces wrought with emotion.

"Brothers and sisters, in this time of darkness, we must band together, now more than ever. For it is only through our unity that we can survive the evils out there and keep our children safe." Holding Chloe on his arm, Mayor Thorpe turned to a giant statue of woven sticks. Covering its head was a spiky wreath of antlers. "Tomorrow night Lord Father is returning. And we will show him that his children will do whatever it takes to protect what he built."

The townspeople raised their fists and cheered.

Mayor Thorpe led them into singing the song to honor Lord Father. Feeling glory in his heart, Inspector Zano sang along with them.

* * *

Five miles from the reservation, Eric followed a heavily wooded road down to the lake. He parked near the moonlit water and killed the engine. This looked like the spot the girl had suggested. On either side of the road were public campsites with picnic tables and fire pits. Thankfully, no campers tonight. He checked his wallet to make sure he had a spare condom. Yep, locked and loaded with two Trojans. Eric had learned long ago that the best way to get over a woman was to find an immediate replacement. Despite being a small, backwoods town, Hagen's Cove had a few Danish hotties.

In his rearview mirror, headlights approached. His leg bounced with anticipation. A convertible Jeep pulled up beside him. Behind the wheel sat Nadine, the foxy brunette from the boat rental shack.

She smiled and waved. "Hiya."

"Hey there."

They both got out and walked in front of their vehicles. Nadine was wearing a halter top and cut-off shorts, which showed off her dark tan. Damn she had nice legs. She brought a twelve-pack of Moosehead, just like he had asked. Maybe this was the girl he should marry. His stepfather would freak if Eric brought home a country girl.

Eric and Nadine sat on the hood of the Hummer, drank beers and got better acquainted. Girls typically liked to move slow at first, until they felt safe, then it was anything goes. Safety tip number one: let her pick the make-out spot. Eric understood the female of the species and knew how to play their games. Mostly all it took to seduce a girl was patience and listening skills. Making them laugh always escalated their attraction.

Nadine was young, ripe and innocent—one of those rare beauties who grew up in a town full of hicks. Those were the easiest girls, because they were always looking for an escape from their boring lives. Nadine giggled at his stupid jokes and kept tucking her hair behind her ear. All good signs.

"I'm glad you called, Eric." She had the same accent as all the locals.

"Did you have big plans tonight?"

She shrugged. "Just laundry and watching reruns of Grey's Anatomy."

Eric slid his finger up her arm. "Well, I'm happy you chose spending the evening with me over Dr. McDreamy."

She laughed and sipped her beer. "You've watched the show?"

"Caught a few episodes." Jessica had DVDs of every season. He wasn't crazy about the show, but to understand women you have to pay attention to their interests.

He sat back against the Hummer's windshield, and Nadine did the same, looking at him sideways. The moon reflected in her large brown eyes. Eric leaned in and kissed her. She kissed him back with an eager tongue. His lips moved down her neck, and Nadine moaned in his ear. Eric pulled away. "I'm sorry. I'm moving too fast."

She touched his arm. "No, it's okay."

"You're over eighteen, right?"

"Of course."

"Do I need to check your ID?" he teased.

She pulled down her halter top, unveiling her ample breasts. "Does this look like I'm old enough for you?"

This was going to be a good night after all.

* * *

Kyle and Jessica followed Elkheart into the tiny room behind the bookshelf. Elkheart hit a button and the shelf rotated and closed behind them. He opened a trap door on the floor. "This chamber has always been kept secret by the elders. Ray doesn't know it exists. By bringing you in here, I'm fully trusting you'll keep it secret."

"You have my word."

"Mine too," Jessica said.

Elkheart climbed down iron rungs. Kyle followed. Ten feet down he landed on concrete. As Kyle helped Jessica down, his father hit a switch.

Three light bulbs partially lit a narrow passageway that ran about twenty yards.

Their boots echoed as they followed the tunnel. At the end of it, Elkheart opened a metal door that was six inches thick. He hit another switch, revealing a long, rectangular room with concrete walls.

"A bomb shelter?" Kyle asked.

"The elders built it in the Fifties."

Kyle and Jessica looked at one another as they stepped into the underground shelter. It was fully stocked with food, a kitchenette, twin beds, a couch and an old TV.

"It's quite cozy," Jessica said, doing her best to reduce the tension, but the fact that his father and grandfather had kept this place secret all these years worried Kyle. What other secrets were they keeping?

At the far end of the room a second set of rungs led up to a door in the ceiling. It had a round wheel like a submarine hatch.

"Where does that lead?" Kyle asked.

"The garage. It's an escape route." It was also where his father kept his Ford Bronco parked.

Elkheart walked to a corner where a tall metal cabinet stood beside stacked wooden crates. He turned the dial of another combination lock. "Before the members of our tribe abandoned this place, they always lived in fear of Macâya Forest. The elders, including your grandfather, kept quiet about what they knew. The people of Hagen's Cove call Macâya Forest 'the Devil's Woods' and would never talk about it."

"They know about the creatures too?" Kyle asked.

His father nodded. "I've dedicated my life to understanding the secrets of those woods." He opened the cabinet. The shelves were stuffed with boxes, video tapes and binders. He pulled out a binder labeled, *Macâya Forest*.

"You remember the legend?" Elkheart asked.

"Yes," Kyle said. "Back in the 1880s lumberjacks explored a green mist inside Macâya Forest and were slaughtered by some kind of beast. The legend's true, isn't it?"

"The Macâya really exists." His father opened the binder. It was a photo album of his expedition team excavating a cave. It looked like some kind of subterranean burial ground. In one picture Elkheart was pouring plaster into large footprints in the mud. Kyle recognized the purple mushrooms from the mineshaft. A second photo showed his father and Amy Hanson standing in the rainforest, holding up casts of foot impressions that were long and narrow with spiked toes.

"Is that from one of those things we saw today?" Jessica asked.

"Yes. We found footprints like these throughout Macâya Forest, especially down in the caves."

Kyle said, "What kind of animal is it?"

"We don't know exactly. Our ancestors called the Macâya a shape-shifting devil. A beast that reflects man's fears. It can form into a human, animal or something in between. The tribe has always respected its territory. Only an elder, like your grandfather, has the spiritual strength to enter the forbidden woods and not be seduced by the Great Trickster."

"But you went in there."

"Foolishly." He gazed down at a group photo of archaeologists and mercenaries. His arm was around Amy Hanson. "I should have never taken my team in there, especially Amy. Had I known what we'd encounter…"

"Did you love her?"

His father looked up, acting surprised that Kyle knew his relationship with Amy Hanson was more than just professor and student.

"Amy kept me grounded. I believe she's still alive in there. Down in one of the tunnels. My men and I have spent the past few weeks trying to find her." Elkheart sighed and looked at Kyle with humble eyes. "I'm glad you're here, son. I've always wanted you kids to understand my mission." He flipped to the back of the binder to black-and-white photos from the 1880s. The same ones Kyle and Jessica had seen hanging on the walls at the Beowulf Tavern. "There's more to the legend than Grandfather and I told you. And no matter how outlandish this all sounds, I need you to believe me."

Kyle said, "After what I've witnessed these past three days, I'll believe just about anything."

Elkheart tapped his finger on a grainy photo of Hagen Thorpe standing with several bearded men in front of a fallen tree. "When the lumberjacks went into the forbidden woods, Hagen didn't survive the attack, as the legend goes. The Macâya killed him and then shape-shifted into Hagen. The beast returned to the town where the women and children were waiting. It killed all the boys and started breeding with the women." Elkheart picked up a crowbar and began prying open one of the wooden crates. "We excavated a burial ground inside Macâya Forest." He lifted the lid. Inside the crate were monstrous skulls. "These were some of the devil's offspring."

* * *

At the funeral home, Wynona Thorpe woke in a dark room. She was lying in her bed under the covers, still dressed in her clothes. Still alive! She cried tears of joy. Perhaps Hugo loved his mother enough to convince the others to keep her around. But she knew there was no love in that man's heart. He needed her to run the funeral home and handle all the domestic duties and that was all.

Climbing out of bed, she tiptoed to the door and opened it a crack. Hugo was on the couch eating pizza and watching a sitcom. He erupted with laughter.

Wynona closed the door and locked it. The moonlight shining through the window provided enough to see. If she moved fast, she could escape without notice. She rummaged through her closet, grabbed a loaded .38 Special, checked the six-shot cylinders. Full as the night Jon Elkheart loaded the gun and hid it within a hollow cutout inside her Bible. Wynona snapped the chambers home.

They won't stop me this time.

She tossed clothes into a small bag and pulled a shoebox full of money from the closet. Over three thousand dollars saved. Enough to start a new life somewhere far away from Hagen's Cove. Florida maybe. She stuffed half the cash in her bag, the rest in her pockets in case she lost the bag.

Wynona changed into jeans and a black sweatshirt to blend in with the night, although it wouldn't make much difference. She slipped on her tennis shoes then tied her hair back. If there was anything Wynona learned from having an affair with a survivalist, it was how to survive. She remembered when she and Elkheart were still together. All the plans they'd made. He had promised to take her away from this godforsaken place as soon he had uncovered the secrets of Macâya Forest. They had talked of moving down to the Florida Keys. But those dreams had shattered the day Mayor Thorpe found out.

She looked at the clock. 9:55 p.m. Not much time before the mayor and his men would be back. If she stayed, she might not live to see tomorrow.

Her car was still parked outside. She contemplated whether to go through the house, and deal with her son, or climb out the window and down the lattice, risking the chance of falling and breaking her neck. She decided to sneak out, but as she moved to the window, the phone rang.

She stopped in the gloom of her bedroom. The old bell phone rang a second time then was answered by Hugo.

Easing the phone's receiver off the cradle, Wynona listened.

"…your mother went to the reservation yesterday," said Mayor Thorpe's angry voice. "She tried to warn them. Now Elkheart's back."

"Is that so?"

"We're having a town meeting at the church tonight to regroup."

"Can I come over there, Father?" Hugo asked.

Mayor Thorpe said, "Yes, but first you have to kill your mother. She's told too much already. If she escapes—"

"Wait a minute," Hugo interrupted. "I think somebody's listening on the other phone."

Wynona heard his receiver set down. Feet walked across the wood floor. The doorknob twisted. Wynona dropped the phone.

Hugo pounded on the door. "Mother, it's not nice to eavesdrop. You'll have to be punished."

Wynona regretted ever conceiving the boy. For thirty years she had put all her love into Jensen Thorpe's illegitimate son and had never gotten an ounce back. He was too much like his father.

"Mother! Open the fucking door!" Hugo pounded again. The wood cracked in the center.

Wynona raised the gun, hands shaking.

Something scraped the other side.

Claws, she thought. *My son can grow claws.*

He growled through the door.

She placed the gun inches away and fired three shots, punching as many holes through the flimsy wood. Peering through a hole, she saw Hugo's quivering body on the floor. Wynona yanked open the door and let him see the shame on her face.

Black ooze seeped from two fissures in his chest. The face of the thing lying on the floor vaguely resembled her son. Hugo stretched a knobby, claw-tipped hand toward her, speaking like a child, "Mother, you shot me… Why?" His voice deepened again. "Why, you *bitch*?" He lurched toward her and received a bullet in the eye.

Hugo lay paralyzed momentarily, as his mottled skin began to shift and contort. Not having much time, Wynona poured a bottle of brandy over his writhing body. Then lighting a cigarette, she flicked it at his chest. Her son burst into flames.

Wynona found her keys and hurried for the car.

* * *

Elkheart pulled one of the skulls out of the crate. "This is what the Macâya's offspring look like in their natural form."

Kyle ran his fingers along the juts and ridges of the skull's broad cranium. Jagged fangs filled its wide jawbones. The eye sockets were surprisingly small and set deep. The skull looked so alien there was nothing in the animal kingdom he could compare it to. The only things that it resembled were the creatures from his nightmares. Some of the skulls had horns.

Jessica picked up what looked to be a baby skull. "Amazing. These creatures really exist?" The scientist in her seemed to be reveling in the discovery of a new species.

Kyle, on the other hand, felt a knot in his gut as he realized who the Devil's offspring were. "Everyone in Hagen's Cove can change into one of these?"

"Just those born from the Thorpe clan," his father said. "I call them 'shifters'. When they're in public, they wear their human masks and blend in quite well. But when they roam the woods, they shape-shift into these monstrosities."

"Even Sam Zano?"

Elkheart nodded. "All the Mounties in the area. They shield the crimes that happen here. When the girls are abducted, Zano makes sure no one ever finds them."

Kyle sat on a twin bed as the gravity began to sink in. "And Ray Roamingbear?"

"Human. But he helps the cult abduct women. In return, he can live out his sick fantasies with his captives, and Inspector Zano turns a blind eye."

Jessica shuddered. She put the baby skull away and joined Kyle on the bed. "What about Wynona?" she asked. "She came here trying to warn us. I thought she was crazy."

Elkheart's face turned somber. "Wynona's not crazy. She was probably terrified for you."

"But why?" Jessica asked.

"Because no woman who enters Hagen's Cove is safe."

Jessica's breath hitched.

"So Wynona's not part of the clan?" Kyle asked.

"Not by choice. Years ago, when she was seventeen, she ran away from home. Wynona hitchhiked to Hagen's Cove to work as a waitress at the tavern. That position is how the town lures in women. If the 'help wanted' ads don't draw any flies to the web, Hugo and Thorpe's truck drivers scour the highways for girls hitching. They like runaways because it's easy for those girls to vanish without a trace. I think Ray has been helping the townspeople collect women. Maybe they let him keep a few of his own."

Jessica squeezed Kyle's hand. He put an arm around her.

"All of the men here murder women?" Jessica asked.

Elkheart shook his head. "The men of Hagen's Cove don't kill the women. They breed with them. The girls are divvied up at the church auction. Some are chosen by the town's men for child-bearing domestic slaves. Most end up committing suicide."

Jessica asked, "Why are they taking women?"

Elkheart put the horned demon skull back. "It's an act of survival. They need to prolong their race. Thorpe's clan has a genetic defect that won't allow them to breed with each other. If two shifters mate the result is always a stillborn. To keep their population growing, they've been kidnapping women for over a century and mating with them. Even the females born into the clan have to find human men to mate with. These women can shape-shift into any man's fantasy. They are highly seductive. Madu and I call the females 'Black Widows.'"

* * *

As Eric sat on the Hummer's hood, drinking another beer, Nadine did a little striptease in the beams of the headlights. She removed her halter top and cut-offs. He cheered her on when she got down to a black thong. She toyed with the straps, spinning around, showing off her tight little ass. And then she slid her panties off and held up her arms. "Ta-da!"

Eric clapped and took in the perfection of her body. He was so hard now his zipper was about to bust. "Climb on up here, hot stuff." He started to put on a condom, but she said, "No, I like it natural."

"We have to be careful then."

"Don't worry, I'm on the Pill." She climbed onto the hood like a prowling jaguar and straddled him. He entered her and she bounced on his lap.

Nadine was a howler. She gripped Eric's shoulders as she rode him on the hood of the Hummer.

He felt himself building, building. "Okay, babe, I'm about to come." He started to lift her off.

"Noooo!" She looked at him with fierce eyes and pinned him to the windshield. She pressed her hips down, grinding harder. The girl was surprisingly strong. She howled, arching her back. Eric exploded into her. Their bodies spasmed and then they collapsed together against the windshield.

He wiped his sweaty brow. "Damn, Nadine, you're an animal."

She giggled in his ear. "Can you do it again?"

"Sure."

"Good. Will you do a special favor for me?"

"What's that?"

"Will you fuck my girlfriends, too?"

Eric heard footsteps through the high grass. Three gorgeous women stepped into the head beams. The redhead in the middle said, "Hey, cowboy, remember me?"

* * *

Not seeing another car on the road, Wynona sped through Hagen's Cove in her Buick. All the buildings were dark, even the Beowulf Lodge and Tavern. She smiled, knowing all the townspeople were at the church.

Zooming past the town limits sign—*Welcome to Hagen's Cove, population 466 and counting!*—Wynona laughed and toasted the sign with her flask, then took a celebratory gulp of brandy. She had finally escaped. She drove along the winding backwoods road that would eventually reach the Trans-Canada Highway. From there she would continue on to Calgary, then to Toronto to see if her mother was still alive.

Wynona had been one of the lucky ones, because Mayor Thorpe chose her for himself. He had provided her with a home, plenty of food, an unlimited supply of fine brandy to drown her sorrows, and a job working for the town's undertaker. When Wynona turned eighteen, Thorpe impregnated her with Hugo. She remembered how hideous the baby had looked after birth. Its infant claws and featureless face had made her faint. In the first few months, its face was just a mouth in a pool of gray flesh. It had tiny sharp teeth that made breast feeding torture. Then, as her baby learned to shape-shift, it began to look like a hybrid of its mother and father. But her son's human features had only been a mask that hid its true nature. Wynona had done her best to love her son, but he had never loved her in return. Now her lifelong burden was lifted as it lay dead in her living room, burning with the rest of the house.

My son is dead.

She pressed down harder on the pedal, relieved she had destroyed the small part of herself that she would have left behind. The full moon lit up the night with a blue-gray luminance. The trees stood on either side in jagged silhouettes. The empty road stretched in front of her. Another half hour and she'd be out of these woods and Toronto bound.

She thought of the other abducted women still trapped in this hell town. The ones who tried to escape were given to Ray Roamingbear to be his playthings. But the worst were the girls chosen for the ritual, which happened once every ten years. Tomorrow night marked the tenth year. "Those poor, unfortunate girls," she said, thinking of Jessica and Shawna.

But there was nothing Wynona could do for them now. She took a swig of lukewarm liquor, let it trickle down her throat, then set the flask between her legs. When she got far enough away to start her new life, her first goal was to quit drinking.

Lights gleamed in her rearview mirror, like wicked eyes in the night. Two trucks raced side by side, advancing at an incredible speed.

Wynona pressed the gas pedal to the floor.

Something scuttled up ahead.

She flashed her brights to see a dark lupine figure standing in the road. It spread its long arms. She swerved to the left, as claws scraped her passenger door.

Headlights glared behind her. A truck rammed her bumper. She jolted forward. The flask landed under her feet.

A truck filled with men in the back raced alongside her. Baseball bats and crowbars pounded her hood, smashed her windows. Wynona screamed. The roadster slammed into her side. Her car slid onto the shoulder, tires rumbling over tall grass.

She got back onto the road. The truck on her left scraped against her door. Something heavy thumped onto her roof. A hand smashed through her side window in a storm of glass. Talons swooped at her face. Wynona ducked, leaning toward the passenger side.

Ahead, two police SUVs formed a roadblock. Sam Zano and his

Mounties aimed their rifles.

Wynona swerved hard to the right as shots shattered her back windows. Her car barreled into the forest, bumping over logs and ditches. Branches scratched the roof and the beast on top flew off. Her Buick rocketed downhill between the scattered pines. Much too fast. She tried to brake, but something was under the pedal.

Her flask!

Wynona fought the wheel. The right front bumper struck a tree, jolted her sideways into a pine. Her door caved inward. The impact hurled her against the passenger door. Shaken but alive, she pushed open the door and climbed out. Her shoulder ached and the forest was spinning.

The trucks stopped, lights stabbing through the pines. Bodies jumped from the beds of the trucks. Doors flew open. The men's angry voices turned to growls.

Wynona raced through woods.

Something snarled off to her left. She turned to see a white-eyed demon running through the trees. Holding back her scream, Wynona veered to her right.

Several growls sounded behind her.

How much longer could she run? Her lungs felt as if they would explode. Fear kept her going.

The forest went silent. She glanced back. Nothing chased her. Had she lost them?

Getting her bearings, she spotted the lake. There were houses along the water's edge. Maybe she could steal one of the boats. She came into a section of the woods where the trees spread apart. She slowed to catch her breath, her side aching.

Laughter off to her left seized her heart.

Turning, Wynona spotted Mayor Thorpe standing ten yards away, his eyes reflecting the moon. He stood with his hands on his hips. He was still dressed in his suit, complete with cowboy hat and boots. "My dear Wynona, how foolish you were to think you could ever escape us." Thorpe smiled impossibly wide, his mouth filled with shark's teeth. Behind him dozens of white dots appeared in the darkness. The devil who had fathered her child shouted in the ancient language.

The demons charged from all directions, pouncing on Wynona. Clawing, tearing, devouring—erasing her very existence.

Chapter Twenty

In the underground shelter, Kyle and Jessica watched a video of the night Elkheart's crew was attacked in Macâya Forest. It was dark, chaotic footage of people running around a campfire. Kyle winced at the screams, gunshots and animal growls as the team was overtaken. A monstrous hand swiped at the camera and the footage ended.

As his father ejected the tape, Kyle remained seated with Jessica on the couch, absorbing everything. The abductions, the murders, a town made up of shape-shifting demons—it was all too much to fathom.

Jessica was visibly shocked and hadn't spoken in a while. Kyle wanted to say something to make her feel safe, but no comforting words came to mind. He put his arm around her shoulder and kissed her temple.

His father locked the metal cabinet that concealed all his research. "For now, I don't want either of you mentioning anything about the shifters to Eric. The last thing we need is for him to go off half-cocked."

Kyle squeezed his fists to keep himself from panicking. "What are we going to do? My plane is parked at the marina."

"Tonight, we sit tight. We'll be safe within the circle of torches Grandfather and I have set up."

Kyle stood. "You think you can keep those things out with magic?"

"Our tribe and the shifters have honored each other's territories for over a century. Our ancestors put sacred laws in place to protect us." Elkheart placed a reassuring palm on Kyle's shoulder. "You two, go get a good night's sleep. Tomorrow, Madu, Scarpetti and I are going back to Macâya Forest to find your sister and Amy. After that, we'll figure out how to escape."

* * *

Kyle and Jessica returned upstairs to the loft in silence. There was still no sign of Eric and that worried Kyle more than he let on. He had convinced himself earlier that Eric had just gone for a drive to cool off and would return after an hour or two. Despite their differences, Kyle still considered his brother family, and the idea of losing him was just as heartbreaking as losing Shawna. Gripping the rail, he did his best to hold himself together.

Jessica quietly packed a suitcase. She didn't cry or panic or demand to be taken away from here. No hysterical theatrics from this woman. In moments of crisis, she displayed an inner strength that Kyle admired. It made him love her all the more. Love? Yes, his feelings for her were that strong now. He would die before he let Ray or anyone lay a hand on her.

Kyle leaned over the rail that overlooked the dark den. Elkheart had retreated upstairs to his room. The mercenaries were on patrol outside, standing watch on the front and back porches. All they could do was wait now. Kyle thought of his plane parked at the marina. They would have to go through Hagen's Cove to get to it. Would the townspeople let them leave? Tomorrow his father and the mercenaries were going to sneak into the mineshaft and search for Shawna and Amy. If by chance they were successful, then Elkheart said the Thorpe clan probably wouldn't let them leave without a fight. Kyle's mind couldn't even go there. He wanted to erase everything he had just learned. Wanted to be back home in Seattle, taking Jessica out on their first date, starting a new life with her. Now, the chances of either of them ever leaving these woods were slim.

He turned around and saw Jessica was standing by the bed, staring at him. They looked at one another for several seconds, saying nothing, but speaking volumes with their eyes. Her brave façade began to crumble. Her face trembled as she teared up.

Kyle put his arms around her.

"I'm so scared," she whispered.

"It's okay," he said, doing his best to soothe her fears.

She sniffed. "I don't want to die."

"That's not going to happen."

"I was just getting to know you."

"Jess..."

She looked up at him, her eyes glossy. "I'm so afraid of losing you."

Kyle pressed his forehead to hers. "I'm staying right here with you."

They kissed, more desperately than before. Jessica pulled off her shirt and her bra. Kyle removed his shirt and shorts, and then she helped him out of his boxers. While sucking her breasts, he slid her shorts and panties down her legs. Both naked, they embraced, kissing, making their way to the bed.

She lay on her back. Kyle climbed on top of Jessica and embraced her. He kissed her again, longer, deeper, and then she was guiding him inside her. As their flesh melded, his entire being seemed to expand with hers. In that moment, all thoughts and fears vanished. They became a union of the animal and the divine—flesh pleasuring flesh, souls merging into ecstasy.

* * *

Elkheart retreated to his bedroom for some much needed quiet time. Sitting on his bed, his aching body relished the comfort of the mattress and pillow. It had been an age since he last slept in a bed. He lit one of his cherished Cuban cigars and puffed. "Man, I love a good cigar." Smoking was the only thing that relaxed him.

He leaned back against the headboard. His whole body ached. If he closed his eyes, he could probably sleep for days. Elkheart touched the other side of the bed, remembering when Amy had slept there six weeks ago. Their fling had been brief, but intense. One of his best archaeology students at the University of Vancouver, Amy Hanson had volunteered to assist him on his latest expedition. Working beside one another for long hours at the campus had led to them sleeping together. They had too many years between them to be anything more than lovers. Elkheart was fifty and Amy, twenty-three. Her youth and eagerness to learn from him had breathed new life into him. She also helped him get over the loss of Wynona. Now *there* was a woman Elkheart could have spent his life with, had she not been a prisoner to Hagen's Cove.

Mayor Thorpe had disapproved of Elkheart's relationship with Wynona, so the mayor and their son, Hugo, had locked her away for several months. Elkheart had wanted to take Wynona away from Hagen's Cove, but the men of the Thorpe clan were relentless and would kill to protect their women. Now they had Amy as well. She was being kept somewhere down in the tunnels beneath Macâya Forest.

Elkheart had been horrified to learn that Ray Roamingbear had invited his kids here. Now Ray had taken Shawna. Losing his daughter fueled Elkheart's rage. Puffing his cigar, he blew smoke rings toward the ceiling. The Thorpe clan had destroyed his marriage, run off his tribe and taken the women he cherished most. Tomorrow, Elkheart planned to show the people of Hagen's Cove that they had crossed the wrong Indian.

* * *

Kyle lay on his back with Jessica's head on his chest. He stared up at the stars through the skylight and remembered their first night on the balcony, looking through her telescope. At that time, his chance of ever being with her had seemed as remote as the stars. Now she lay naked in his arms. The feeling of her skin touching his sent ripples of euphoria up his body to the top of his head. He could feel her heartbeat, her breath on his chest. Shrouding this heavenly moment was a dark cloud of fear that Jessica was going to be snatched away and lost to him forever. It wasn't fair. He had endured two years of loneliness while mourning his wife's death. He had survived his own suicidal tendencies, faced Death while standing on the ledge of his balcony fifteen stories above the city. He had kept going, hoping he would one day experience love again. He deserved to be happy. Now that he had found Jessica, there were so many things he wanted to do with her, so many places to take her, if only given the chance.

"You're awfully quiet." She lifted her head. "I need you to talk to me."

"About what?"

"Anything." Her eyes showed that she was more afraid than she was letting on. "Just take my mind away from here."

"Okay…I was just thinking how I wish we were alone together on some tropical island."

She smiled at this. "Yeah? Like where?"

"Tahiti. Just imagine it, Jessica, sandy beaches, crystal-clear water, sunny weather. We could stay in one of those huts that stands over the water. Dive right in from our bedroom."

"We could go snorkeling."

"And swim with dolphins."

She laughed. "Sounds wonderful."

Kyle stroked her back. His fantasy was interrupted by images of demon skulls, of his father's expedition team being slaughtered by beasts attacking from the darkness. This sent a wave of shivers through him.

"What's wrong?" Jessica asked.

"Just a chill." To keep the dark thoughts at bay, he concentrated on the fantasy of traveling the world with Jessica. "What's your dream vacation?"

"I've always wanted to go to Paris. Visit the Louvre, the Eiffel Tower, the whole bit."

He pictured the two of them walking the streets of Paris. "I know the perfect little bistro where they make the best crepes. We can sample every kind on the menu."

"And drink lots of French wine and go dancing."

"I could take you to Paris."

"Seriously?"

"If you'd go with me."

"I'd go anywhere with you." Her eyes were dead serious.

"Then consider it a date...after we have our first one in Seattle, of course."

"You're on." Jessica smiled. "How about taking me to Paris *and* Tahiti?"

"Okay, now you're pushing it." Kyle rolled Jessica over and kissed her, caught up in the fantasy that they could have a happy future together. But at the back of his mind, his thoughts returned to the present. A terrible ache burrowed at the center of his chest as he thought of his sister still out in the woods somewhere, or, God forbid, down in the cave. As a shockwave of fear coursed through him, Kyle turned away, hiding his face.

"What's it is?" Jessica asked.

"Nothing."

Her hand touched his shoulder. "Please, talk to me. We need to be strong for each other."

"I..." Kyle did his best not to tear up. "I'm afraid for Shawna."

"She's going to be all right. Your father and his men will find her."

Jessica's stare tried to convince Kyle that there was still some hope left. He wanted to believe that everything was going to work out. That Shawna and Eric would return to the cabin safely. But the stark reality was even if his family was all back together, the people of Hagen's Cove might not let them leave these woods alive.

* * *

Eric lay spread eagle on the ground, as the four women held him down and took turns with him. At first, the arrival of Nadine's friends had been a man's fantasy come true. Each woman looked as if she had stepped out of a centerfold. A redhead, brunette, and two blondes who looked like twin sisters. Celeste Thorpe, clearly the alpha female, took charge, climbing on top of him, mauling him with her hungry lips.

Eric had wanted to fuck this redhead badly yesterday at the bar, and tonight he got his wish, only he didn't enjoy it as much as he'd hoped. Sex had always been a sport he played on *his* terms. He loved the thrill of the hunt, the seduction, the conquest. He also liked being in control, his women submissive. Celeste, Nadine and the twins wouldn't let him leave when he was finished. They drained him and replenished him over and over. At last, he passed out from exhaustion.

Eric awoke some time during the night. The headlights of the Hummer blazed in his eyes. The four women were lying together naked in the grass, intertwined. By the rise and fall of their ribs, they appeared to be sleeping.

He crawled to where their clothes lay scattered on the ground—bras, panties, denim cut-offs, high-heel shoes, a leopard skirt. He found his shorts and slipped them on. Then his hiking boots. He couldn't find his shirt. *Screw it! Just get the hell out of here.* He climbed behind the wheel of the Hummer and locked the doors. He turned the key in the ignition. It revved but wouldn't start.

The four women raised their heads, eyes reflecting the beams of the headlights.

Eric twisted the key again. "Come on!"

The naked women approached, circling the vehicle. Celeste put her hands on the hood. "Where do you think you're going?"

Nadine dragged her nails down his side window. "Baby, don't leave us."

The blonde twins pounded the back window.

"Go screw someone else!" Eric pumped the gas pedal.

The women howled, their skin darkening. Their bones stretched.

"Holy shit!" Eric turned the key again. *Rev, rev, rev.*

Nadine flattened her palm against the window. Claws split the tips of her fingers.

Celeste leaped onto the hood, her bat face growling at the windshield.

"Shit, shit, shit!" The engine turned over finally. Eric drove forward, barreling toward the lake. He slammed the brakes and the Celeste-thing flew into the water. In the rearview mirror he saw the other three running toward him.

Eric yanked the gear-shift into reverse and flattened his foot on the pedal. He backed over one of the twins, the wheels rolling over her with a crunch. "Oh, fuck!" He smashed into Nadine's Jeep. Spinning the wheel, Eric did a U-turn and sped up the narrow road.

The women ran through the high grass like a pack of hyenas, laughing as if enjoying the hunt. One of them leaped, crashing through the passenger side window. Nadine opened a mouth full of fangs. She clawed at his arm and ribs. Eric gripped her forehead and held her back. Her legs hung out the window.

Eric lost hold of the wheel, swerving. The Hummer sideswiped a tree, cutting the girl in half. Her upper body fell into the passenger seat.

On the verge of tears, Eric kept driving until he reached the main road and stopped. Nadine's lifeless head lay in his lap. Her blood covered the dash and passenger side.

"I killed her. Fuck! Fuck! Fuck!"

He had to get rid of her. He opened the passenger door and pushed Nadine's severed body into the high grass. On the dirt road behind him, he heard angry growls. He spotted two loping shadows.

Eric stomped the gas and fishtailed onto the paved road. He looked in the rearview mirror. The two she-beasts stopped in the middle of the road, their feral eyes glowing in the night.

* * *

The interior of the cabin was kept dark so no one from the woods could see inside. Porch lights lit up the front and backyard. All around the main house, the circle of torches continued to burn. Moths flew around the flames. A few got too close and caught fire.

In the kitchen, Jessica made a pot of coffee for the men. Next to her, Kyle prepared bowls of leftover stew with cornbread. Jessica's whole body tingled every time she brushed up against him. In all her life, she had never felt more secure with a man. She rubbed his back. He gave her a brief smile and then returned to his cooking. All the joy from their lovemaking had left his eyes. For a brief second, Jessica felt her heart drop, a foolish insecurity creeping in that he didn't really love her. *He's just worried about his sister.*

Jessica prayed that Ray hadn't done anything to hurt Shawna. A vision of the rapist flashed in Jessica's head, remembering how she felt when he dragged her into the shed.

"They like the pretty ones," Ray had said. *"They'll be coming for you soon. But first, you and I get to have a little fun."*

Her wrist still ached from when he had shackled her to the mattress. The thought of that monster still roaming the woods gave her the shivers. Thankfully, the mercenaries were keeping constant watch, and Kyle kept his rifle within reach. *I'm safe now,* she kept telling herself. She wanted to believe it, but the feeling she was getting from Kyle and the others was that they were in far greater danger than ever. Maybe killing Ray's dogs was enough to scare him away. *Or maybe he'll seek revenge.* As a precaution, the men planned to stand watch in shifts tonight.

Jessica took cups of coffee to Scarpetti and Madu. "Some java to keep you boys awake."

"Now that's what I call hospitality." The Italian soldier leered at her.

The South African soldier just bowed and gave her a big grin. He had an innocent smile with a large gap between his front teeth. Madu was so quiet and shy. She figured he was in his mid-twenties. He stood over six feet and had a lean, muscular build. When Madu wasn't smiling, he looked menacing, like he could stare down a lion. He sipped his coffee as he stood at a back window and watched the woods.

In an alcove that would be considered a second living room, Elkheart was sitting in a chair facing the front windows. Jessica set down a steaming cup on a table beside him.

"Thanks." Kyle's father kept his focus on the front yard.

"Mind if I join you?" she asked.

He nodded to the chair next to him. "Be my guest." Wearing wire-rimmed glasses, Elkheart had a face that looked both intellectual and hardened by tragedy. She could see some resemblance to Kyle and Eric, but their father had stronger Cree features.

Grandfather Two Hawks paced across the front porch, shaking a rattle and chanting.

"What's he doing?" Jessica asked.

"Warding off evil spirits. He's an old-school medicine man. That's how he protects our village." Elkheart smiled and raised his rifle. "I take a more modern approach."

Jessica decided she liked Kyle's father. "So how did you meet Madu?"

Elkheart looked over his shoulder at the dark-skinned mercenary. "About ten years ago, I was working on an archaeological expedition in South Africa. My team was having trouble with lions, so we hired a few Zulu warriors to protect us. Madu was sixteen then. An orphan who'd seen his parents murdered. Guess you could say he's like a son to me." He winked. "Don't let Kyle or Eric know that."

Headlights beamed through the front windows. The Hummer parked and Eric hurried to the door and knocked. "Let me in!"

His father opened the door. Eric stumbled inside. In the ambient light, Jessica could see he was shirtless and bleeding. He had slashes on his arms, chest and ribs and fresh nicks on his face.

"What happened to you?" asked Elkheart.

"I was freaking attacked." Eric went to a kitchen cupboard and pulled out a bottle of vodka. His hands shook as he poured a drink.

"By what?" Kyle asked.

"I don't know. I was sitting in the car by the lake and this animal jumped through my window." Eric gulped the vodka. "I think it was a mountain lion."

Jessica grabbed her medical kit. "I'll clean those wounds."

He glared at her. "No thanks, I'd rather bleed to death."

"She's just trying to help you," Kyle said.

"This is all I need right here." Eric raised his Stoli bottle.

"Stop being a horse's ass," Elkheart said. "You're bleeding all over my kitchen floor. Now sit down and let me dress those wounds."

* * *

While his father patched up Eric, Kyle stood post at the front windows. He felt awkward around his brother as guilt began to settle in that he'd slept with Eric's ex-girlfriend.

When Eric went into the bathroom to shower, Kyle signaled Jessica over. He whispered, "We should keep our PDA to a minimum."

"You mean I can't do this?" She held his hand.

Kyle smiled. "I don't like it either, but anything else is rubbing his nose in it. Hopefully at some point he will forgive us and see this is for the best. In the meantime we should sleep in separate beds."

She made a sad face. "I know you're right, but I'll miss you."

"It won't be for long."

"He didn't love me. And who knows how many bloody times he was unfaithful?"

"I know, but Eric has a lot of pride." And a bad temper.

She nodded. "Okay, hands off 'til we get back to Seattle. But as soon as I move out, you and I are going on a date."

"I won't let you out of my sight."

Jessica waved goodbye. "I'll just be in the next room fantasizing."

As she started to walk away, Kyle pulled her to him. "One last kiss." He gave her one to think about until they returned home. Then they separated to opposite ends of the den. It was going to be damned hard keeping his hands off of her.

His brother came out a few minutes later, wearing a fresh set of shorts and bandages. Eric remained shirtless as if showing off his battle scars. Kyle didn't believe the mountain lion story, but he was happy to see his brother had made it back alive. Now all they had to do was find Shawna and they could get the hell away from this place.

Kyle turned his attention back to the window. He thought he saw movement out in the woods. A shadow moved from one tree to the next.

"Dad, there's somebody out there!" He grabbed his rifle.

Elkheart came to the window. "Where?"

Kyle pointed. "Just past that…"

The forest seemed to come alive as dozens of silhouettes sifted through the pines. Kyle's heart seized as men carrying axes gathered at the edge of the burning torches. At the front of the crowd, wearing a suit and cowboy hat, stood Mayor Thorpe.

Chapter Twenty-one

Kyle felt Jessica behind him as they looked out the front windows. Outside, at least fifty loggers had gathered. More kept coming from the forest. They circled the cabin. Many held axes, crowbars and baseball bats. They remained just outside the burning torches, their faces cast in shadows.

Eric backed to the center of the den. "Oh fuck, what do they want?"

Elkheart said, "Madu, Scarpetti, go upstairs and wait for my signal."

The two soldiers hurried up the staircase.

"You kids, stay inside." Elkheart started for the door.

Kyle grabbed his father's arm. "Are you crazy? They'll kill you."

"I've dealt with them before. They won't cross the sacred fire. See?"

Some of the lumberjacks tried to enter the ring of fire and jumped back as if hit by an electric current.

"I'm going with you then."

"Fine," Elkheart said. "But let me handle the talking."

Eric remained by the fireplace, clutching a log poker.

Kyle's and Jessica's eyes met. "Go upstairs with the soldiers," he said.

"I don't want you to go out there." She touched his hand.

"I can't let Dad face them alone. Hurry upstairs. We'll be back inside in a minute." Gripping his rifle, Kyle stepped out onto the front porch and stood next to his father. Grandfather was there, too, praying and shaking his rattle.

"Stay on the porch," his dad said.

Kyle's heart beat wildly as he watched his father walk across the yard. He stopped twenty feet from the crowd. "Mayor, you know your people aren't supposed to be trespassing."

"You're one to talk, Mr. Elkheart," Thorpe said in his thick Danish accent. "Your curiosity has put us all in a rather dangerous predicament. When Lord Father returns tomorrow, he won't be happy about the bones you took."

Kyle tightened his grip on the rifle. He saw the ghost of Nina Whitefeather appear from the crowd. She walked along the circle of torches, watching the standoff.

Elkheart squared off against the mayor. "You want your filthy bones back? You can have them. First, you bring back my daughter. And Amy too."

"Sorry, but they've already been spoken for. They belong with us now."

"You son of a bitch, if you don't bring back those girls, I'll burn Hagen's Cove to the ground!"

Mayor Thorpe raised his palms. "Calm down now. Let's be civilized."

"The bones for the girls…that's my final offer."

Thorpe grinned. "Oh, we're not here for the bones, Mr. Elkheart. We want that woman you got in the cabin."

Kyle stepped forward and aimed his rifle at the crowd. "You stay the fuck away from her!"

Elkheart said, "Son, lower the gun! We don't want to escalate this."

Kyle lowered his rifle. His body shook with rage.

Mayor Thorpe smiled in the glow of the torches, revealing sharp teeth. "Maybe we'll take your young man too, for our females. He's got *vigor*. They like that."

Elkheart said, "Son, go back to the porch."

Kyle backed away, keeping his eyes on the Thorpe clan.

Their leader, dressed in his suit and cowboy hat and wearing a smug grin, crossed his arms. "Kyle, did you ever wonder why you were invited back? You can thank your father for that. Around here, when a Cree crosses our town, the sins of the father fall upon his children."

"You leave my kids out of this."

"We both know that isn't possible."

"Mayor, you see that window up there?" Elkheart pointed. "Right now, my snipers have you in their scopes."

Two red laser beams stretched from second-story windows to Thorpe's chest. The mayor growled, his eyes burning with white fire.

Elkheart said, "Unless you want to die on Cree soil tonight, I'd suggest you take your clan and get the hell off our property."

"We need the woman, Mr. Elkheart. If you don't give her over to us by dawn, then Lord Father is going to be full of wrath tomorrow. He'll come for all of you. We'll take that woman, one way or another. It's up to you whether we take your sons, as well." The mayor tipped his cowboy hat. "Something to think about." He walked back into the forest.

The loggers challenged Kyle and Elkheart with angry stares and then followed the mayor.

Shaking with adrenaline, Kyle joined his father in the center of the yard.

Several shadowy faces turned and looked back, their eyes blazing white dots. Then they all faded into the darkness.

* * *

Thunder rumbled in the distance. Flashes of lightning branched over the treetops as storm clouds began to darken the sky. Wind rattled the windowpanes.

While Elkheart and his mercenaries conversed in heated whispers in the kitchen, Kyle sat with Jessica on the loveseat, holding her hands. After what they had just experienced, Kyle wasn't about to let her out of his sight. She kept looking at him with horrified eyes. "Why me?" she whispered.

He wanted to say something to ease her fears, but there were no words. He was more afraid of losing her than of being taken himself. He would fight to the death before allowing anyone to hurt Jessica.

A loud commotion came from up in the loft. Eric cursed as he lugged three suitcases down the stairs and headed for the front door.

His father stepped in front of him. "Where do you think you're going?"

"Driving the hell out of here. If anyone else wants to go, now's your chance. Jess, you coming?"

She shook her head.

Eric made a face as if she had just slapped him. "Suit yourself then."

"What about Shawna?" Kyle asked. "You're just going to abandon her?"

Eric said, "There's nothing we can do for her sitting around here."

"We have to find her," Kyle said.

"Then go play Rambo," Eric said. "I'll drive to Calgary and tell the police. Let them come search for her."

Elkheart remained in front of the door. "You're staying right here."

"The hell I am! Out of my way, old man."

Their father shoved Eric backward. "Listen, goddamn it! There's one road out of here and they'll have it blocked. If you drive off, you'll be dead by morning or worse."

Eric's face twisted. He looked like he might cry. His voice cracked. "I don't want to die out here."

"None of us do." Elkheart took one of his suitcases. "This is the safest place."

"What do we do now?" Kyle asked.

"The only thing we can do. Wait until dawn."

"We'll be dead by then," Eric said.

"Listen, every one of you," their father commanded. "Those things out there feed off fear. They can find your weaknesses and use them against you. If you believe in God, now would be a good time to start praying."

Jessica squeezed Kyle's hands. He gazed into her eyes, knowing what she was thinking. This was going to be the longest night of their lives.

* * *

In the kitchen, Eric poured himself another glass of vodka. It burned his throat, but did nothing to stop his body from shaking. Peering into the den, he noticed Kyle and Jessica sitting close to one another. She was crying, and Kyle was stroking her hair and talking to her in whispers.

What the fuck is this? Grabbing the Stoli bottle, Eric stepped into the den. Kyle and Jessica quickly moved apart.

Eric sat down at the fireplace. A fire in the hearth burned behind him, heating his back. He took a swig from the bottle, staring at Kyle and Jessica on the loveseat. "You two sure have gotten chummy."

"She's scared," Kyle said. "I was just consoling her."

"Is that so? Because it sure looks like you're moving in on my woman."

"How can you think about that right now?" Kyle asked.

The logs in the hearth popped and crackled.

"Tell me. Did you two fuck while I was gone?"

Kyle glared. "That's enough, Eric."

"I have a right to know if my brother's been fucking my fiancée."

"Ex-fiancée," Jessica said.

"So you jumped into bed with my brother?"

Kyle stood and took her hand. "Come on, let's go to another room."

Eric followed them. "Man, was I an idiot to invite you two on this trip. Kyle, I'm not surprised that you would try to get into Jessica's pants. But, Jessica, I had no idea that you were such a whore."

When Kyle wheeled around and decked him, Eric felt an explosion of pain as the fist struck his face. Next thing Eric knew, he was flat on his back with Kyle on his chest. They rolled on the floor, grappling with one another. Kyle's forearm pressed down on Eric's throat, cutting off his oxygen. His vision turned fuzzy.

"Stop it!" Their father and Madu pulled them apart.

Elkheart stood between them. "This is exactly what the shifters want. For us to turn on one another."

"We should just give them what they want," Eric said, rubbing his throat. "They're going to come back and take her anyway."

Kyle charged Eric again, but Madu held him back.

Eric stood and picked up the Stoli bottle.

Elkheart took it away from him. "We need you sober."

"This is all *your* fault," Eric said to his father. "We're going to die tonight because of you."

"I won't let that happen. Come with us. Madu and I have a plan."

* * *

Everyone but Grandfather and Scarpetti gathered down in the bomb shelter. With its steel doors and thick concrete walls, Kyle felt safer down here. His father unlocked a door to a second, smaller room. Inside was an arsenal of submachine guns, assault rifles, shotguns and pistols. Enough weapons to arm a cult of religious fanatics, or in this case, defend themselves against one.

"Jesus Christ," Eric said.

"Madu and I have been preparing for this for a long time. I didn't plan for you two being here, but we could sure use your help."

Kyle picked up a sawed-off shotgun.

"That's good for close range," his father said. "I'd also take one of these." He pulled a black sniper rifle off the rack. "Just put the red laser on your target and fire."

Kyle aimed the rifle, placing a laser on the wall.

"What are you planning to do?" Jessica asked.

"We have to defend ourselves," Elkheart said. "If Thorpe's clan wants a war, we'll give them one." Kyle's father had a crazed look in his eyes, like he was looking forward to a showdown.

Eric backed away from the gun closet. "I don't want any part of this."

Elkheart said, "You got two choices, son, fight or die. It's time to man-up."

Eric's face was a mask of panic. "Why don't we just stay down here and lock ourselves in?"

"They would just wait us out. Up top, we can shoot them before they reach the house."

Eric jabbed a finger at his father. "You're nuts if you think a few guns are going to stop that many men."

"I know them better than you think. Before you boys were born, our tribe got into a feud with Thorpe's clan, and after we killed a few of them, Thorpe backed off."

"Maybe Eric's right," Jessica said. "Maybe I should go with them. Then no one has to risk getting killed."

"No way," Kyle said. "They're not taking you anywhere. Dad, I want Jessica to stay down here where she'll be safe."

"Good. The rest of us will load up guns and ammo and take turns standing watch. Are you in, boys?"

Kyle and Eric nodded.

"Madu, will you instruct them on how to kill the shifters?"

The mercenary pulled out one of the demon skulls. "They are difficult to kill." He knocked on the cranium. "Very thick, like a bear. Their bones deflect bullets. You have to shoot them through the eye or the heart."

"A gut shot won't stop them," Elkheart added. "These creatures heal amazingly fast. They won't bleed to death. But they do have one major weakness. They hate fire. Their skin is highly flammable. That's why I built this." He pulled out a makeshift flamethrower. He slid the canister pack on his back and gripped the nozzle. "I call it 'dragon's breath.'" Elkheart grinned, an unlit cigar tucked at the corner of his mouth. "With this baby I can barbecue shifters from twenty feet away."

Their father went on to explain that the men would all stand watch for the next hour, then take two-hour shifts throughout the night so the others could sleep. As Elkheart, Madu and Eric left the shelter, Kyle hung back with Jessica. "Lock the door when I leave. It's six inches of steel. Nothing's getting in here unless you let it. Our code is three knocks."

"I want to fight alongside you," she protested. "I grew up on a farm. I know how to shoot a gun."

He shook his head. "The mayor's men want *you*. I couldn't concentrate knowing you weren't safe. I want you down here."

She nodded and put her arms around his waist. "Stay with me."

Kyle kissed her forehead. "I wish I could, but they need me up top. When my shift is over, I'll come check on you."

She rested her head on his chest. "I don't want to lose you."

He held her against him. "You're not going to Paris by yourself."

* * *

In the dark cabin, each man stood post near a window in different rooms. Kyle and Madu went upstairs, while Elkheart and Scarpetti remained in the den. Eric took the study, feeling safer that he could jump down into the underground tunnel if he needed to retreat. Holding a Glock pistol, Eric stared out the window. The porch lights and circle of burning torches provided plenty of light to see the perimeter.

He tried to figure a way out of this nightmare. His old man was crazy if he thought he could take on this town. Four of their women had nearly kicked Eric's ass earlier. Against fifty men, they wouldn't last five minutes. Eric wasn't about to go down with the rest of Elkheart's group. He needed a plan. He considered sneaking out a window and running into the woods. Maybe he could hike his way past the roadblocks. But he had no clue how far it was between here and the Trans-Canada Highway. It could take days. He would need provisions, a bedroll, a flashlight and a compass. He couldn't collect all that without Elkheart finding out. And what if Eric got lost out there? These woods were full of bears, wolves and now demons… It was a bad plan.

Eric shook his head, disbelieving the situation he was in. When Nadine, Celeste and the twins had attacked him earlier, he had sworn they had rufied his beer and he had hallucinated them turning into demons. This was all just a bad trip, he hoped. The drugs would wear off soon and he'd wake up to find that he had imagined this whole cult standoff.

He saw a flash of white outside.

Eric… a woman's voice spoke inside his head.

Celeste stepped out of the woods, wearing a sheer negligee. Her red hair hung across her bare shoulders. She walked along the torches, leering at Eric. Damn, this bitch didn't know when to quit. She waggled a finger. *Come to me, baby.*

The pull to obey her was damned strong. Eric backed away. "Stop it. Stop!"

I'll satisfy your every fantasy.

"Stay away from me!" He went into the hall bathroom and locked the door. He looked at his reflection in the mirror. He saw a man who looked beaten and battered, with two black eyes and a busted lip. His torso and arms were covered in slash marks.

In the reflection, Celeste stepped out of the shower behind him, dripping wet. She whispered in his ear, *There's one way you can escape, baby.*

He turned around, but she wasn't there. Eric slumped against the sink. He stared down at the Glock in his hand. All he had to do was put the barrel in his mouth.

Eric put a fist to his forehead. *I have to get the fuck out of here.* He returned to his post, his whole body shaking. In the darkness, someone whispered his name. He turned to see Ray Roamingbear standing in the corner of the study, aiming a crossbow at Eric's chest.

* * *

Upstairs in the room where Shawna and Zack had stayed, Kyle sat in a chair by the window. Beside him several guns were propped against the wall. He twirled the wedding ring around his finger. The sight of his sister's guitar only added fuel to the rage burning inside him.

They belong with us now, Mayor Thorpe had said of Shawna and Amy.

Like his father, Kyle wanted revenge. He wasn't afraid of dying. Death had become his near constant companion. It haunted his home, lay beside him in bed, even whispered in his ear each night as he slept.

As he thought about his late wife, Stephanie appeared outside the glass door that led onto the balcony. She looked as beautiful as the day he had married her. She placed her palm to the glass. Like Kyle, she was wearing her wedding ring. "I still need you," she said. "It's lonely on this side without you."

"I know." Kyle stood and put his palm to the glass, matching hers.

Stephanie looked so real. So alive. "Honey, we don't have to be apart." Her eyes filled with tears. "I miss you."

"I miss you too." So many emotions flowed through him—grief, guilt, sadness, desire. How many nights he had cried himself to sleep, longing to be with his wife. Wishing he had died with her.

"I can't come back to you, Kyle," she said. "But you can come to me."

He looked at all the guns. A single shot from any one of them would transport him into her world.

"There are beaches here," she said, smiling. "We could collect shells together, then make love on the sand." Memories of their honeymoon flashed through his mind.

He thought of Jessica, the new love for her now burning inside him. He had finally met a woman he could love.

Kyle pulled his hand away from the glass. "I'm sorry, Steph, but I've made a promise to someone else." He walked over to an open window. He slid off his wedding band. "I wish you well on the other side." He kissed the gold ring and then set on the windowsill. When he looked back at the glass door, his wife was gone.

* * *

In the gloom of the study, lightning flashed behind Ray Roamingbear. He put a finger to his lips. "Shhh... Set your gun down, gently."

Eric did as he was told.

"I don't want to hurt you. See?" His cousin lowered the bow and raised one hand. "I'm on your side. They sent me to protect you."

Eric swallowed. "Can you help me escape?"

"I can get you off the reservation before things get hairy."

"What about back to Seattle? I want to go home."

"I'm afraid that's not possible. They'll never let you leave Hagen's Cove. But they'll let you live, if you join the ranks like I did."

"I don't want to be a part of some cult."

"Oh, it's not what you think. It's paradise here. There's nothing but love between our brothers and sisters. We were living peacefully until your father started stirring up trouble. Do you want die for his sins?"

"Fuck no."

"Just think about it," Ray said. "You and I would make a great team. I could mentor you. Teach you how to serve Lord Father and the clan. And you know what you get in return?"

Eric shook his head.

"You see them out there?" Ray pointed out the window.

Celeste and several beautiful women stood at the edge of the forest.

"They'll help you live out every fantasy you ever imagined. The women back in the city will never satisfy you like our sisters can."

"I don't give a fuck about them. I just want out of here. I'll do anything, Ray. Just get me the fuck out."

His cousin thought for a moment. "I can convince Thorpe to spare you...*if* you help us."

Eric's eyes remained transfixed on Ray. "What do you want me to do?"

* * *

The storm crackled above the cabin. In the upstairs bedroom, Kyle glanced at a digital clock on the nightstand. After midnight. He wanted to check on Jessica, but he had another hour on his shift.

Rain started pelting the roof and windows. Then a heavy drizzle fell, dousing the ring of fire. One by one the torches went out.

Kyle grabbed a rifle and shotgun and hurried downstairs. He found his father standing by a front window in the den. Lightning flickered on his face.

"Dad, will the protective circle hold up in this storm?"

"It should. Grandfather is very powerful. He's out there now, speaking prayers to keep the demons out." Elkheart smiled confidently. "Thorpe's clan members know better than to mess with your grandfather."

A shot fired and one of the porch lights burst.

Kyle and Elkheart dropped to the floor, as several more bullets hit the house.

"That's for killing my dogs!" Ray shouted and shot again. Another light exploded. Darkness pressed against the windows. With the heavy cloud cover, there was no moonlight tonight, just random flickers from the electrical storm.

Elkheart broke a windowpane and took a few blind shots at the forest.

They waited a few moments, but didn't hear another word from Ray.

"Christ, I don't see Grandfather," his father said. "Scarpetti, do you see him?"

The mercenary looked out the window. "Not on the back porch either."

"I'll check the backyard." Kyle ran hunched into the kitchen and peered out the sink window. The rain was coming down like a monsoon now, shaking the pine branches. Lightning flashed, and he spotted Grandfather sitting in his rocker in the middle of the yard. Four arrows stuck out of his chest and throat.

* * *

Jessica tried to sleep on one of the twin beds in the vault. Her mind wouldn't stop worrying about Kyle and the others. The men upstairs might die because of her. She kept picturing all the townspeople outside, surrounding the cabin. *We want the girl you got in the cabin,* Mayor Thorpe had said. If Elkheart didn't turn her over by dawn, the town would be back to get her. She tried not to think about what they would do to her.

Tapping...

Jessica rolled over, listening.

Kyle had said three knocks. These taps were steady. *Tap, tap, tap, tap...*like a hammer against metal. And they weren't coming from the door. The sound came from the back of the room, which was dark. The lamp by her bed only lit up a small circle around her. Jessica opened the drawer of a nightstand and found a flashlight.

The tapping stopped.

She walked toward the back of the room. Her flashlight beam found a black metal cabinet and several wooden crates. That's where the bones were stored. One of the demon skulls still sat on top of a crate.

Shifters heal amazingly fast, Elkheart had said.

If their flesh could regenerate, Jessica wondered if the bones could too.

The tapping returned again, startling her. It came from above. Her light followed a set of iron rungs that led up to a square steel door in the ceiling.

Tap, tap, tap, tap...

The hatch vibrated and dust sprinkled down. Someone was trying to get in.

Jessica backed away.

At the door behind her echoed three solid knocks.

"Oh, thank God." Jessica opened the door ready to throw her arms around Kyle. Her heart dropped when she saw Eric.

* * *

Kyle reeled at the sight of Grandfather's body. "Dad, he's dead."

"No..." Elkheart crossed the den and looked out the window. Growling, he raised his automatic rifle and unleashed his fury on the woods. Then his father stopped and collapsed against a wall, breathing heavily. He punched the wall. "Fuck!"

Kyle watched for Ray Roamingbear, eager kill the bastard himself.

Rain continued to fall, thumping against the porch awning. The forest erupted with howls and screeches. Kyle's heart quickened. In the strobe lights of the storm, tall shadow shapes with elongated arms moved between the pines. Some shifters walked on two legs, others loped on all-fours like apes.

"They're coming!" Scarpetti screamed and opened fire with his automatic rifle.

Demons broke the tree line, running past the unlit torches.

Kyle peered through the scope of his sniper rifle. Lined his red laser on the chest of one charging across the yard. *Boom!* The shot knocked it down. The rifle's kick hurt his shoulder. Ignoring the pain, he whipped the beam to the next moving shadow and pulled the trigger, hitting its massive shoulder. The thing kept coming, shrieking toward the sink window. Kyle put the red laser on its face. *Boom!* The shifter dropped and smacked the wall of the house.

More demons burst from the trees. Footfalls thundered like a herd of bison.

Elkheart and Scarpetti sprayed the backyard with wide arcs of bullets. The shadows scattered, circling the cabin. Shots echoed upstairs as Madu started shooting.

"I've got the back!" Elkheart shouted. "You two take front!"

Kyle and Scarpetti ran to a row of windows. Out front, dozens of shifters tore through the trees. The beasts rammed against the vehicles, fists smashing the windshields. A car alarm sounded. Combined with all the gunshots firing, the noise was maddening. The air stank of hot sulfur.

Heart pounding, Kyle aimed his red laser left and right, trying to target the advancing shadows. "They're attacking from all sides!"

Scarpetti fired rapid bursts with his rifle. "Keep shooting!"

Kyle shot repeatedly, hitting a few moving targets, missing others. Some creatures ran at the house and stopped halfway, baring their fangs like baboons. Others remained in the forest, howling.

"The goddamn things are taunting us!" Scarpetti shouted.

Kyle kept shooting until his rifle clicked empty. He searched his pockets for a fresh magazine.

Scarpetti's clip emptied and he stopped to reload.

Some of the shifters they had shot got back up.

"Shit!" Kyle's shaky hands struggled to swap out the rifle's magazine.

A tall shadow walked toward his window, spreading arms that stretched as it morphed from man to beast. Its palms fanned out with long, branch-like fingers.

Kyle dropped the rifle, reached behind his back, and pulled the sawed-off shotgun from its holster. A fiendish face growled at the window in front of Kyle. He shot point blank. Its head exploded. Its body crashed through the glass and landed at his feet. From the gaping hole in its neck black blood spewed onto the floor. Kyle backed away.

Scarpetti fired madly. "Come on, you motherfuckers!"

Fists hammered at the front door. Kyle turned and blew two holes through it.

Madu ran down the stairs. "There's too many of them!"

Outside, a horde of shadow shapes charged the cabin from all sides.

Elkheart yelled. "Retreat to the study!"

The four men ran down the hall toward the downstairs office. Windows shattered in the den behind them. Kyle joined Scarpetti and Madu in the study. Where was his father?

Kyle looked back down the hallway. Elkheart had stopped midway and was shooting a long, orange-blue flame down the hall. Two shifters wailed as they caught fire and fell into a tangle of clawing limbs. On the other side of the burning heap, more creatures hissed and exposed their fangs. Elkheart kept blasting them. Flames spread up the walls to the ceiling, raging around his father. Kyle and Madu ran down the hall and pulled Elkheart into the study.

"Everyone, down below!" Elkheart commanded, but the bookcase wall was closed. In the fire glow, he struggled to find the book to open it. Lightning flashed. Beasts shaped like black scarecrows stood at every window. Kyle, Madu and Scarpetti stood back to back, firing their guns, as long arms broke through the glass.

The bookcase swiveled open.

"Move! Move! Move!" Elkheart ushered them into the secret room. Then Kyle's father spread an arc of fire around the study, torching the beasts at the windows.

Kyle hurried down the rungs first. Animal cries and rapid shots continued to echo above. His father climbed down. "Keep going!"

Their heavy breathing echoed off the concrete walls as they raced down the tunnel toward the bomb shelter. His father collapsed against a wall, wheezing. He pumped asthma medicine into his mouth.

Kyle ran back to help him.

"Don't worry about me. Get into the shelter!"

The steel door stood open. Kyle ran into the dark room and flipped on the lights.

"Jessica?!" He searched the gun closet, but she wasn't there. At the back of the room, the hatch in the ceiling was open. His whole body shaking, he climbed up the rungs to the garage. The door was up. Kyle ran out into the storm. "Jessica!"

As lightning flashed again, he spotted Eric pushing her toward the forest.

"Stop!" Kyle chased after them. Rain slapped his face. Lightning lit up a forest filled with moving shadows. "Eric!"

His brother turned and fired his pistol. The shot pinged the garage.

Kyle kept running. "Bring her back!"

Eric and Jessica disappeared into the trees.

"Nooooo!" Kyle called after them.

Something roared and slammed into Kyle. He rolled across wet grass. A beast with a gargoyle face and curvy horns pinned him down. Fangs opened up as it shrieked inches from his face. A boot kicked its ribs, knocking it off Kyle. Elkheart aimed a shotgun and blew the shifter's head off.

"Jessica!" Kyle jumped back up and started down the hill, but his father and Madu grabbed his arms. "We have to go after her!"

"It's too late!" his father yelled.

"No!"

They dragged Kyle back into the garage. Scarpetti's gun unleashed a barrage of bullets on a wave of charging shadows. Then he brought down the garage door.

A small demon slipped through, smashing into a tool bench. It leaped ape-like on top of the red Bronco's hood, screeching. The thing kept shifting before their eyes. Horns jutted from its head. A tail sprouted from its backside and whipped over their heads, slicing Madu's cheek.

"Get down!" Scarpetti yelled and fired shots at the creature.

Elkheart pushed Kyle down the hatch, then climbed down himself. Madu and Scarpetti fired rounds above and then scrambled down the rungs. Scarpetti landed on the floor beside Kyle. As gray hands clawed for Madu's face, he pulled the hatch closed, chopping off the fingers. Black blood sprayed the wall and the mercenary's shirt. Severed fingers rained down around Kyle. They squirmed on the floor like maggots. Screaming, Scarpetti stomped them, mashing the fingers with his boots.

Madu spun the wheel and sealed the door to the ceiling then jumped down and collapsed. The four men lay on the floor, gasping for air. Above them, the demon wailed and pounded on the hatch.

* * *

"Let me go!" Jessica cried and kicked at Eric's shins.

He shoved her against a tree and pressed the pistol barrel to her head. "Stop it, goddamn it!"

"Eric, don't do this," she pleaded.

"Babe, you chose the wrong guy to fuck with." He gripped her arm and brought her into a clearing. "Here she is!" he yelled at the woods.

Ray Roamingbear approached, holding up his crossbow. "That's my boy. We'll take her from here." He made clucking sounds with his tongue.

A large animal burst through the clearing. It snatched Jessica in its arms and disappeared with her in the dark forest. Her screaming trailed off.

Eric collapsed against a tree.

Ray cuffed him on the shoulder. "Don't worry about her. You done good. Welcome to the clan, my new brother. Tonight, the females are all yours."

A coven of beautiful women surrounded Eric, pawing him with eager hands. Celeste came to the front of the crowd and caressed his face. She smiled with sharp teeth. "Darling, you have earned a night you will never forget."

Part Eight

Fear Wears Many Skins

I had never loved a woman with so much intensity that I would risk my life for her. My very soul. That I would cross over into forbidden spirit realms to protect her from the evils that walk between worlds. And then the Hollowers took my Elena and nothing else seemed to matter, except finding her.

—Detective Alex Winterbone

Chapter Twenty-two

Kyle dreamt he was running with the elk again. Moonlight lit the winding trail that carved through the forest. The herd led him to the Great House where Kyle heard drumming and chanting. The windows were aglow with orange firelight. He entered the community building. At the center of the long room, several Cree elders and younger men sat around a fire.

Grandfather Two Hawks spoke, "The great war approaches. Those that live beneath the earth are growing stronger. We must prepare our spirits for battle."

As Kyle walked toward the circle of men, all their heads turned toward him.

Grandfather motioned with his hand. "Come, Kyle."

He sat next to his grandfather, awestruck by the strength and fierceness in his eyes. He looked twenty years younger. "It's time you learned how to use your gift."

Grandfather's hands began to glow with bluish-white light. He placed his palms on Kyle's head. Then he woke up...

...back inside the bomb shelter. Bluish-white light illuminated the darkness. As Kyle's eyes adjusted to the gloom, he realized the light was coming from his hands. Sparks swam across his palms like silverfish. The strange phenomenon faded quickly and the room went dark again. Kyle lay back against his pillow. "What the hell?"

* * *

The next morning, Kyle, Elkheart, Madu and Scarpetti gathered as many weapons as they could carry. As Kyle stuffed shells into his sawed-off shotgun, he fought back the urge to break down. His heart felt as if it were being ripped apart. He had failed to protect Jessica and now she was lost in the Devil's Woods.

His father gripped his shoulder. "She's still alive. We'll find her. Shawna and Amy too."

Scarpetti said, "Sir, I think your son should hang back here."

Kyle shook his head. "No way. I'm going."

"You'll slow us down," Scarpetti said.

"I can hold my own."

The ex-Delta Force soldier squared up to him. "You ever been in combat inside a cave? It can royally fuck with your head, man. In Afghanistan, I saw trained soldiers go crazy and start killing their own men. Last thing I need is to be worrying about you down there."

"We need him," Elkheart said, stepping between them and getting in Scarpetti's face. "We need every man who can shoot, and my son is a damned good shot. He goes with us. End of discussion." He passed around caving helmets, radio headsets and night vision goggles. Elkheart showed Kyle how to wear the goggles and turn on the infrared illuminator to see in pitch-dark. To demonstrate, Elkheart turned off all the lights in the bomb shelter. The infrared illuminator created enough ambient light to see details of the room. Kyle could see the others moving about. "Amazing."

"You'll need one of these too." Elkheart handed him a tiny flashlight. "In this mode it's a high-powered flashlight. When you push the button, it shoots out a strobe and temporarily blinds your target. When those bastards go underground, their eyes get extra sensitive."

Scarpetti said, "Yeah, they hate this shit."

Kyle flashed the strobe a few times, and bright flickering light created chaos in the darkness not unlike the strobes at a nightclub.

Elkheart went over a plan that sounded impossible to pull off. Kyle had been down in a cave only once in his life, and that had been with a teenage guide and a busload of tourists taking pictures. He'd suffered severe claustrophobia and vowed never to enter a cave again. He kept that to himself. The more his father talked, the more Kyle thought their mission sounded insane. Four men against a cult of shape-shifting demons. A better plan would be to drive out of here and bring back a hundred-man rescue team who knew how to maneuver through caves. But there wasn't time.

Elkheart lit a candle at an altar. "Before entering Macâya Forest, we must purify our minds." He touched the flame of his lighter to a bowl of sage. He looked at Kyle. "Ask Great Spirit, or whatever you call God, to free your mind from fears and channel your anger into the courage of a warrior. Call in your animal guides. To fight these demons, we must be strong physically, mentally and spiritually." Elkheart chanted in Cree. With a crow's feather, he wafted the smoke over his head and around his body and then passed the bowl to Madu. Kyle had never been much for praying, but if he was ever going to start this seemed the time. "Yea, though I walk through the valley of the shadow of death, I will fear no evil…." It was the prayer that his mother had taught him as a kid. He whispered it softly. Then he asked for the safe return of Jessica, Shawna and the others. Finally, he called to his animal spirits, the elk of the forest. "Run beside me, brothers. Lend me your strength, swiftness and courage."

Elkheart raised his large elk-horn knife over his head and sang to Great Spirit. Madu kneeled and held his machete flat against his chest, whispering his own prayer. Scarpetti kissed his cross and rosary and then crossed his chest. To close the ceremony, his father blessed a crate of Stoli bottles filled with reddish-brown liquid that gave off a potent smell. Then his men stuffed each bottle with a kerosene-soaked rag.

"What are those?" Kyle asked.

Scarpetti smiled. "Molotov cocktails with a shamanic kick."

"One of your grandfather's concoctions," Elkheart said. "Vodka, gasoline, elk's blood and his prayers."

Kyle felt his adrenaline pumping as he put on a vest loaded with shotgun shells. The leather holder strapped to his back allowed him to reach back easily and grab the sawed-off shotgun. He also chose a 9mm MP5 submachine gun with a night vision scope. The gun was small, light and had a shoulder strap.

Scarpetti grabbed a monster submachine gun. "M4 Carbine with a grenade launcher." He grinned at Kyle. "Size does matter."

"We've got one last surprise for our demon friends." Elkheart pulled out two black vests and handed one to Madu. As they put them on, Kyle's father reached into the pockets and pulled out a clay brick and a timer. "C-4 explosives. We're going to make those fuckers wish they hadn't messed with us."

Kyle shook his head, looking at the father he had always thought was just a bookish professor who liked to dig up bones. "Dad, since when did you become a soldier?"

Elkheart puffed on a cigar. "Years ago, when I was working a dig in Cambodia, I came across a temple with demons carved into the stone. The glyphs showed them worshipping a larger devil that had many faces. I kept finding signs of its existence in the jungles of Africa and South America. This devil made its way into Christian art and mythology, but it doesn't look like anything like a red man with horns and pitchfork. The

Great Shape-shifter doesn't hold any one form. It just mimics people's fears."

"How did it come to exist?" Kyle asked.

"I have no idea of its origin. All I know is the beast has been around since man started carving symbols into stone. Our tribe has always called it 'Macâya'. It's not breeding only with women here, Kyle, but in other parts of the world, as well. Madu and I fought some of these demons in Africa."

"They killed my family," Madu said. "And took my sisters."

"We believe this nomadic devil travels through a subterranean tunnel system that connects all the continents. Every ten years it returns to Macâya Forest to breed. The clan throws a religious ceremony and prepares an offering of women to the one they call 'Lord Father.'"

Kyle felt knots in his stomach. "It's returning today, isn't it?"

His father nodded and lugged on his flamethrower pack. "They hold the ceremony inside the copper mine." He checked his watch. "We need to leave now. At dusk, one or more of the captives will be chosen as the Macâya's mate."

* * *

Floating.

Jessica opened her eyes to blinding sunlight.

Blue sky above. Blurred faces. Singing.

For a moment, she thought she was dead.

Her vision cleared slowly. Faces moving out of the haze. Men and women smiled down at her. Sang in a language she didn't understand. Jessica felt water in her ears. She lifted her head. She was half-submerged in a lake, wearing someone else's long white gown and nothing else. The townspeople cradled her back, her legs, her feet. Two women held her hands to their hearts and sang to her with tears in their eyes. A redheaded woman placed a bouquet of sticks and dried flowers on Jessica's chest.

Who were these people? Whatever drug they'd given her, her brain returned to sharp awareness all at once. She panicked and began to struggle. The men held her in place. She was crying, helpless. Her body shivered uncontrollably.

Through a gap in the swaying bodies, she saw another group was gathered around another floating girl. She looked Jessica's way. Their eyes met. Lindsey Hanson's petrified expression mirrored Jessica's terror.

The gap closed as more people crowded around Jessica. Mayor Thorpe's face loomed over her. He cupped her head in his hands and spoke in another language, his tone punctuated like a preacher. She felt water being sprinkled on her forehead. It mixed with her tears. The mayor smiled down, eyes beaming, and dunked her head underwater.

* * *

Kyle followed the mercenaries out of the bomb shelter, prepared for an ambush. There was none. The study and downstairs hallway had burned to the ground, leaving a gaping hole. Sunlight streamed through the missing wall. They checked the house and surrounding woods, but the shifters had left the village. They had removed the bodies of the ones shot down, leaving no evidence behind. They had done their damage, though. Demolished the Hummer and turned the Jeep on its side. All the windows downstairs had been shattered. Glass and broken furniture were strewn across the smoking floor.

Elkheart and Kyle picked up Grandfather's rocking chair, which still had his body in it, and moved him to the center of the cabin. They put his sacred pipe in his lap beside his favorite tobacco. They each said a prayer to the great man who had helped shape their lives. Honoring Grandfather, they lit the cabin on fire.

As Kyle watched his childhood home turn into a giant bonfire, Grandfather's ghost emerged from the flames. The old man gazed at Kyle and his father for a long moment, then Grandfather shape-shifted into the spirit of a great elk and ran off into the woods.

* * *

The two mercenaries kept their guns trained on the woods as they followed Kyle and Elkheart down the hill to the garage. Parked inside, the red Ford Bronco was still intact. They loaded up their gear and weapons. Before leaving, Elkheart took Kyle down the road and showed him how to operate the MP5 submachine gun. "This is how you swap out the clips. This is how you shoot." He demonstrated, shooting at the wall of the stables, and then let Kyle fire off a few rounds to get a feel for it. The bullets shot out in rapid succession.

"Got the hang of it?" his father asked.

Kyle nodded. His arms shook with adrenaline as he thought about

Mayor Thorpe and his clan taking Jessica. "I can't wait to use it on those fuckers."

"It may take more than bullets to stop them."

"What do you mean?"

"These demons don't just exist on the physical plain. They are connected to other dimensions and can attack us on a spiritual level."

Kyle saw movement through the trees. His father reacted faster, spinning with his gun. Standing at the edge of the tree line was the ghost of Nina Whitefeather, looking at them curiously. Behind her several other ghosts appeared, including Zack, who gazed at them with vacant eye sockets. Elkheart was staring at them too.

"You can see them?" Kyle asked.

His father nodded. "Just like Grandfather, I can see into the spirit realm and call in animal guides, what our elders called *manitou*. Every generation has one tribe member born with the gift of second sight. When you were just a kid, you used to talk to animals and imaginary people. I knew then it was you."

"My whole life I thought I was crazy."

"So did I when I saw my first ghost. I was just a boy, and a dead medicine man walked into the village and put his hands on my head and started speaking to me. I ran screaming to my mother." His father chuckled. "No, son, you're part of a long lineage of spirit warriors. This gift can serve you in dealing with dark forces. You can call in the manitou as your guides. They've helped me many times. If we had more time, I would train you how to fight drawing power from other dimensions."

Spirit warriors? Other dimensions? Kyle had so many questions.

His father frowned. "I'm having second thoughts about you going back to Macâya Forest. I started this war with the Thorpe clan. There's no reason you—"

"I'm not afraid to die," Kyle said, but the crack in his voice betrayed him and made him sound like a child trying to prove something to his father.

"You'd be risking more than your life. Mayor Thorpe is a powerful trickster known as a Soul Eater. When a demon kills a man, Thorpe absorbs his soul, and his imprisoned spirit haunts these woods."

Kyle observed all the lost souls gathering in the forest.

His father's eyes filled with concern. "I don't want you to end up like them."

"I'm going with you, Dad. You won't talk me out of it."

"I see you've got my stubborn streak too." His father sighed. "All right, but follow my orders."

Kyle nodded, gripping his submachine gun.

His father pulled out his favorite hunting knife. "I want you to have this." The long blade with the elk-horn handle had been given to Elkheart by his father. "It's been blessed by many generations of elders. May our ancestors of the Great Elk Tribe watch over you."

Kyle held the knife, feeling a strong vibration in its handle. "What about you? You need their protection too."

His father smirked. "They've been watching over me long enough."

* * *

They rode in silence as Elkheart drove the Bronco down the bumpy dirt roads. Sitting in the backseat holding the MP5 between his knees, Kyle imagined they were going deer hunting. He shut down all fears and got into the mindset of a hunter.

His father parked at the wall of trees that bordered Kakaskitewak Swamp. He turned the vehicle around, facing the dirt road that led back to the village. Ready for a fast getaway. The four men got out and loaded their bodies with weapons, ammo and equipment. Putting the caving helmets on, they tested the radio headsets. Kyle spoke into the small mike that hung in front of his mouth. The crackling voices of the other three chirped in his left ear.

Scarpetti tweaked the volume on Kyle's headset. "These radios are for if we get separated down there. Keep the chatter to a minimum."

Madu said, "Demons can hear for long distances and use sound waves to target prey. Like bats."

Kyle nodded.

Elkheart pulled out a hand-drawn map and spread it across the hood. It looked like a Y-shaped tree with a few smaller branches. He whispered, "This is the tunnel system for the copper mine. The rails run down about fifty yards and then split off here." He tapped the center of the Y. "The left tunnel goes down to where the females have their den. The right leads down to where we think the males gather. We've never explored that far."

"What are these tunnels?" Kyle asked, pointing to the smaller tributaries.

"Offshoots," his father said. "There's a maze of tunnels running beneath Macâya Forest. We need to stay as close to the mine as possible or we'll get lost down there."

* * *

Kyle switched on the light of his caving helmet as they entered the mine shaft single file. His father took the lead, carrying the flamethrower. Scarpetti went next, then Kyle. Madu followed last. The machete handle jutted out from behind his back. He met eyes with Kyle and nodded. The Zulu warrior's face looked fearless.

No one spoke as they walked.

Kyle's helmet beam spotlighted mossy green walls. Hordes of purple mushrooms glistened in the dank tunnel. Every twenty feet, Elkheart stuck a glow stick in the wall so they could find their way back out. The tunnel curved and continued to descend. Gravity pulled at Kyle's legs, causing him to walk a little too fast. He felt as if the black hole was sucking him downward. He thought of Jessica, lost somewhere in this subterranean labyrinth, and his drive to find her gave him courage.

They reached the juncture where the shaft split into two tunnels. Elkheart, who had memorized the map, chose left. He occasionally shot out a dragon's breath of flames to see what lay ahead. They passed a few intersecting tunnels. Kyle felt on edge as his light shined into them. He whipped his submachine gun left and right, half-expecting demons to lash out. Where were they all?

Kyle heard moaning ahead. The sound echoed in the tunnel. He fingered the trigger of his MP5.

Somewhere in the darkness water splashed. Female voices giggled and screeched.

Elkheart paused and gave Kyle the look he used when they hunted together. His serious stare said, *Are you ready for this?*

Kyle nodded.

As they curved around the mine shaft tunnel, the right wall opened up. Their helmet beams disappeared into infinite darkness. The splashing sounds grew louder, echoing like an indoor swimming pool.

Feeling a sudden childish fear of the dark, Kyle kept his back against the walls as they followed a ledge. It sloped down ten feet into a pit of slimy water. The female demons undulated in the soup, like spawning fish. They had the female body parts, but their bones were long, and their skin, charcoal gray. They seemed too preoccupied to notice the four men standing above them. The demons' eyes were rolled back to whites. They moaned as if in ecstasy.

Cast off to the side among the debris of floating sticks was a gray husk with Eric's face. All the blood had been drained from his shriveled body, the eyes, lips, and genitals eaten away. His brother had died screaming.

Kyle fell back against the wall. The sight weakened his legs and his chest felt like it was caving in. Despite their differences, to see that Eric had died suffering was too much to bear.

He's gone.

Madu grabbed Kyle's wrist and gave him a hard look. This was no time to break down.

A man groaned from the darkness.

Panning their lights, their beams found Ray Roamingbear in the middle of the orgy. He drifted in the viscera. Females swam over and under him like hellish mermaids. He was alive, his face blissed out, grinning with pleasure. His eyes opened, staring up at the four gunmen. Ray floated helplessly as Kyle aimed his gun. Rage replaced his sadness. He wanted this kill. Wanted to see the bastard suffer. Kyle thought of Nina and all the girls Ray had raped and murdered. His betrayal to the tribe, to his family. Gripping his submachine gun with tense hands, Kyle looked at his father, who gave a nod. Kyle blew a hole in Ray's bulging stomach. He cried out in pain.

The females around him shrieked and dove under the oily surface of the pool.

Ray screamed in agony and clung to a rock island in the center.

"Finish him off," Elkheart said.

Kyle felt sick to his stomach. He'd never shot another human being. "I can't."

Elkheart raised his rifle and fired. The side of Ray's head burst and his limp body sank down into the pool. Then Elkheart glared at Kyle. "Down here it's kill or be killed. Got it?"

Kyle nodded. When he looked down, he spotted a female with a bat face climbing up the muddy bank toward his feet. He fired his gun on impulse, hitting the creature in the face.

All at once the female demons popped their heads up out of the slime. They shrieked together.

"Now, men!" Elkheart shot a twenty-foot flame across the pit, torching the demons closest to the edge. Scarpetti yelled like a madman as he strafed them with bullets. Kyle and Madu lit Molotov cocktails and hurled them farther outward. Orange-blue flames spread across the muck. The she-demons screamed as the fire engulfed them. Dozens swam for the shore, climbing up the slope.

The four men shot down at them. The demons tumbled and splashed, but more kept swimming toward the muddy shore below. Kyle held down the trigger. Rapid-fire bullets shredded torsos and heads. A slimy hand gripped his ankle. A female creature's face surfaced. He jammed the barrel into its eye socket and blew a hole through the back of its skull.

Flames continued to spread across the oily water. The females fled to the far wall, disappearing into holes.

"Let's hurry!" Elkheart continued around the pool. Dead she-demons floated in the mass grave, as the flames melted their flesh. The cavern reeked of death.

Kyle followed the men into another tunnel, this one narrower than the opening to the mine shaft. In the tighter places, the damp walls rubbed against his shoulders and he had to step sideways. The railcar tunnel came to a T-section, and the metal tracks ended. The floor of the intersecting passage was all rock and mud.

"Shit, which way now?" Scarpetti asked.

"Let's try left." Elkheart sounded uncertain as he placed another glow stick in a crevice.

Going left felt wrong. "Wait, Dad." Kyle looked down both tunnels. He felt a strong pull to go right. He touched the walls and heard ghostly echoes coming from that direction. When he released his hand, the screaming stopped. "We should go this way."

"You sure?"

"The spirits are telling me to take this tunnel instead."

Elkheart touched his palm against the rock wall and nodded.

Scarpetti rolled his eyes. "Seriously? That's what we're going by?"

They headed down the tunnel that Kyle had suggested. Their boots squished through mud. Tiny waterfalls dribbled down lime-green walls. Kyle's helmet occasionally bumped the low-hanging ceiling. Water dripped down the back of his neck. He glanced back to make sure Madu was still following. The black mercenary gave a reassuring gap-toothed smile.

Up ahead, an unlit torch jutted from the wall. Elkheart pulled it off the wall and lit it. "Let's save our batteries."

They switched off their helmet lamps, and the darkness seemed to wrap itself around Kyle. The only light now came from the torch his father carried. They passed a few empty chambers. Twenty feet down the passageway, Elkheart lit a second torch and handed it to Kyle. His flame illuminated a hole in the ceiling. A female face with milky white eyes peered down at them.

"Shit!" Kyle jabbed his torch up the crevice, and she hissed, her wide mouth full of sharp piranha teeth. An arm lunged from the hole, claws scraping his helmet.

"Stand back." His father aimed his flamethrower and blasted up the hole. The female demon screeched and fell between them in a fiery heap. She writhed and wailed on the tunnel floor, the talons on her hands and feet slashing the air. Madu ended her cries with a whack of his machete.

Kyle leaned back against the wall and exhaled. "Shit."

"Be wary of every hole and crevice," his father said. "That's where they sleep."

Kyle's sister's voice called from the darkness ahead. "Hello? Is someone out there?"

"Shawna?"

"We're down here! Help us!"

Kyle started down the tunnel, but his father grabbed his arm. "Hold up. These things are tricksters. They can mimic voices."

As they crept toward Shawna's pleading voice, Kyle's heart filled with hope. *Please let Jessica be with her.*

Their torches lit up a rocky chamber. On the floor, a thatch-work of sticks covered a pit. Beneath the slats, muddy girls shielded their eyes. One of them had tattooed arms.

"Shawna!"

"Kyle!" She reached up and grabbed his hands. "Thank God!"

Madu chopped at the wood covering. Seconds later, they pulled Shawna out. She was naked and covered in mud. She cried uncontrollably on Kyle's shoulder.

"Here." He took off his jacket and put around his sister.

Elkheart leaped down into the pit and embraced Amy Hanson. "You're still alive," he said, his voice full of emotion. His father had been looking for her down here for the past six weeks. He covered her with a windbreaker. When he brought her out of the pit, Kyle reeled. Amy's swollen belly looked as if she were pregnant.

Shawna guzzled a bottle of water, then poured some on her face and wiped away the mud mask. She only had a few scratches and bruises, but her eyes looked haunted. Kyle couldn't fathom what she'd been through down here."

Kyle searched the chamber for a second pit, but only found a rock wall. "Where's Jessica?"

"Some men took her somewhere," Shawna said. "They took Amy's sister too."

* * *

Following the path of glow sticks, the six of them journeyed back without seeing another demon. The females seemed to have retreated deeper within the cave. Stepping out of the mine shaft, Kyle was grateful to see sunlight again. He drew fresh pine air into his lungs.

It took Shawna and Amy a moment to adjust their eyes. They all hiked back through the jungle-thick forest and crossed the swamp in the canoe. Back at the red Bronco, the men pulled off their packs and gave the women sandwiches that they'd brought from the cabin. Kyle, Elkheart, Madu and Scarpetti ate quickly, knowing they had to go back down. Kyle checked his watch. Late afternoon. Another few hours and it would be dark. He felt his hope of finding Jessica waning. "We need to get going."

Elkheart nodded, looking both physically and emotionally worn out. He hugged Amy and then the daughter he hadn't seen in twenty years. He gave Shawna a shotgun and the keys to Big Red. "Stay in the Bronco. If we're not back by sundown, you two drive the hell out of here." He gave the girls quick directions, and they nodded.

"What about road blocks?" Kyle asked.

"Today, everyone in town will be down in the cave for the ceremony."

Shawna punched Kyle's shoulder. "You better come back."

"We will." Kyle hated leaving the girls, but two more needed to be rescued.

Amy said, "Please find Lindsey."

"We'll find her and Jessica." Kyle hugged his sister. "You'll be okay?"

Shawna gripped the sawed-off shotgun. "I can take care of myself. Go on. I'll look after Amy." His kid sister was tougher than he'd thought. Kyle kissed her forehead and then followed the mercenaries back to the canoe.

When they reached the split-off point inside the mine shaft, this time Elkheart and his men veered right. Kyle took the rear, counting the glow

BRIAN MORELAND

sticks his father stuck in the walls. The rail-car track curved downward into a black abyss. This tunnel seemed to go deeper than the previous one. Kyle felt the temperature dropping the farther they descended. A chill began to seep into his bones. Every so often they passed thick wooden planks that kept the shaft from caving in. At one point the ground leveled off, and the mine opened up wide enough for the four men to walk in pairs. A few railcars were parked along the sides of the tracks. Kyle imagined that over a century ago miners had used these for transporting copper out of the shaft. They must have been surprised to discover that they weren't alone down here.

The cavern narrowed into a tunnel shaped like a tube. Elkheart aimed his flamethrower and shot a flame into the passageway. Nothing lurked in there except clusters of purple mushrooms. The smell of burnt fungus was heavy in the air. Kyle wondered if just breathing the spores would cause him to hallucinate.

His father entered the tunnel first, followed by Scarpetti and Madu. Again, they had to walk single file, this time hunched over. Kyle hated tight places. His breathing became more labored. His headlamp lit up walls covered in green lichen. Water continuously plinked on his helmet and dripped down his face. His waterproof jacket kept his upper body dry, but his jeans were soaked from all the moisture.

The tunnel opened up into a chamber that had more head room. The metal track came to a dead end at a flat wall. Unlike the natural cave walls, this one was made of large gray bricks, as if constructed by masons. Etched into the stone were strange symbols, similar to hieroglyphics. The wall continued high into the darkness.

His father whispered, "These are the ruins my team found. It's similar to the ones we discovered in Cambodia and the Congo." He reached up and wiped moss off the wall. "This is the demigod the shifters worship. Their Lord Father, the Macâya."

Their headlamps illuminated a relief of a creature sitting cross-legged like Buddha. Six arms fanned out from its torso, spreading fingers tipped with daggers. Its head had a demonic face.

At the bottom of the brick wall a small archway led into a black tunnel. The arch stood only three-feet high. Kyle squatted and pointed his flashlight's beam into the small opening. *Great, another tight passage.* This one looked like the interior of a damp sewer pipe overgrown with algae. A few feet in, the stone floor sloped into water.

"What's this lead to?" Kyle asked.

276

"We don't know. This is as far as we've ever gone."

Kyle took in another deep breath and exhaled. "After you."

* * *

Shawna sat behind the wheel of her dad's beat-up Ford Bronco. She was jonesing for a cigarette. She searched the glove compartment, but her father only smoked cigars and chewed tobacco. She hit the steering wheel in frustration.

As dusk approached, the sun kept moving toward the western mountains. The forest grew a shade darker. In less than two hours it would be night. Shawna wished the men would return. She wanted to get the hell of out of these woods, but she didn't want to leave the others behind. She feared for Jessica and Lindsey. Most of all, Shawna feared losing her big brother and her father. Now that Eric was gone, they were the only family she had left.

Sitting in the passenger seat, Amy kept crying. That was all she had done down in the pit, especially after the men took her sister. Poor Amy had spent six weeks inside that cave. Shawna glanced at Amy's swollen belly.

"It's growing inside me," she said, looking at Shawna with red eyes. "I can feel it."

Shawna looked away.

"They grow faster than normal babies," Amy said. "It doesn't take nine months."

Shawna felt a knot in her own stomach. She had been raped. Had felt the beast shooting its seed inside her. She could be pregnant too.

* * *

At the brick wall with the arched tunnel, the four searchers removed their packs and began crawling in six inches of water. It was slow going. Kyle had to push his MP5 and a Molotov cocktail bottle ahead of him, crawl a few inches, and then repeat the task. The others moved along far ahead of him, and soon all Kyle saw was a long, black tube ahead. His heavy breathing echoed off the stone. His helmet kept scraping the ceiling. The tunnel seemed like it was closing in around him. At one choked section, the rock walls rubbed against his shoulders. He wedged his way through, only to hit another tight spot. Claustrophobia kicked in. His throat constricted. "Dad!" Kyle lay flat on his stomach, hyperventilating. His hands wouldn't stop shaking. He needed to get out of here. A voice screamed in his head to retreat.

"Kyle?" His father's voice sounded in the radio headset. "Son, you can do this. The tunnel only goes another fifty feet or so. We've already made it out. Just keep coming."

"Okay." Kyle kept his eyes closed for a moment and just breathed. He thought of Jessica, lost somewhere down here. He concentrated on her face, her voice, the way she had felt in his arms. He'd rather die than know he'd left her down here. He squeezed his fist. He opened his eyes with renewed determination and continued crawling.

He made it to the end of the tunnel and the others pulled him to his feet. Kyle stood beside his father, Scarpetti and Madu in a cavern of impenetrable blackness. The Zulu soldier put a finger to his lips. The four men remained silent for several seconds, probing the surrounding gloom with their flashlights.

Chittering sounded from above.

Something wet and slimy hit Kyle's shoulder.

Everyone tilted their beams up a high brick wall and spot-lit a rack of fangs dripping saliva. The lights hit a dark face with white-membraned eyes. The demon shrieked and leaped through the air into the darkness.

Scarpetti backed up. "Shit, where'd it go?"

Kyle and the others stood back to back, their lights panning the void above them. Kyle's mind felt electric down here, as if this cave was awakening some deep part of his brain. He saw a vision of the four of them from high above, as if seeing through the creature's eyes. He sensed where it was hiding.

"There!" Kyle raised his light beam. The demon was crawling lizardlike down a pillar. When the lights hit its eyes, it released a high-pitched growl and dove at them.

Kyle and Madu opened fire. Bullets tore into its flanks. Kyle ducked as the thing flew over his head and crashed into the wall. It rose, standing over seven feet. Their lights spot lit a sinewy torso with a protruding rib cage. Horns jutted from its shoulders. Its eyes began to glow white, as if illuminated from within.

Scarpetti raised his gun. The beast smacked him sideways. He skidded into the gloom. Madu attacked next, the machete raised over his head. The demon picked him up and hurled him. It roared at Elkheart, who backed away. Then it turned and charged toward Kyle. An arm too long for its body knocked him back against a pillar. As the demon attacked again, Kyle yelled, holding the trigger down on the submachine gun. Bullets stitched up the creature's chest and neck, knocking it backward. It howled in pain, bleeding black blood.

Kyle discharged his gun again, hitting the demon in the face, bursting one of its glowing eyes. It fell at his feet. His father finished it off with his flamethrower. The carcass glowed with orange embers.

Scarpetti walked back, rubbing his jaw. He kicked the charred corpse. "Fucking bastard."

Elkheart examined its monstrous head. "This breed's different than the shifters. Look at the sizes of its claws."

"Must be a dweller," Madu said.

Kyle was almost afraid to ask. "What are 'dwellers'?"

Madu said, "Demons born in the cave. They live their whole lives down here."

Elkheart nodded. "We believe the shifters living in Hagen's Cove only represent a fraction of the demons that exist in these tunnel systems. They've been mating with humans for centuries, maybe since the beginning of man. Our theory is that most of these creatures live belowground and only come out at night to hunt."

Madu cut off a black claw and passed it to Kyle. "You're one of us now."

The eight-inch claw looked like an obsidian blade. Kyle squeezed it and picked up an imprint of the creature's memories. Seeing through its eyes, he caught flashes of it running with a pack of demons through the forest at night, attacking a herd of deer…dragging a screaming woman into the cave, mating with her…at the edge of the Cree village, retreating from Grandfather Two Hawks, who fended off the demons with glowing hands. Memory after memory flooded Kyle's head. He smelled the blood of its prey, the sweat and skin of the women it raped, felt its fear of Grandfather.

A hand grabbed his wrist, bringing Kyle back to the present.

His father looked at him with knowing eyes. "What did you see?"

Kyle wiped sweat off his face. He recounted the memories. "This demon's at least a couple hundred years old. One of the original guardians of Macâya Forest. It was also one of the pack that attacked your camp and took Amy."

Scarpetti looked at Kyle sideways. "How the fuck do you know that?"

Kyle ignored him and followed his father back toward the high wall. "Dad, why were they afraid of Grandfather?"

"Because he knew how to fight them."

"I saw his hands glowing. How is that possible?"

"Cree spirit warriors have the ability to tap into other dimensions and draw power from them. Your grandfather was a master at it. That's why the Thorpe clan left him alone."

"Can you draw power into your hands?"

"Not very well. My years of drinking really screwed up my gift. Your ability is stronger."

Kyle looked at his palms. They tingled as he thought about the power hidden deep within his cells. "All I know how to do is pick up imprints."

"It takes years of training to learn how to use your gift. I had intended for Grandfather to teach you, but..." He shook his head, as if ashamed that he had failed Kyle as a father.

Scarpetti approached them. "I hate to interrupt this father-son bonding, but we don't got all goddamn day down here."

Elkheart nodded and placed another glow stick above the small archway to mark their exit. He checked his watch. "One hour before sundown. The ceremony will be starting soon. Let's move."

They continued through a chamber that had a flat stone floor. Their beams panned across giant pillars carved with hieroglyphs and reliefs of demons mating with women. Again, Kyle saw stone depictions of their demigod. "What is this place?"

"A subterranean temple," Elkheart whispered, his tone awed. "This would have been one of the greatest archaeological discoveries of this century." He stuck a C-4 brick to the base of the pillar.

"Now which way?" Scarpetti asked. "This place is a fucking maze."

Elkheart looked at his son, giving him a nod.

Understanding, Kyle placed his palms on one of the stone columns. In his mind's eye he saw warped images of a group of people carrying torches through the temple. They were cloaked in fur robes and masks of goat's heads. With lengths of vines they pulled Lindsey behind them like a slave. The girl was blindfolded and dressed in a white gown that ended at the middle of her thighs. Lindsey's legs were bleeding from scrapes.

Kyle searched for Jessica, but couldn't see her.

A goat-faced figure jerked a tether hard and a girl fell to her knees. The cry of pain was Jessica's. Rage and fear coursed through Kyle, heating his blood. He pulled away from the pillar. "We have to hurry."

* * *

For the first time in her life, Jessica understood what it was like to be blind. Hours had passed since she'd last seen light. Or any kind of detail. Was this what death was like? A continuous awareness of nothing?

No, she believed in God. Believed life after death began with the soul traveling to some heavenly place. There'd be sunshine, gardens, waterfalls—and celestial beings. And if she had her way, she'd be surrounded by the souls of all the people she loved. She would get a hug from her Gramm every day. Jessica had always felt her grandmother's spirit was watching over her and would be waiting on the other side when Jessica crossed over. Her Gramm's arms would be open and she'd have that big smile on her face like she did whenever Jessica had come for a visit as a girl.

No, not dead yet. She could feel her heart beating. Could feel the fabric of the gown they had dressed her in. The scratchy wicker sandals on her feet. She lay on a cold stone slab. Wooden bindings held her wrists and ankles in place, the skin beneath them torn from her repeated attempts to get free.

While her vision had left with their torches, her hearing remained acute. She heard every drop of water splash into a puddle. Every skitter. Every screech. When the darkness fell silent, like now, she heard her own breathing. And the girl, Lindsey Hanson, sobbing somewhere nearby.

"Hey," Jessica whispered. "Lindsey."

Sniffles. "Yes?"

"It's going to be okay."

"I'm...so...scared. I hate the dark."

"When I was a little girl," Jessica said, "I used to be deathly afraid of my closet when my room was dark. At bedtime, my parents would turn out the lights, but I could never fall asleep right away. I'd sit there in bed holding my doll, Matilda, and watch the closet. I swear that door opened a crack. And the more I watched it, the more that door opened just a little bit more."

"And? What happened?" Lindsey asked.

"Well, at first I got really scared and hid under my blankets. Each night I got braver, though, and would stare at the closet a bit longer. After about a week, I realized there's nothing to be afraid of. The dark can't hurt me."

Lindsey sniffled. "It's not the dark I'm afraid of."

"My friends will come for us. I know they will." She pictured Kyle's face in her mind, the look he wore when she caught him staring. It was so tender that it brought tears to her eyes. "Think about what you'll do when we get out."

"Take a bath."

Jessica laughed. That the girl could still joke was a good sign. "What else?" she asked, encouraging Lindsey to keep talking.

"I don't know. I can't see it. What about you?"

"I'll finish getting my medical degree. Travel with Doctors Without Borders. I am scheduled to visit Ecuador this fall and work with the children there." She'd seen pictures and she let herself imagine their faces now. God still had a purpose for her. She believed that. Her life wouldn't end here in this cave.

The waiting continued. The maddening nothingness. Endless black. Like that gap in her closet, the door opening ever wider. The darkness leering at her.

Stare it down, Jess. Keep thinking positive. She thought of Kyle. She tried to imagine their first date in Seattle, wondering where he might take her. Dinner and a show, perhaps. A kiss at the top of the Space Needle would be nice. The fantasy vanished as wet fingers stroked her legs. Jessica gasped. All the fears she had buried crawled across her skin like spiders.

Seconds later, Lindsey screamed.

A match struck. In a flash of blinding light, Jessica glimpsed a man with a bull's head. He lit a torch and touched the flame to a metal bowl on an altar. A small fire spread, illuminating a statue of woven sticks with a demon skull.

Then she heard the call of bugle horns.

* * *

Somewhere in the darkness ahead of the four men, horns blew. They droned on, sounding like ships lost in the night. Kyle's heart quickened. He followed the mercenaries through a low doorway and saw faint, shimmering light in the distance.

Elkheart raised his fist, instructing the team to stop. He turned off his helmet and flashlight and peered through night vision binoculars. "Kill your lights. We're here."

"Jessica?" Kyle asked.

"Alive. Now gear up."

They turned off their headlamps and put on night vision goggles. Kyle switched on the infrared illuminator. The world turned pale green in the goggles. He could see some details and the glow of flames rippling in the distance. His father, Madu and Scarpetti looked like specters. Kyle's peripheral vision disappeared. The blackness at the edge of his vision stirred up his claustrophobia. He breathed, trying to control the fear flapping in his chest. *Just focus on finding Jessica.*

He inserted a fresh clip into his submachine gun. He checked to make sure his strobe light was still strapped to the barrel. For protection, he gripped the antler handle of his knife and called in his spirit guides. Again, it vibrated in his hand.

Madu's eyes met Kyle's. No smile this time. The Zulu warrior looked fierce and ready for battle. Scarpetti looked agitated. Elkheart stuck another C-4 brick on a pillar and signaled the rest to move deeper into the cave.

The rescue team maneuvered between the pillars. Through his goggles, Kyle saw that some of the columns had been built into cave walls pocked with catacombs. A shadow-shape moved in one of the crevices. Madu shown his light into the cave hole, but the creature was no longer there.

Walking alongside his father, Kyle used his instincts to search for Jessica. He still couldn't see her, but he could feel her up ahead. *I'm coming for you, Jess.* He sensed another presence in the chamber where she and Lindsey waited. It was a very different vibration than he had gotten off the shifters and the dwellers. This beast felt like darkness eternal, like the embodiment of all of humanity's hatred and fear. A demigod created from pure evil. The things it wanted to do to Jessica and Lindsey made Kyle sick to his stomach. Fueled his fury. He walked faster toward the flame glowing in the distance.

The bugle horns trailed off. Then Kyle heard what sounded like a thousand cawing crows.

The squad stopped at a ledge that overlooked the corner of a stage. Kyle spotted a giant wood statue with a monstrous skull. On a stone platform below it, a cloaked figure waved burning incense over two women in white gowns. The sight of Jessica lying on a block of granite caused Kyle to gasp with fear and relief.

* * *

The cawing that echoed off the stone walls was deafening. Jessica wished she could cover her ears. Her wrists fought against the bindings.

The fur-robed figure standing a few feet away pulled off the bull's head mask. Mayor Thorpe grinned at her. His pale face was painted with red symbols. He dropped his robe, standing naked before her. Strange hieroglyphs covered Mayor Thorpe's face, arms and legs. He raised his palms—each decorated with an all-seeing eye.

The crow sounds stopped. Then Jessica heard the scrapes and footsteps of bodies moving in the darkness behind her. The temple filled with growls and ghoulish moans. She was thankful she couldn't see the hellish congregation.

Mayor Thorpe opened a thick book and shouted out strange words, as if speaking in an ancient language no longer spoken. His voice boomed inside the cavern. As he gave his sermon, his fingers glided up Jessica's leg and arm. Caressed her cheek. He did the same to Lindsey, walking full circle back to the altar. Then he turned to face a set of stone steps that ascended into blackness. He yelled some form of incantation. Behind Jessica, the demons chanted. "*Va-lak, Va-lak, Va-lak...*"

Above the stage, an archway lit up with a pulsing green light. Fog drifted down the staircase. Pounding footsteps approached. A shadow took form in the glow.

Lindsey screamed.

Jessica looked at the teenage girl tied to the stone slab five feet away. *Stop screaming!* she wanted to say. *You'll draw the thing.*

Iridescent green light swirled around the statue of the demon god. The cool mist clouded Jessica's vision. Then the chamber filled with a sound like a mallet pounding stones. In the dim light, she made out a tall form descending the steps. She saw legs covered in dark fur. Knees that bent the wrong way at the joints. A massive head covered in black thorns.

Mayor Thorpe kneeled at the foot of the stage. "*Store Fader, Valak!*"

A large hand with too many claws touched the mayor's shoulder. Then the great beast turned toward Jessica.

She snapped her eyes shut.

The footsteps drew closer.

The devil was breathing right above her now. *Stare it down, Jess.*

She opened her eyes again, saw its face and screamed.

* * *

As green fog drifted across the platform, Kyle lost sight of Jessica. In the mist, a giant silhouette had walked down the steps. Kyle caught glimpses of multiple arms sprouting from its torso. A swooping tail. The Macâya crossed the stage.

One of the girls cried out. Jessica.

Kyle rushed forward.

The mercenaries grabbed him, pulling him back behind a pillar.

Elkheart got in Kyle's face. "Not yet. We go on my command."

Demons cackled from the dark pit beneath the stage and surrounding catacombs.

The sounds of the girls wailing caused Kyle to panic. "We have to do something."

"Follow my lead." Elkheart gave hand signals to Madu and Scarpetti. They split off and took high positions, aiming their guns at the pit.

Kyle and his father moved from pillar to pillar until they were directly behind the stage. Through the smoke, Kyle watched in horror as the Macâya's body stood over Jessica and Lindsey. Their screams drowned out all the other sounds.

Elkheart barked into the radio headsets, "Strobes on!"

In the distance, Madu and Scarpetti switched on their strobe lights. The chamber turned bright. In the chaotic flickers, Kyle saw a large gathering of demons inside a rectangular pit below. They reeled at the lights, growling. Some backed into the void. Others charged up the steps toward the mercenaries. Madu sprayed the horde with rapid fire. Scarpetti launched grenades. The demons shrieked as explosions of shrapnel tore through them. Severed limbs, gore and bone fragments scattered through the air. All across the pit, shredded bodies collapsed into piles, but the legion seemed endless as more demons kept attacking from the dark.

Kyle ran into the pulsing green mist that covered the stage. His father lit a Molotov cocktail and hurled it into the pit. Flames spread across several creatures near the stage. Dozens more rushed from the blackness. Elkheart torched them with his flamethrower. "Help cut the girls loose!"

Kyle searched the fog. "Jessica!"

"Kyle! Help!"

He found Jessica and Lindsey lying on stone tables, their hands and wrists bound by vines. He ran toward Jessica.

The giant beast rose in the smoke behind her. Six arms flexed from its torso. Enormous wings spread from its back. The Macâya roared.

Kyle reeled and aimed his submachine gun, his arms shaking. His strobe light flashed across a thorn-covered head that constantly shifted with faces. The flickering light blinded its many eyes that appeared and disappeared in the dark pool of its face. A wing swooshed around, shielding its head and torso.

Kyle charged the demigod, firing rapid shots into its body. A whip of its tail knocked him to the ground, dazing him. His vodka bottle rolled over a ledge, into the pit. The smoke drifted over him. Seconds passed as Kyle tried to stop his vision from spinning. All around him gunshots, explosions and animal cries echoed in the cavern. In the pulsating lights, Elkheart and Scarpetti fired a barrage of bullets into the pit below. Flames burned across a heap of dead creatures. The air stank of burning flesh. The horde surrounded Madu on the temple steps. He slashed with his machete, but the demons overtook him, dragging him down into the darkness.

Somewhere in the smoky chaos, Jessica and Lindsey cried in terror.

Elkheart turned his flamethrower on the Macâya. It screeched, flew upward and disappeared into the blackness above them. Then Kyle's father lifted him to his feet. "Help me cut the girls loose." Elkheart ran to Lindsey.

Kyle found Jessica still tied to the stone slab. He pulled out his knife and sliced the vines binding her. She threw her arms around his neck. He hugged her shaking body. "Thank, God."

Jessica's eyes were full of tears. "Kyle."

"Come on. We have to go." Kyle pulled her up the steps. Elkheart and Lindsey followed with Scarpetti firing shots behind them.

At the top of the stairs, Elkheart pressed a switch on a C-4 charge and a digital timer started counting down. "We got twenty minutes 'til this whole place blows. Let's go!"

The five of them raced between the pillars. Something screeched off to their left. Kyle stopped Jessica and aimed his strobe. Up in the catacombs demons were perched on ledges, growling, fangs exposed.

Elkheart blasted a flame up the stone walls. The demons retreated into their holes. He pushed against Kyle and Jessica. "Keep mo—!" Something grabbed Elkheart and hurled him several feet. He rolled and smacked a wall.

"Dad!" Kyle rushed to his father. He lay on the ground, unconscious. Blood soaked the back of his head.

Twenty feet away, the girls screamed as the beast with large wings flew through the air. The Macâya's many arms clawed for them, but missed as the girls ducked behind a pillar.

Scarpetti yelled and kept shooting until his submachine-gun clip emptied. "We gotta get out of here! Go! Go!" He pushed the girls toward the exit. "Kyle, come on!"

"I can't leave my father! Take the girls out!"

Scarpetti marched over. "Leave him. We have to go—"

Blood splattered Kyle's shirt.

Scarpetti looked at him with shocked eyes. Claws jutted from his chest. Then he was pulled up into the darkness.

Kyle stood, petrified. He didn't want to leave his father behind.

Jessica and Lindsey ran over to Kyle and clung to him, shivering. He had to get them out of here. He spotted the glow stick that marked the exit. "Come on." As he hurried the girls toward the tunnel, he heard something breathing behind him. Tentacles wrapped around his legs and yanked him off his feet.

"Kyle! No!" Jessica reached for his hand.

He clawed the ground as something dragged him away from her.

* * *

The sun began its descent behind the mountains.

In the Bronco, Shawna looked in the rearview mirror at the darkening forest. "Come on, guys."

"They're not coming back," Amy said.

"Yes, they are."

"We should just go."

"No, it's not nightfall yet."

Amy doubled over.

"Another cramp?" Shawna asked.

"It feels like the baby's coming."

"Oh, shit. Not now."

"I need to get to a hospital."

"Okay, okay. Give me a few more minutes." Shawna touched the girl's shoulder. "Wait here. I'll be right back."

"Hurry…" Amy released a plaintive whimper.

Carrying a shotgun, Shawna hiked through the thicket of trees that bordered the swamp. She walked down the pier that stretched over the black water. She listened, but the only sounds were croaking frogs. On the opposite shore, she could see the trees nailed with animal skulls, marking the entrance to Macâya Forest. The canoe was still lying on the bank.

"Kyle?!" she called. "Dad?!"

Amy screamed in the distance.

Shawna hurried back through the clinging branches.

The Bronco's passenger door was ajar. The empty seat soaked.

Amy's water had broken.

Shawna searched the woods, calling her name.

* * *

Kyle rolled across the brick floor. Whatever creature had dragged him deep into the temple, it had released him. His whole body ached. He lifted his head, dazed, the pillars spinning green. His night vision goggles hung crooked. As he sat up with a groan, something in the shadows growled. A hand shot into his viewfinder and ripped the goggles off Kyle's face. His world went pitch-black, and every childhood fear came rushing in. He scooted backward against cold stone. *It* was with him in the darkness. The thing that had killed Scarpetti. Kyle could feel its presence nearby. Could hear its breath. Fingers brushed his cheek. Kyle gasped and kicked blindly at the air. He fumbled with his caving helmet and switched on his headlamp. The light caught movement as a body recoiled into the blackness.

Kyle felt the floor around him. He had lost his submachine gun. "Shit!" He reached back and pulled off his short-barrel shotgun.

A beeping sound echoed close to his ear. On a pillar beside him a C-4 charge timer was counting down. Less than fifteen minutes. Panic launched him to his feet. He had to find the girls and his father and get the hell out of this cave. He searched the gloom for the exit.

"There's no escape." Mayor Thorpe's voice reverberated in the cavern. "You belong to us now."

Howling echoed from the catacombs. Kyle jerked his head upward and his headlamp beamed across dozens of hands slapping the walls with a thundering cadence. Black faces with luminous white eyes gleamed down at him. The demons could easily pounce, but for some reason they remained in the pocked walls, chanting as one maddening cacophony.

Then all at once they hushed.

Kyle took a step back, turning his beam left and right. For several seconds, the only sounds were his heavy breathing and his boots scraping stone as he fumbled through the temple.

Which way was the exit? He felt so disoriented in this warren of pillars.

The bugle horns droned again, deep and menacing.

He felt the air of wings flapping above him. Claws scraped his helmet. The Macâya was taunting him.

Up ahead came the echo of dozens of feet padding through mud.

A flame lit up a torch on the platform at the center of the temple. Once again, the bowl at the altar caught fire, illuminating the demon statue that overlooked the stone tables.

At the top of the steps, Kyle raised his shotgun. Terror shook every fiber of his being, but his anger was stronger. He walked down the steps, blasting shots at the giant winged creature gliding over the stage. The Macâya flew high up to a balcony and sat on a throne that was mostly hidden in shadow.

Off to Kyle's right, Mayor Thorpe stepped into the fire glow. His naked body was painted from head to toe with red words and symbols. In his hands, he clutched the decapitated heads of Madu and Scarpetti. "Soon, you and your father will join them." Thorpe tossed the heads into the dark pit and Kyle heard the demons swarm, grunting like overzealous hogs in a feeding frenzy.

Kyle pumped another round in the shotgun.

The clan leader circled him. Thorpe's eyes reflected the torchlight like a wolf to the moon. He spoke inside Kyle's head in a dreamlike voice, "We knew the day would come when you would return." He gestured to the calligraphy scrawled on his chest. "The prophecy foretold that one of Elkheart's sons would one day rise against us. All this time I thought your brother was the gifted one." He chuckled, as if amused by some irony. "He was no match for our sisters." Thorpe pointed a long finger at Kyle. "Turns out *you* were the enigma. We've been trying to decipher you for years, but your grandfather was shielding you. Too bad he's no longer around to protect you."

Kyle backed up to the edge of the pit, wary of the damnable audience below. The Macâya remained on his throne, like a king watching a show.

Behind the mayor, two demons brought Jessica and Lindsey onto the stage.

Kyle caught Jessica's gaze and charged across the stage toward her. Thorpe raised his tattooed palms. His eyes rolled back to whites.

Kyle was halted by a stabbing pain inside his head. He could feel Thorpe penetrating his thoughts, scouring his mind for weaknesses and fears. He drudged up childhood traumas...Kyle, five years old, almost drowning after falling through the ice covering a pond, seeing his first ghosts in the freezing black water...ten years old, hiding under the bed with his brother as their parents screamed at one another in a drunken rage...riding in the station wagon's backseat with his crying siblings as their mother and new boyfriend Blake drove them away from the reservation...the turbulent teen years, being abused by his God-fearing stepfather, Blake's leather belt whipping Kyle's back.

As each painful memory spiraled through his head, Thorpe's features morphed in and out of faces. First he became Blake scowling at Kyle, then Eric, his eyes black holes, his mouth a rictus of tortured pain as he died. Seeing his dead brother stirred up grief alongside Kyle's anger and fear. "Get out of my head!"

Then the shape-shifting of Thorpe's face quickened, resembling the nightmarish creatures that had ended up in Kyle's books. One horror after another snarled and snapped at the air with fangs. When Thorpe found the memories of Stephanie fatally wounded from the car accident, his face shifted into her lacerated face. He spoke in her voice, "You should have killed yourself when you had the chance, Kyle. Now, he's going to skin you alive and eat your soul." Her wicked laugh turned into a man's as she shifted back into Thorpe's grinning face. "That's just a glimpse of the suffering I'm going to put you through. But first, you're going to watch."

He hissed at the demons holding Jessica and Lindsey. The creatures took them back to the stone slabs.

"No!" Kyle's rage sparked from his palms. He mentally pushed back, sending his own thoughts into the symbol-scrawled man who stood before him.

Thorpe's hands went to his temples, as Kyle invaded the chambers inside the Soul Eater's head. Kyle drummed up visions of demons feasting upon men and women—Nina, Zack, Wynona and countless others—and Thorpe walking among the dying, sucking their souls into his body. The ghosts roamed Macâya Forest and the caves beneath, and Kyle saw where silver cords chained them to Thorpe like slaves. He was drawing power from them.

Kyle raised his palms, but only a few sparks came out. "Ah, hell." He aimed his shotgun and pulled the trigger.

Thorpe stumbled backward as a bloody hole opened in his stomach. A second shot ripped open the center of his chest. The wounds sealed within seconds. Thorpe glared. Claws shot out of his fingertips like switchblades. His mouth split open wide, exposing rows of pointed teeth.

The beast roared and charged Kyle, smacking him backward, into the pit.

* * *

Elkheart awoke with a massive headache. He felt the blood on the back of his head. "Christ."

His pain was forgotten as he realized Kyle and the others were gone.

Elkheart jumped to his feet, his joints cricking. He stumbled against a wall, still woozy from the concussion.

Up ahead, pillars were half-lit from a fire glowing in the nave. He could hear the demons chanting. The mating ceremony was back on.

As he hurried through the temple, he came across Scarpetti's headless body. "Shit." There was no time to mourn. Elkheart checked one of the many explosives he'd stuck to the pillars. The timer was counting down.

Under ten minutes now.

* * *

The short drop to a muddy floor knocked the wind out of Kyle. Bottle rockets of pain shot through his ribs. He stood, realizing he was now down inside the pit beneath the stage. The bodies of burnt demons were piled in smoking heaps.

Up on the stage, Mayor Thorpe was going through some kind of metamorphosis, his bones growing longer. The iridescent green smoke swirled around him, drifted across the stage. Kyle lost sight of Jessica.

He searched the mud floor for his shotgun, but he'd lost it in the fall. He pulled out the elk-horn knife and concentrated on his gift.

I call in the manitou of the Elk Tribe. Grandfather, please help me.

Kyle's hands began to glow. A great power surged into the knife, as he felt the presence of Grandfather's spirit channeling through him.

The sound of feet squishing through mud made him jerk his light. Behind him demons were emerging from the blackness. Kyle sliced the air in a circle, keeping them at bay. They seemed to fear the light emanating from his hands.

Thorpe leaped from the stage and kicked Kyle in the back. He tumbled across the muddy ground. He aimed a palm at the approaching beast, but the power wasn't enough to stop it.

Thorpe pressed a foot against Kyle's chest, pinning him. He growled at the other demons and they slinked back into the shadows.

Kyle twisted, shining his headlamp upward.

Mayor Thorpe loomed seven feet tall now. His face, more devil than human, stared down with luminous red eyes. "Your soul belongs to me now." Tentacles grew from Thorpe's chest, snaking through the air toward Kyle. At the tip of each appendage, a parasitic mouth chomped. Feelers latched on to his legs and began sucking at his life force.

Kyle yelled in agony. He stabbed the knife into Thorpe's calf. The Soul Eater wailed and backed away. Its tentacles released and swooped wildly around its body as it circled Kyle with a limp.

"Get the hell away from my son!" Ten feet away, Elkheart fired a pistol, blowing off Thorpe's ear. The angry beast's feelers shot through the air and attached to Elkheart's chest. He arched his back, crying out in pain.

Kyle's hands flared up with cobalt-blue fire. He raised his palms and sent all his fury into the Thorpe-demon. The power knocked it loose from his father, who fell to the ground.

Thorpe faced Kyle, his eyes full of shock.

Kyle could hear the lost souls screaming inside Thorpe's body. Kyle connected his mind to their spirits. "Fight back," he commanded. Their faces and hands pushed from within Thorpe's abdomen. An arm stretched outward from his cheek. More arms jutted from his chest. Thorpe growled, as if in pain, and shook his head. The mottled flesh began to bubble and tear open as the ghosts clawed their way out. Kyle called them into his body. The glow in his hands intensified. He channeled their rage. The Thorpe-creature shrieked as blue flames engulfed its torso. Fiery tentacles swooped through the air. His burning flesh opened with a thousand holes, and a thousand voices screamed.

Kyle attacked with the knife and sliced open Thorpe's belly. White light spilled out as more souls escaped their prison, their cries echoing in the temple. The demon that had been Mayor Thorpe fell to its knees inside the storm of swirling ghosts. They clawed at his face like angry birds.

Kyle grabbed a knot of Thorpe's hair. The wailing devil face shifted back to a man with scorched skin and eyes melting like wax. Kyle cut Thorpe's throat, sawing through the flesh and bone until the head severed from the neck. The demon's body collapsed, pumping out black blood. Yelling like a warrior, Kyle raised the head so the demons could see their leader had been slain. They backed away from him. He hurled Thorpe's head in the direction of the Macâya and pointed his knife toward the balcony.

As the ghosts swarmed the king demon, Kyle ran to his father. He was dazed, but alive. All around them, demons screeched, but kept their distance. Kyle and Elkheart hurried up the steps, into the haze that covered the stage. The Macâya glided over them, disappeared into the fog, and carried off one of the girls in its multiple arms. Flying up the stairs, it escaped with her through the glowing green archway.

Kyle ran up the staircase. "Jessica!" He reached the doorway and halted at a ledge over a dead drop. The winged devil spiraled down a deep chasm that was illuminated by emeralds embedded in the walls. Lindsey wailed in the Macâya's arms as they disappeared into a dark abyss far below.

Kyle ran back down to the mist-shrouded stage and called Jessica's name.

She yelled back. As he searched the fog, she barreled into his arms.

Elkheart came over to them. "Less than six minutes. Come on!" He led them back to the archway marked by the glowing stick. Elkheart entered the tunnel first, then Jessica. Kyle hurried through the narrow tube on hands and knees, urging Jessica to keep moving. Voices shrilled behind him. He glanced back and saw glowing eyes moving toward him.

At the other end, his father yelled, "Three more minutes! Hurry!"

Kyle wiggled through the tight rocks and made his way out the drainage pipe. He followed Jessica and Elkheart up the mine shaft. As they neared the exit, his father pulled another C-4 brick out of his vest and stuck it onto one of the wooden beams. He set the timer. "Thirty seconds now."

Demon cries echoed behind them.

Kyle guided Jessica out of the mine shaft. Night had fallen. The rainforest was pitch-black now. Kyle's father remained inside the cave, firing his flamethrower and yelling like a madman.

"Dad, come on!"

"Keep going!"

Kyle and Jessica ran down the wooded path. A blast shook the ground like an earthquake and the two stumbled to the forest floor. Debris filled the air. Jessica crawled into Kyle's arms. They lay in a bed of wild ferns for several moments, as the ground continued to tremor from deeper explosions. Kyle held her head to his chest, thankful she was alive.

Then he felt a familiar vibration from the pines and heard droning sounds. White lights shimmered through the forest. He shielded Jessica as ghosts entered the moonlit clearing, surrounding them.

Kyle stared in awe. "Do you see them?"

"See who?" Jessica asked.

Dozens of specters took form. The ghosts of his ancestors. Among the Cree people stood lumberjacks from a century ago and countless men and women, including Nina Whitefeather, Zack, and Eric. Madu and Scarpetti. The luminescent eyes of the ghosts looked at Kyle, then one by one the spirits flew upward to the sky. Kyle felt a hollow in his chest as Eric went with them. Nina remained behind. She floated over to Kyle and touched his arm with icy fingers. The Cree girl smiled. Then she, too, floated upward.

Chapter Twenty-three

After the last of the ghosts disappeared, Macâya Forest turned dark again.

Kyle helped Jessica to her feet. He heard the slap of branches and then his father emerged, covered in soot, but very much alive. "Let's get out of these damned woods."

As they paddled the canoe across the swamp, Kyle heard beastly howls coming from Macâya Forest. They had survived the cave, but now they had to get back to the plane. Kyle prayed they could reach Hagen's Cove before the shifters caught up to them.

The three arrived at the Bronco only to discover Shawna and Amy missing.

Kyle called out, "Shawna!"

"Over here!"

He found her sitting in the dirt road, cradling the shotgun and sobbing. Kyle kneeled beside her. "You okay?"

She shook her head.

"Where's Amy?" Elkheart asked.

Shawna pointed to the woods that bordered the road. Blood covered the high grass.

"No…" Their father ran into the trees.

Kyle helped his sister to her feet and walked her to the Bronco. He pulled her and Jessica into his arms, grateful to have them back.

Howls echoed behind them, sounding closer.

"Oh my God, they're still coming," Jessica said.

"You two get in the truck. I'll get Dad." Kyle grabbed Shawna's shotgun and followed the bloody trail. Twenty yards into the forest his flashlight shone on his father's back. He was on his knees. Over his shoulder, Kyle saw Amy. Her eyes were closed and she appeared to be unconscious or dead. There was so much blood covering the ground and her legs. Kyle's light followed an umbilical cord. Feeding at Amy's breast was an infant with glistening gray flesh. It turned its head. A face with only a sharp-toothed mouth screeched back at them.

Elkheart yelled and knocked it off Amy's chest. The newborn demon rolled into the grass. His father held out his hand. "Give me the shotgun."

Kyle handed it over.

As the baby shifter raised its head and cried, Elkheart aimed and blew the hell out of it. He dropped the gun and took Amy in his arms, shaking her. "Amy…" He caressed her face. "Wake up, Amy, wake up." His voice was full of tears.

Kyle touched her wrist. No pulse. He put a hand on his father's shoulder. "She's gone."

"No, she can't be." Elkheart pumped her chest, trying desperately to revive her.

"Dad, we have to go."

His father wailed and pounded his fist on the ground beside her body.

As the howls drew nearer, Kyle helped his shaken father back to the truck and sat him in the passenger seat. He was in no shape to drive. In the backseat, Jessica and Shawna watched out the back windows, urging Kyle to hurry.

The sounds of water splashing echoed from the swamp. Branches snapped, as glowing eyes moved through the thicket of trees.

Kyle leapt behind the wheel, floored the gas, and tore up the dirt road.

* * *

Only darkened trees filled the rearview mirror as Kyle drove the Ford Bronco through the empty Cree village and past the main cabin. His childhood home had burned to the ground and was now just foundation, ash and billowing smoke. There was nothing for them here anymore. This land belonged to the Macâya. And the half-human shifters who worshipped the ancient beast.

Kyle's hands still felt electric as he drove down the reservation road. He was only beginning to understand the nature of his gift. If he survived this, he made a vow to learn how to use it. In the passenger seat his father remained silent, a man shell-shocked by sudden loss. In the backseat Shawna leaned against the window, her eyes closed. If they made it out of these woods, his kid sister would never be the same. None of them would.

Looking in the rearview mirror, Kyle met eyes with Jessica. They stared at one another for a long moment, riding in silence. While there were no comforting words that could be conjured after what they'd just been through, the look between them was all Kyle needed to keep going.

As he sped along the dirt road, the headlights carving a swath through the night-shrouded trees, Kyle thought about the best way to escape. His seaplane was still parked at the marina at the edge of town. But in what condition? The townspeople could have destroyed it, torn out the engine. Or they could be waiting in Hagen's Cove, ready to ambush anyone who tried to escape. Driving back into town was too risky. As much as Kyle loved his plane, he would have to leave it behind. The only other option was to follow a backwoods road around Lake Akwâkopiy, about thirty kilometers. Once they reached the Trans-Canada Highway, they would be safe. They could drive on to Calgary.

Having a plan gave Kyle hope. At the T-section where the dirt road met the paved road, he turned left and sped towards the highway. A mile later he passed another dirt road and a sign: *Thorpe Timber Mill: Delivering Lumber Products Since 1882.* It occurred to him that Thorpe's timberland, which neighbored the reservation, backed up to Macâya Forest. That must have been how the townspeople traveled back and forth to the mine shaft. Kyle wondered how many other cave openings there were along the mountain. He imagined the loggers returning to their vehicles. A deadly convoy racing up the dirt road.

The thought made Kyle shudder. He pressed the pedal to the floor. Driving around a curve, he saw an obstruction up ahead and slammed on the brakes. A giant pine tree lay across the road, blocking their escape route.

"Shit!" Kyle punched the steering wheel. He looked at his father. "Are there any other roads that lead out?"

"This is the only one."

"Fucking great," Shawna said.

Jessica gripped Kyle's shoulder. "What are we going to do?"

"We have to get to my plane or steal a boat."

"We're going back into town?" Shawna said.

"It's our only choice," Kyle said.

Something growled in front of them. A shifter ran on all fours across the top of the fallen pine. The headlights reflected in its eyes. It flashed its fangs.

Kyle jammed the gearshift into reverse, backed up and turned the Bronco around, throwing everyone sideways. Tires screeching, he drove pell-mell towards town. He passed the reservation sign as an army of shadows burst from the trees. Kyle swerved. Claws scraped the doors and windows. Shawna screamed as a beast rammed her side, causing the truck to fishtail. Kyle spun the wheel, clipping a creature with the front grill. Another shifter clung to the back bumper and was dragged a hundred feet before dropping away, its body rolling across the asphalt.

Dozens of shadows with glowing eyes loped down the road after them, but the Bronco moved faster and gained distance, leaving the pack far behind.

Kyle barely caught his breath before he passed a police car on the side of the road. Flashing red lights came on. The patrol car chased after them, its siren wailing.

"Goddamn those bastards!" cursed Elkheart. He cocked the sawed-off shotgun. "Keep driving."

The police car rammed their back bumper. While one Mounty drove, Kyle saw Inspector Zano leaned out the passenger window with a pistol. Shots fired from behind.

"Duck down!" Kyle swerved the Bronco as a bullet pinged the back door. A second shot blew out the rear window.

The girls screamed.

"Stay down!" Kyle yelled.

"Move to the left side!" Elkheart spun with the shotgun and fired out the window. "Let 'em pass!"

Kyle let off of the gas. The police car pulled up alongside them. Inspector Zano stood halfway out the window, shooting wildly.

Elkheart shot the driver point-blank in the face. The man's head exploded, splattering black blood across the windshield. The car careened off to the side of the road, into the forest.

Kyle floored the accelerator.

His father sat back in his seat. "Everybody all right?"

Jessica and Shawna said they were okay.

Kyle raced the Bronco past a green sign: ten kilometers to Hagen's Cove. He watched the mirrors, but nothing else chased after them.

* * *

Hagen's Cove was a ghost town, every log building dark and silent. The bells of the old church started clanging, echoing along the empty streets. To Kyle it sounded like a distress call. He worried that someone might be at the top of the bell tower, ringing the bells to summon the loggers from their homes. He imagined cave dwellers climbing out of sinkholes in the forest, responding to the alarms. But his rational mind reminded him the bells rang on the hour. It was ten o'clock.

The shifters running on foot were probably still miles down the road.

That left a short window to escape.

At the marina docks, Kyle helped Jessica board the seaplane. He checked the engine and everything seemed intact. When all the instrument lights came on, he released a sigh of relief. The townspeople must have been confident that no survivors would make it this far.

His father remained on the dock, gripping his flamethrower. Shawna stood with him, her head on his shoulder. They both watched the road that led up to the Beowulf Lodge and Tavern. In town, all was still quiet.

"We're leaving in one minute," Kyle told them. "Shawna…"

Elkheart kissed her forehead and then told her to get on the plane.

Kyle helped his trembling sister into her seat and touched her face. "You're gonna be okay. You're safe now."

"I won't feel safe 'til we're back in Seattle." She looked out the window, resting her hands on her stomach.

As Kyle headed back outside, Jessica grabbed his hand and pulled him to her. She kissed him and pressed her forehead against his chest. Since rescuing her in the cave, they'd barely had a moment together.

"Still want to go to Paris with me?" He offered a smile.

She laughed through tears. "I'll go anywhere with you."

"Buckle up then. First, I'm taking you home." Kyle stepped out of the plane and began untying the ropes from the dock. "Dad, let's go."

"Just a minute." His father opened the back of his Bronco and pulled out a black duffle bag. "This has all my research. Every video we shot." He held it out to Kyle. "Deliver this bag to my department at the University of Vancouver."

"Deliver it yourself."

"Don't argue with me, son. Here…" He pushed the bag into Kyle's chest. "They'll know what to do with it."

"Stop talking crazy."

"My mission's not done here."

"Dad, come on."

"Get those girls out of here." His father turned and walked toward his truck.

Kyle felt a mix of anger and grief. "This is suicide. Get back here."

"Stop wasting time. This town won't be empty for long."

Kyle followed him.

"Son, just—"

For the first time in his life, Kyle hugged his father. "Don't do this."

Elkheart stiffened and patted his back. "I'm not changing my mind. Now, get that bird up in the air." He pushed Kyle away. "Go on."

"You always were a stubborn son of a bitch." Kyle walked to the end of the pier. He tossed the duffel bag onto a seat, then pushed the Otter seaplane away from the dock and leaped onto the pontoon.

"One more thing, son…"

Kyle looked back at his father, who was now sitting behind the wheel of the Bronco. "You hang on to Jessica. She's a keeper."

* * *

Elkheart whistled as he drove down Main Street, pouring out a can of gasoline onto the road. He ignited Molotov cocktails and hurled them through windows. At the center of town, he went inside the old white church. The bells had stopped clanging and it was quiet now. He lit the kerosene rag soaked in his last Stoli vodka bottle. "This is for Amy and Wynona." He threw it at the wood statue of the Lord Father. The woven sticks caught fire. The head with the wreath of antlers torched and caved in on itself.

As Elkheart walked down the aisle towards the exit, he swept the nave with a dragon's breath of flames. The pews burned. The pine walls rippled with undulating waves of orange as wildfire spread toward the steeple.

Then he stepped out onto the front porch and crossed the lawn. The cool summer night had gotten warmer as he felt the heat from the surrounding buildings. Hearing complaints from his sore back and ribs, he took a seat on the curb beside his Bronco. He felt dog-tired. He was getting too old for this life. Elkheart stuck the tip of a Cuban against a flame from his barrel. Then he puffed the cigar and waited. "It won't be long now."

The main street reeked of gasoline fumes. In the distance sirens wailed. As the headlights from a convoy of police cars and pickup trucks entered town, Elkheart stood and raised his flamethrower. He waited until the lead vehicle, driven by Inspector Zano, got close enough. Then Elkheart shot out a burst of fire to the gas-soaked road. An orange-blue flame snaked toward the oncoming vehicles.

* * *

Kyle flew the seaplane over the lake. Down below, several burning buildings lit up the town of Hagen's Cove. A chain of fire engulfed the convoy of trucks, one after the other, causing them to crash into buildings.

Kyle shook his head. "Crazy son of a bitch."

On the country road, the headlight beams of a dozen more cars and trucks barreled between the pines. Kyle didn't know who had better odds, but he had faith that his father wasn't fighting this war alone. If demons could exist on earth, then so could angels. Kyle had experienced that miracle firsthand. He looked across at Jessica, sitting in the copilot's seat. She put a comforting hand on his leg and gave him a look that was both saddened and full of hope. Kyle drew strength from this Aussie woman's spirit.

Below them, flames continued to spread across houses and trees. The Beowulf Lodge and Tavern caught fire. The church's steeple collapsed in the blaze. Jon Elkheart was leaving his mark upon Hagen's Cove.

Not wanting to see the final showdown, Kyle looked away from the burning town. He thought of his father, the man he had barely known—alcoholic, warrior, myth chaser—and willed himself not to cry.

Feeling the power of a spirit warrior in his hands, Kyle angled the plane high above the forest and soared upward, into the night sky.

Epilogue

Six weeks later...

Hell wasn't such a bad place after all, Lindsey thought as they fed her another purple mushroom. That was what she had eaten mostly for as long as she could remember. Mushrooms that grew in abundance from the cave walls and along the mud floor. Occasionally, when she was on her best behavior, they gave her strips of raw meat and honey-flavored mead, which made her drunk. For now, the cave dwellers only dangled mushrooms over her mouth. She bit into another cap. With each earthy crunch, she felt happier and giggled.

It was warm down here, tropical. Steam issued from vents in the craggy walls. Iridescent green light emanated from glowing emeralds embedded into the rock. Fog floated over the mud floor. Lindsey's skin was constantly damp from the heat and the moisture that dripped from spikes that hung from the ceiling. But the bedding they had made her was soft and comfortable.

We take care of our own, her caretaker had said while brushing Lindsey's hair.

There were others like her in the cave. The new girls always cried like she had the day she'd arrived. They were terrified they were going to die at the hand of the devil that walked through the mist. Once the new girls saw the beast take its human form and gaze at them with its luminous eyes, they realized Valak wasn't going to kill them.

The den mother, a middle-aged woman with silver hair, watched over the girls. When they were all gathered in a circle, she taught them about how to adapt to living among the clan, and their important roles. *"You are the chosen ones,"* the den mother had said. *"Only the lucky women get to bear a child from Great Father."*

The cavern suddenly became noisy with a crying baby.

The den mother, who was also their midwife, entered the chamber holding a bundle against her chest. "Look what I have for you," she said, smiling. "You have a son."

She handed the infant over to Lindsey, who cradled it and caressed its wet gray skin. The face was smooth as clay. It had no eyes. No nose. Just two air holes over a lamprey mouth filled with spirals of tiny sharp teeth. It found Lindsey's milk-swollen breast. She grimaced as its teeth locked on to her nipple. Her son suckled greedily, taking in more than just milk.

"Will my baby always look like this?"

The older woman put a comforting hand on her arm. "In time he will learn he has the gift to change skins. His features will grow to look like you."

Lindsey nodded. Being a mother among the clan was all so new.

The infant's whipping tail wrapped around her arm, and she was surprised by the motherly bond she felt. Her fingers explored the strange webbing and bones covering her baby's back. The skin flapped at her touch. "My baby has wings?"

The den mother nodded. "A child from Great Father is very special. One day your little one will grow up to rule his own clan. It is his destiny." She pointed to a wall engraved with ancient hieroglyphs and a painting of the demon god that had fathered Lindsey's child. The den mother smiled. "Your son will help lead his brothers and sisters when all the clans rise out of the darkness to fulfill Great Father's prophecy."

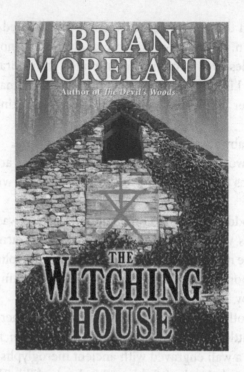

BRIAN MORELAND

Author of *The Devil's Woods*

THE WITCHING HOUSE

Some houses should be left alone.

In 1972, twenty-five people were brutally murdered in one of the bloodiest massacres in Texas history. The mystery of who committed the killings remains unsolved. Forty years later, Sarah Donovan is dating an exciting man, Dean Stratton. Sarah's scared of just about everything—heights, tight places, the dark—but today she must confront all her fears, as she joins Dean and another couple on an exploring adventure. The old abandoned Blevins House, the scene of the gruesome massacre, is rumored to be haunted. The two couples are about to discover the mysterious house has been waiting all these years, craving fresh prey. And down in the cellar they will encounter a monstrous creature that hungers for more than just human flesh.

"A book for all horror fans . . . *The Witching House* reads like your favorite horror movies."
—**Hayley Knighten, Booksaredelicious.com**

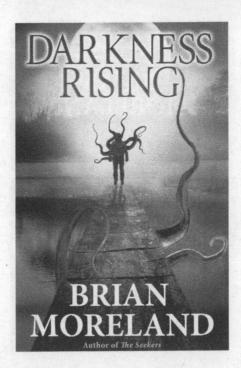

Darkness runs deep ...

Marty Weaver, an emotionally scarred poet, has been bullied his entire life. When he drives out to the lake to tell an old friend that he's fallen in love with a girl named Jennifer, Marty encounters three sadistic killers who have some twisted games in store for him. But Marty has dark secrets of his own buried deep inside him. And tonight, when all the pain from the past is triggered, when those secrets are revealed, blood will flow and hell will rise.

"Moreland has assembled a masterpiece novella that I cannot recommend enough. Upon first reading, this is easily one of my favorite horror releases of the year."
—Horror Underground

"I really enjoyed *Darkness Rising*...If you are a fan of Moreland or the genre, you owe it to yourself to add this to your collection."
—Horror After Dark

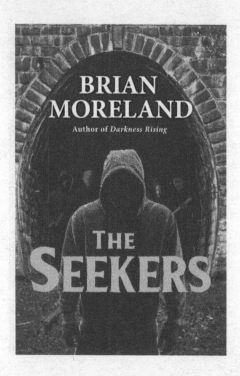

Beneath the city of Boston, evil is gathering.

While living under a bridge with the homeless for six months, journalist Daniel Finley witnessed something terrifying. Something that nearly cost him his sanity.

Now, two years later, he's published a book that exposes a deadly underground cult and its charismatic leader who preaches a dark prophecy. Down in the abandoned subway tunnels exist unimaginable horrors. And in a church of darkness, the cult's numbers are growing. Soon Daniel's worst nightmares are coming true. A fanatical army is rising to shed blood on the streets of Boston.

"Brian Moreland has crafted a unique and thrilling vision of horror that left me both satisfied and wanting more. I strongly encourage you to pick up this novella. "
—**Ravenous Monster**

About the Author

Brian Moreland writes dark suspense, thrillers, and horror. His books include *Dead of Winter, Shadows in the Mist, The Witching House, The Seekers, Darkness Rising, The Devil's Woods* and *Tomb of Gods.*

Brian loves watching all kinds of movies, reading stories, cooking, hiking, traveling the world, and enjoying life to the fullest. As a wandering free spirit, he's lived in Hawaii and Florida, backpacked across Europe, Australia, New Zealand and Costa Rica. He grew up in Texas and now lives in Tennessee where he is having fun writing suspenseful novels and short stories.

Join Brian's mailing list: http://www.brianmoreland.com/

Follow on Twitter: @BrianMoreland

Facebook: https://www.facebook.com/BrianMorelandWriter

Brian's blog: http://www.brianmoreland.blogspot.com